The Great Game

Book II
of the Royal Sorceress series

ALSO BY CHRISTOPHER NUTTALL

The Great Game

Book II
of the Royal Sorceress series

Christopher Nuttall

Elsewhen Press

The Great Game
First published in Great Britain by Elsewhen Press, 2013
An imprint of Alnpete Limited

The use of the typeface Goudy Initialen was
graciously permitted by the designer, Dieter Steffmann.

Elsewhen Press, PO Box 757, Dartford, Kent DA2 7TQ
www.elsewhen.co.uk
British Library Cataloguing in Publication Data.
A catalogue record for this book is available from the British Library.
ISBN 978-1-908168-27-6 Print edition
ISBN 978-1-908168-37-5 eBook edition

Printed and bound by CPI Group (UK) Ltd, Croydon, CR0 4YY

To Pauline, Catherine and Kate

Prologue

THE TIMES, LONDON

TO THE EDITOR OF THE TIMES

Sir,–As a retired military officer and sorcerer in the Royal Sorcerers Corps, I am writing to express my grave concern – nay, dismay – over the decision of HIS MAJESTY'S PRIME MINISTER, THE DUKE OF INDIA to appoint LADY GWENDOLYN CRICHTON as Royal Sorceress. The Duke's record of service to our Empire is, of course, beyond any question. Nonetheless, I believe his decision here is not fortunate. It is not one, I feel, that is in the best interests of the British Empire.

No one can deny that LADY GWENDOLYN has shown the pluck and determination expected of an Englishwoman in a sticky situation. Her heroism contributed significantly to ending the Rebellion, a rebellion whose end was in my opinion not marked by an adequate number of hangings of the traitors who launched it, before there was further loss of life.

However, the fact remains that LADY GWENDOLYN is profoundly unsuited to any position of authority. Like any girl, she is far too delicate for this burden to be placed upon her. The sheltered upbringing of a lady of her station does not cover the areas that any sorcerer would need to know. For example, it will occasionally be needful for the sorcerer to command a party including other ranks. The exigencies of battle occasionally require the officer leading the engagement to motivate other ranks with stiff words, words with which a lady of her station would assuredly be unaware, let alone be prepared to use.

Furthermore, although there are no detailed reports, there are disturbing rumours from her childhood that suggest unpleasant thoughts about her conduct. I shall say no more about those!

Even if she was physically and mentally capable of holding her own in thaumaturgic combat, she is only sixteen years old [ED – LADY GWENDOLYN is seventeen as of writing]. There is no way that she can command the respect and admiration that MASTER THOMAS commanded from the sorcerers who served under him. If there is a conflict of wills within the Corps, a woman, nay a girl of sixteen, can hardly be expected to stand firmly behind her position and compel men three or even four times her age to carry out the decisions that she will of necessity have been supplied *sotto voce*.

It runs against the grain for any man to take orders from a woman, let alone a girl whose past experience with life will have been playing with dolls, learning the arts of the feminine home economy, and casting the most demure downcast glances toward future suitors. The sorcerers of the RSC will have no doubt that LADY GWENDOLYN is far less knowledgeable – let alone experienced or competent – than themselves. That is the nature of the world; that men lead, and women do as they are told while being grateful that they are not asked to perform unnatural acts involving leadership, courage, or rational thought. At best, LADY GWENDOLYN will be repeatedly embarrassed by her elders; at worst, she will have to dress up as a man and lead the RSC onto the battlefield, no fit place for a woman! I submit to you that forcing a young girl to undergo this humiliation is cruel and unnecessary.

Nor is there any reason to allow an accident of birth to dictate the holder of the post of Royal Sorcerer. MASTER THOMAS'S true genius lay in his organisation skills; he, more than anyone else, shaped both the Corps and the Royal College. There is no true requirement for a Master Magician to hold the post; the old belief that the holder should be the most powerful and capable magician in service has been discredited. Do we really expect a General to be physically stronger than a Sergeant?

In this era of instability, with the very strong possibility of yet another war with France, the last thing we need is uncertainty in the ranks of the Royal Sorcerers Corps. I therefore call upon the government to reconsider its position and find a more suitable person to serve as Royal Sorcerer. Certainly, there are any number of men within the Corps who, by virtue of their male birth, are intrinsically more competent than is this girl, LADY GWENDOLYN.

I am, Sir, your most obedient servant
COL. SEBASTIAN, Blazer (Ret. 1830)
2nd Warwickshire Yeomanry Regiment   May 1, 1831

Chapter One

t's a shame you can't hide your chin," Olivia said, as Gwen studied her own reflection in the mirror. "Without it, you'd fool even a sharp-eye."

Gwen snorted. Her adopted daughter had grown up on the streets. Physically, she was somewhere around ten years old – it was impossible to be sure – but mentally she was well over forty. Children grew up quickly on the streets and those unlucky enough to be born female tended to suffer more than most. Gwen had railed against her own upbringing, but she'd been lucky – very lucky – compared to Olivia. A few more years and she would no longer have been able to pass for a boy.

"Use an illusion," Olivia added. "You could pass for a man without the outfit."

"True," Gwen agreed. Creating illusions was easy. "But I might not be able to fool a Sensitive."

She studied herself thoughtfully. The black jacket and white shirt she wore – the very latest in male fashion – had been carefully designed to hide the swell of her breasts, while the top hat disguised her short blonde hair. She'd had to cut it short while she'd been training under Master Thomas, but she'd kept it short even after she'd succeeded him as Royal Sorceress. It was short enough to pass for a slightly-effeminate male hairstyle, or so she hoped. Elaborate wigs, which would have hidden everything, were currently out of fashion. Even her mother, who would have fainted if she'd realised that Gwen was dressing up as a man, hadn't been able to see when wearing wigs would be fashionable once again.

Most importantly of all, she looked nothing like Lady Gwendolyn Crichton, Royal Sorceress.

"You'll certainly fool those toffs you're going to see," Olivia assured her, with the certainty of one who knew. "That lot never look very closely at someone wearing the right clothes. I know conmen who profited simply by dressing the part."

Gwen took one final look in the mirror and then turned, picking up the cane that had been passed down to her from Master Thomas. The elderly magician had left her almost everything he'd owned, including money, property and a set of notebooks that were written in a scrawled hand that was almost impossible to decipher. Looking down at it, Gwen felt herself feeling the same ambivalence she always felt towards the memory of her mentor. Master Thomas had plucked her from her boring life and trained her as a sorceress – and she would always be grateful – but he'd also been responsible for unleashing a nightmare on London to defeat the Swing. Gwen was one of the very few people who knew the truth, even though it was something she would have preferred to forget.

There was a knock at the door. "Begging your pardon, My Lady, but Inspector Jude is downstairs," the maid said. "He awaits your pleasure."

Gwen nodded to Olivia and walked to the door. Cavendish Hall was massive, with several entrances that allowed her to leave unseen. She might have been the Royal Sorceress, with the formal power to deal with all legal and military matters involving magic, but the remainder of the Sorcerers Corps was unsure how to deal with her. If they'd had another Master Magician, Gwen knew, she would have been expected to stand aside for him. But they hadn't. Some of the traditionalists were even making noises about appointing a committee of magicians to take Master Thomas's place. Only the newcomers supported her without reservation.

Inspector Jude stepped out of the carriage and nodded politely to Gwen. Like her, he'd dressed up in the garments of a young nobleman, one of the many who were born and bred outside London and gravitated to the capital city when they came of age. She had to admit that he wore the clothes better than she did, complete with a hint of stubble that gave him a daringly rakish look. No one would have taken him for a Bow Street Runner, at least not on first sight.

"They're definitely having a meeting tonight," he said, as she climbed into the carriage and sat down. "We saw the Worshipful Master heading for the hall barely an hour ago."

"Good," Gwen said, tightly. She *always* felt nervous before walking into trouble, even though she was fine once the trouble actually began. "Let's hope that it isn't just another false alarm."

The Worshipful Order of Ancient Wisdom had seemed, at first, like just another craze spreading through legions of aristocratic men who refused to do anything useful with their lives. Most of them were second or third sons who wouldn't inherit either land or property, leaving them living in considerable luxury without any real goals in life. Those who had the inclination joined the army, or the navy, or even the Colonial Service. The remainder just idled around London, enjoying an endless series of parties, hunts and other diversions. It wouldn't be the first time that they'd started trying to play around with magic.

But there were rumours about the Worshipful Order, disturbing rumours, and it was Gwen's task to investigate. They'd become more blatant in the six months since the Swing, since Master Thomas had died, as if they didn't expect Gwen to hold them to account. She'd known that she would have to do something the moment she'd read the file. But punishing young aristocrats required a far higher level of proof than punishing common people.

The carriage rattled noisily as it crossed the bridge and headed into Pall Mall. Once, it had been the most expensive part of London, but that had been before the Swing, before rebels had held the capital city long enough to destroy many of the hated symbols of wealth. Now, several dozen buildings were being rebuilt, yet the richer part of the population had started to gravitate to areas outside the city. Gwen's brother had informed her that flats in Pall Mall were actually going surprisingly cheaply these days.

Inspector Jude didn't bother with small talk as the carriage turned the corner and headed down towards the Worshipful Order's hall. Gwen felt her stomach tighten as she checked both the cane – which concealed a sword – and the hidden revolver she carried in her jacket. There would be policemen, and a Talker, waiting near the building, but she'd had enough experience by now to know how quickly a situation could get out of hand.

"Here we are, My Lord," Inspector Jude said. "Remember to swagger as you jump out of the carriage."

Gwen smiled as the carriage lurched to a halt, a moment before one of the doormen opened the door and waited for the occupants to step outside. She jumped down, silently relieved that she no longer had to wear skirts at all, no matter how scandalous her mother and her friends found it, and strode up to the door with all the confidence she could muster. Lord McAlister, her *alter ego*, wouldn't allow anything to stand in his path. Gwen kept walking and the doormen simply melted away. They knew that the Worshipful Master *loved* inviting the other aristocrats to his little coven. Anyone who knew about it, they assumed, had been invited. Gwen had no intention of correcting them just yet.

"Ah, *Laird* McAlister," the Worshipful Master said. Gwen braced herself as his gaze flickered over her, but he looked away without seeing anything suspicious. The smell of brandy suggested that he'd been fortifying himself before the meeting actually began, unsurprisingly. Some of the party set could drink all night and never notice any ill-effects in the morning. "Welcome, welcome; please, take a place in the hall."

Gwen nodded and headed into the main room. It had been heavily altered to suit the Order's needs, complete with two stone tables in the centre of the room, one much larger than the other, and five heavy chandeliers hanging high overhead. They spun slowly, casting odd shadows over the spectators – and the robed members of the Order.

Apart from the Worshipful Master himself, they all wore masks to conceal their identities. It was another sign that they were pushing the limits, even for men with fine aristocratic families. They really *didn't* want to be caught.

The room filled up slowly. As Gwen had expected, there were twelve members of the Order openly decked out in their ropes, and around forty unrobed men who seemed to be nothing more than spectators, all instantly recognisable to someone who had grown up within the aristocracy. The unrobed men were drinking heavily, served by maids who walked from person to person carrying glasses and bottles while doing their best to avoid groping fingers. There didn't seem to be any aristocratic women in the room, for which Gwen was grateful, knowing that one of them might have been able to see through her disguise. Besides, aristocratic women were prone to a different sort of silliness than the men.

"Welcome, one and all," the Worshipful Master said. The doors slammed closed with a heavy thud. "Today, we will crack open the secrets that lead to magic and invest ourselves with the power of sorcerers!"

He produced a book and placed it down on the smaller table. Gwen recognised it at once and had to fight to keep her face calm. The volume, written by a mad Arab, was well known in the occult world, but it was all nonsense. Certainly, none of the spells within the volume had worked when the Royal College had tried them, back during the early days of magic. And none of the *known* forms of magic had been listed in the book.

"We shall summon an entity from the ninth plane of hell," the Worshipful Master said. He certainly sounded as though he believed what he was saying, although Olivia had once told Gwen that sounding sincere and honest was a vital requirement for being a conman. "To prepare the room, we will chant a summoning rite. Join us, once you pick up the words."

He clicked his fingers, and then started to chant in a language Gwen didn't recognise. A moment later, the other brothers joined in, creating a sonorous, almost hypnotic effect. It was nonsense – magic simply didn't work that way, as Gwen knew better than anyone – and yet it was captivating. The rhythms were easy to learn and follow; one by one, the audience slowly joined in with the brothers. She exchanged a brief look with Inspector Jude and started to mutter the words herself, wondering which language they were using. Or maybe the Worshipful Master had made them up. It wouldn't be hard to come up with a few dozen nonsense syllables and recite them with apparent sincerity.

The chant seemed to change once everyone had picked up the words. Gwen listened as the Worshipful Master added his own words, his voice echoing out over the background, while the brothers kept repeating the same mantras. He would have made a good singer, she considered, if he'd been able to go on stage, but it would have been a major scandal. It wouldn't do for the scion of an aristocratic family to stand up and sing like a common music hall jockey.

Finally, a bell rang and the Worshipful Master fell silent. The chant slowly died away, leaving them standing silently in the midst of the room.

"We have been heard," the Worshipful Master said. "He *hears* us. He is *coming*."

A dull thump echoed through the hall. Despite herself, Gwen tensed. There was so much they didn't know about magic; it might just be possible that the Worshipful Master and his Order had stumbled into something new. But all of her instincts told her otherwise, despite the shiver running down her spine as another thump shook the building. And then a door opened at the far end of the room and two more brothers, robed and masked, walked in, carrying a girl between their shoulders. She was naked, but didn't seem aware of it. One look and Gwen knew that she had been drugged. The dull expression in her eyes was proof of that.

"We will offer this life to the dark one," the Worshipful Master said quietly, as the Brothers helped the girl onto the larger stone table. "She will die and we will be rewarded with power beyond imagination."

Gwen glanced at Inspector Jude, who nodded, one hand

reaching into his jacket for his concealed revolver. Nodding back, she closed her eyes and sent a single thought to the Talker outside the building. *Come.*

"With this blade," the Worshipful Master said, "we will send her to the afterlife and..."

Gwen stepped forward and reached out with her magic, yanking the knife out of the Worshipful Master's hand. He stared at it, and then at Gwen, his face twisted with disbelief and shock. Gwen caught the knife in one hand – one glance at it told her that it came from John Wells, a well-known fake magician – and slammed it to the floor. It shattered into a spray of stone fragments.

"You are all under arrest," she said, drawing on her magic to illuminate her form. They'd see through her disguise now, so she pushed as much Charm into her voice as she could. "Sit down and wait quietly until the police get here."

Some of the aristocrats, too weak-minded or drunk to shake off the Charm, complied at once. The others, already panicking, kept running, heading for the doors that led to the outside world and freedom. None of them could afford to be caught. A handful produced weapons and hesitated, unsure if they should be pointing them at Gwen or at the Worshipful Master. Gwen had no doubt that they were wondering if they could convince their families that they were actually spying for the government...

The Worshipful Master snarled and produced another knife, throwing it at Gwen with lethal force. Gwen caught it effortlessly and threw it back, angling it right between his legs. He let out a yelp as the knife sliced through his robes and fell over backwards, just as two other bystanders opened fire on Gwen. The bullets bounced off her magical shield and ricocheted around the hall. One of the Charmed aristocrats on the floor let out a yell as a bullet grazed his shoulder.

"You are under arrest," Gwen repeated, as Inspector Jude produced a pair of handcuffs and cuffed the Worshipful Master. Down below, policemen were flooding into the building, rounding up everyone inside. No doubt most of those arrested would claim to have nothing to do with the Order; some of them might even be telling the truth. But Gwen found that rather unlikely. "Tell me; just what did you expect would happen when you killed the poor girl?"

The Worshipful Master glared at her. "I would have been granted power far superior to yours," he snarled, finally. Gwen couldn't tell if he was serious, or if he was still trying to con her. He really should have known better. "And then I would have ruled the world."

Gwen shook her head as two burly policemen arrived. "Have him taken to the cells, somewhere separate from the rest of his Order," she said. The remaining members of the Order had surrendered without a fight and, once they'd been cuffed, their masks had been removed. Gwen recognised all, but one of them as scions of powerful families. Their arrest was likely to lead to a power struggle between the King's Government and their relatives, all of whom would be outraged at their children being arrested. "And keep them separate as well."

"Certainly, My Lady," Inspector Jude said. The policeman beside him gave Gwen a sharp look, as if he hadn't realised that she was female until Jude had pointed it out. "I trust that you will be taking the case directly to the Home Secretary?"

"I will," Gwen said. Master Thomas could have dealt with everything on his own authority – but he'd had sixty years of experience and knew where most of the bodies were buried. Gwen had much less latitude... and many more political enemies. The ones who didn't consider her a foolish female – never mind the fact that Queens tended to be better for the country than Kings – believed that she was too young to do her job.

"And, Inspector, I want you to find out where she came from."

A police doctor was already looking at the intended sacrifice. "She's been drugged, probably with a light dose of chloroform," he said. "It would probably be better to let her recover here and then transfer her to one of the hospitals, where she can be interviewed."

"See to it," Gwen ordered. "I can write a chit for a

Healer's services, if necessary."

She took one last look at the Worshipful Order of Ancient Wisdom and then walked out of the door, back onto the streets. A small army of policemen were identifying, booking and finally marching off the aristocratic witnesses, using kid gloves. Gwen found it hard to blame them; even a very junior aristocrat could file a complaint that would ruin a constable's career. The Bow Street Runners might have been purged of the worst of the corruption after the Swing, when they had failed to keep the streets under control, but there were still bad apples in the barrel.

Taking a copy of the arrest list from Inspector Lestrade, who could never have passed for an aristocrat, she walked off in the direction of the Houses of Parliament. If she knew Lord Mycroft, he'd still be working on papers in his office until midnight and he'd need to see the arrest list as soon as possible. The Worshipful Order of Ancient Wisdom would create a political nightmare as soon as they were released from custody.

But there had been no choice. Sacrificing a human being was very definitely crossing the line, even though Gwen had *known* that it would be futile. They'd had to be stopped, even if it meant risking the stability of the government – or even if it meant risking her own position.

Because if she *couldn't* stop well-connected men murdering members of the lower orders, what had Jack died for anyway?

Chapter Two

uring the Swing, Whitehall and the Houses of Parliament had been extensively damaged by the rebels. After the fighting had come to an end, the government had started a long-term project to rebuild the heart of the British Establishment, allowing the government departments to be extensively reorganised – and, Gwen had been told, to be purged of a great many officials who had outstayed their welcome. Lord Mycroft, who had lost his flat in Pall Mall when the rebels had firebombed it, had moved into Whitehall and taken effective control of the government. These days, he rarely left his offices.

Gwen smiled to herself as the policemen on duty waved her through the gates. At first, they'd been suspicious of a young girl visiting Whitehall, certainly one without any male escort. Now, they just let her through without asking any questions, apart from a handful of requests to show off her magic. Gwen had been puzzled at first, until Inspector Jude had reminded her that the Royal Sorcerer was supposed to provide magical support if the Bow Street Runners ran into trouble. A display of competence on her part was always welcome.

Lord Mycroft's office occupied the entire second floor of the Home Office. Somehow, it still managed to seem crammed with files, books and boxes, allowing Lord Mycroft instant access to any or all of the government's archives. Gwen had never seen him actually having to *look* at the files; like Doctor Norwell, Lord Mycroft possessed a perfect memory and an undeniable gift for seeing connections in the information that would be missed by almost anyone else. He was easily the most intelligent man that Gwen had ever encountered. The thought of what would happen to the government when he died or retired was chilling.

"Lady Gwen," Lord Mycroft said. He was seated on the far side of a massive desk, splitting his attention between a government report and a chessboard where a puzzle had been laid out for his attention. "I trust that matters went well?"

Gwen nodded as she sat down. "The so-called Worshipful Order of Ancient Wisdom is in custody," she said, as she passed him the arrest list. "How could anyone be so stupid as to believe such nonsense? Summoning a demon *indeed*!"

Lord Mycroft snorted. "We have been allowing people to believe all kinds of nonsense about magic, ever since Professor Cavendish first codified it," he reminded her. "For all they know, maybe you *do* get your powers from the devil."

"Too many people believe that," Gwen muttered. She'd been ignorant about the true nature of magic before Master Thomas had taken her as his apprentice. Maybe an outsider, with nothing more than rumours to go on, would believe that magic came from the devil – or, for that matter, that someone could be turned into a frog just by a magician snapping their fingers.

"But not, alas, enough of them," Lord Mycroft added. "We do know that the French have definitely started to build their own force of trained magicians. A present from Master Jackson, I do believe."

Gwen rubbed her forehead. The French had originally believed that magic was of demonic origin, if only because magic had allowed the British to beat them soundly in 1800 – and, lacking the insight provided by Professor Cavendish, they had been unable to codify magic for themselves. But then they'd allowed Jack to reside in France and he'd taught them how to find and train new magicians. Gwen had no doubt that, whatever the Pope had to say about it, the French would have no hesitation about using their own Sorcerers Corps. After all, Master

Thomas hadn't hesitated to fly in the face of convention and recruit *her* when he'd needed an apprentice.

Magic had given the British Empire a major advantage in 1800. Talkers had allowed the coordination of military forces all over the world, while it had taken the French weeks or months to get orders and reports to various far-flung outlets. Blazers had ignited wooden sailing ships before they could fire a single shot towards the Royal Navy. Even Sensitives – the weakest form of magic - had offered the British an unfair advantage. No wonder the French had called magic demonic – and no wonder that they'd accepted Jack's offer with alacrity. They needed to master magic for themselves.

"So have the Turks," Mycroft added. "And *they* have help too."

Gwen gritted her teeth. The last report had placed Lord Blackburn in Cairo, working with the Sultan of the Ottoman Empire. Lord Blackburn might have been nothing more than a Charmer – which didn't stop him being very dangerous – but he knew enough to put the Turkish research program into magic onto a very sound footing. Gwen had disliked him intensely even before she'd realised just how deeply entangled he'd been with the farms and other programs intended to keep magic firmly in upper class hands.

Maybe I should be glad he fled before the end of the Swing, she told herself, firmly. *He would have been pardoned at the end, like everyone else.*

It was strange to consider such matters. A year ago, she'd wanted – desperately – to explore her own powers and do something *useful*. Now, she was the foremost magician in the land, the leader of the Royal Sorcerers Corps and Chairman – *Chairwoman*, she supposed – of the Royal College. Powerful men hung on her every word, just as she'd imagined when she'd been a child, experimenting with the magic that had both blessed and blighted her life. But she'd never realised just how far her responsibilities would stretch until it was too late to change her mind.

Or, for that matter, how many people would refuse to

take her seriously.

"And so have the Russians, we assume," she said, tartly. "Or have you heard anything different from them?"

"Nothing," Lord Mycroft said. "But the Russians have always been good at keeping secrets. They could have a small army of magicians by now and we wouldn't know about it, at least until we saw them in combat... perhaps in Central Asia."

Gwen nodded, visualising the map in her mind. Britain ruled all of India and was pushing northwards through Afghanistan; Russia was pressing southwards, building a colossal network of roads that would allow the Cossacks to ride to their destinations far quicker than ever before. Sooner or later, the two empires would meet and clash. By then, the Russians would need magicians of their own if they wanted to prevail.

"Or Europe," she said, after a moment. "They might end up breaking the treaty with France..."

"Unlikely," Lord Mycroft said, with authority. "The recent royal marriage between Paris and St. Petersburg will give them some incentive to avoid outright war, even if they are disagreeing over the precise division of the German states. I have it on good authority that diplomats on both sides are strongly suggesting that they leave the Germans independent as buffer states, particularly as few believe that the Germans could ever become a major threat to both empires. Besides, if they do go to war, the only winners would be right here in London."

"Because whoever won would take a generation to recover," Gwen said, to show that she had been paying attention. The six months since she'd become Royal Sorceress had required a great deal of cramming. "Better to expand into Africa and Central Asia."

"Much better," Lord Mycroft confirmed. "On the other hand, we don't want either power establishing a firm foothold in Turkey – or Persia. And Parliament will give us a hard time if anything happens to block the slave trade from exploiting North Africa."

Gwen fought the impulse to scowl. There were parts of the British Empire, notably the islands in the Caribbean and the American South, that depended upon slavery – and the slave trade, where Negroes were enslaved in Africa and sold to the highest bidder. She had never truly grasped the realities of slavery until after she'd become Royal Sorceress, despite the horror she'd seen in London before the Swing. Countless men and women, taken from their homes by rival tribesmen, shackled in cramped holds where many of them would suffocate before they reached their new homes. And if one of them hadn't developed magic and accidentally set fire to a boat in London, Gwen would never have known that the slaves had even been there.

Slavery was an abomination, as horrifying in its way as the conditions of the poor that had helped fuel the Swing. But the slaveholders had considerable political power and even the most enthusiastic reformers had been unable to ban the slave trade, let alone stamp out slavery within the Empire. One day, Gwen suspected, the slaves would revolt...

"Politics," Lord Mycroft reminded her. He seemed to be good at following her thoughts, even though he was no Talker. "We do what we can, when we can. And we keep the interests of the Empire firmly in mind."

He tapped the chessboard. "It isn't the single pieces" – his fingers brushed lightly over the white queen – "that are important, so much as how they fit together," he added. "Our priority is to keep the Empire intact. And the way politics has been shaken up recently..."

"The Swing," Gwen said. "You told the King that the Reform Act would be better for the Empire in the long term."

"I did," Lord Mycroft confirmed. "And it will be. But that doesn't stop us from having teething problems as the Reformers try to change everything at once and the Conservatives try to keep the Empire in a state of stasis. Neither side can be allowed full rein, but maintaining the balance is not easy."

It took Gwen a moment to follow his logic. If a reforming Parliament moved against slavery – and only a few individuals within the Reform Party had truly taken an antislavery stance – the slaveholders would unite with the Conservatives. Given a few decades, perhaps something could be done, but until then...

"I suppose it doesn't matter to the pawns," she said, with more bitterness than she had intended. "Most of them don't get to be queens."

"Certainly not in less than six moves," Lord Mycroft said. He quirked an eyebrow at her as he swung the chessboard around until the white pieces were in front of Gwen. "The long-term is what matters. Master Thomas was Royal Sorcerer for sixty years. You might hold the post as long..."

Gwen privately doubted it. Master Thomas had remained remarkably spry for a ancient man, to the point where Doctor Norwell had wondered if he'd been subconsciously Healing himself all along, but he'd been... well, a *man*. And he'd had no replacement in sight, until he'd turned, out of desperation, to Gwen. *She* had a private suspicion that if another Master Magician – a *male* Master Magician – happened to show up, she would be pushed into resigning by the Royal Committee. *None* of them, even the more forward-thinking, were comfortable taking orders from a young girl.

"... And, in any case, the Empire will be here long after we are both dead," Lord Mycroft continued, seemingly unaware of her thoughts. "We must ensure that we do not sacrifice long-term security for short-term gratification."

He tapped the board, meaningfully. "Would you like to play?"

Gwen had to smile. Chess was not considered a ladylike game; certainly, none of the truly great players in London were female. But then, *magic* wasn't very feminine either. And her brother had taught her how to play, years ago.

"Too tired," she said, after a moment's hesitation. David had been good, but Lord Mycroft was an absolutely brilliant player. He would be. Even refreshed, Gwen doubted that she could manage anything more than a brave showing before he swept her pieces off the board. "And I have to be up early tomorrow."

"Indeed," Lord Mycroft said. He looked up, his sharp

eyes suddenly meeting hers. "And do you *want* to go to the ceremony tomorrow?"

Gwen refused to look away, even through his gaze was piercing. "I believe that I have no choice," she said, icily. She didn't *want* to go at all. "We are going to be telling the entire world a lie."

"We all have to do things we hate," Lord Mycroft reminded her, coldly. "Telling a lie, as you put it, is far preferable to the... problems we would face if the truth came out. And our political system, even *reformed*, could not survive the explosion. It would shatter the Empire and leave us vulnerable to our enemies. The truth can remain buried for centuries."

"Lost in the files," Gwen commented, sarcastically. One of the things she'd discovered while doing the paperwork only the Royal Sorcerer could do was that the government was very good at losing things. They were written down and then buried in the files, where they could be safely forgotten about. "And what happens when it comes out?"

"By then, one way or the other, it shouldn't matter," Lord Mycroft assured her. "But believe me, your... *detractors* are facing the same problem."

Gwen snorted. Her detractors, on and off the Royal Committee, only had to put up with a seventeen-year-old girl holding the most important position in the British Empire. She had to tell a lie... and then do whatever it took to *maintain* that lie, knowing that the consequences of the truth coming out would be worse. And if her detractors, the ones who didn't know who'd issued the original orders, ever found out that she'd lied, they would claim that it was yet another reason why a girl could never hold a position of responsibility. How could they trust a known liar? The fact that male politicians lied all the time wouldn't bother them in the slightest.

"And many of them are trying to cope with the Trouser Brigade," he added. His lips formed, very briefly, a smile. "They *hate* that too."

"And blame me for it," Gwen said. "And for once they're even right."

There was no way she could fight in the long dresses

that had been fashionable for Young Women of a Certain Age and Martial Status, even if the Royal Committee had been prepared to listen to people in skirts. Instead, she'd had a dressmaker prepare an outfit for her that was almost identical to Master Thomas's suit, complete with trousers and top hat. The only real change had been some tailoring to fit the female form...

Gwen had never considered herself either a setter or a follower of fashion. Lady Mary, Gwen's mother, worked hard to keep up with the latest fashions, but Gwen had never been interested in following her mother down that path. Now, however, she had *set* a new fashion. Upper-class women were walking around in trousers and shirts, looking for all the world as if they were dressing up as their fathers. The staunchly-conservative sections of society were horrified, but their quiet – and sometimes not so quiet – disapproval had failed to halt the trend. Indeed, it had only given it momentum.

Not that it was entirely useless, Gwen considered. Many of the upper-class women wanted to do something *useful* besides marrying and giving birth to the next generation of aristocrats. It was customary for many wealthy women to become involved with charity work, but the trouser brigade had taken it one step further and actually gone to work. A surprising number of them had even gone into the hospitals that Gwen had helped establish for the poor. Their future husbands would have heart attacks when they found out.

"The older you are, the harder it is to accept that the world is changing," Lord Mycroft said. "And there is a strong impulse to simply dig one's heels in and refuse to tolerate even the merest change. Give them time."

Gwen snorted. "How much time?"

The Swing had ensured that all males over twenty-one got the vote. It hadn't extended the same right to women, something the trouser brigade found hideously offensive. They'd started campaigning at once, demanding enfranchisement... Gwen had no idea where *that* would end up. She'd felt nothing but contempt for women like her mother, who were quite happy to leave such matters to the men, yet she had no idea if women would be wiser when it came to voting properly. How could someone whose main interest lay in dominating the social scene be trusted to direct the country's future? But then, similar arguments had been used against granting all *men* the vote. Where did one draw the line?

"Enough," Lord Mycroft said. He rose to his feet and half-bowed to her. "You have done well today, even if it will cause political problems. But we can come to some agreement with their families."

Gwen scowled as she stood up. No doubt the members of the Worshipful Order of Ancient Wisdom would be given slaps on the wrist, although she trusted Lord Mycroft to ensure that they had a scare before they were allowed to go. They'd come within inches of murdering a young girl...

"Just make sure they stay out of politics," Gwen advised. "And I'll see you at the ceremony tomorrow."

"I will not be at the ceremony," Lord Mycroft admitted. "However, the Duke is looking forward to seeing you, I believe. He is quite grateful for some of your innovations."

Gwen nodded. Somehow, she wasn't surprised that Lord Mycroft wouldn't be coming to the ceremony. The last thing that had caused him to alter his daily routine had been an armed uprising in the centre of London. But the reminder that the Duke of India, the Prime Minister of Great Britain and her Empire, was on her side made her smile. Not every older man saw her as a threat to their position, or as a silly girl playing with forces she didn't understand.

No, she thought, as she turned to leave. *Just most of them.*

Chapter Three

ady Gwen?"

Gwen swallowed a very unladylike curse as she opened her eyes. She'd asked Martha to wake her at seven o'clock – the ceremony was meant to be at ten – but right now she just wanted to go back to sleep. Her maid peered at her nervously, one hand carrying a steaming mug of imported coffee. Even after several months, Martha was still unsure of her position in Cavendish Hall.

"I'm awake," Gwen muttered. The temptation to just skip the ceremony was overpowering; she had to grit her teeth and push it aside. "Put the coffee on the table and then run me a bath."

"Already done," Martha assured her, wryly. "You must have been sleeping like a log."

Gwen nodded. She should have gone to bed as soon as she returned to Cavendish Hall, but she'd had to write a quick report for the files. It had been past midnight when she'd finally entered her rooms and collapsed on the bed, without even bothering to get undressed. Her suit, unsurprisingly, felt uncomfortable and filthy.

"Thank you," she said, remembering her manners. She'd scared too many servants away when they'd realised that she'd had magic, even as a young girl. "Please remind Olivia that she doesn't have to attend the ceremony."

She watched her maid go and then took a sip of the coffee. It tasted unpleasant, but she had to admit that it woke her up properly. Master Thomas had introduced her to it, claiming that it would one day replace tea as the foremost drink in the British Empire. Gwen had her doubts. It just tasted vile.

Shaking her head, she swung her legs over the side of the bed and stood up. Master Thomas had set up the suite for himself, years ago; Gwen was still privately amazed that Cavendish Hall had largely survived the Swing, rather than being burned to the ground. Her best guess was that Jack had felt sentimental, which seemed unlikely. His memories of Cavendish Hall would have been tainted by the truth of his own origins. Or maybe he'd planned to assimilate all the knowledge stored within the Hall before destroying it.

One advantage of wearing a suit, Gwen had decided long ago, was that it was considerably easier to take off than the formal dresses most girls were required to wear. The trouser brigade probably agreed. Pulling off the suit and placing it in the basket for the maids to collect for cleaning, she walked into the bathroom and looked down at the tub. Hot and cold running water was a feature of stately homes in London – and running water would be made available to everyone, once the pipes were in place – but *she* had no hot water. Master Thomas had told her that it was an excellent test for young Blazers. It was difficult to harm oneself with one's own magic, yet if the Blazer happened to overheat the water he'd burn himself. Gwen had learned rapidly to be very careful when heating her own water.

"Pain is the great teacher," Master Thomas had said, the first time she'd burned herself. "And why didn't you think to put in more cold water?"

Gwen flushed at the memory as she climbed into the tub and relaxed, allowing the water to cleanse her skin. Magic was so useful that it was difficult to realise that it had limitations, at least until the magician came face to face with them. Or, for that matter, that not thinking could have disastrous consequences. One young Blazer had tried to heat the water while he was *in* the bath. If Lucy hadn't been in the building he would have died before anyone could save his life.

It was tempting just to close her eyes and sleep, but there was no time. Instead, she pulled herself out of the bath and used a towel to dry her body. Martha knew better than to touch the suits she'd left in the wardrobe, but she'd laid out a set of underclothes on the bed. Gwen sighed as she pulled them on, followed by another suit, practically identical to the one she'd slept in. She didn't have the time or the inclination to design other suits for herself.

Besides, she thought sourly, *the dressmakers would be happy to design them for me, just so they could say that I was one of their customers.*

Pushing the thought aside, she stepped out of her suite and walked down towards the dining hall. Months – it felt like years – ago, she'd had a food fight with some of the young male apprentices, back before the Swing. They'd been offended by the mere thought of a *female* joining the Royal Sorcerers Corps, let alone that she was Master Thomas's apprentice. Now... some of them were dead, killed in the Swing, or promoted upwards. There was less time for *fun*.

Not that you thought it was fun at the time, she reminded herself, as she sat down at the High Table, reserved for the Senior Magicians. Even the youngest of them was ten years older than Gwen herself – and *he'd* spent most of his life in India, before being brought back to Britain to fill a dead man's shoes.

The hall was almost empty, save for a handful of students who would be spending the day desperately cramming for their exams. Gwen had brought in a number of students from lower-class backgrounds, attempting to replace the sorcerers who had died in the fighting. Unfortunately, they rarely knew how to read or write, let alone the basics that every upper-class pupil was expected to know. Tutoring them was an additional expense, but one Gwen thought would be worthwhile. Not everyone agreed.

She accepted a plate of bacon and eggs from one of the servants and started to eat. No one was quite sure of the relationship between magic and food, but almost every magician found himself hungry after working magic – and it was very rare to see a fat magician. Gwen ate more than her mother ever had and yet she was almost painfully thin.

Or perhaps it was the physical exercise. Master Thomas had been a keen believer in that too.

"Lady Gwen," a voice said. "Good morning to you."

Gwen nodded politely as Sir James Braddock sat down next to her. He was a tall man, handsome in a bland kind of way, with short blonde hair and a strong chin that would probably have sent her mother into fits of delight. A strong chin, she'd once claimed, was the mark of a true hero. If she'd been there, she would probably have encouraged Gwen to marry Sir James, even though he was ten years older than her. Sir James was a true hero. Everyone said so.

"Why, Sir James," she said, tightly. "Is it not a positively *delightful* morning?"

It wasn't really Sir James's fault, but she resented his presence – and that of the rest of his team. The Royal Committee had recalled Merlin – the Empire's foremost team of combat magicians – from India after the Swing, in hopes of using them to replace Master Thomas. Gwen couldn't argue with the logic, but she suspected that they'd seen it as a way to express their lack of confidence in her, no matter how they managed to justify it publicly.

And besides, Sir James could irritate her at times.

Which makes him better than most of the Royal Committee, she told herself, sharply. *They manage to irritate you all the time.*

"We're being tapped to provide security for the ceremony," Sir James said, as if Gwen didn't already know that. She'd signed the papers personally, after reading them carefully. "And I understand that the Duke of India wishes to talk with us afterwards."

"Maybe," Gwen said. Master Thomas's death had opened up a great many possibilities, particularly for those in power who thought that the Royal Sorcerers Corps had been allowed too much independence for too long. "But you *will* attend the other ceremony."

Sir James looked at her sharply, then nodded. At least he didn't seem inclined to complain to her face, although God knew how he talked about her behind her back. Gwen had ended up sacking one prominent Blazer outright after he'd stepped well over the line, which had earned her more enemies – and a persistent critic who wrote a new letter to *The Times* every week. She couldn't understand why the newspaper kept publishing them.

They finished breakfast in silence. Several of the other senior magicians, the ones who didn't live in Cavendish Hall, would be making their own way to the ceremony. Gwen was silently grateful for that, even though Master Thomas would have had them all coming to Cavendish Hall first, just so they could show their respect. At least she wouldn't have to put up with their company in the carriage.

"I'll see you at the ceremony," she said, as she stood up. "And remember – try not to start a fight with any of the former rebels."

She saw Sir James scowl – and, briefly, allowed herself a moment of amusement. The general amnesty that had followed the end of the Swing hadn't sat well with most of the more conservative members of the aristocracy, who would have preferred to ensure that anyone who dared raise a hand against them had it cut off. There had been no choice – even if the Redcoats had eventually crushed the rebellion, it would have devastated much of Britain – but they didn't really believe that. They'd been in power for too long.

"I won't," he promised.

Gwen would have preferred to fly to Soho under her own power. But it would have been far too undignified for the Royal Sorceress. Instead, she rode in a carriage that at least allowed her some privacy – and a chance to get her feelings in order. It had been six months since she had last set foot in Soho, during the height of the Swing. Since then, the area had been burned to the ground – rebels and Redcoats working in harmony, for the first and probably the last time – and every last undead monster had been destroyed. Or so they hoped. The undead were a puzzle, even to theoretical magicians like Doctor Norwell. They shouldn't have managed to 'live' and shamble around, let alone spread like a virus.

There were already massive crowds waiting patiently as

the carriage pulled up beside the others. Gwen climbed out without the help of the coachman and looked around, unable to avoid noticing how many of London's great unwashed had come to see the ceremony. After all, it was theirs as much as it belonged to the upper classes – although neither side really knew the truth about what had happened in Soho. She caught sight of a handful of aristocrats she knew and allowed herself another brief moment of humour. They looked as if they wanted to hold their noses but didn't quite dare.

Soho had been abandoned after the first Cholera outbreak had killed thousands of civilians, something that – in hindsight – should have warned people that the government had an interest in leaving it that way. They'd used the rotting disease-ridden buildings to conceal a great secret, one that had come far too close to destroying London utterly. And Gwen was one of a very few people who knew the truth.

These days, Soho had become a garden. The greatest landscape artists and sculptors of the Empire had competed to turn the remains of the district into a fitting monument for two heroes; Master Thomas and Jack. Gwen rolled her eyes as she saw the two statues, towering over the humans thronging through the park. Master Thomas might have looked that dignified in real life – he'd certainly been the most dignified man Gwen had ever met – but Jack had never had so many muscles on his arms. The sculptor had placed him in working class clothes, reminding everyone that Jack had chosen to fight for the poor.

The official version of the story blamed everything on France. But then, it was *easy* to convince the British public that the French were behind every last problem that beset the British Empire. After all, if the French could do something as diabolical as sending a monkey to spy on Hartlepool, who knew what *else* they could do? They would certainly have no difficulty manipulating Jack and Master Thomas into going to war with one another... and then unleashing the revenants to ensure that London was completely destroyed. Yes, everything could be blamed on the French.

Gwen looked up at the statues, shaking her head slowly. What would the adoring public, rich *and* poor, say if they ever found out the truth? Master Thomas had *unleashed* the revenants at the command of the British Government, hoping to ensure that the Swing was terminated before it was too late to save the Empire. He and Jack *hadn't* allied to fight the revenants; Master Thomas had *commanded* the small army of undead monsters. And Gwen herself... the official version had her bridging the gap between the two men. No one knew that she'd effectively betrayed her tutor to stop him from wiping out the entire city.

Perhaps it is better that way, she thought.

But she couldn't help thinking that it was likely to come back to haunt them sooner or later.

Someone was burning a French flag in the crowd, waving the flaming cloth around to general amusement. The downside of the official story was that it encouraged hatred and rage towards the French – and made people wonder why the British Empire hadn't declared war. And the French, knowing perfectly well that the revenants *hadn't* been their fault, were protesting their innocence loudly to anyone who would listen to them...

"Lady Gwen," one of the organisers said. "If you would care to join the Duke of India..."

Gwen nodded and allowed him to lead her to the stage. The Duke of India – the man who'd conquered the subcontinent, opening up a whole new world for the Empire – was a tough man, dedicated to his profession. Being Prime Minister didn't agree with him, but he'd been the one man that King, Parliament and the public had been able to agree on. Gwen had heard that he was actually very popular among his troops, even if he swore like a navvy half the time. If nothing else, he enlivened Cabinet proceedings with his bluntly expressed view of the world.

He nodded to Gwen as she sat down beside him. "I wanted to thank you for the additional Talkers and Seers for the army," he said, without preamble. "They will make future deployments considerably easier to control, even if they do also make it easier for people to look over the commander's shoulder."

Gwen nodded, knowing just how the Generals and Admirals must feel. But they were better off, surely? The old days, when a squadron could be sent out on a mission and no one would know what had happened for weeks or months afterwards, were gone. Now, ships could be directed from place to place as easily as a man could order dinner. The days of command independence were also gone – and she knew that the commanders resented it. How could someone in London truly understand the situation on the ground?

"I'm glad you took them," she said, honestly. The Duke of India was one of the few who didn't care about her sex, or her age. He saw the world in terms of people who were useful and those who weren't. As long as he considered Gwen useful, he wouldn't turn on her, or support her enemies. "Convincing the Corps to accept lower-class magicians was difficult."

"There are no such thing as bad men, merely bad officers," the Duke grunted. He'd led an army made up of men recruited from the dregs of society, honing them until they were a shining rapier in his hand. The Kings and Maharajahs of India hadn't known what had hit them until it was far too late. "And magicians are too useful to turn down."

He cleared his throat as silence fell over the crowd. "I must speak," he said, crossly. He disliked public speaking at the best of times. "We'll talk later about future deployments. Thomas was fond of giving advice, even when unasked. You need to give advice yourself."

Gwen nodded inwardly as the Duke rose to his feet and stamped over to the podium. At least *she* wasn't being called upon to speak. Royal Sorceress or not, the only women who spoke in public were those of the trouser brigade – or very upper-class women, trying to convince their fellows to give money to their charity. Very few women would ever speak to a crowd composed mainly of the lower orders. Why, they might be exposed to bad language. Or the savage nature of those raised without perfect breeding and manners.

She gritted her teeth as she caught sight of Colonel Sebastian in the crowd, his gaze fixed on her face. Sebastian *hated* her, although she wasn't sure if it was because of her sex, her age or because he thought that *he* should have been Royal Sorcerer. Certainly, reading between the lines of his letters to various newspapers, she thought it was the latter. But Sebastian was not a Master Magician and could never have filled Master Thomas's shoes.

And besides, she thought, *he would just have restarted the Swing.*

She leaned back in her chair and tried to relax. The ceremony might have been based on a lie, but was important – and yet it wasn't as important as the second ceremony, the one she'd arranged herself, insisting that most of the senior magicians attend, no matter what other commitments they had. They'd complain, loudly, but she had the authority, at least on paper, to compel them to attend.

And if they refused, she would not forget.

Or forgive.

Chapter Four

he house sat within a garden, behind a solid brick wall topped with iron spikes. Gwen had taken a look at them, when she'd first visited the building, and decided that they made escape almost impossible. The building didn't *look* like a prison – from the outside, it looked like just another large house bought by a family that was going up in the world – but it was a prison, in all but name. Those who lived and died within its walls had no hope of escape.

Gwen walked through the gates and stopped in front of the small crowd of senior magicians. Apart from Lucy, who was standing to one side with a grim expression on her face, they were all male – and none of them seemed willing to meet her gaze. There were truths that a properly brought up young lady wasn't supposed to know – and the existence of the building, and the others like it, was one of them. It still shocked Gwen, sometimes, to realise just how ignorant she'd been, even though she'd been better read that most of her peers. And theoretical knowledge was nothing like genuine experience.

Good, she thought. *They're all here.*

Sir James looked thoroughly uncomfortable as her gaze swept over him and his comrade, Peter Wise. Gwen had never asked if Sir James had known about the farms – she hadn't wanted to know – but she suspected that he had. A Mover so powerful would not have been allowed to risk his life in India without siring a few children first. The fact that most of the women within the farms had been there against their will might not have bothered him as much as it should have done. After all, they weren't upper-class women.

Beside him, Bruno Lombardi kept his gaze firmly fixed on the ground. Gwen knew that *he* had been to the farms before his marriage – and that he might still be going there, if Gwen hadn't shut the whole program down. She would have preferred to promote the shy Italian to a position on the Royal Committee – at least he didn't seem inclined to give her trouble over her sex – but it was unthinkable. An Italian, even an Italian in exile, was not to be promoted over the heads of British citizens. Besides, with the French firmly in control of much of Italy and the Pope a prisoner in the Vatican, it might have been unwise. Who knew *what* Lombardi would do if they found a way to pressure him?

Lord Henry Brockton looked back at her, his face tightly controlled. He hadn't made any secret of his disdain for her, even though he was more polite about it than his former superior, Colonel Sebastian. Gwen found him a constant trial, even though he never quite crossed the line that would allow her to fire him. Besides, he *was* experienced and dedicated to the Corps – and a war hero, as evidenced by the scar crossing his swarthy face. His service in Ireland was unimpeachable.

Gwen kept her face under control herself as she met Earl Jason Amherst's eyes. He was a tall thin man, with the same supercilious expression all Charmers seemed to share – and the awareness that he could talk anyone into anything, given enough time. Gwen distrusted him, at least partly because he was related to Lord Blackburn, who'd had the same general attitude. The Darwinists had been keeping their heads down over the past six months, but she was sure she knew who led them now. Even if he hadn't been unfortunate in his choice of relations, she wouldn't have trusted him anyway. Charmers were never trusted.

Finally, her gaze found Doctor Norwell. "Well," she said, into the silence. "I trust that everything is ready?"

Doctor Norwell nodded. As a theoretical magician, he could never hope to hold a high position in the Royal Sorcerers Corps, but he'd helped to expand the theoretical underpinnings of magic. And he'd been one of Gwen's tutors... she doubted that he coped well with her sudden promotion; indeed, he had better reason to resent her than anyone else in the Royal College.

Life isn't fair, she reminded herself, coldly.

No one was quite sure who'd been behind the farms. Gwen had been tempted to blame it all on Lord Blackburn, but the Charmer had been thirty-two when he'd fled the country and the farms had been in existence for much longer. The files, which were normally thorough and detailed, were vague on that point... unless Doctor Norwell had seen fit to destroy some of them rather than give the files to Gwen. She could only wonder if it had been Master Thomas, or one of the long-dead Masters, or someone else. And if that person was still around...

She pushed the thought aside and cleared her throat.

"Years ago," she said, in the blunt matter she'd learned from the Duke of India, "the Royal Sorcerers Corps, desperate for manpower, started to commit a series of crimes. Young male magicians, born to poor families, were taken away for adoption. Their mothers and fathers – and their sisters – were taken to buildings like this one, where they were turned into baby machines. They were *raped*" – she smiled at their reaction to a word upper-class women were not supposed to know, let alone understand – "until they became pregnant. If their children happened to be male, they were adopted by trusted couples and brought up as upper-class magicians. If they were female, they were used to further the breeding program.

"The program's value was very limited," she added. "Of all the children... *produced*, only a quarter of them became magicians. And only one of them, despite much enthusiasm, became a Master."

Jack had known, Gwen knew. He'd come from the farms – and it had been discovering the truth of his origins that had driven him away from his mentor. It was quite possible, although no one knew for sure, that he'd even been Master Thomas's son. Later, before the Swing had truly started, Jack had blown up one of the farms, along with everyone inside, the innocent as well as the guilty.

Maybe he'd thought that he couldn't get the girls out before Master Thomas arrived... or maybe he'd lashed out at the reminder of his own origins. There was no way to know for sure.

"And the fact remains that it was a crime," she said. "I chose to shut the program down because it was a ghastly reminder of just how far we could fall. We have enough magicians – and new ones coming – to no longer require the farms. I want you all to witness the end of this building."

She concealed her amusement at their expressions. Some of them – Brockton and Amherst, certainly – would have wanted *her* to go to the farms. If her father hadn't been so well-connected, Gwen might well have ended up a prisoner herself, drugged to keep her docile while she produced child after child until her body gave out. Hell, there had been no need, according to the files, to *kidnap* children. Poor parents of magical kids would have been happy to take a few coins in exchange for never having to see their witch-touched children again.

And besides, losing one child might allow them to keep the rest alive.

She turned and walked towards the entrance. The heavy wooden door had been left ajar, allowing her to step inside without hindrance. Inside, everything of value had been stripped from the walls; they'd even taken the carpet from the floors. The building felt as if it had been abandoned years ago, rather than a mere four months. It had taken that long to organise the distribution of the surviving women and children from the farms.

The clerks who managed finances for the Corps had complained about the cost. Giving each magician a stipend to keep them loyal wasn't too big a drain, it seemed, but ensuring that every woman from the farms didn't have to go onto the streets was too much. Gwen had eventually ended up adding funds from Master Thomas's legacy to ensure that the girls were safe, even though she'd been warned that most of them would probably lose it quickly. And many children had been left orphaned... she'd had to arrange for their adoption too.

They'd be the last of the farm generation.

She stopped outside an opened door and peered into the room. It was bare, apart from a single bed in one corner. Manacles hung from each corner, ready to hold someone down if they resisted... some of the girls, she'd read in the files, had been particularly determined to escape, even after the drugs and beatings. The chains looked strong enough to hold an elephant.

Bracing herself, she opened her mind...

The images assailed her at once, blasting through her mind so powerfully that they drove her to her knees. They blurred together into a single liturgy of horror and torment; there were so many of them that she couldn't pick out specific images. If she'd been a Sensitive, she might have been driven mad by the exposure... as it was, it took her several minutes to bring her mind back under control. No *wonder* that so many Sensitives, particularly those who developed their powers in isolation, ended up in Bedlam. They didn't stand a chance.

Damn you, she thought. A very unladylike word – and one her mother would have slapped her for using, if she'd said it in public. *How could you do this to anyone?*

She walked through the rest of the building, keeping her mind tightly closed. Most of the beds had been abandoned, even the bedding, such as it was, had been left there. The women would have been permanently trapped, without even books to keep them distracted. She'd hated her life, hated the restrictions that being born female put on her, yet she'd been far luckier than the girls in the farm. They would have given their souls to trade places with her.

Master Thomas had taught her to pay attention to small details. Something caught her eye as she glanced into the final room, drawing her towards the wall. Someone had chipped into the stone, bit by bit, a pair of names and a message. ALI AND PRU, 1827. GOD SAVE OUR SOULS. Gwen felt a lump in her throat as she stared down at the sole memento of two girls who had shared the room, both probably long dead by now, only remembered in the files. If they could write, no matter how badly, they might not have been lower class at all. Where had they come from?

You can't stay here, she told herself, angrily. The building was deserted. All that were left were the ghostly images burned into the surroundings, just waiting for a Sensitive to pick up.

Carefully, feeling oddly unsteady, she walked back down to the lobby and closed her eyes, drawing on her magic. It swirled inside her, ready to be used, just like it had that day when she'd discovered that she was a magician. Even without knowing the basics, she'd managed to learn quite a bit on her own. Her ability to combine the different talents was remarkable, according to Master Thomas. But then, she had never truly realised that there *were* different talents.

"Burn," she whispered, opening her eyes.

The air grew warmer around her as she projected her magic outwards. Wallpaper started to blacken, then catch fire; the wooden staircase began to glow with light as flames leapt up the banisters and crawled through the plaster covering the stone walls. And yet, Gwen kept pouring on the magic, until the stones themselves began to crack under the heat. A roaring holocaust started to rage through the house.

She drew on her magic again, forming a protective bubble around her body, and waited. The fire was completely out of control now, obliterating the scanty bedding and melting the metal beds into puddles of molten iron. A giant rafter crashed down from high overhead as the flames destroyed the buildings supports, followed rapidly by one of the storage chests that had held what food and drink were offered to the captive women. It was already blazing with eerie green and blue flames.

Something must have been left inside, Gwen realised, as the staircase collapsed into a heap of flaming debris. She looked up, just in time to see cracks forming above her head as the ceiling started to follow the staircase into destruction. The flames grew brighter for a long second, then the ceiling caved in. Pieces of flaming debris bounced off Gwen's protective bubble and crashed to the ground.

She heard – or felt – a dull creak echoing through the house as one of the walls started to collapse. Moments later, large parts of the roof collapsed inwards, smashing through the remaining parts of the upper floor. Gwen saw, for one brief moment, a body, just before it vanished within the flames. She'd given orders that all of the bodies were to be destroyed – it was standard procedure to cremate the dead, now that necromancers could bring new life to rotting corpses – but one had clearly been missed. Or maybe it had just been very well hidden.

There was a final crash as the rest of the roof fell in on her, landing on top of the protective bubble. Gwen kept her thoughts under tight control – panicking now would be disastrous – and altered the shape of her bubble. The rubble was pushed aside, allowing her to levitate herself up and out of the destroyed building. To the sorcerers outside, she had to look like an angel rising out of the flames.

A Blazer could have destroyed the building, particularly if he was smart enough to realise that direct beams of magic would be less effective than making fire. A Mover could have protected himself and then escaped the holocaust. But Masters could use both powers – and so much more, besides. Whatever Colonel Sebastian might say, there was a very good reason why the Royal Sorcerer had to be a Master Magician.

The grass was smouldering, she realised as she dropped to the ground in front of the senior magicians, but the flames were unlikely to spread. Instead, without her magic or much left to burn, the flames were already dying down, leaving nothing more than a pile of charred rubble. All of the evidence of the farm's existence had been destroyed.

"The fire brigade will be on their way," Sir James said. There was a round of nervous chuckles from some of the magicians, although others were watching Gwen coldly, perhaps regretting the end of an era. "What do you want to tell them?"

Gwen shrugged. Both the fire brigade and the Bow Street Runners had been given specific instructions to ignore the farms, leaving the guards stationed there to handle any problems. She honestly had no idea if that had changed, but it hardly mattered. Right now, a word from Sir James would suffice to distract interested policemen – and the fire was already dying out.

"You can tell them that we corrected a mistake," Gwen said, finally. It was true enough; besides, the Royal Sorcerers Corps took the lead in anything involving magic. "And you can leave it at that."

She put a little Charm into her voice, just enough to ensure that they would all hear her. "I want you all to understand that things have changed," she said, as calmly as she could. "We no longer need the farms and *I will not* tolerate their existence. Nor will the Government."

Lord Brockton looked as though he were about to argue, but thought better of it.

"The other farms will be destroyed in turn," Gwen continued. Perhaps she wouldn't do it herself. There were some young Blazers who were doing well in their schooling and deserved a reward. Wanton destruction would probably suit them just fine. "Once they are gone, that part of our history will be buried."

She smiled at them, somehow. Master Thomas had kept himself going for hours, but she felt tired and worn now that she no longer needed to maintain the bubble. But she didn't dare show weakness in front of them, not when too many of them already saw her as a weak and frail female.

"We will go back to Cavendish Hall, where you can all join me for lunch," she concluded. She would have preferred to eat alone, but protocol was protocol. Besides, some of them would be better off under her eye for a while. "And then we will hold the next meeting of the Royal Committee."

She watched them go, then turned back to stare at the blackened ruins. A final wisp of smoke rose up from the debris, then faded away into nothingness. She was tempted to try to open her mind again, to see if all the impressions had been burned away, but she didn't quite dare. Doctor Norwell, when he'd been her tutor, had once speculated that *all* humans were Sensitive, some were just more sensitive than others. Maybe all the stories about ghosts were really nothing more than undiscovered Sensitives walking into an area that had been magically tainted by bad events.

"I don't think they were convinced," Lucy said.

Gwen nodded, without turning round. Lucy had been Jack's mistress and Gwen honestly wasn't sure how she felt about that. She'd *kissed* Jack... what would have happened if he'd survived the Swing? But then, Lucy had told her that Jack had been partly intent on his own self-destruction, if it meant the destruction of the society that had shaped him. Gwen, remembering his behaviour, could hardly disagree.

"I know," she said, quietly.

They respected her power, but they didn't take her seriously. How could they?

Someone – she couldn't remember who – had once told her that legitimacy consisted of being there long enough so that no one could remember anyone else. Maybe she'd just have to be patient. Sooner or later, most of Master Thomas's appointees would be gone.

But it seemed a very long time to have to wait.

Chapter Five

wen allowed herself a smile as she stepped into the Royal Committee's chamber. The designers had placed it right at the top of Cavendish Hall, allowing light to shine through the skylight and illuminate a long wooden table, where the members of the committee sat. A smaller table held two bottles of wine and several glasses, while a bookshelf held copies of the Corps' accounts. The walls held several portraits; a regal portrait of King George IV, a joint image of the first three Master Magicians and a large painting of Queen Elizabeth, a droll reminder that a woman had once done an extremely good job of ruling the entire country. At the far end of the room, the original *Battle of Philadelphia* hung on one wall, showing the surrender of George Washington and his army of rebels to the British Redcoats.

The members of the committee rose to their feet as she entered the chamber. Gwen nodded politely to them, took her seat at the end of the table and motioned for them to sit down. She couldn't help noticing that several of them had taken wine from the table, but others had chosen to try to keep a clear head. That was good, she supposed. Magic and alcohol didn't mix very well. Besides, if she had taken a glass for herself, people would have *commented*.

"The meeting is now in session," she said, primly. They didn't like having a chairwoman, any more than Gwen liked attending the meetings in the first place. If Master Thomas had told her that the post included so many worthless discussions, she would have had second thoughts about accepting his offer. "God save the King."

"God save the King," they echoed back.

Gwen nodded. It was customary to start the meeting like that – and it also reminded them that King George, who had taken a much stronger interest in governing his country after the Swing, was one of her supporters. Not everyone *liked* the King, or respected him, but they'd be careful not to show disrespect in public. They never knew who might be listening.

"Before we start," she continued, "do we have any urgent business?"

Sir James cleared his throat. "Ambassador Talleyrand has requested permission to visit the Royal College," he said, shortly. "It is my very strong advice that permission be denied."

There was a general rumble of agreement. Talleyrand was France's Special Envoy, the man King Louis used to handle diplomatic incidents... and one of the smartest men in the world. Gwen doubted he was smarter than Lord Mycroft, but it hardly mattered. Allowing him to see the Royal College might have unforeseen consequences in the future. Who knew what piece of intelligence he'd find that could be put together with something else to create disastrous results?

But it was Gwen's decision... and if her refusal caused a diplomatic incident, she'd be blamed.

"We could organise his tour so that he sees nothing useful," she mused, aloud.

"It would be difficult to be certain," Sir James said. "As you know, I have recommended that we move out of the city entirely..."

Gwen scowled as the old argument washed over her. After the Swing, when Cavendish Hall had been attacked and captured by the rebels, several of the younger magicians had advocated moving out of London. Cavendish Hall could serve as their headquarters, the Royal College could continue its research... but most of the magicians would train and live out of the city, where they would be less vulnerable to enemy attack. And, for that matter, less tempted by the pubs and fleshpots of London.

"But that would seem like a defeat," Lord Brockton insisted. He'd said the same thing at a dozen earlier meetings. "We cannot run from our own capital city."

Sir James scowled at him. "It isn't a retreat," he insisted, icily. "If we did our training outside the city, if nothing else, we would..."

"... Not be able to call on a reserve of magicians, if necessary," Amherst said. "Besides, many of our trainees have other... requirements. We should not take them from London."

Gwen tapped the table, exasperated. Had the senior magicians given Master Thomas so much trouble? "That is a debate for another time," she said. Personally, she was inclined to agree with Sir James; moving the training facilities out into the countryside would give them much more room to operate, as well as keeping the young magicians away from London's temptations. "For now, we shall deal with the French Ambassador."

She was tempted to insist that Talleyrand be allowed to visit, knowing that it would annoy them, but it would be pointless spite. And Sir James did have a point.

"We shall politely deny his request," she continued. "However, he may attempt to pressure our superiors into allowing him to visit. In that case, we shall conceal as much as possible before he arrives."

She didn't need to be Sensitive to sense their irritation. She'd compromised – just like a woman. Master Thomas would have said no and made it stick, but Master Thomas had had influence and knowledge no one else could match. Even if Gwen had been born a man, she couldn't have wielded so much influence. And they would probably still have resented her.

"The first issue on the agenda, then, is recruitment," she said, changing the subject. "Mr. Norton?"

Geoffrey Norton looked up from where he sat at the far end of the table. Like Doctor Norwell, he had no magic of his own and hence no vote on the committee – but he did have influence. Master Thomas had put him in charge of recruitment and personnel; the files stated that Gwen's old mentor had believed that a magician would be likely to favour his own branch of magic over the others. Six months of wrestling with the senior magicians had convinced Gwen that he'd been right.

"The next intake of magicians are scheduled to enter the Royal College in two weeks," he said, calmly. "That's ninety-two magicians, mainly Blazers and Movers..."

Lord Brockton interrupted. "How many of them are from the lower classes?"

"Seventeen," Norton said. If he resented being interrupted, he didn't show it. "The remainder come from the upper classes or... adoptive families."

The farms, Gwen thought, coldly. If there was one detail that had convinced her that the whole program was useless as well as morally disgusting, it was the simple fact that only one in four of the children ever developed magic. No one was quite sure how magic was passed down through the generations, but it was quite common for a magician to have children who didn't seem to have magic. Or, for that matter, for two non-magicians to produce a magical child. Gwen's parents had no magic and yet they'd produced a Master Magician.

"Seventeen," Lord Brockton repeated. He looked over at Gwen and scowled. "And what will they do to the morals of the other magicians?"

Gwen couldn't hide her irritation. They'd gone over the same issue at every single meeting Gwen had chaired, without even coming up with new arguments. By now, she could have argued their side – and the other side – in her sleep. And it never seemed to go away.

The Royal College and the Sorcerers Corps had started by only recruiting magicians from the upper classes – or the middle classes, if the magician in question was powerful enough to allow them to overlook his origins. Lower class magicians were rounded up and sent to the farms, which – unsurprisingly – encouraged the ones who escaped to stay underground. Many of them had joined Jack's rebellion when he'd made his desperate bid to overthrow the government, if only in self-defence. They could expect no mercy if they were caught.

In the aftermath of the Swing, the Royal College had

agreed to relax the barriers to entry, allowing lower-class magicians to enter formally and train with their social superiors. It hadn't always gone well.

"I seem to recall," she said tartly, "that nine out of ten of the last discipline issues that reached my desk concerned upper class students. And it wasn't a lower class student who had to be expelled for stealing from his classmates."

"But such matters were not a problem before lower class students joined the Royal College," Lord Brockton insisted. "The morals of the next generation of magicians are being corrupted."

Gwen rather doubted it. *She'd* had a hard time during her first few weeks of training- and there had been no lower class students at the time – but then, she'd been the only girl to enter the Royal College. In many ways, she had been very isolated. No one had asked her to go out for a night on the town. It just wasn't done.

But he was right about one thing. Upper class students picked on the lower class students... and vice versa. And yet it was hard to see what could be done.

She smiled, sweetly. "Would you wish us to stop recruiting Healers?"

Lord Brockton's face purpled. No one knew why, but all seven of the Healers discovered since the Swing were lower class. The Royal College tested hundreds of potential candidates every month, yet they'd been unsuccessful in finding an aristocratic Healer... In hindsight, Gwen suspected that they would have found Healers earlier if they'd abandoned their reluctance to recruit from the lower classes before the Swing.

And all but one of the Healers were female.

"Healers are a different issue," he said, finally. "They certainly cannot be trained with the other students."

Norton cleared his throat. "We shall graduate forty new magicians this year," he said, defusing the tension in the room. "Most of them are already earmarked for the military, but the police have expressed an interest in additional Movers, should they be available."

"Tricky," Sir James pointed out, quietly. "We took losses during the Swing."

Gwen nodded. The uprising had killed nearly half of the magicians who had been in training at the time, as well as a number of experienced tutors. In some ways, the problems Lord Brockton had complained about had been caused by the Swing; Master Thomas, whatever else he'd done, hadn't ensured that there were tutors held in reserve. Given time, Gwen was sure that the problems would be overcome, but time seemed to be in short supply.

"The military comes first," Lord Brockton insisted. "We may be at war with France by the end of the year."

"True," Gwen agreed. "On the other hand, we can keep a reserve of magicians in the capital and assign them to support the police."

Surprisingly, there was no disagreement.

Sir Benjamin MacIver, Head of Changers, coughed for attention. "We must face facts," he said, dispassionately. "We need more magicians."

"Hence the decision to recruit from all classes," Gwen reminded him, tartly. Sir Benjamin was less pointlessly obstructive than Lord Brockton, which made him all the more dangerous to Gwen's position. "We need to find more magicians as quickly as possible."

"Indeed we do," Sir Benjamin said. "And while I share your disdain at the whole farm program, it was successful in providing us with additional magicians. Right now, however, we are dependent upon nature to provide us with new recruits."

Gwen fought down the flash of rage that threatened to overcome her. Was she going to be fighting the same battle over and over again? Oh, she could see their point – magic had made the British Empire supreme and that supremacy had to be maintained – but it didn't change the fact that the farms had been grossly immoral. And of questionable value.

"I believe that we can compromise," Sir Benjamin oozed. "We have considerable funds available to us. It would be quite simple for us to pay women to have children with selected fathers and to supervise their upbringing. Should they have magic, we could take them into the Royal College from a very early age."

"But such a program would be public," Doctor Norwell pointed out. "It could hardly *avoid* being public. And then we'd be risking..."

"Very little," Sir Benjamin stated. "There are plenty of women from the lower classes who sell their children. We would merely be purchasing the ones who... meet our demands."

Gwen took advantage of the argument to concentrate her mind. She couldn't show her anger openly or they'd just dismiss her as an emotional women, too emotional to be allowed anywhere near a position of power. Cold logic was required to outmanoeuvre Sir Benjamin, yet cold logic suggested that he was right. Why *not* pay women to have children with the right fathers?

As Royal Sorceress, Gwen had been asked to patronise a number of charities, including one intent on keeping fallen women off the streets. She'd looked into it before committing herself and discovered that the charity had a high failure rate. Puzzled – she would have accepted any offer that took her off the streets, if she'd lived there – Gwen had asked Lucy about it. And Lucy had pointed out that there were two factors that the high and mighty upper class women, who had never worked a day in their lives, had failed to take into account.

The first was economic; prostitutes earned more from prostituting themselves than they did by working in the jobs the charity had offered to them. And the second was pride; no one liked to be talked down to by a handful of condescending women who knew nothing of the reality of life on the streets. Or, for that matter, from churchmen who seemed to believe that they had a right to claim tithes from men and women who had little to spare.

"It seems a workable scheme," Lord Brockton said. "We could study the possibility and then decide if we wanted to commit ourselves."

"I suppose we could," Gwen said, keeping her voice under tight control. "But have you considered the social impact?"

Sir Benjamin stared at her. "The *social* impact?"

Gwen allowed herself a smile, then looked directly at

Norwell. "How many of our graduated magicians, the ones who would be expected to *father* those children, have wives and families of their own?"

Doctor Norwell blinked in surprise, but answered the question. "Almost all of them," he said. "We increase the stipend for magicians who marry and produce children, so they have strong reason to be fruitful and multiply."

Gwen looked back at Sir Benjamin. "The married magicians will have very unhappy wives if they father children with other women," she pointed out, mildly. "*Proven* adultery can be used as ground for separation, even divorce. You cannot order a magician to impregnate another woman – and even if you did, his wife would still be furious. I think the results would be disastrous for morale at the very least."

"Adultery is hardly unknown," Sir Benjamin said.

"There is a considerable difference between something that can be overlooked and something that is so blatantly public that it cannot be ignored," Gwen said, fighting to keep her voice under control. "You seem to expect that every wife will accept her husband fathering children with other women. Take my word for it; they will *not* take it calmly."

She allowed her gaze to move around the table, gauging reactions. Lord Brockton was looking thoughtful; clearly, he thought the idea was worth developing. Doctor Norwell seemed to agree with him, which was a pity. Gwen would have preferred him to be supporting her. Others, however, seemed to recognise Gwen's point. Women might have no political rights, but that wouldn't stop them from making their husband's life a misery if he acted *too* badly.

"Perhaps we could work on the project with unmarried magicians," Sir Benjamin said, perhaps suspecting that he'd overplayed his hand. "Or maybe we could just bury the details of who fathered who in the files."

"That worked out *so* well for Master Jackson," Gwen said. She held up a hand. "Your proposal is worthy of further study."

And hopefully it can be studied to death, she added, in

the privacy of her own mind.

The discussion moved on to the next few items on the agenda. Several people had reported seeing large, yet intelligent animals in Liverpool, suggesting the presence of Weres. Gwen rather doubted it – they could have come forward and joined the Royal Sorcerers Corps – but it had to be investigated. A pair of combat magicians were detailed to Liverpool to see what they could find out. At least there had been no reports that suggested that the Weres had gone feral. When they did, they were always the most dangerous of animals.

"The members of the Worshipful Order of Ancient Wisdom are threatening to sue us," Norton said, when she asked if there was any other business. "Apparently, we broke up a perfectly harmless meeting."

We, Gwen thought, sourly. She liked that.

"Not a good sign," Lord Brockton observed. "How many of them are well-connected?"

Gwen didn't bother to hide her anger this time. "They were on the verge of murdering a young girl for *nothing*," she snapped. "I don't know why they believed that murder would grant them powers beyond imagination, but all it would have done is left them with a dead body. We – I – had to stop them."

"Quite right," Lord Brockton said. "But the manner you chose to stop them caused embarrassment."

"How much more embarrassment would it have caused them," Gwen demanded, "if they had killed the girl and *then* got caught?"

She looked around the room. "Our job is not just to use magic for the defence of the realm," she reminded them. "We are also meant to protect the realm from magic, real or faked. And as for those... fools who thought they could murder a girl and get away with it, they had to be stopped too. And that is part of our job."

On that note, the meeting ended.

Chapter Six

aster Thomas would have joined the senior magicians for a drink after the committee meeting, Gwen knew. It was a chance to talk with them on a more informal basis – and relax, after getting his way in the meeting. But it wasn't an option open to her. Even if she hadn't been female, she was still much younger and less experienced than the men she was supposed to lead. And besides, she preferred to spend time alone rather than with other people. After spending much of her life in isolation, she had become used to it.

Back in her office, she looked down at the endless pile of letters and documents awaiting her signature. Master Thomas had had a secretary to help with his mail, but the poor man had disappeared during the Swing and Gwen hadn't wanted to find a replacement. Lord Mycroft had offered the service of one of his confidential clerks – the men who handled top secret papers buried in the government's vaults – but Gwen had learned the hard way to make sure that she read everything she signed. Giving that much power to someone else, when she had too many enemies, struck her as dangerous.

Most of the letters, thankfully, were simple enough. A handful were rather more complex, touching on legal matters; one of them addressed the pros and cons of using Talkers to interrogate suspects in prison. Gwen read it with some interest, noted the conclusion and then signed it with a flourish. It might be more *convenient* to have Talkers do the interrogations, but she couldn't think of anything more likely to cause a massive backlash against magicians in general. No one liked the idea of having their thoughts read.

We need to find more Sensitives, she thought, once she'd put the letter in the box for delivery. *They'd be better with interrogations, without intruding on someone's privacy.*

She contemplated it for a long moment, before putting the thought aside and turning to the next set of letters. They were reassuring missives written to the parents of young magicians, assuring them that their children would be perfectly safe at the Royal College. Two of them had been written specifically for a pair of mothers Gwen knew by reputation, who'd written to demand that their sons were not to have anything to do with low-born magicians. They were going to be disappointed, Gwen knew; there were no social barriers in the classroom. Besides, she happened to know that at least one of the sons went out drinking and wenching every night.

The next box contained letters sent to her personally. Several of them came from charities, including two that she'd already politely declined to publicly support; she put them aside for later consideration, when she had time to deal with them. A number questioned her competence as Royal Sorceress; she picked them up with her magic and tossed them into the fire. Two claimed to have found new forms of magic and she read them carefully, before putting them in the box to go to Doctor Norwell. The letters could be hoaxes – they'd certainly had hoaxes before – but they would have to be investigated. Everyone had thought that Healers were a myth until Jack had found one.

She gritted her teeth in irritation as she opened the penultimate letter. It was from another regular correspondent, who never seemed to notice that Gwen didn't write back to her. The elderly woman found the thought of her granddaughter wearing trousers – and working in the hospital – to be horrifying and insisted that Gwen do something about it. How, the letter demanded, could the young girl expect to find a proper husband if she had a reputation for walking around without a chaperone?

"Idiot," Gwen muttered. Even if she'd been inclined to help, she didn't run the hospitals and she didn't have any legal authority over non-magicians. Besides, it was the place of the girl's father to object and he didn't seem to have any concerns – although, with a mother-in-law like that, he might just be allowing his daughter to go to the hospital to annoy her grandmother.

The final letter was from her mother, inviting her to attend yet another fancy dress ball and hinting that a number of eligible young men would also be attending. She'd never quite given up on the thought that Gwen would marry, one day; she didn't seem to realise that it was unlikely that anyone would want her. What sort of man wanted a woman who was more powerful than himself? Gwen was, as far as she knew, unique. There were no other Master Magicians known to exist.

She sighed and pushed the letter towards the fire. Lady Mary would just have to do without a second wedding, at least for a decade or two; she could wait until her grandchildren were old enough to marry.

There was a knock on the door. Gwen reached out with her magic and opened it.

"Begging your pardon, milady," Sergeant Brandish said, "but there are two miscreants here to see you."

Gwen pursed her lips together in annoyance. She'd forgotten that she had to deal with students who had become a bit *too* unruly. At least Sergeant Brandish – who'd been recommended by the Duke of India – could keep them under control while she found the notes she'd been sent by their tutors. They were buried somewhere under the hundreds of other notes she was expected to read.

I probably should get a clerk, she thought, sourly.

One of the miscreants was in big trouble – or should be in big trouble. The other wasn't a student at all. Gwen scowled down at the note - there was no way to avoid the fact that she was about to lecture a man twice her age on behaving himself – and then looked up at the Sergeant.

"Send in the first one, please," she said.

Jonathon Dulcimer was handsome – and, judging by the way he swaggered into Gwen's office, knew it. He had black hair, cropped close to his skull like almost every other magician including Gwen herself, and a smile that suggested that he didn't really think he was in trouble. And he had a pedigree that would have convinced Gwen's mother to point her at him... if she hadn't been magical herself. Someone like Dulcimer would be *horrified* at the thought of having a wife who was more powerful than himself.

He reached for the chair on the other side of Gwen's desk, without bothering to ask permission. Gwen used her own magic to hold it in place, then glared at him until he stepped backwards, although he still held the air of irritating self-confidence. Did he really think that she would tolerate any disrespect? He was lucky he wasn't dealing with Master Thomas.

"Your tutors inform me that you have been molesting the maids," Gwen said, with an icy sharpness that should have warned him that he was in deep trouble. "I have no less than *five* complaints from different maids about your conduct. Do you have anything you wish to say for yourself?"

Dulcimer blinked in surprise, perhaps expecting nothing more than a droll lecture – if that. "I did nothing that they didn't want me to do," he said, quickly. "And I paid..."

Gwen cut him off. "You used your talent to pinch one of the maids," she said, unable to hide her scowl. Pinching a girl without touching her was an old Mover trick. It had been tried on Gwen, back when she'd been Master Thomas's apprentice. But she could retaliate. The maids had no such protection. If Dulcimer had had the sense to pinch them when there was another Mover around, they wouldn't even have known who to blame. "She had to be *Healed*."

She pressed on before Dulcimer could say a word. "And you tried to lure two other maids into your bed," she continued. "When they refused, you tried to molest them. Did you think that would go unnoticed?"

But it might have done, if the maids had been too terrified to speak. Or, if Dulcimer had used his brain, he might have realised that some of the maids were *happy* to share their charms with the student magicians, as long as they got paid. Gwen disapproved, but apparently nothing could be done to stop it. She'd seriously considered simply removing all the maids, before realising that they were necessary. Perhaps she should just hire older women instead.

She could expel Dulcimer – and part of her wanted to do just that. But they *needed* Movers... and expelling one for nothing more serious than playing with a maid would give the committee more ammunition to use against her. None of *them* would take the maid's objections seriously, not when they'd been deeply involved in running the farms. For all she knew, they might even *encourage* the maids to sleep with the students.

"They're just maids," Dulcimer objected. "Everyone knows..."

"Shut up," Gwen hissed, pushing Charm into her words. His mouth snapped shut with an audible click; he stared at her in mute horror. He hadn't really *believed* that she had power, she realised; it just hadn't made its way through his mind. "You will go tell the Sergeant that I am *thoroughly* displeased with your conduct and that he is to take immediate correctional measures."

She held his eyes, silently daring him to look away. "And you will *not* touch any of the maids, ever again," she added, lacing her words with more subtle Charm. Perhaps his mind was strong enough to break the compulsion, but if she was lucky, he'd never even question why he was staying away from the women. Lord Blackburn, whatever else could be said about the traitor, had given her a solid grounding in Charm – and in how the human mind could be quite inventive in concocting justifications for accepting it.

"Yes, Milady," he said.

"Go," Gwen ordered. "And send in the other miscreant."

She watched him leave, looking rather less self-confident than he had when he'd entered the room. Part of her felt like a bully, remembering all the tutors she'd scared off before Master Thomas had invited her to become his apprentice; part of her thought that Dulcimer thoroughly deserved it, just as he deserved the thrashing the Sergeant would give him. Maybe there was a good man in there somewhere. Maybe.

There must be something about power that makes it so easy to abuse, she thought, tiredly.

The door opened again, revealing an older man. Sam Davis was, according to the file, around thirty years old – but he looked at least forty. The file had stated that he'd been a Mover in the British Army in India and had fought bravely, before turning to drink in the aftermath of the Sikh War. And now he was in deep trouble for public drunkenness – and for threatening to destroy a pub when the owner refused to serve him more beer. If he'd carried out his threat, Gwen knew, nothing could have saved him. He would have been hanged after a short trial to determine his guilt.

He limped as he inched forward, the legacy of a wound suffered in India. Gwen discarded the thought of making him stand to attention and used her magic to push the chair towards him, allowing him to sit down. Up close, it was clear that he hadn't bothered to wash for a few days – or weeks; indeed, the policemen who'd found him had reported that he'd been sleeping rough. And to think that he had enough money in his RSC pension to pay for a flat, even in London. But he spent it all on drink.

"You need to clean up your act," she said, softly. Master Thomas would have yelled at him, but Master Thomas had been much older than the crippled Mover. Gwen felt absurdly like she was telling off her father. "Public drunkenness isn't good for the soul."

"As if they care about my soul," Davis said. He was middle-class; in his prime, he'd been a more powerful Mover than Cannock, who'd taught Gwen how to use her talent. But once he'd been crippled, the Corps hadn't bothered to find him another position. "I am nothing to them."

Gwen knew how he felt. If a male Master Magician were to be discovered, she could easily see the Royal Committee trying to ease her out of her position. Davis should have been offered more of a pension; hell, they could have put him in the farms and he would probably have been happy. Instead, they'd just left him to rot.

And that wouldn't be her problem, if he hadn't been a magician.

"Listen to me," she said. "There are Healers now. You could go to them and get Healed..."

"And then go back to the war?" Davis demanded. "You think I want to fight again? I can find other employment in London and..."

He stopped, abruptly. "But you're just a chit of a girl," he added. "You wouldn't want to know about that, would you?"

"Probably not," Gwen said. A Mover could find work anywhere, even if he didn't want to work for the Royal Sorcerers Corps. And if he cleaned up his act, *she* wasn't going to destroy his career by denying him permission to work outside the Corps. "One moment."

There were just too few Healers to heal *everyone* who might need treatment. Gwen had prioritised magicians who were injured in the line of duty, then insisted that everyone who could pay a reasonable fee had to pay. It never failed to irritate her how many aristocrats, men and women who had enough money to buy houses in the centre of London, tried to avoid paying to be Healed. Didn't they realise that, six months ago, there were some wounds and diseases that were literally beyond all help? Or, for that matter, that a wound that might be an inconvenience to an aristocrat could be disastrous to someone without enough money to fall back on when they lost their job.

She wrote out the slip quickly, then passed it to Davis. "That slip will get you a session with a Healer," she said, simply. "Your leg can be healed, then you can take up employment with whomever you want. I won't stand in your way."

Davis stared at her, as if he didn't quite believe his good fortune. "But... but I'm a *drunk*."

"You can ask the Healer to do something about that too," Gwen said, although she had her doubts. Years ago, an aristocrat had ordered a Charmer to ensure that his son never touched opium again. The young man had committed suicide shortly afterwards, for no apparent reason. Doctor Norwell had speculated that the opium had filled a need in the young man's mind, one that had never found something else to replace the drug.

"Thank you," Davis said, still staring at her. "But..."

He stood up and bowed to her, then limped towards the door, one hand clutching the slip of paper as if it promised salvation – which, in a way, it did. Gwen sighed, shook her head as the door closed behind him, then turned back to her papers. Moments later, there was yet another knock on the door. Wearily, she pulled it open.

"Sir James," she said, in some surprise. "What can I do for you?"

Sir James gave her a brilliant smile. "Merlin has been given orders to be on alert when the French visit the Palace," he said. "We're assembling here tomorrow morning. I was wondering if you wanted to run the gauntlet with us."

Gwen eyed him, thoughtfully. The gauntlet was the final testing ground for combat magicians, men who had been taught to work as a team. Maybe they couldn't be Masters, but Merlin had years of experience in combining their abilities for best results. And yet they had little experience in *fighting* Masters. Sooner or later, there was going to be another Master Magician who wasn't loyal to the British Crown.

"You want to try and catch me," she said. *She* needed the experience too – and besides, she wanted to work off some frustration. It wasn't as if she had another Master to pit herself against either. "It might be a good idea."

"Splendid," Sir James said, rubbing his hands together. "You know, you really should spend more time with us, rather than the committee. They're dreadfully boring."

"*You're* on the committee," Gwen pointed out.

"I'm an exception," he assured her. "And I won't be there for much longer. The Iron Duke will find a magician who can speak for the military and I'll go back on active service."

Gwen nodded. "I'll see you tomorrow morning," she

said. It had been months since she'd last gone through the gauntlet. It was designed for small groups, not a single magician who could evade most of the traps with ease. "How many of the traps are you going to leave there?"

"None," Sir James said. "Just you and us. How does that sound?"

"Fun," Gwen said. One way or another, she could let off her frustrations – and no one could object, at least not publicly. There were no other Master Magicians, after all. "See if you can pin me down."

"We won't hold back," Sir James assured her, mock-seriously. "We *know* how dangerous women can be."

"Out," Gwen said, unable to hide her amusement. "I'll catch up with the paperwork tonight and give you the whole morning tomorrow."

She watched him go, then turned back to the papers, working her way through them one by one. Nothing seemed to be out of place, but still... she worried that, one day, she would sign away something important. And yet if the paperwork kept rising up, she would eventually be buried under the weight.

"Boring," she muttered aloud. "I need something else to do."

Chapter Seven

wen couldn't help a thrill of anticipation as she washed, dressed and ate breakfast the following morning. The Royal Sorcerer was supposed to be a fighter, but she'd done very little *fighting* since the end of the Swing and she was surprised to discover just how much she'd missed it. Fighting was rough and tumble, with the very real danger of serious injury... and yet it was much simpler than the political and bureaucratic skirmishes she had to wage every day. Even the prospect of taking on Britain's foremost team of combat magicians couldn't dull her excitement.

Several buildings near Cavendish Hall had been destroyed during the Swing, allowing the Royal College to snap them up in the aftermath and add their grounds to the training area. One of the buildings was being rebuilt to serve as extra living space for the magicians and their servants; the other piles of debris had been taken away or used to help build the Gauntlet. On the face of it, it was nothing more than a makeshift village – more of a hamlet – that served as the training ground. Anyone who walked into the hamlet without taking due precautions, however, would swiftly wind up in trouble. The hamlet was designed to trap magicians.

We're not invincible, Gwen reminded herself, as Sir James escorted her around the edge of the hamlet to where she would enter the Gauntlet. Merlin would enter from the other side, with instructions to capture Gwen before she could make it out. Excited as she was, she also knew that she could get hurt; the six combat magicians who made up the team wouldn't hold back, and they were far more experienced than Gwen herself.

"I'd wish you luck," Sir James said, "but..."

Gwen had to smile. "I understand," she said, dryly. "I could always wish you bad luck, couldn't I?"

Sir James laughed and walked away. Gwen watched him go and then turned her attention back to the Gauntlet. The edge of the training area was marked by trees, each one large enough to provide a surprising amount of cover – and conceal the training exercise from prying eyes. No one was supposed to enter until they got the word, whereupon... she'd have to get through it, rather than just beat the combat magicians. She could take out five of them and still lose.

Choose your attacks carefully, she reminded herself. *And try to shape them towards the person you're fighting.*

She shook her head and waited. Patience might be a virtue, as her mother had remarked more than once, but it wasn't one of *hers*. How long would it take for Merlin to get ready to move?

A thought touched her mind. *Go.*

Bracing herself, Gwen stepped through the trees and into the hamlet, crouching low. A handful of buildings, none of them much larger than a backyard shed, greeted her, providing a limited amount of cover. But anyone who relied on them for safety would run into trouble; the tall grasses surrounding them concealed hidden pitfalls and other dangers. Concentrating, she tried to pull an illusion of nothingness around her. It wouldn't make her completely invisible, certainly not in broad daylight, but it should make her harder to see.

She briefly considered throwing herself into the air and making a run for the far edge – she would win by escaping, even if they all survived without being taken out – before dismissing the idea. It wouldn't work, not when there was absolutely no cover in the air. They'd see her and then their Movers would pull her out of the sky. Or simply disrupt her magic and let gravity do the rest.

In the distance, she could hear the sounds of birds calling as she inched forward. She couldn't hear anything that suggested that Merlin was advancing on her position, which suggested that they were sticking close to the exit. It made sense, she knew; they won by stopping her and she *had* to reach the exit to win. Sweat trickled down her face as she kept moving, reaching out with her senses. If there was someone lying in wait, she might just be able to sense them before they jumped her.

Nothing materialised to block her path. She passed two small buildings, carefully checking them out from a distance, yet there was nothing. Where *were* they? The third building seemed, just for a moment, to be occupied, before she realised that she was sensing a fox, hiding out in the city. There was more wildlife in London than many people realised. She smiled... and then she sensed their presence.

She closed her eyes, concentrating. There were at least two magicians ahead of her, but she couldn't tell which ones. Sir James was smart and experienced; who would he send forward to flush her out? Gwen would have sent the Blazers, knowing that they'd have the best chance to win quickly. But it was quite possible that he had something else in mind. And there was no time to think.

Quickly, she created an illusion of herself and sent it forward. It wasn't quite right, but if they acted quickly they wouldn't have time to realise it. There was a brilliant flash of light as one of the Blazers shot a beam of magic at the illusion, exposing his own position in the process. Gwen fired a beam of her own back at him and heard a handful of colourful curses, none of them suitable for female ears. Tagged, the Blazer would have no choice, but to withdraw.

She pulled her magic around her, forming a protective bubble, and ran forwards. The second magician was infusing magic into the ground, preparing a minefield. Gwen saw the magic destabilising and threw herself into the air, rising up as quickly as she could. The ground exploded with blue fire a moment later, a trick she'd seen before, but rarely performed so well. If she'd been a mere Blazer, she would have been caught in that second.

A powerful force struck her bubble and sent her falling back towards the ground. She pulled the bubble around her as strongly as she could, then winced in pain as she felt the feedback when the bubble hit the ground. It popped a moment later, forcing her to concentrate to re-establish it. She hesitated, then ran around the building, almost running right into another Mover. He wrapped his own bubble around him as she fired another blast of magic into his face, then ramped up the brightness. Gwen heard him curse as he covered his eyes, fighting to maintain his bubble. She drew on her magic and skimmed away across the ground, hoping that he'd be too distracted to notice that she'd gone, at least for a few seconds.

Flames roared up in front of her and she stopped dead, before realising that they had to be an illusion. The other Blazer was a skilled master of illusions, according to his files; flames were simple, easy to produce. She ran through them, feeling nothing, and looked around for the Blazer. He was nowhere to be seen... and yet he couldn't be too far away. Very few illusions lasted longer than a few seconds if the magician just left them alone.

Idiot, she told herself, a moment later. She called on her magic and blazed away, lashing out at random. The Blazer was so skilful that he could probably hide in plain sight. A moment later, he fired back at her, clearly aware that there was no place to hide. Gwen smiled as it bounced off her bubble, then struck him with her own beam. He made a show of collapsing to the ground, dead.

"STOP," a voice barked. "FREEZE!"

Gwen froze as the command slammed into her mind. *The Charmer*, she realised; *he must have been waiting for a chance to Charm me.*

She cursed inwardly, fighting the command. It was powerful, more powerful than anything she'd experienced before, even from Lord Blackburn. But the more obvious it was that someone was using Charm, the easier it was to fight it. Magic sparkled in front of her and his control over her body snapped, allowing her to jump forward and throw herself right at the Charmer. He lifted a hand, as if he expected her to hit him with her fists, and she knocked him into a wall with her magic. She watched him crumble to the ground...

... Something wrapped around her legs and pulled, hard. Gwen lost her balance and started to fall, before realising that she was dangling from an invisible rope. Sir James had finally shown himself, slipping his power through her defences while she took care of his team mates – he *was* good at it. Gwen thought desperately as she saw him, standing in the middle of the grassy field, daring her to stop him before it was too late. Catching sight of some rubble on the ground, she picked it up with her magic and hurled it towards him.

Her aim was bad and she missed, but the debris came close enough to force him to lose his concentration and Gwen had a moment to break free. She fell towards the ground, barely catching herself before she would have landed badly. Even Lucy, the most skilled Healer in the Corps, wouldn't have been able to put her back together again. Gwen picked herself off the ground and threw a powerful bolt of magic towards Sir James. He might have been only a Mover, but he blocked it effortlessly. A moment later, he threw the debris back towards her.

Gwen muttered unladylike words under her breath as the debris bounced off her bubble. Sir James had taken advantage of her distraction to run towards her, slamming his power directly into hers. She winced in pain as her bubble wavered under the pressure; he had much more experience with his specific power, even if she possessed the full power set. He winked at her, then altered his magic. His protective bubble became a set of needles poking into *her* bubble. Gwen stared in disbelief. She'd never even *thought* that was possible.

For a second, absolute panic held her spellbound, then she threw herself backwards as her bubble started to collapse. Sir James pushed forward, refusing to give her any time to recover; Gwen forced herself to push the remains of her bubble right at him. The magic hadn't faded completely, turning the remnants into needle-sharp fragments that sliced into his protections. But they weren't powerful enough to overcome him completely.

She lifted her hand, generating light again... but Sir James just kept coming forward, covering his eyes. He might not have the powers of a Sensitive, yet he didn't need them; his power pervaded the air, allowing him to locate her without much difficulty. She gritted her teeth, reached out with her magic and tore into the ground, pulling up great clods of earth and throwing them at him. The effort strained her to the limit, but forced him to slow down, just long enough for Gwen to turn and run. If she could find cover, just for a second...

A flash of light passed over her head, narrowly missing her. The other Blazer, she realised; a confident man who'd impressed her more than she'd wanted to admit. She twisted and threw magic back at him, but he ducked and evaded it. Cursing, Gwen pulled a new bubble around herself and fired a second blast at the blazer. And then Sir James caught her again.

Not this time, she thought, as his magic wrapped around hers and lifted her up into the air, despite her protective bubble. He flipped her upside down... did he really think that would discomfit her? She'd learned how to fly, even upside down, months ago. Gwen concentrated and hardened her bubble, feeling his magic crawling over hers. This time, he wouldn't be able to break her protections so quickly...

... And then his magic flickered. Gwen frowned, puzzled, just as the pressure on her started to intensify. How could *anyone* generate so much power? It would take... she saw it a moment later and cursed her own mistake. She should have made sure that the other Mover was down and out before she ran into Sir James. There were *two* of them pouring pressure on her shield. She shuddered as she felt their magic crowding her, shaping needles that were slowly burning into her bubble. It wouldn't be long before it popped and she was defenceless...

Desperately, she called on her Charm.

"Let me go," she ordered, pushing as much power into her words as she could. "Let me go!"

The pressure lessoned, just long enough for her to hope that she'd succeeded, then tightened again. Naturally; Merlin had a Charmer on the team and they would have practised resistance until Charm barely affected them. Gwen had done the same, although she was far less practised. She gritted her teeth, trying to hold out, but she was rapidly reaching the limits of her endurance. And then her bubble burst and she fell.

Sir James caught her a moment before she hit the ground, slowing her fall so she landed gently. She felt his magic crawling over her, holding her down, as he walked over towards her and tapped her on the forehead.

"I think we win," he said. He had the grace to sound a little ashamed about it. "But you didn't do badly,"

Gwen could barely move, even after Sir James's magic had faded away. She didn't think that she was physically injured, beyond a number of minor bruises that would heal quickly, but she was completely exhausted. And he thought that she hadn't done badly? If she'd had to face Master Thomas alone, she would have been beaten in short order. She took the hand he held out to her and allowed him to help her to her feet, feeling the world blurring around her.

"Here," Sir James said. He pushed something against her mouth and she sipped gratefully. "Drink this."

The water tasted pure and, at that moment, like ambrosia. Gwen leaned on him long enough to recover her bearings, then gently let go of his arm. He gave her an understanding look; she didn't dare show weakness in front of the committee. If she gave them any excuse to think of her as a weak and feeble woman...

I almost won, she told herself, angrily. *I'd like to see the Committee do so well.*

But she knew that it wouldn't matter.

"You would have beaten any one of us," the Charmer said. Gwen couldn't remember his name at the moment, if only because she preferred to have as little to do with Charmers as she could. "We had to work together to overwhelm you."

"And should have stayed closer together," Sir James grunted. He looked tired too; Gwen felt a little better when she saw the sweat dripping off his brow. "We could have won quicker if we hadn't wanted to catch you away from the exit."

Gwen pulled herself upright as they stepped through the trees and out onto the lawn. Refusing to waste such a fine day, the cooks had offered to prepare a garden lunch for the magicians and Gwen had accepted, before realising just how worn out she was going to be after the fighting. It had really been too long since she'd fought properly. Perhaps she could convince Lord Mycroft to keep Merlin in London for a few more months. There *were* other teams of combat magicians and India didn't need them as much as Britain.

She pushed the thought aside as she sat down on one of the rugs and accepted a chicken leg and a bowl of salad from one of the servants. Sir James joined her and chatted happily about nothing, while two of his team mates went over to the students and started telling them exaggerated stories – or at least Gwen *hoped* they were exaggerated – about service in India with the British Army. Most of the new recruits would *go* to the army afterwards, Gwen knew; the threat of war could not be disregarded, even on such a lovely day.

"You did extremely well," Sir James said, loudly. "You came very close to beating us."

Gwen glanced at him in surprise, then realised that Lord Brockton had come close enough to listen to them without making it obvious. Praise from Sir James for her wouldn't make Lord Brockton feel any better, but at least it would make him less sure of his allies on the Committee. Gwen looked back at Sir James and wondered if she could count him an ally – and, if so, for how long. He wouldn't remain in London indefinitely.

Perhaps His Lordship should consider himself lucky, she thought, ruefully. *Master Thomas would have killed him by now*.

She finished eating, said her goodbyes and walked back into Cavendish Hall, heading back to her suite. Martha had, thankfully, already laid out another suit; Gwen simply had to undress, wash herself quickly and then get dressed again. Her body was covered with bruises, as she had expected, but they would heal quickly. There was no point in asking Lucy to Heal them.

There was a frantic tapping at the door. "Come in," Gwen called.

A maid, panting slightly, stepped into the room. "Your Ladyship," she said, between gasps. "Lord Mycroft has arrived in his carriage. He requests that you accompany him."

Gwen blinked in surprise. Lord Mycroft rarely changed his routine for anything or anyone, even the King. Whatever the matter was, it had to be urgent. War? Had France declared war?

"I'll grab my coat," she said. Thankfully, she was washed, dried and dressed. She didn't want to ride in a stuffy carriage while she was still unclean. "Tell him I'll be with him in two minutes."

Chapter Eight

re we at war?"

Lord Mycroft regarded Gwen gravely as she climbed into the carriage and sat down facing him.

"Not yet, but we could be soon," he said. He rang a bell and the carriage lurched into life, the coachman cracking the whip to make the horses move faster. "A situation has developed that requires your presence."

Gwen studied him, thoughtfully. He looked... *mussed*, as if he'd been forced to leave the office on very short notice. Coming to think of it, she reminded herself, he rarely ever left the office. Whatever had happened had to be urgent – or disastrous.

Lord Mycroft leaned forward, resting his hands on top of his cane. The pose reminded Gwen so strongly of Master Thomas that she felt an odd sense of *déjà vu* for a long moment, before firmly reminding herself that Master Thomas was dead. She missed him, even with what had happened in his final hours. If she'd had more time to learn the ropes, and impress the Royal Committee, would she have had so many problems now?

"Tell me," Lord Mycroft said. "Have you ever heard of Sir Travis Mortimer?"

Gwen hesitated, thinking hard. "Not that I recall," she said, finally. He didn't sound like one of the men that Lady Mary had tried to convince her would make a suitable husband – and he wasn't one of the people she dealt with as Royal Sorcerer. It wasn't really surprising; there were so many people knighted in the British Empire that she couldn't hope to be familiar with them all.

"He *was* one of your people," Lord Mycroft said, with a single raised eyebrow. "But, to be fair, he spent the Swing in India, so you might not have met him personally."

Gwen flushed. She *didn't* know every magician in the Royal Sorcerers Corps – and probably never would. The sorcerers that had been sent to India or America or South Africa were on very long-term deployments. Some of them might not even have heard that Master Thomas had died, to be replaced by a slip of a girl. Even with Talkers, it took months for news to reach everywhere in the Empire.

"He was a Sensitive," Lord Mycroft added. "Quite an unusual fellow, really."

Gwen nodded, tightly. Sensitives were uncommon – and they tended to be predominantly women, rather than men. Doctor Norwell had admitted, when pressed, that men *liked* having the big and noisy powers, but preferred not to talk about possessing the more *subtle* powers. Charm was less effective if the victim knew that he was being Charmed... and Sensitivity sounded disgracefully feminine. *Men*!

But, masculine or not, it could be a very useful talent.

"A powerful Sensitive," she mused. "What happened to him?"

Lord Mycroft scowled. "Sir Travis was discovered dead this morning," he said, grimly. "I was informed immediately, naturally, and came at once to Cavendish Hall. Your presence is required."

Gwen winced. Losing a magician *hurt*, even if she hadn't known him personally. Maybe Master Thomas had been able to accept losing his people calmly, but she felt as if she would never master *that* skill. She wasn't even sure she *wanted* to.

"I see," she said, thinking hard. "What killed him?"

"A blow to the back of the head, according to the report," Lord Mycroft said. "Do you see why that is odd?"

"Yes," Gwen said, slowly. "A Sensitive should not have died that way."

When she pushed her limits, she was almost completely aware of her surroundings, right up to the point where the sudden influx of information threatened to overwhelm her mind. A Sensitive, with only one talent, would either go mad or learn to live with it – and if he succeeded, he'd have a formidable tool. It was impossible to lie to a Sensitive, or prevent one from reading you, no matter how much you tried. Even keeping one's mouth shut didn't hide the reaction that betrayed your innermost thoughts.

No Sensitive had a comfortable life. They rarely slept well – a single noise could awake them – and their marriages tended to end poorly. Gwen knew, from watching her own parents, that there were matters her mother and father never discussed openly, but that option would never be available to a Sensitive. Master Thomas had urged her to develop her Sensitivity, but never to rely on it. A Sensitive could be crippled by a sudden loud noise.

She looked over at Lord Mycroft and frowned. "Sir Travis was in *India*?"

"Indeed he was," Lord Mycroft confirmed. "And yet he managed to keep from being overwhelmed by the exotic."

"Impressive," Gwen admitted. Maybe she would have liked Sir Travis, if they'd ever had a chance to meet. Or maybe he would have been as smug and full of himself as many of the senior magicians. "What do you want me to do?"

Lord Mycroft smiled. "I want you to investigate his death," he said, calmly. "*That* is one of your roles as Royal Sorceress."

Gwen blinked. "I am no detective," she pointed out. "Surely your brother..."

"My brother has... other matters to concern himself with," Lord Mycroft admitted. "But even if he were free, it would still be your responsibility. A magician is dead, seemingly murdered. We must know the truth before time runs out."

Murdered, Gwen thought. It didn't seem likely. Sneaking up on a Sensitive was impossible, unless the magician was drugged and comatose. Sir Travis would have known if someone with murderous intentions approached him – or, for that matter, if someone had been

Charmed into serving as an unwitting cat's paw. How could a murderer have got close to him?

Maybe he was tricked, somehow, she thought. If nothing else, they would have to solve the mystery to ensure it could never happen again. But she honestly didn't know where to begin.

"Start with the crime scene," Lord Mycroft advised. "And then see where it leads you."

Investigating magical crimes *was* part of the Royal Sorcerer's job, Master Thomas had told her, but he'd never given her any formal training. There just hadn't been enough time... and there might not have *been* any formal training. Gwen had watched Lestrade at work long enough to know that he had a habit of chasing the blindingly obvious or finding himself unable to work out how to proceed. Scotland Yard just didn't seem to have very many detectives.

But any one of them would be better prepared than Gwen.

"The police will be supporting you," Lord Mycroft assured her. "But you *do* have to take the lead. It is *expected* of you."

Gwen scowled. If she pushed someone else forward, even Mycroft's brother, the Royal Committee would snicker and claim that she was shirking her responsibilities. And if she did try to find the killer, if there *was* a killer, they would claim that she was shirking her *other* responsibilities. Master Thomas hadn't had to deal with so much backchat...

... *Or maybe he did*, she reminded herself. She'd never attended any formal meetings of the Royal Committee before he'd died, merely the emergency meetings before the Swing had gripped London and the government had had to flee the city.

"Send me a couple of clerks," she said, resignedly. If she could shuffle the paperwork onto someone else – at least the task of filtering out the unimportant letters from the hundreds she received each day – it would make life a little easier. And perhaps she could pass some decision-making down to the senior magicians. She didn't *have* to approve their training schedules, did she?

"They will be at Cavendish Hall later today," Lord Mycroft assured her. "And don't worry. They know how to be discreet."

The carriage rattled to a stop. Gwen almost jumped as a hidden panel appeared behind her head, revealing the face of the coachman. "The police are blocking the road up to the building, sir," he said, to Mycroft. "They insist that you have to walk."

"Unsurprising," Lord Mycroft said. He stood up, opened the door and clambered out with remarkable agility for a man his size. "You can wait with the other cabs until I come back."

Gwen jumped down beside Mycroft and glanced around. Like most aristocratic houses in this part of London, Mortimer Hall was surrounded by a brick wall that served more to mark the owner's territory than provide a barrier. Gwen could have scrambled over it without using magic; given that she could see apple trees rising up on the far side, she had a feeling that the young men in the district probably raided the garden regularly. Olivia had told her that it was a common rite of passage among the young men unfortunate enough to grow up in the Rookery. Raiding an aristocrat's garden made them feel like they were fighting back, even though it was petty and pointless.

Lord Mycroft led the way down towards the gates, which were guarded by a line of burly policemen in blue uniforms. She winced as she saw a handful of reporters already there, shouting questions towards the policemen and a handful of men in black suits, who probably worked for Mycroft. Some reporters were decent people, she was prepared to admit, but others had a remarkable skill for twisting the truth into something unrecognisable, without ever actually telling a lie. The freedom of the press was yet another consequence of the Swing – there were over two *thousand* new newspapers founded in London in the last six months – but there were times when she thought that it had gone too far.

And they recognised her, of course.

"Lady Gwen," one reporter shouted. "Do you have any

comments?"

Gwen ignored them as best as she could, even though the questions were growing more and more absurd. Hardly anyone seemed to know that Sir Travis was a Sensitive – which did make a certain amount of sense – and half of the reporters seemed to have decided that a magician had killed him. It hadn't been *that* long since Jack had terrorised the aristocracy, after all. A couple of rogue magicians could easily break into a house and kill the inhabitants...

She pushed the thought aside as Lord Mycroft led her through the gates. Mortimer Hall was smaller than Gwen's own home, built in a dark gothic style that had been all the rage a hundred or so years ago. It seemed to have survived the Swing with very little damage, but she couldn't help noticing that a number of windows were boarded up and the Garden had been allowed to slip out of control. The handful of statues – all angels weeping and covering their faces, as if they were trying not to see the evil of the world – sent a shiver running down her spine.

"I believe that Sir Travis's mother died while he was in India," Lord Mycroft said. "His father died when he was very young, leaving her to bring up their child on her own. She refused to move back with her family, even though there was no hint of scandal tainting the birth. Instead, she stayed here."

Gwen nodded, sourly. Magical children *terrified* the non-magicians; God knew she'd terrified hundreds of servants into giving their notices and seeking employment elsewhere before Master Thomas had taken her to be his apprentice. A Sensitive wouldn't accidentally burn down the house or go flying, but he'd still have too much insight and a complete lack of discretion. Gwen suspected that Sir Travis's mother had decided, after one or two incidents, that it was safer to keep her child isolated.

She could have given him up for adoption instead, she thought, realising that she would probably have liked her, if they'd ever met. But then, *Gwen's* mother had never seriously considered giving her up, even after her social reputation began to suffer. Maybe she'd underestimated her mother all along.

The doorway was wide open, but guarded by two more policemen. "The Inspector is awaiting you in the study," one of them assured Lord Mycroft. The other was staring at Gwen, as if he couldn't quite grasp how she was wearing male clothing. "Do you require an escort?"

"I have been here before," Lord Mycroft said. "But thank you for the offer."

Gwen stared at his back as they walked inside. If Lord Mycroft had been here... Sir Travis had to have been *important*. Maybe it made sense to have the meeting away from Whitehall, where a Sensitive would find it hard to avoid being overwhelmed by his surroundings, but if that had been a problem, how would Sir Travis have been able to operate in India?

She couldn't ask when there were so many policemen around, so she concentrated on looking around and studying the interior of the building. It was surprisingly bare; she could see places on the walls where portraits had hung, before they had been taken down and stored elsewhere. There were definitely signs that *someone* had been trying to keep the place tidy, but it was clear that they were losing the fight. Dust was everywhere, particularly in places few men would notice. Maybe, Gwen told herself, Lady Mary's lessons on how to run a household hadn't been wasted after all. It was clear that Sir Travis hadn't been a married man.

The stairs seemed reassuringly solid, even though half of the carpeting had been removed and the rest had ugly marks from where dozens of policemen had tramped up and down. At the top, two doors had been forced open by the policemen, revealing rooms so dusty that it was clear that no one had been inside them for months, if not years. The pieces of furniture in the opened rooms were covered with cloths, providing some protection against the ravages of time. Somehow, Gwen doubted that they would still be in good condition anyway.

"Sir Travis saw no need to use the rooms," Lord Mycroft explained. "They were closed off, one by one."

He stopped outside a larger room and peered inside.

"Lestrade," he said, by way of greeting. "I trust that the crime scene remains undisturbed?"

"Yes, Your Lordship," Lestrade said. He looked understandably nervous; the last time aristocrats had started to die, he hadn't managed to catch the killer either. But then, he wouldn't have *wanted* to catch a Master Magician without some heavy magical support. "Sir Travis is lying right where he fell."

Gwen braced herself as she stepped into the room. Few people in London would have been comfortable allowing a woman to look at dead bodies; she still remembered the incredulous looks the policemen had thrown at her and Master Thomas when they'd thought they couldn't be seen. Now, part of her was used to seeing corpses... London had been littered with bodies by the time the Swing was over. And it was part of her job.

Sir Travis looked to have been decent, she decided. He was surprisingly pale for a man who had been in India and Turkey, but that might not have been surprising. A Sensitive would prefer to avoid the sun where possible. He was clearly healthy, wearing a thin nightshirt and trousers that would have allowed him to host meetings without bothering to get properly dressed. There were some people – Lady Mary, for example – who would have complained about such informality, but a Sensitive could be counted upon to know his friends.

"That's the cause of death," Lestrade said, pointing to the back of Sir Travis's head. Blood matted his hair, revealing a nasty crack in his skull. Even a Healer couldn't have saved someone whose skull had been caved in. Death, Gwen suspected, would have been effectively instant. "Can you sense anything from the wound?"

Gwen gritted her teeth and knelt down beside the body. Carefully, she opened her senses, bracing herself for a rush of memories and impressions burned onto the world by the trauma of Sir Travis's death. Instead, there was nothing...

... apart from an alarmingly familiar scent.

"Wolfbane," she said. "Someone wanted to block a werewolf's nose."

"Yes," Lestrade said. "Anything else?"

Gwen hesitated. "No," she said, finally. There should have been *something*, unless Sir Travis had been taken completely by surprise. But if that were the case, how could someone have sneaked up on a Sensitive? "I take it that he couldn't have committed suicide."

Lestrade gave her an odd look. "Suicides normally shoot themselves, or stab themselves, or take poison, or jump off bridges," he said. "I don't see how he could have killed himself in such a manner."

Gwen stood upright and looked around. There were no signs of a struggle, apart from a broken object – a vase, she guessed, as there were several other intact vases in the room – that had been flung against the wall. Could it have been the murder weapon? She walked over and picked up one of the pieces, only to discover that it was almost eggshell-thin. It would have shattered on a person's skull, without inflicting any real damage.

"I shall leave you to your task, Lady Gwen," Lord Mycroft said. He looked over at Lestrade. "See to it that she gets all the help and support that she requires."

"Of course, Your Lordship," Lestrade said. "But we have already arrested a suspect."

Gwen blinked. "A suspect?"

"The one other person in the house when Sir Travis met his untimely end," Lestrade said. "His maid. She is currently in the kitchen, being interrogated..."

"I think I should talk to her," Gwen said, shortly.

"A good idea," Lord Mycroft said. "I shall see you in Whitehall, Lady Gwen."

He bowed and left the room, twisting slightly so he could pass through the door. Gwen watched him go, then looked back at Lestrade. She could understand why he'd arrested the maid, but how could someone have harboured murderous intentions for so long and yet remained undetected by her master? A Sensitive would know better than to treat a servant as part of the furniture...

"Take me to her," Gwen ordered.

Lestrade bowed and led her out of the room.

Chapter Nine

ir Travis's mother died just after the Swing," Lestrade said, as they made their way down to the kitchen. "The maid was left in the house all alone until Sir Travis returns from India – and he dies bare weeks later. I don't think that was a coincidence."

Gwen scowled, keeping her thoughts to herself. Lestrade was as tenacious as a bulldog, which wasn't always a good thing. When he came up with a theory that fitted the facts, he rarely gave up on it easily, to the point where he twisted or ignored later facts so he could keep his original theory. She had to admit that two deaths in the same house looked suspicious, but it didn't necessarily follow that the maid was a murderess.

"Maybe," she said, finally. "How did Sir Travis's mother die?"

"Cold, the doctor claimed," Lestrade said. "She did have a hard life – plenty of family heirlooms had to be sold off to provide for her son. And many of their cousins called her a traitor."

Gwen nodded. Every aristocratic family with a high opinion of itself – which was almost all of them – prided itself on passing houses, land, paintings, jewels and worthless tat picked up overseas down to its distant descendents. There were aristocratic families, having trouble making ends meet, that could have solved their problems by selling off some of their family collections. But that wasn't the done thing in Polite Society. Sir Travis's mother would have been accused of throwing away her son's heritage, even though she would have had no choice. It wasn't as if his relatives had helped her when she needed it.

She glanced over at Lestrade and asked a question. "There was only one maid?"

"I don't think they could have afforded to keep others," Lestrade said.

Gwen blinked in surprise. Sir Travis's family had been poorer than she realised, if only because house help was *cheap*. Gwen's mother had never had any difficulty hiring servants, even though they'd heard rumours about Gwen herself. A regular aristocratic family would have a small army of servants, ranging from cooks to coachmen. You weren't anyone in society unless you had a horse and carriage of your very own.

She scowled as Lestrade led her into the kitchen. It was smaller than she'd expected, smaller than the one she remembered from back home – and clearly not designed for feeding more than a handful of guests. A gas stove sat in the middle of the room, flanked by two tables and a free-standing set of shelves loaded with cooking tools. Gwen had never really cooked anything in her life – her mother had been outraged, the sole time she'd asked if she could learn to cook – and she didn't recognise half of the tools. At the far end of the room, there was a giant fireplace that looked large enough to roast a whole cow. It was so barren that she realised that it hadn't been used for years.

The maid was seated in the middle of the room, her hands cuffed behind her back. She was a tiny thing, wearing a white dress that had clearly seen better days – and contrasted oddly with her dark skin. Gwen had seen coloured men before, but the maid was the blackest person she had ever seen. The whites of her eyes stood out against her face, which appeared to be bruised where someone had hit her, perhaps more than once. And she couldn't have been more than fourteen years old.

Gwen met her eyes... and saw nothing, but outright terror. She found it impossible to believe that this frail girl could be a murderer, or that she could have got the better of Sir Travis, who had been a strong man as well as a

Sensitive. And yet... what was she doing here? There had been a craze, some years ago, for black butlers, but the girl was clearly no butler...

"She was taken off a slaver when she was a child by the Royal Navy," Lestrade said. "The Captain was one of Lord Nelson's former officers – and you know Lord Nelson's position on slavery. She was taken back to Britain, trained as a domestic and eventually sent to work for Lady Mortimer. It was the best they could have done for her."

"Right," Gwen said. She couldn't help noticing the girl staring at her when she heard Gwen's unmistakably feminine voice. "Take your men out of here and leave us alone."

Lestrade gave her an odd look, but nodded and started to bark orders to his men. One of them seemed concerned about leaving Gwen with a potential murderess; the other pointed out that the girl was cuffed – and besides, Gwen had powerful magic to defend herself. Gwen watched them go, then knelt down beside the girl and studied her face. Up close, it was clear that the policemen had been beating her to try to force a confession. And, because of the colour of her skin, no one would complain.

Lord Nelson had beaten the Barbary Pirates, who'd raided British shipping and sold British citizens into slavery, by personally leading the invasion of Tripoli. Afterwards, he'd joined the antislavery campaign, pointing out that slavery was the lifeblood of Britain's North African enemies – and anything that hampered slavery worked in Britain's favour. The slaveholders in the British Empire did not agree... and even a man as famous as Lord Nelson could only get so far. If the Royal Navy hadn't been so stubborn about the right of a Captain to do whatever he pleased on his ship, the Captain who'd liberated the maid might have been in serious trouble.

"Hello," Gwen said, as lightly as she could. "My name is Gwen. What's your name?"

"Polly," the maid said. Her voice was surprisingly upper-class, which surprised Gwen until she realised that the only person Polly would have talked to for years was

Lady Mortimer. "I didn't kill him!"

"I didn't say you did," Gwen said. She *hated* watching women cry, even though Polly had more reason than most. "Take a deep breath and calm down."

A powerful Sensitive wouldn't have needed to compel anything. He would have known if someone was trying to lie to him. But Gwen didn't have anything like the skill Sir Travis must have shown. Carefully, hating herself, she laced her voice with Charm.

"I need you to tell me the truth," she said, softly. It was always difficult to tell just how much effect Charm had on its intended target, but Polly – who would have been trained to follow orders – should be vulnerable to the magic. "Did you kill Sir Travis?"

"*No*," Polly snapped. She pulled at the handcuffs, futilely. "I didn't kill him!"

"I believe you," Gwen said. There was no hint that Polly was resisting the Charm, let alone that she was aware of its existence. Shaking her head, Gwen stood up, walked around the chair and used magic to unlock the handcuffs. "I need you to answer some questions."

Polly stood up and started to rub at her wrists. The handcuffs had been on so tightly, Gwen realised, that her wrists had started to swell. Making a mental note to ensure that the two policemen were disciplined, she helped Polly to another – more comfortable – chair and found her a glass of water. The maid didn't seem inclined to run, but then she had nowhere to go. She probably knew next to nothing about London, let alone where she could hide if slave-hunters came after her.

"All right," Gwen said, squatting next to her, "what happened last night?"

Polly looked at her, through tear-filled eyes, and began to explain.

"The Master – Sir Travis – often had late-night meetings with some of his friends," she said, softly. "Some of them were secret; I wasn't supposed to know about them. I didn't know why he was so worried about me..."

Gwen could guess. In Turkey, or any other foreign country, the servants were not always trustworthy. The host country often used them to spy, even though it was technically illegal and could be relied upon to cause a diplomatic incident if they were caught at it. David had grumbled about diplomats who forget that simple fact when he'd moved from business to government service. English servants could be trusted; foreign servants tended to have two sets of masters.

"He was very apologetic about it," she added, "but he'd lock me in my room whenever he had such visitors. I didn't really mind that much; there was always something to do in the house, but if I was locked up I couldn't actually do it... last night, he had several visitors coming to see him. He locked me up as soon as the sun started to set."

She gave Gwen a half-shy, half-amused grin. "I still knew who had come to see him," she added. "He didn't keep *that* much from me."

Gwen resisted the temptation to roll her eyes. Servants saw *so* much more than their masters and mistresses ever realised. And to think that Lady Mary had wondered how rumours of her devil-child kept getting out into Polite Society.

"But he normally came to unlock the door after he'd finished," Polly continued. "Instead, when I fell asleep, the door was still locked. I woke up in the morning and discovered that he *hadn't* unlocked the door. And I had to make him his breakfast. I picked the lock and sneaked upstairs to see if he was still awake. Instead, I found his body and... and I called the Police. And they blamed *me*."

"He would have known that you picked the lock," Gwen pointed out, mildly. "Why didn't you just stay there?"

"The Master was always demanding a very early breakfast," Polly explained. "I was supposed to bring it to him in bed, every day."

"My brother was much the same," Gwen admitted. She wondered if Laura had cured David of demanding his breakfast in bed, before deciding that it wasn't something she wanted to think about. "The Police came and then...?"

"The rat-like man ordered me arrested," Polly said. She rubbed the bruise on her cheek. "And they just kept shouting at me..."

"They won't shout at you any longer," Gwen assured her. The rat-like man was Lestrade, she guessed; there had always been something a little ratty about his face. "How did you stay in the house after Lady Mortimer died?"

"Her Ladyship insisted that I dedicate myself to the house," Polly said. "She taught me how to read and write and do figures – and made me promise that I would keep the house as clean as possible for the next generation. And her son just kept me here."

Gwen felt a flicker of sympathy for the young girl. She'd been a child when she'd been enslaved, then liberated, and then moved to a different kind of slavery. Her wages wouldn't have been very high, if they'd existed at all. And one person, no matter how experienced, couldn't hope to keep the entire house clean indefinitely. Mortimer Hall needed a small army of servants just to keep it free of dust. No wonder so many rooms were locked up. Polly had had no time to clean them at all.

And she'd been alone for at least five months. Gwen could understand *that*.

"I think you should get something to eat," she said, finally. Polly *had* to be starving; Lestrade probably wouldn't have allowed her anything to eat or drink while she'd been under arrest. "And then I need to have a few words with the Inspector."

"Thank you, Milady," Polly said. "Do you want anything to eat? Should I make food for the policemen?"

"Maybe later," Gwen said. The nasty part of her mind was tempted just to say no, but the police would have to guard the house for several days. "Eat whatever you need to eat, then we can talk about what your master was doing before he died."

She left Polly in the kitchen – after satisfying herself that there was no way out of the room that wasn't guarded by a policeman – and found Lestrade studying some documents he'd found in a room on the ground floor. One of them was Lady Mortimer's will, which noted that Mortimer Hall and its remaining contents were to be passed down to her son, but her jewellery collection was to be given to Polly.

Judging from the descriptions, Polly should have found herself a few thousand pounds richer once they were sold, enough to convince London to overlook the colour of her skin. Assuming she'd ever received them...

"A motive for murder," Lestrade said, in a tone that suggested that he found the case closed. "She would have inherited the jewels..."

"She would have inherited them without having to kill Sir Travis," Gwen pointed out, coldly. Her mother had gone over writing a will with her, pointing out that it was a skill young ladies desperately needed. "There's nothing written here to suggest that Polly would have to wait until after Lady Mortimer's son was dead."

She scowled down at the Inspector, allowing some of her anger to leak into her voice. "I Charmed her," she added. "She wasn't the murderer, Inspector."

"Maybe Sir Travis insisted on keeping the jewels," Lestrade insisted, stubbornly. "Wouldn't *that* have provided a motive for murder?"

"She isn't the murderer," Gwen repeated, feeling her patience starting to snap. Lestrade might have had a point, but she doubted that Polly had it in her to be a killer. "Besides, we don't even know if she *knew* she was going to get the jewels. She would hardly be the legal custodian of the estate."

Lestrade grimaced at her for a long moment, then bowed his head. "Someone would have to serve as custodian while Sir Travis was in India," he said. "I shall have him located and then we can ask about how the will was handled. But if the jewels went elsewhere..."

"I can pay for a lawyer, if necessary," Gwen said, tartly.

Her mother's lessons had been very clear. There were certain circumstances in which a particular bequest in a will could be overturned, but if the jewels in question had been Lady Mortimer's, there should have been no grounds for refusing to pass them to Polly. Polite Society might want to balk at passing anyone to a black girl, particularly one of such questionable origins, yet they wouldn't want to create a precedent that could be used to overturn other wills.

She smiled, remembering one of the stories her mother told. A will had gone missing and the property had been divided up according to law – and then the will had been rediscovered, several years later. Much of the property had gone to the wrong person. It had taken nearly a decade of legal wrangling before the property had been divided up again – and, in the meantime, two great families had practically been torn apart.

"But if not her," Lestrade said, "then *who*?"

"A very good question," Gwen agreed. "I plan to spend several hours speaking to Polly and learning everything she knew about her master's business. Hopefully, that will give us some clues to follow. Meanwhile, I'd like you to have a few words with the constables who... interrogated her. They're both fined one month's salary."

Lestrade stared at her. She rarely asserted herself so bluntly.

"Ah... one of them has a family," he protested, finally. "Losing so much salary would be a grievous blow."

"And yet he tortured a young girl in the hope he would learn something useful," Gwen reminded him. "Would anything she said have been useful, if she said it just to make the pain stop? And the real killer would have made his escape while you were busy putting Polly in front of a judge, who would sentence her to be hanged."

She frowned, then relented – slightly. "Half of his salary for the month," she said. "And made it quite clear that I gave him that as a mercy, because of his family."

"Thank you, Milady," Lestrade said.

Gwen skimmed through the rest of the will. Most of it was legalese, but it seemed fairly straightforward. Sir Travis would inherit everything passed down from his father – Lady Mortimer would have been the custodian, rather than the owner – and most of his mother's personal possessions. There were no charitable bequests or donations to the King, unsurprisingly; Lady Mortimer hadn't had the financial resources to give much away on her deathbed.

She looked up at Lestrade. "Did Sir Travis leave a will?"

"We have yet to find one," Lestrade admitted. "He had a locked safe in his bedroom, but we have been unable to open it. We think it has a magical lock."

"I'll deal with it," Gwen promised. That was going to be tricky. Magical locks could be incredibly difficult to pick, even for a Master Magician. But there was no choice. No mundane safecracker could break into a safe that had been sealed with magic. "Once Polly is ready to attend, we'll start going through his papers."

"He may have left a will with a lawyer," Lestrade added. "We've started some enquiries..."

"You might want to ask Lord Mycroft," Gwen suggested. "If Sir Travis was working for him, it's quite possible that any papers of his were stored in the government's vaults."

"He would probably give them to you," Lestrade reminded her. "But I don't think he would allow me to see the papers."

Gwen had been told – by Mycroft's brother – that in any crime scene it was important to look for three things; means, motive and opportunity. Put together, they always pointed to the most likely suspect. But right now, all she really had was the opportunity. Polly had been locked in her room, unable to interfere as the murderer entered the hall...

... And yet, how had he managed to prevent Sir Travis from noticing him until it had been far too late?

"Have the body moved to the hospital and ask Lucy to take a look at it," Gwen ordered, as she passed the will back to Lestrade. "And then we'll see what we can dig up."

Chapter Ten

ir Travis's suite was the cleanest part of the hall, Gwen decided after the body had been removed, leaving behind a chalk outline to signify where it had been. The bedroom was definitely intended to be regal, complete with a four-poster bed, while the bathroom was surprisingly modern for such an old house. It even had hot running water, something that she suspected that Polly would have found a mercy. The only alternative would have been to boil the water in the kitchen and then carry it up three flights of stairs to the bathroom.

The bedroom reminded her a little of David's bedroom, back at Crichton Hall. Gwen had spent enough time sneaking in and out of her brother's room – mainly to borrow books that her mother felt were unladylike – to know what a boy's bedroom was like – apart from fewer books and more toys, there was little difference between this one and her brother's room. Sir Travis had left his model soldiers on a table, even if he hadn't played with them in years. Perhaps the adult had found it comforting to sit and contemplate the time when all that mattered was playing with toys.

She picked up one of the model soldiers and frowned. One of her detractors had sent her – anonymously, although she suspected Colonel Sebastian – a set of expensive dolls, handmade by craftsmen in Surrey. It had been intended as a mocking reminder that she'd spent most of her childhood playing with dolls, like any other well-bred young lady... but men spent time playing with dolls too. Only they called them toy soldiers, not dolls. The difference escaped her, unless the adults thought that they taught valuable life skills. Given how poorly Gwen had treated her dolls, it was easy to believe that she would make a very poor mother.

The wardrobes were almost empty, apart from a number of trousers and jackets so outdated that they had to have belonged to Sir Travis's father. There was very little that seemed to belong to Sir Travis, which struck Gwen as odd. Most upper-class men had considerable wardrobes, even the ones who professed to disdain fashion; one never knew when one might have to change suddenly. Even if Sir Travis had only had his salary from Mycroft, he should have been able to buy more suitable clothes. Perhaps he just didn't care enough to bother.

Or maybe he didn't want to be lumbered, she thought. She'd had to attend the departure ceremony for Lord St. Simon, the new Viceroy of India, and he'd taken seven trunks of clothing with him. But Sir Travis might have been smart enough not to want to drag so much gear with him, wherever he went.

She stepped back and peered over at the portrait of George III on the wall. The King looked like he had in his youth, before the mental troubles that had eventually caused him to collapse into madness – a curse, some said, put on him by an American rebel. George had been the backer of Professor Cavendish when he'd been systematising magic, his redemption for his disastrous decision to dismiss Pitt the Elder years ago. If Pitt had remained Prime Minister, France would have been defeated so utterly that she would never have been able to challenge Britain again.

"It's behind the portrait," Polly said, as she entered the room. "It took several days to install it properly."

Gwen nodded, running her hands down the side of the portrait until she found the lever. There was a click and the portrait swung open, revealing a metal safe blurred into the wall. A Changer had been involved, Gwen realised, as she studied his handiwork. It would be very difficult to hack it out of the stone and cart it off to open at leisure.

"The key only worked for him," Polly explained.

"When he died, I think it was meant to stop working."

Gwen scowled. That was... odd, even in the most paranoid government departments. If someone died unexpectedly, there should be at least one other person with access to the safe – or the contents would be lost forever. Lestrade had left Sir Travis's keys on the desk when he'd had the body removed, so Gwen used her magic to call them to her – Polly's eyes went wide when she saw them flying through the air – and pushed the key into the safe. Nothing happened.

For the key to work, it has to be held by the right person, she reminded herself. *For the lock to work, it has to have the right key, which has to be activated in turn. And it can only be activated by one person. Very secure.*

"I think it did," she said. There was no point in pressing the dead man's hand against the key; the magic woven into the object wouldn't recognise the corpse as its rightful owner. "I'm going to have to break into it."

"You can't," Polly objected. "The Master was very certain that no one could break in."

Gwen smiled. A Mover could have opened the safe – if he could see what he was doing, which the magic would render impossible. But a Mover and a Seer, working together... it wasn't possible for anyone other than a Master Magician. And it would be difficult even for her.

"Let me concentrate," she said, pressing her hand against the safe and closing her eyes. The safe seemed to glow in her mind's eye, warded with enough magic to make opening it a nightmare. Whoever had done the Infusing had done a very good job. "And don't let anyone into the bedroom while I'm working."

She pushed her awareness towards the safe, wishing that she'd spent more time practising Seeing. It had its own dangers; like Sensitives, far too many Seers ended up in the madhouse when they lost control of their gifts. The safe looked oddly translucent in her mind's eye, as if it wasn't quite there. And it wasn't, in a sense. She could send her awareness drifting right through it.

Concentrate, she reminded herself, as she studied the lock. It was incredibly complex; if she hadn't seen watchmakers at work, she would have suspected that magic had been used to build the mechanical side of the safe. The right key would open it; the wrong key would jam the lock permanently, if pushed too far. And the wrong sort of magic...

She realised the danger in the next second. Someone had been *very* clever and woven enough magic into the safe to trigger a fire if a Seer got too close. Not a protective rune, created by an Infuser, but something more basic. Gwen cursed out loud – she heard Polly gasp at the language – and reached out desperately, trying to pull the magic out of the safe. It was reluctant to bend to her will, but she pulled at it until it snapped. The rush of energy tore through her body and flashed out, smashing against the far wall. Polly let out a cry of shock, which Gwen barely heard. Instead, she sucked in the remaining magic and turned the key again. This time, the safe opened effortlessly.

"Lady Gwen," a voice shouted. A strong hand grabbed her arm. "Are you all right?"

Gwen nodded, although her legs felt uncomfortably wobbly. No normal magician could have done that – and Gwen had never even known that it was possible. Doctor Norwell would be pleased, she told herself crossly. More data for his endless research into the limits of magic.

"I think so," she said. She opened her eyes and saw Lestrade staring at her. "The safe should be open now."

"And you wrecked the wall," Polly said. "What happened?"

Gwen looked over towards the far wall. It had been shattered, glowing embers littering the floor. She'd been very lucky that she hadn't accidentally set the whole house on fire.

"I sucked the magic out of the safe and discharged it," Gwen said, finally. "Inspector, can you see to dealing with the remains of the embers?"

"Certainly," Lestrade said, gruffly. He seemed to have remembered *why* she was the Royal Sorceress. "But I do need to see the papers."

Gwen nodded as she turned back to the safe. The

interior was smaller than she had expected – everything looked funny from the Seer's viewpoint – and crammed with documents, mostly written in a dreadful scrawl. Her lips twitched as she remembered the handwriting lessons her mother had forced David to take, insisting that he would never get anywhere in life until he mastered the art of using a pen. It had annoyed him that Gwen had proven to be better at handwriting than himself – and would probably annoy him more if he ever saw Sir Travis's handwriting. It was incredibly difficult to read.

"Help me spread them out on the desk," she ordered, passing half of the papers to Polly and taking the rest for herself. Behind the papers, she saw a small metal box; carefully, she picked it up using magic and put it on the desk. Inside, she discovered four medals and a set of gold coins she didn't recognise. "What are these?"

Lestrade peered at the coins. "International Gold," he said, seriously. "They're very rare, outside the Diplomatic Service. Those coins are pure untraceable gold."

He picked up the medals thoughtfully. "These two are from campaigns in India," he said. "This one is from China, I think... one of my detectives served in the Battle of Taipei and his medal looks similar. I don't recognise this one at all."

Gwen did. The silver medallion with an engraving of a sword was only ever given to magicians who had distinguished themselves in combat. *Gwen* had one, awarded to her after the Battle of London. She was the only woman who had earned such a medal.

"He must have picked it up in India," she said, thoughtfully. Sir Travis had been a Sensitive... and yet he'd gone into battle? Remarkable. "Let's have a look at the papers."

One leather-bound book was a journal, written – like so many others – for later publication. It was a common practice, all the more common now that the censors had largely stopped trying to control the thousands of new publications coming onto the market every month. A famous explorer or soldier could expect to sell hundreds of copies of his memoirs, using them – if he saw fit – to launch a political career. Sir Travis might have had political ambitions... or he might have intended to warn his fellow countrymen of a danger which he alone saw looming. It was an old tradition, one enthusiastically embraced by Colonel Sebastian; his book, *Moving Mountains in the Empire*, could easily have been entitled *1000 Reasons To Hate Female Magicians and Lady Gwen in Particular*.

Gwen glanced at the journal, resolving to read it properly later. Sir Travis had been more of a sketch artist than a writer, she realised; the first couple of pages were decorated with sketches of elephants, tigers and a woman who seemed to be wearing a scarf around her head and nothing else. She couldn't help flushing as she turned the page, then put the journal down. Thankfully, neither Lestrade nor Polly seemed to notice.

The other papers were confusing, all written in a hand that was nearly impossible to read – and sometimes shifted into code. Gwen parsed through them slowly, but none of them made any sense, apart from a reference to visiting a house in Whitehall. It nagged at her mind until she realised just who it referred to – and why. Clearly, Sir Travis had had no problems going into the heart of the British Establishment. And someone who didn't have insider knowledge wouldn't have a clue what it meant.

"Look at this," Lestrade said. He tapped the top of the papers, where there was a date and a single number. "There are some papers missing."

Gwen silently cursed her own oversight under her breath. He was right; the papers were numbered and dated and several pages were definitely missing.

"Sir Travis was doing something for Lord Mycroft," she said, out loud. "And it had to be something important, or Mycroft would never have stirred himself to come out here with me."

She looked over at Polly. "Do you know Lord Mycroft?"

"The fat man," Polly said. Her face softened, just slightly. "He was always polite and he used to tip me..."

"Good for him," Gwen said. "When did he last visit?"

Lestrade coughed. "You cannot consider *Lord Mycroft* a suspect," he objected.

"I don't," Gwen assured him, with the private thought that if Mycroft had turned to crime, he could do something bigger than murdering one Sensitive – even if it was a remarkable feat – and there would be nothing left to suggest that the crime had even taken place. "But we do need to know who might have had a motive to want him dead."

She looked back down at the papers. Deciphering them would take weeks, even if she found someone who could break the code. And if Sir Travis had been working for Lord Mycroft... she could simply ask Lord Mycroft for help in breaking the code. He might just insist on taking the documents – Gwen knew that she wasn't entrusted with *all* the Empire's secrets – but at least she'd *know*.

"Polly," she said, slowly, "who came to visit on the night he died?"

Polly hesitated, took a brief look at Lestrade, then tried to answer the question. "There were three visitors, I believe. Augustus Howell" – Lestrade started, as if he recognised the name - "Ambassador Talleyrand and the Special Undersecretary of State, David Crichton."

Gwen stared at her. "David *Crichton*?"

"Yes," Polly said. "Weak-chinned fellow, odd eyes, paid no attention to me on his first visit..."

"Oh," Gwen said. David, her *brother*? What was *he* doing mixed up in the whole affair? "Do you know why he came to visit?"

"The first time was a month ago, before Sir Travis went off to foreign parts," Polly said. "He came with the fat man; I served them brandy and little cakes I cooked myself. I think it was just an introduction, because he came back a night later while I was locked in my room."

"Surely the Ambassador is a more important figure," Lestrade said. He might not have been the smartest policemen in the world, but he would have been able to recognise Gwen's brother's name. The police were taught to remember all of the aristocratic families, if only to ensure that they knew who had to be treated gently when arrested. "What could *he* want with Sir Travis?"

"He made the appointment earlier in the day," Polly explained. "The messenger didn't give me a reason."

"He probably didn't know," Gwen muttered. She'd heard enough about how Talleyrand dealt with the world to be sure of it. Somehow, he'd managed to keep his position through several successive periods of unrest in France. "And Mr. Howell?"

"A businessman," Lestrade growled. There was something unpleasant in his voice that suggested it wasn't a safe topic. "I don't know *why* he would come to visit Sir Travis."

"He visited a day earlier, while Sir Travis was out," Polly put in. "I think he... I think he was..."

"A thoroughly unpleasant person," Lestrade said.

Gwen looked from one to the other, then put the question aside. "Which of them visited last?"

"I don't know," Polly confessed. "But whoever came last has to be the killer, doesn't he?"

Gwen nodded. If one of the three was the killer, and the other two were innocent, the killer had to be the last one to visit or the person following him would have raised the alarm. The last visitor had opportunity... and yet, they would still have to get the better of a Sensitive. There were no signs of a struggle on Sir Travis's body. Indeed, he'd looked remarkably peaceful. Drugged?

But it should be impossible to drug a Sensitive, she told herself.

She couldn't see David as a killer. Her brother was stuffy – at least in public, although she knew that he'd flirted a bit with the wild side before taking a proper job – and had a very promising future ahead of him. A conviction for murder would ruin his career, his family... and Gwen's career too. Ambassador Talleyrand had diplomatic immunity – he'd have to be sent home, rather than hang for murder – but his career would still be over if he were accused of murder. France would be looking for a scapegoat to appease the British public.

And that left Howell. Who was *he*?

"I'm going to take the matter to Lord Mycroft," she said,

standing up. After his exertions, he would probably be at the Diogenes Club eating a hefty lunch. "Perhaps he can clear up some of the issues here."

Lestrade gave Polly a sharp glance. "And her?"

"She can stay here, if she wants," Gwen told him. She'd have to speak to Norton and get him to recommend a lawyer to make sure that Polly actually got the jewels she was owed. "Or we can find her a guest house if she doesn't want to stay."

"I'll stay," Polly said, quickly. "I promised Lady Mortimer that I would take care of her house."

Gwen nodded and left the room, walking down towards the lobby. Someone was arguing with two of the policemen, pushing forward by sheer strength of will. Lestrade stepped past her and raised his voice.

"What," he demanded, "is going on here?"

"Inspector Lestrade, I presume," the newcomer said. "My name is Charles Bellingham, *Sir* Charles Bellingham. I am Sir Travis's close personal friend. Perhaps you could explain, Inspector, just what you are doing in my friend's home?"

Gwen concealed her amusement at Lestrade's reaction. Charles Bellingham was a household name.

"Your friend was found dead," Lestrade said. "If you will come with me, I shall explain in the drawing room."

We may have questions for him, Gwen thought, and followed them into the drawing room.

Chapter Eleven

nlike most men, Sir Charles Bellingham didn't do a double-take when he saw through Gwen's male attire and realised that she was female. Instead, he merely took Gwen's hand and kissed it lightly, smiling in a manner that reminded Gwen of Jack, the day he'd shown her what lay beneath the prosperity of the British Empire.

"The Royal Sorceress," he said. There was more than a trace of India in his voice. "Travis would be delighted to know that such an esteemed personage was investigating his death. He was a Sensitive, you know. And he was always quite sensitive about it. I only found out because he kept beating me at cards."

Gwen collected herself as Lestrade motioned for Sir Charles to sit down, which he did in a manner that suggested that he owned the building. He was tall, with long blonde hair that hung down over a tanned and rugged face. Lady Mary would have said that he had *character*, just before encouraging Gwen to start casting him downcast glances in the hopes of interesting him. After all, *everyone* knew Sir Charles Bellingham. The adventurer had a gift for self-publicity that outshone even Lord Nelson.

She'd read the dispatches Sir Charles had sent back to Britain to be printed in the newspapers, back before Master Thomas had taken her on as his apprentice. Sir Charles had spent most of his life in India, serving the British Crown; he'd done everything from negotiating with Indian princes to donning a disguise and travelling into the heart of Afghanistan, even spending two months living with the tribesmen there. None of the dispatches Gwen had read had mentioned Sir Travis, at least as far as she could remember, but maybe that wasn't surprising.; someone like Sir Charles couldn't afford to praise others too much, or they might steal his fame.

"I don't think you ever mentioned playing cards in your dispatches," Gwen said, slowly. It wasn't the right thing to say, she realised a moment later. He'd managed to fluster her. "Did Sir Travis play often?"

"We spent weeks riding through India and sleeping in the open air," Sir Charles said. He gave her a wink that made her blush. "There wasn't much else for us to do, so we cracked open the pack and played for hours. He kept winning."

Gwen nodded. Master Thomas had told her that Sensitives, Seers and Talkers were discouraged from gambling – they had unfair advantages – but the rule had never been properly policed. She could easily imagine a Sensitive as capable as Sir Travis having absolutely no problem winning game after game, at least until his opponent caught on.

"Well, until I realised the truth," Sir Charles added. "Then things were a bit more even."

He smiled at her. "He really did have a gift for talking to the Indians," he said. "The man could speak almost all of their languages like a native, far better than myself. It took him a mere six months to master the dialect of one particular tribe and become great friends with their leader. He even managed to convince them to put aside their fear and join the campaign against the Thugs, bad cess to the lot of them."

Lestrade coughed, meaningfully. "When did you last see Sir Travis?"

"Two weeks ago, just before he went to Istanbul," Sir Charles told him. "We'd gone before, but this time he had to go alone – some geezer in the Foreign Office thought it would be better for this particular meeting to be on a low key. Or something like that. I was busy having my book edited, so I didn't object when he told me he was going alone. In hindsight, perhaps I should have gone. Those

Turks really take insults seriously."

"They do," Lestrade agreed. "Did the Turkish Government have a reason to feel insulted?"

"Not that I know," Sir Charles admitted. "Travis was *good* at making people like him, even when he had come to dismantle their kingdom and incorporate it into British-administered territory. I believe that they were hammering out the details of some agreement, but he never told me about it."

Gwen frowned. "You were such close friends and yet he didn't tell you what he was doing?"

"Oh, we shared a lot," Sir Charles said. "But Travis was a man of honour. His orders were not to discuss it with anyone else and he followed them, unhesitatingly. Even when we were in Istanbul together, he went to quite a few meetings alone."

Gwen wasn't quite sure what to make of *that*. In her experience, friends shared everything... although she had had few true friends in her life. The magicians she got on best with were mostly male – and she couldn't share everything with *them*. Perhaps, if Jack had lived, she would have had a close friend...

She pushed the sudden burst of heartache aside and looked up at Sir Charles. "When did you first meet him?"

Sir Charles smiled brilliantly. "He came over to India with a commission in his pocket and instructions to visit a number of allied monarchs," he said. "I ended up being volunteered to escort him from kingdom to kingdom – I saved his life a few times and he saved mine – and we became good friends. And then I saved him from the Fishing Fleet."

Gwen blinked. "The Fishing Fleet?"

Lestrade coughed, embarrassed.

"Quite a few young women come out to India in hopes of snaring a husband," Sir Charles told her, casting a sidelong glance at the Inspector. "Most of them have few prospects, which doesn't stop them trying to lure young men into their clutches..."

"Thank you," Gwen said, feeling heat spreading through her cheeks. She could guess the rest of the details, if only from overhearing some of her mother's discussions with her friends.

"That said, a few of them did very well in the Red Tree Siege," Sir Charles added, mischievously. "Fought as well as any man, they did."

"Your dispatches made it sound as though you won the battle single-handedly," Gwen reminded him. She couldn't help liking him. "Or was Sir Travis there too?"

"Oh, I beat the enemy leader in single combat and convinced the rest of his tribe to swear allegiance to King George," Sir Charles said. He chuckled, convincing Gwen that he wasn't entirely serious. "Sir Travis sneaked through the enemy lines and guided the reinforcements to a position where they could have broken the siege, if I hadn't won already."

"As fascinating as this discussion is," Lestrade said gruffly, "there are details we have to cover. Do you know what Sir Travis would have done with his will?"

Sir Charles hesitated, thoughtfully. "Most of us Indiamen leave basic wills with the Foreign Office," he said, after a moment. "*I* certainly do – Travis, on the other hand, had a noble estate. He might well have kept a lawyer on retainer to handle the transfer of property when he died."

Gwen cleared her throat. "Do you know what Sir Travis wrote in his will?"

"Not a clue," Sir Charles assured her. "Travis never asked me to witness it, so I don't know what it said. I imagine that he intended to rewrite it after marrying – that's fairly standard too, as the wife would need some provisions in the will – but I was never consulted. And why should he have consulted me?"

Lestrade leaned forward. "He was planning to marry?"

"He was engaged to Lady Elizabeth Bracknell," Sir Charles said. "It wasn't announced openly; they were planning to announce it after Lady Elizabeth turned eighteen and completed her schooling." He looked at Gwen. "Do you know her?"

Gwen shook her head. Most aristocratic children in London knew one another – the thought of playing with *commoners* would have shocked their parents – but Gwen had always been fairly isolated. She couldn't remember, offhand, if her mother had ever said anything about the Bracknell Family. There wasn't a Bracknell on any of the committees Gwen had to deal with as Royal Sorceress, but that didn't mean that they weren't important.

And they'd waited for their daughter to complete her schooling before marrying her off, she noted. That spoke well of them. Most girls were, at the very least, introduced to London society when they grew into womanhood; every season, London was filled with aristocratic daughters and their mothers, looking to meet potential husbands. Where marriage was as much an alliance between two families as it was between a husband and wife, few couples could avoid having their parents involved right from the start.

Gwen had never had her Season. But then, who would have wanted to marry her?

"I will certainly speak to her," Gwen said. "Do you know how well she knew Sir Travis?"

"There was no hint of scandal," Sir Charles said. "I believe they were introduced at her coming-out ball, then attended several later balls together – the latter two holding hands. Sir Travis approached her father two months ago, then proposed to her formally. She accepted."

Gwen winced, remembering her mother's lessons. A woman could refuse a proposal, but even *having* an unwelcome proposal was a strike against her, because she would be assumed to have encouraged it. Given how hard it was for young men and women to read one another, it was quite easy for one women to believe that she wasn't showing interest – and the man to believe that she *was* interested. Or, if they did want to marry and the parents refused to grant them permission, they would have to wait until the girl turned twenty-one – or run off to Scotland to get married. The latter would certainly cause a scandal... and if the girl happened to give birth within a year, High Society would tut-tut and say that they only married because the girl fell pregnant.

Which is meant to be difficult, Gwen thought, ruefully.

They were never meant to be left alone together.

She felt a moment of sympathy for Lady Elizabeth. *She* would be tainted by her fiancé's death, even if it was nothing to do with her. Rumours would follow her for the rest of her life... just as they'd followed Gwen, with far more cause. But there was nothing Gwen could do about that, apart from urging the girl to ignore Society's whispers. Who *cared* what they thought?

"Sir Travis was murdered," Gwen said, flatly. "Do you know anyone who might have wanted to kill him?"

"I don't think that there was anyone in London who would have wanted him dead," Sir Charles said, after a moment's thought. "He did have his fair share of enemies in India, but it would be unusual for Indian feuds to spread back to the motherland. India sometimes makes people act... poorly."

"We will follow up on it anyway," Lestrade said through gritted teeth. "What about the Bracknell Family?"

Sir Charles snorted. "My dear sir, the Bracknell Family agreed to marry their daughter to Travis," he said. "They would hardly have needed to kill him to refuse permission, particularly as the marriage was not officially announced. All they would have had to do was send back the marriage contract and it would be at an end."

Gwen frowned, considering it. Breaking an engagement, even an unannounced one, was sure to lead to a scandal if it became public. But then, if the Bracknell Family had wanted to end it, they would not have made it public – and it was rare for a man to sue for Breach of Promise. A woman might well sue, if only because a broken engagement made it harder for her to make another, but men rarely had *that* problem.

"Tell me something," she said, slipping as much Charm into her voice as she dared, "did Sir Travis have a mistress?"

Sir Charles slapped his thigh. "Blunt *and* direct," he said, looking right at Gwen. "I like it!"

"Answer the question," Lestrade ordered, as Gwen flushed.

"Travis had no mistress in London," Sir Charles said.

"In India..." He cast Gwen an odd look, as if he were pretending to be reluctant to talk. "In India, there was never any shortage of mistresses for unattached Englishmen. Having one was often a good way to improve one's grasp of the local tongue. Can you believe that most of the straight-laced officers can barely say '*get me a gin and tonic, boy*' in Hindi?"

Gwen shrugged, lowering her eyes to hide her embarrassment. Young men were taught French as well as Latin in schools – and she'd picked up a great deal from her tutors, before she'd scared them away – but she'd never wondered how officers and men in India picked up the local language. But they *had* to learn; the dispatches she'd read often dwelled on how untrustworthy the natives were, even the interpreters.

"But I don't know if that would have mattered to the Bracknell Family," he added. "What happens in India stays in India. Besides, I wouldn't have been surprised to discover that Lord Bracknell had his own mistress in London. Lady Bracknell is a... sour-faced old prune."

"No doubt," Gwen murmured. Women were not supposed to have sex before marriage and definitely not *outside* marriage – and those who did were forever shamed by Polite Society. But the rules were different for men, as long as they were discreet and took care of any little unintended consequences. She'd known about it since she'd been old enough to work out what really happened to create children, but she hadn't realised the scale until she'd looked at Doctor Norwell's notes. Quite a few of the girls who ended up in the farms had come from illicit relationships.

And upper-class women weren't supposed to have *any* interest in sex.

She pushed that thought aside too and concentrated on the matter at hand. "It does seem unlikely that they would have wanted to murder Sir Travis to end the marriage contract," she said. "Unless... was there anything particularly special about the contract?"

"I never saw it, but I would be surprised if there was," Sir Charles said. "Lady Elizabeth isn't exactly a ruling

Queen."

Gwen nodded. He was right; there shouldn't have been anything in the contract that made murder a more attractive option than simply breaking it off. Or, for that matter, penalising either party, particularly if it were the parents who chose to end the agreement.

"We'll look into it," she said. Maybe she should ask her mother first. "But for the moment..."

She leaned forward, pushing Charm into her voice. "You have absolutely no idea who might have killed Sir Travis?"

"None," Sir Charles said. "It's a complete mystery."

Gwen frowned. For once, she couldn't tell if the Charm was having any effect at all – let alone if he'd noticed her attempt to use it. A strong-willed person might shrug off the Charm without even noticing it... and yet, he *was* answering the question.

"We may wish to speak to you later," Gwen said, tiredly.

"So don't leave London," Lestrade added.

"Of course," Sir Charles said, with another brilliant smile. For a moment, his eyes met Gwen's. "I shall be at your service, should you wish to see me."

"Thank you," Gwen stammered. There was something about him that attracted her... maybe it was because he was handsome, or perhaps because he seemed to treat her as an equal. Part of her wanted to see him again, even though the rest of her knew that it would be dangerous.

"There is the issue of the funeral," Sir Charles added, bluntly. "Will you see to it that I am informed of who is handling the arrangements?"

"Of course," Lestrade said. "Once we locate the will, we will see what provisions have been made for his funeral."

Gwen watched him escort Sir Charles out of the room, then looked down at her hands. Her emotions made no sense to her at all; her heartbeat suddenly felt very loud in her chest. Was this what it was like to fall in love? Or was it merely attraction? Her mother had never covered *that* with her daughter. Did she like Sir Charles or was she *imagining* that she liked Sir Charles?

And if I do, she asked herself, *who do I talk to about it?*

Lady Mary would be useless, of course. She would start planning the wedding at once, even though she had no idea if Sir Charles liked her. Coming to think of it, just what was her legal status? Master Thomas had effectively adopted her before his death; now, was she a free woman or had her legal guardianship gone back to her father? Lord Rudolf Crichton hadn't tried to claim control over the considerable wealth that Master Thomas had left to her, but marriage was a different story.

Stop it, you idiot, she told herself, a moment later. *You're acting like a love-struck fool.*

Standing up, she picked up the papers and walked out of the drawing room, down towards the gates where a handful of carriages were waiting for the policemen. The reporters had left, she saw with some relief, apart from a couple who were still hanging around in the hope that something interesting and newsworthy would happen. Gwen scowled at them, climbed into the nearest carriage and issued orders. The coachman cracked the whip and the carriage jerked into life.

Gwen sat back and concentrated on controlling her emotions. Whatever she had felt, when she looked at Sir Charles, she could not allow it to get in her way. Someone had murdered Sir Travis and she had to find him before he struck again. And if Lord Mycroft couldn't shed any light on what Sir Travis had been doing for him, Gwen would have to start interviewing suspects and hope she learned something useful.

And one of them was her own brother.

She couldn't help gritting her teeth. *That* was going to be an awkward conversation.

Chapter Twelve

he Diogenes Club was near Whitehall, but not close enough to be automatically considered part of the Establishment. Indeed, most of the Club's regular members were unaware of its true purpose, unwittingly providing a certain degree of cover for its activities. The Diogenes Club provided a place for government ministers and agents to meet and talk in private, without bringing them to Whitehall. After all, *talking* was one thing that would never be associated with the Diogenes Club.

There had been no female members until Gwen had inherited Master Thomas's membership – and she had a quiet suspicion that it had only been Lord Mycroft's intervention that had allowed her to *keep* the membership. The average member of the club came to the Diogenes to get *away* from the wife and children, according to Master Thomas; they didn't even permit female *servants* within the club's walls. Even so, Gwen didn't visit very often. The club's atmosphere only appealed to a certain type of man.

She jumped out of the carriage and walked up to the doorman, who recognised her at once. The Diogenes had no membership cards; the only way in was through the main door, forcing everyone to pass under the doorman's gaze. He knew everyone who was allowed into the club and would have denied entry to anyone else, unless they were accompanied by a club member. The doorman nodded to her and stepped aside. Gwen nodded back and stepped into the club.

Absolute silence fell as soon as the door swung closed

behind her. Talking was forbidden within the club, except in a handful of isolated and heavily sound-proofed rooms. Members who spoke out loud – or even ate too loudly - could be fined or, as a last resort, evicted from the club permanently. Very few former members were ever allowed to reapply.

The receptionist looked up at her as she approached, one eyebrow lifted questioningly. Gwen picked up the book of members and tapped Lord Mycroft's name; the receptionist turned and pointed to a diagram on the wall, indicating that Lord Mycroft was in one of the private dining rooms. Gwen smiled at him, nodded in acknowledgement and headed for the stairs. At least she wouldn't have to face him in one of the larger rooms, where the slightest sound could bring the guards.

She glanced into the first floor as she walked up the stairs. A handful of chairs were scattered around, with men sitting in them reading the newspapers or a handful of heavy books. Most of them were smoking heavily, the stench making Gwen's nose twitch unpleasantly. Healers had proved that smoking Tobacco was bad for human lungs, but they hadn't managed to discourage very many smokers from continuing to smoke. Gwen hadn't even *tried* to ban magicians from smoking.

The third floor was divided into a handful of rooms, ensuring absolute privacy for the diners and their guests. Gwen smiled as a steward intercepted her before she could reach Lord Mycroft's room. She held up her card, which he read quickly, blinking in surprise. Between her suit and the darkened corridor, her femininity had simply passed unnoticed. He must be new, Gwen decided, as he took the card down the corridor. If Lord Mycroft refused to see her, the stewards would evict her with as much force as necessary. The club took very good care of its members.

He returned a moment later and beckoned her forward, past a long series of closed doors, to one door that had been left on the latch. Gwen opened it and stepped inside, spotting Lord Mycroft on the other side of a large table. He was splitting his attention between a dinner of roast beef and a small pile of paperwork from the office.

"Lady Gwen," he said, as the door clicked closed behind her. The door was locked; only the right key could open it from the outside. "Would you care for something to eat? Or drink? They do a very good roast beef here, with excellent potatoes..."

Gwen sat down facing him and picked up the menu. Recently, there had been a fashion for Turkish food sweeping London – a reaction to Turkey's recent defeat of a French-backed revolution in Greece – but the Diogenes paid no lip service to such brief fads. The menu was typically English, with only a handful of dishes that came from outside the British Isles. For most of the club's members, she knew, the haggis would be exotic enough.

"A beef sandwich, I think," she said, marking it on a sheet of paper and dropping it down the tube to the kitchen. They'd send the meal up through the dumbwaiter, minimising contact between the staff and the club members. "What was Sir Travis doing for you?"

Lord Mycroft didn't object to her interrupting his dinner. "Diplomacy," he said, simply. "As a Sensitive, he was very capable of seeing what the other side actually *wanted* in negotiations."

Gwen nodded. Diplomats always started out with exaggerated demands and then allowed their counterparts to whittle them down, until they arrived at a compromise both sides could live with. It probably hadn't been easy for Sir Travis, she reflected; the British Empire held the whip hand in India and had no intention of allowing any mere prince to claim even a local victory. On the other hand, if she believed everything Sir Charles had written in his dispatches, a recognition or honour from King George was enough to convince some princes to allow the British to oversee the affairs of their kingdoms.

"My brother was one of the people who saw him before he died," Gwen said, tartly. "Did you know that he was involved in the affair?"

"It was a possibility," Lord Mycroft said, blandly. "He *was* certainly meant to have seen Sir Travis on the night he died."

Gwen glowered at him, not bothering to hide her

irritation. "And you didn't think to tell me about *that* little detail?"

Lord Mycroft lifted one elegant eyebrow. "It may interest you to know," he said, "that there are some matters *outside* the purview of the Royal Sorceress. Those include secret diplomatic talks that could cause no end of problems if they became public too early. And yes" – he pointed a finger at her – "they include the work of said Sorceress's brother."

"You have ordered me to find the killer of Sir Travis Mortimer," Gwen snapped. "The list of suspects includes my own brother. How is that *not* important to me?"

Mycroft sighed. "Because I needed you to view the evidence blind," he said. "And because, like the rest of us, you are expected to put personal feelings aside and serve your country."

He cut another piece of beef and chewed it, thoughtfully. "What have you found out?"

Gwen put her thoughts in order and outlined everything she'd discovered, starting with Polly's innocence and ending with the missing papers. Lord Mycroft studied the ones she'd brought with her carefully, clearly recognising that some were missing. It was hard to read his face, but Gwen could tell that he was very concerned. The missing papers were clearly important.

"You had to break into the safe," he said, when she'd finished. "Could another magician have done the same trick?"

"Only if he were a Master," Gwen said. She'd given the matter some thought while the carriage had been rattling towards Whitehall. "Even Merlin couldn't have cooperated closely enough to open the safe without destroying the papers inside."

"But that leaves us with another puzzle," Lord Mycroft pointed out. "Either we have another Master Magician running around London or Sir Travis opened the safe himself. Could he have been Charmed into opening the safe?"

Gwen hesitated. "I wouldn't have thought so," she said, finally. "The more... unnatural a particular act is, the harder it is to use Charm to force someone to do it without them realising what's happening. Even if the Charmer were powerful enough to overcome resistance, there should still be some signs of a struggle on his face."

Mycroft frowned. "Even with someone as powerful as Lord Blackburn?"

"There should still have been some trace of a struggle," Gwen said, remembering how Lord Blackburn had taught her how to resist Charm. It would be nice to find the traitor in London and arrest him, but it was unlikely that the Turks would ever send him back. "And if there were a Charmer massively more powerful than Lord Blackburn, he'd be running the world by now."

"There are all sorts of suggestions about the new Sultan," Lord Mycroft commented. "But people have been very charismatic for centuries before magic came into the world."

There was a chime from the dumbwaiter. Gwen stood up and walked over to the hatch, opening it to reveal a large sandwich crammed with beef, vegetables and horseradish. Her mother would have been offended at such fare, but Gwen found it hard to care, not when using magic often left her feeling half-starved. She picked up the plate, carried it back to the table and sat down to eat. It tasted extremely good.

"But there is a simpler explanation," Lord Mycroft said. "Sir Travis took the papers out of his safe and had them on his desk when he was murdered. The killer then took them with him when he left."

Gwen scowled. Why hadn't *she* thought of that?

"But that raises another puzzle," Lord Mycroft added. "Your brother wouldn't *need* to steal the papers, Ambassador Talleyrand should never have been allowed to *see* the papers and Howell wouldn't have risked murdering anyone. And yet, the papers are worthless – unless one happens to have the key to unlocking the code. And to do that, you'd have to know what the papers were in advance."

He frowned. "Unless, of course, the killer just took the papers relating to specific dates and times," he concluded.

"*That* would make a certain kind of sense."

Gwen nodded. "Who is Howell?"

"Almost certainly uninvolved, although his presence in this affair is worrying," Lord Mycroft said. "You should leave him out of your calculations."

Gwen kept her opinion of *that* to herself, but silently resolved to investigate Howell as soon as possible.

Mycroft cleared his throat as he pushed his plates to one side. "You may have realised that there is more to this case than I have told you," he said. "I would go so far as to say that it is of national importance. It is vitally important that we find the murderer and establish just what happened to those papers before it is too late."

"You said it might lead to war," Gwen said. "How likely is that?"

"The French were blamed for the undead epidemic in London during the Swing," Lord Mycroft reminded her, dryly. "Right now, there are questions being asked in Parliament as to why the new government hasn't declared war on France. The Duke of India is hard-pressed to explain, if only because he cannot command Parliament as easily as he can command his army. And the Honourable Members are hearing from their constituents. The general public loathes France right now. If there were a handful of defections in the Commons, the Prime Minister's position would be fundamentally weakened and we would go to war.

"And then there's the proposal from Governor Arnold in Philadelphia," he added. "Our American subjects want to invade Northern Mexico, if only to liberate the white settlers who fled there after the end of the rebellion. And several in the Admiralty support them, Lady Gwen. Do you understand why?"

Gwen shook her head. The Army worked closely with American Militiamen, even if there was still a lingering sense of distrust after the attempted rebellion, but the Navy had much less to do with America apart from escorting slavers across the Atlantic. Admittedly, there were several squadrons based in America, or the West Indies, that might have developed close ties to Americans...

"The French and Spanish hold Panama," Lord Mycroft explained. "Some bright spark at the Admiralty has realised that a canal, dug through the country, would make it much easier to redeploy Royal Navy squadrons to the Far East, should we ever have need to intervene in China or Japan. And we really should consider the latter. The Japanese are far too like us for comfort. If they get organised as a nation, we could be in some trouble."

Gwen struggled to remember geography lessons that had never quite gelled in her mind. "They're just a small set of islands," she pointed out, finally. "How much trouble can they cause us?"

"*We're* a small set of islands," Lord Mycroft countered. "And yet we rule a quarter of the globe. The French can never focus completely on us because they have to control Europe – given time, the Prussians might turn into a serious threat to their control. The Russians have too many internal problems to deploy all of their strength against an outsider, at least as long as Russia itself is not invaded. The Turks have too many problems controlling the territory they hold."

He smiled, but it didn't quite touch his eyes. "What would happen if those factors no longer applied?

"My... predecessors were horrified at the mere *prospect* of France joining the American Revolutionaries in their war, particularly when they realised just how badly Lord Bute had mishandled our relations with Prussia and the rest of the German states. If the Americans had kept the war going, I have no doubt that the French would have joined them – and the results would have been disastrous. We had alienated Prussia too badly to count on them to support us."

Gwen looked down at her hands, remembering the fighting in London at the end of the Swing.

"If we did go to war," she said, "could we win?"

"We would win at sea, if not easily," Lord Mycroft said. He shook his head in wry amusement. "One has to admire French persistence. They've been beaten successively in naval wars and yet they keep rebuilding their navy. Right now, we have reports that suggest that they too are experimenting with steam-powered vessels, which could be a major problem in future. But we could isolate the different parts of the French Empire and pick off the smaller colonies.

"Beating the French in Mexico, on the other hand..."

His face twisted into an odd scowl. "It would be difficult," he admitted. "Ever since the French and Spanish united their Crowns, they've actually been working on developing Mexico into a proper power base. They've even managed to make progress towards giving the locals a stake in maintaining the *status quo*. And Mexico couldn't simply be isolated and left to starve. We'd have to invade."

"Or they might invade us," Gwen said.

Mycroft nodded. "The Americans think that they can win quickly," he said. "I'm not so sure. No one has fought a major war with modern weapons since 1802. And the French may well have some unfair advantages. There are plenty of Mexicans in New Orleans – and the French who used to live in Quebec."

He shook his head. "I would prefer to avoid such a war, if possible," he concluded. "Sir Travis was working on a project that might convince the French not to push too hard. But his death may have scuppered that plan."

Gwen leaned forward. "What *was* the plan?"

"You need to talk to your brother," Lord Mycroft said. "He can tell you everything – I'll give you a note to that effect. And you can confirm his innocence."

"They might not trust my opinion," Gwen said. A young lady was always expected to support her family, right or wrong. "And..."

"This isn't going to go public," Lord Mycroft said, sharply. "I trust your opinion."

He reached for a notebook and scribbled a note, then pulled a cord that would summon a steward to collect it. "This could be important for you too," he added. "You know how many people there are out there who think that you're nothing more than a weak and feeble woman – no, a little girl dressing up as a man – who had the good fortune to assume Master Thomas's legacy. This is your chance to prove them wrong."

Gwen gave him an icy look. "That hardly seems fair," she pointed out.

"The world isn't fair," Lord Mycroft reminded her. "And besides – you can hardly rail against your fellow women, the ones who expect the men to take care of everything, and then blame men for not taking women seriously. This is your chance to show that you can carry out an investigation on your own.

"Yes, your brother is a suspect," he added. "And yes, that will reflect badly on you. If my brother were to be accused of something – anything – do you think that my position would not be questioned?"

"True," Gwen conceded, flushing.

"And if you bow out now, you know how many people will claim that you gave in to womanish sentimentality. Or that you *knew* that your brother was guilty and chose not to have to convict him. After all, women cannot be legally forced to testify against their relatives."

He was right, Gwen realised. Legally, a wife could refuse to testify against her husband – or a sister against her brother – and nothing would be said, officially. But everyone would wonder, none too quietly, what she'd had to hide. Surely, they'd say, someone who had nothing to fear would stand up, swear to tell the whole truth... and then tell the truth.

But what, a quiet nagging voice asked, *if he really is guilty?*

The steward entered the room and took Lord Mycroft's note. "I have asked your brother to meet you in the Viewing Room," Lord Mycroft said. "Once you have finished speaking with him, you might as well go back to Cavendish Hall and get some sleep. You will need your mind to be in perfect form when you question Talleyrand."

He rubbed his fleshy chin. "And I will send you the file on him," he added. "Talleyrand is the ultimate survivor. Do *not* underestimate him."

Chapter Thirteen

nder other circumstances, Gwen would have rather liked the Viewing Room. It was on the sixth floor, high enough to allow her to stare out over London without having to fly under her own power. Down below, she saw an endless stream of horse-drawn carriages, making their way to and from Whitehall, while street-sellers peddled their wares to pedestrians taking the air. It was easy to believe that the Swing had never taken place, if only because the damaged buildings had been rapidly repaired.

She turned away from the window as the door opened, revealing David Crichton. As always, he looked rather stuffy in his suit, which had been carefully tailored to make him look at least a decade or two older than he actually was. Gwen had puzzled over that until she'd discovered that the older generation of civil servants and government ministers tended to dislike the idea of youth at the helm. David was young enough to be the son of most of the people he had to work with, just as Gwen could have been their daughter. But it was always easier for a man.

"David," she said. David was too old to enjoy being hugged, even by his sister, at least in public. "It's good to see you again."

"And you," David said, primly. "Mother was complaining to Laura about how you never came to see her."

Gwen winced inwardly. Trust David to mention *that*! But Laura, his wife, would probably have reminded him to tell Gwen when he next saw her. Being a daughter-in-law, even one with her own establishment, Laura couldn't escape the dominating presence of Lady Mary. If nothing else, it was unlikely that Gwen would have to put up with her own mother-in-law.

David hadn't been a bad brother, not really. But once upon a time, he'd become a stuffy old man and never really looked back. And yet... he'd given Gwen advice when she'd needed it – and he might have been promoted because of his connection to the Royal Sorceress. Gwen had never dared ask if that was the case. Men, she'd learned by now, resented it when a woman arranged their promotion.

"You've put on some weight," she observed. "Did Laura get a new cook?"

"The new one does a wonderful stewed beef," David admitted. "Laura has been making her practice meals for the child, when he's finally born. Pregnancy seems to have concentrated her mind on preparing a nest."

Gwen had to smile. Maybe her nephew – or niece – would distract Lady Mary from hounding Gwen about marriage, once Laura gave birth. She was certainly nearing her time.

She braced herself. "Did Lord Mycroft tell you why he ordered us to meet?"

David shook his head. "He just said that we had to talk – and that I was excused the rest of the day, if I needed to go home," he said. "Gwen... what is going on?"

"I..."

Gwen hesitated – none of her mother's lessons had ever covered *this* – and plunged forward. "Sir Travis Mortimer was murdered last night. You would have been one of the people who saw him just before he died."

David's eyes opened wide. "Travis is *dead*?"

"Yes," Gwen said. Thankfully, David wasn't the kind of brother who was over-protective of his sister. Besides, he knew she'd seen more horror in the last year than most people saw in their entire lives. "He was murdered. I have been charged with investigating his death."

It took a moment for David to realise the implications. "And you think that I am a suspect," he snapped. It wasn't a question. "What sort of monster do you think I am?"

"I don't think you did it," Gwen assured him, cursing herself. That had clearly been the wrong approach. But then, David guarded his good name as carefully as upper-class women guarded their honour. Any accusation, from *anyone*, would sting. "But I do need to know what happened that night."

David turned, found a chair and sat down heavily. "Lord Mycroft said I could talk to you about anything," he said. "I never thought that it would be... Gwen, what do you know about the Airship Treaty?"

"Absolutely nothing," Gwen said, honestly.

"Good," David said, with sudden force. "Because the whole thing is a state secret. No one was supposed to know about it, outside a very small group. If the secret comes out before it is too late..."

Gwen frowned. "What – precisely – is the Airship Treaty?"

David laughed, rather wildly. "It may never get off the ground," he said. "And if the French know about it..."

"Calm down," Gwen ordered. She walked over to the drinks cabinet, poured a glass of brandy and passed it to him. He sipped it carefully, looking into the liquid as if he expected to find answers there. "David..."

She briefly considered using Charm, but David would be aware of the possibility – and if he was working for Mycroft, he would have been trained to resist Charm, no matter how subtle. And it would destroy their relationship completely if she tried, particularly after the day she'd first used her powers. Gwen barely remembered that day – she'd been six years old - but no one else could forget it. She'd terrified the entire house.

"Turkey is isolated," David said, putting the glass down on the table. "The Russians are threatening them from the north; the French are threatening them from the west. And they have the Persians to the east, who may become a later threat. Their new Sultan has been reorganising their government and military, but they don't have the resources to stand off both Russia and France. We believe that the two powers have already come to an agreement to divide up the Ottoman Empire between them."

Gwen had a feeling she knew where this was going, but she kept her thoughts to herself and let him talk. He'd never liked being interrupted.

"We cannot risk having the French in control of Turkey," David continued, "or the Russians in control of Persia. Either one would expose India to land invasion, an invasion that would be much easier than coming through Afghanistan. We have a strong interest in supporting the Turks. The Airship Treaty was intended to be the first step in building a formal alliance with Turkey."

That, Gwen decided, made sense. "Why is it called the Airship Treaty?"

"Because one of the provisions is for a series of airship bases in the Ottoman Empire," David said. "Getting airships to India isn't easy; the French often refuse to allow us to overfly their territory, which forces them to take the long way around Spain. We used to fly over Egypt until the Sultan took it back into the fold. Now, the treaty would make it much easier to get airships to India. Anyone who heard that much wouldn't think that there might be more to it.

"The secret provisions in the treaty are a military alliance, predominately naval and economic, against France and Russia," he continued. "In effect, we will prop up the Turks and use their territory as a buffer to protect our own. British investments will help the Turks to develop their own industrial base, strengthening Istanbul's hold on its empire. Between us, we can even keep Persia neutral, further safeguarding India, and prevent the French from menacing North Africa. The French will be caught in a vice."

Gwen hesitated, taking a moment to digest the implications. Lord Mycroft had been doubtful about winning a war, if one had to be fought, but he'd certainly been working hard to ensure that Britain was in the best possible position to *win* if it came down to a fight. If Turkey happened to be strong enough to hold the line against both France and Russia – and they'd held their own against the Russians in the last few bouts – the French would be in a very difficult position. They might well swallow their pride and refuse to fight.

But that gave Talleyrand a very strong reason to try to destroy the treaty before it could be signed.

She put that to one side and concentrated on her brother. "What was Sir Travis's role in all this?"

"Sir Travis was the prime negotiator," David said. He seemed to be calmer, now that he had the chance to lecture her. "You see, there are some diplomats who are visible – their mere presence raises suspicions of secret talks between two powers. Sir Travis was nothing more than an adventurer, on the face of it; he was certainly nothing like as prominent as Ambassador Talleyrand. No one would notice him in Istanbul, holding meetings with the Sultan's own confidential diplomats. He was the one who drew up the first draft of the treaty, then hand-delivered it back to Britain. We were working on the final version when he died."

Gwen gave him a considering look. "And the government saw fit to keep it a secret?"

David gave her an odd look. "Gwen, the French would certainly react if they heard about the treaty before it was actually signed," he said. "And even some of our own people would not be too happy about it. One persistent worry was that we might be giving the Turks too much in exchange for too little."

"Too much for too little?" Gwen asked. "Why...?"

"The Turks want more than just a promise of naval support," David explained. "They want help building up their technological base, their own airships... and some assistance in building their own version of the Royal Sorcerers Corps. And we have to refrain from interfering in the Arabian peninsula as they regain control, which is worrying for two separate reasons. We have treaties with a handful of minor states along the coastline and our Islamic subjects in India require access to Mecca. As the Sultan claims to be the rightful overlord of all Muslims, this could cause problems for us in India."

Gwen saw the logic. "We might build the Turks up to the point where they become a threat in their own right," she said.

David nodded in agreement. "That's the way of the world," he said. "The solution to one set of problems becomes another set of problems in its own right."

"Very profound," Gwen said, recalling the world map she had in her office at Cavendish Hall. "Why don't we build up the Persians as well?"

"The Sultan insisted that the treaty formally exclude that possibility," David said. "He wants Persia to remain as a buffer state between us, the Turks and the Russians – he doesn't want the Persians to become a power in their own right. In fact, we'd be committed to going to war with Russia if *they* tried to build Persia up into a genuine threat."

"Which would bring in the French," Gwen said. She had a sudden vision of treaties activating, one after the other, until the entire world was on fire. "David... is this really a good idea?"

"If we let Turkey go under, we risk our own holdings in the Middle East and India," David said. "If Turkey can be built up, there should be an uneasy stalemate, rather than an outright war."

"I don't like that *should*," Gwen admitted. "The French didn't make particularly rational calculations in 1800 either. Nor did the American rebels."

"We can, but try," David said.

Gwen nodded, ruefully. "What happens to the treaty now?"

"I'm not sure," David said. "Sir Travis did the legwork; at the very least, we would have to build up a new relationship between another confidential diplomat and the diplomat the Sultan trusted enough to handle their side of the talks. Someone who wasn't a Sensitive might not get so far in the talks."

"But you have a final draft," Gwen said. "Can't you just have that signed?"

"Not without Parliament mulling over it," David said. "The Prime Minister intended to present it to Parliament in a month, once we had a version that both sides could accept. But it might not happen without Sir Travis. He might have been needed to defend it, you see."

"Ending his career as a secret diplomat," Gwen said.

David nodded, shortly. "He was planning to get married," he said. "After that, he was going to remain in London, probably taking up a more visible position with the Foreign Office. He didn't have the seniority to become Ambassador to Turkey, but we might have sent him there as an assistant, someone who does the real work while the Ambassador attracts all the attention."

Gwen heard the bitterness in his tone and concealed her amusement. David had been angling for a post in Paris, perhaps as the Ambassador's special assistant. But Lord Holloway had rejected him in favour of his best friend's young nephew. *She* could have arranged a position for him at Cavendish Hall, if she'd thought that he would accept it. But he would have hated working under his sister. It was a pity – she could trust David to handle the paperwork – but understandable. Besides, nepotism would have been used against her by her political enemies... even though everyone knew that everyone did it.

"He was intending to marry Lady Elizabeth Bracknell," Gwen said. "Did you know that?"

David gave her a vaguely superior smile. "I was one of the witnesses when the marriage contract was signed," he said, before sobering. "The poor girl really liked him, you know. She's going to be broken-hearted."

Gwen understood. "Was there anything... different about the marriage contract? Anything that might have come back to haunt them?"

"Dear God, Sis," David said. "You *can't* suspect Lord Bracknell. He's a high court judge!"

"I think I have to explore all of the possibilities," Gwen said, tartly. In her experience, judges tended to think twice about counter-signing any warrants signed by the Royal Sorceress. She had never met Lord Bracknell, but if he was anything like his fellows he was a violent, bigoted, narrow-minded old fool. "What about the contract?"

"There was nothing particularly special about it, apart from the clause that insisted that Lady Elizabeth had to complete her schooling before the banns were formally read," David told her. "She was given a small dowry, which would be returned to her family in the event of the contract being broken, unless the affair damaged her reputation – and his. The money was held in trust at Great London Bank – there was a promise of a much larger dowry when the engagement was announced. If Lady Elizabeth did something to compromise herself, the dowry would be left with Sir Travis; however, if the parents broke the contract, they would be required to pay compensation in addition to surrendering the dowry. All fairly standard, really."

Gwen considered it for a long moment. "Nothing about land, property or bank accounts?"

"There would have been a second contract drawn up closer to the wedding," David reminded her. "The contract did state that land and suchlike would be settled on her, in the event of her being widowed, but there was no fixed agreement. As Sir Travis died *without* breaking the contract, I think the dowry would stay with her. There was certainly no provision for him dying before the marriage was... ah, sealed into law."

He frowned, thoughtfully. "I don't know who Sir Travis named as his principle heir," he added. "If he didn't name someone directly, there could be a lawsuit by what remains of his family to reclaim the dowry." He snorted. "But the dowry was really only four hundred pounds. They'd have to spend that much just to reclaim it."

"Poor Elizabeth," Gwen said. She should consider herself lucky. "Were there any possible motives for the Bracknell Family to want to kill Sir Travis?"

"None," David assured her. "If they discovered him... doing something that would invalidate the contract, they could have broken the engagement and kept the dowry. And, seeing that the contract was secret, they wouldn't have been embarrassed in public either."

"Unless Sir Travis made it public," Gwen said, quietly.

"Anything that would serve as grounds for breaking the contract wouldn't be something he'd want to make public," David said, slowly. "Lady Elizabeth would be embarrassed, but it wouldn't be as bad as it could be, later."

"True," Gwen agreed. She cursed mentally as an obvious question suggested itself to her. "Did Lady Elizabeth have other suitors? Maybe someone who decided to get his rival out of the way?"

"Not as far as I know," David said. "But you would have to check with her. I was just the witness."

Gwen shook her head, tiredly. Even if Lady Elizabeth had had another suitor, he would have had to somehow slip through Sir Travis's magic and take him by surprise. Still, it would have to be investigated.

"I'll need to see Sir Travis's will," she said. "Do you know where he kept it?"

"It should be in the Foreign Office," David said. "I'll have a copy sent to you – once he's certified dead, his supervisor will have to see to locating the executor and giving him the will."

"Thank you," Gwen said. She looked up and held his eyes. "I have to ask – did you kill Sir Travis?"

David scowled at her, but shook his head. "No," he said. "And I don't know who did."

Gwen stood up. "Thank you for your time," she said, and meant it. "If you want to go home..."

"I have to go back to the office," David said. "If Sir Travis is dead, someone has to start working on contingency plans."

Gwen rolled her eyes, then walked out of the door, heading down the heavily-carpeted staircase to the bottom floor. The receptionist nodded at her, holding up a single white envelope. Puzzled, Gwen took it and pulled it open. Inside was a single card, with SIR CHARLES written in plain black text. Below, there was an address in Pall Mall. Turning the card over, she saw a handwritten note.

Lady Gwen, it read. *Would you care to join me for a drive?*

Gwen stepped through the door and out onto the street. A single carriage was waiting just past the door, with Sir Charles standing beside it. Gwen felt flattered and confused – and alarmed – at the same time. Royal Sorceress or not, single men were not supposed to pick up single women in their carriages. But then... hadn't she ridden with Lord Mycroft in *his* carriage?

"Please, Milady," Sir Charles said, with another brilliant smile. "Would you care to join me?"

Gwen hesitated, then allowed him to help her up into the carriage.

Chapter Fourteen

I must apologise for meeting you like this," Sir Charles said, as the carriage rattled into life. "But Travis always did things in the most direct manner possible and I assume that you, a fellow magician, would do the same."

Gwen couldn't help feeling flattered. Most men – even magicians – treated her, at best, like a little sister. Talking with them forced her to wrap her head around an entire series of allusions and half-truths intended to keep unfortunate realities from delicate feminine ears. The idea of someone being *direct* with her was remarkable. Even Lord Mycroft was never direct.

"Sir Travis was my dearest friend," Sir Charles added. "I will do whatever it takes to bring his killer to justice."

"I certainly intend to find the murderer," Gwen said. It was harder to concentrate than it should have been. Had he come to find her because he wanted to *court* her? And, coming to think of it, *how* had he known where to find her? "Do you know if Lady Elizabeth had any other suitors?"

Sir Charles considered it. "I do not believe that the young lady had many opportunities to meet young men," he said, after a moment's thought. "Her father was quite controlling, I fear. Indeed, her coming out was long delayed."

Gwen frowned. Now that she'd had a chance to think about it, an unsuccessful suitor for Lady Elizabeth's hand would make a plausible suspect – although it wouldn't explain how the murderer had managed to get so close to a Sensitive with murderous intentions. Had he come in peace and turned murderous so quickly that Sir Travis had no time to react? It didn't seem possible. There should still have been some reaction on the man's face as he died.

And it was quite possible that there *would* be suitors. Even if Lady Elizabeth was an educated woman – and Gwen knew through bitter experience that men didn't always want educated or powerful women – she was still the daughter of a judge. A man like that could open doors in London, boosting his son-in-law's career. Lady Elizabeth might be the ugliest and least charming woman in the world and she would *still* have suitors. And if no one knew that she was engaged, the suitors would keep coming. Maybe her parents had found a better match for her and then had Sir Travis murdered, just to avoid having to break the contract.

But if that came out, it would destroy them...

Too complex, she thought, remembering one of Lord Mycroft's lectures. The more complex any given plan or concept was, the more likely it was to fail; he'd told her, several times, that the simplest solution was often the right one. And she couldn't see the Bracknell Family risking their existence just to avoid the shame of breaking a marriage contract. Their position in society would be dented, but they would survive.

"I wouldn't put anything past a high-ranking family," Sir Charles said. There was an undertone of bitterness in his voice that surprised her. "But the young lady was a decent person and her father... wasn't too bad. Her mother insisted on chaperoning, of course, but Travis never objected to it."

He couldn't, Gwen thought. Being alone with a young man, even for a few moments, could be enough to wreck a young lady's reputation. Sir Travis would have been wise to be relieved that Lady Bracknell was there, even if he did find her presence a little constraining. A smart husband wouldn't want his wife to be the talk of the town, even if he *knew* that she was innocent.

She smiled up at Sir Charles. "Tell me about him," she said. "What adventures did you and he have in India?"

"I shall have to order the coachman to keep circling the

block," Sir Charles said. He rubbed his hands together with delight. "This could take hours..."

His smile grew wider. "There was the time when we were attached to a regiment that was on garrison duty in the Punjab," he said. "The Colonel in command spent most of his time trying to improve his mind by playing polo... he actually managed to get some of the natives interested in the game. Then he tried to play it on elephants, which was great fun but rather impractical. So when a tiger started menacing the local villagers, he sent us after it. I would have thought that the Colonel would have wanted the honour for himself, but... he was too lazy to hunt."

Gwen snorted in amusement.

"So we went to the village and started trailing the tiger," Sir Charles continued. "Not a hard task for a Sensitive, you see; we went into the jungle, completely without thinking. Travis keeps his eyes on the ground, right up until the moment the tiger pokes his head out of the bushes and growls at us. And poor Travis falls over with shock!

"The tiger seemed rather surprised by *that* result, giving me time to shoot him between the eyes," he added, "then drag Travis out of the way. Luckily, I killed the tiger – or he would have mauled both of us."

He hesitated. "No one else knows how close he came to fainting there," he said. "Don't tell anyone, all right?"

Gwen nodded. A Sensitive could be stunned by a sudden loud noise... although she was surprised that the tiger had managed to get so close without Sir Travis realising that it was there. But then, a jungle would have thousands of different impressions for a Sensitive to read – and if Sir Travis wasn't used to hunting tigers, he might not have known what he was sensing until it was too late.

"After that, we started using Judas Goats instead," Sir Charles added. "We tied a goat to a stake at the edge of the jungle, then took turns hiding in the tree with a hunting rifle. Once the tiger showed himself, whoever was on duty shot him – which turned very dangerous when one tiger was wounded rather than killed. I had to trail the blighter through the jungle to finish him off."

Gwen knew very little about hunting, but that sounded odd. "Couldn't you have left him to die?"

"A wounded beast makes a more dangerous enemy," Sir Charles said. "If the tiger had been maddened by the wound, he might have become much more savage to the natives... and it was our job to protect them. No, we had to kill him before he could escape."

He smiled again, then started to tell a different story. "A month or two later, we went on a mission to Bukhara, a state where both us and the Russians were competing for influence," he said. "It was a remarkable city – do you know it dates all the way back to the time of Alexander the Great? But the current Emir was nothing like as capable as his predecessors and the Russians had managed to secure more influence than we'd realised in his court. They caught us and threw us into jail."

Gwen had read part of the story in dispatches, but she had no idea how much of the public version was actually true.

"I told you that Sir Travis was *good* at talking to the natives," Sir Charles continued. "We were both tortured, of course, and we told them nothing, but Sir Travis realised that the Emir's younger son had doubts about his country's attachment to Russia. He prevailed upon the young man to help us escape, then plotted a coup that allowed him to replace the Emir and purge his elder brothers. We were going to kill the Russian advisors, but apparently they had protested when the Emir arrested us. They thought that our deaths might bring the army to Bukhara."

"*That* wasn't the version you sent back home," Gwen pointed out. The version of the story she'd read in the newspapers had stated that they'd made a daring escape, leaving Bukhara in the dead of night disguised as local traders. There certainly hadn't been anything about helping a prince overthrow his father. "Why didn't you tell the truth?"

Sir Charles shrugged. "You think the British Public wants to know the full truth of the Great Game? Our fear is the Russians seizing a land bridge to India... and they are trying to do just that, advancing their borders southwards kingdom by kingdom. We have to do whatever it takes to stop them, even if it means sponsoring coups and dealing with dishonourable men – or tribesmen who would stick a knife in our back as soon as it was turned. But the British Public doesn't want to hear about that. They want to hear about heroics..."

Gwen couldn't disagree with him. After all, she was one of the few people who knew what had *really* happened during the Battle of London.

"Not our only crazy adventure," Sir Charles said. "There was the time when we disguised ourselves as horse-traders and wandered from kingdom to kingdom, gathering intelligence for future operations. We tinted our skin and spoke in accented voices – and yet we were nearly caught more than once by sharp-eyed locals. And then there was the time when we were nearly married to a local nabob's daughters... *that* could have been embarrassing, I tell you."

"Nearly married?" Gwen asked. "Why....?"

"Turned out that the man thought we were royalty, wandering around in disguise," Sir Charles told her. "Apparently, some states have a tradition of the King donning commoner clothes and going out to see what his people were actually saying in the marketplace. We had to leave *that* state in a hurry, believe me."

"That sounds unbelievable," Gwen said. "He didn't even know who you were?"

"He might not have changed his mind if he had," Sir Charles said. "We met a couple of white men who changed their religion and married local girls. One of them was actually a former colour sergeant who became the commander of the king's army. He was actually teaching them how to fight like us... good thing he also had the sense to advise his father-in-law not to resist or it could have become bloody. That army might come in very handy one day."

He scowled. "Still, you can never trust someone who immersed himself in the ways of the orient," he added. "The locals are a shifty lot. If you look weak, they won't hesitate to take advantage of it – and you never know what is going to set them off. A couple of years before the Swing, there was a near-mutiny in the north of India; some travelling faker of a fakir had told the local troops that the cartridges in their rifles had been coated with pig or beef fat. Muslims can't touch pig fat; Hindus see the cow as a holy animal... it was a lie, but it still started trouble for us. If we hadn't managed to summon additional regiments to disarm the mutinous troops and keep the peace, it could have gone badly for us."

Gwen remembered all the whispered rumours about her and scowled. Sometimes, all it took was repetition to get people believing a lie, even if it was absolute nonsense. Even after she'd become the Royal Sorceress, the rumours about her ranged from the absurd to the disgusting – and those were just the one's she'd heard. God alone knew what was being whispered about her in distant India, or America.

She changed the subject. "What was Sir Travis like, as a person?"

"Good companion, always calm and composed... never really seemed surprised by anything the locals did," Sir Charles said. "But... he did have a bit of a weakness for gambling. He'd play cards constantly with anyone fool enough to take him up on it. I eventually had to ask him to stop using his magic if he wanted to gamble with me."

That was... *odd*, Gwen realised. It was simple *not* to use Blazing or Moving, but she'd always had the impression that Sensitives rarely had such fine control over their powers. So many of them ended up in the madhouse *because* they couldn't control their powers. Indeed, there were unwritten laws *against* Sensitives and Talkers gambling, if only because they had an unfair advantage. Had Sir Travis been so capable that he could turn his power off at will – or had he lied to his friend?

"A gambling habit is hardly unusual," she mused, deciding not to mention the latter possibility. "That wouldn't have served as an excuse to break off an engagement..."

But it *would* have, she realised, if Sir Travis had

effectively been cheating. David had once told her that a man he'd known had been blackballed from all of the gambling halls in London after being caught cheating. Sir Travis might not have been cheating, but with his powers he would certainly be suspected of cheating... and it would be difficult to prove his innocence. He might even have been cheating without *intending* to cheat, if his control over his powers wasn't as good as everyone said.

A Talker could have verified his innocence, she knew. But he'd had so many secrets in his head that his superiors would have been reluctant to allow it.

"He used to play at the Golden Turk," Sir Charles said. "I believe that he first went there to meet a Turkish... ah, representative... and then kept going back. He never played with *me* in London."

Gwen smiled. "What did you play for?"

"Very small stakes," Sir Charles said. "When we were travelling, we gambled over who would wash the dishes or carry the heavier load. In Calcutta, we would play for money with the rest of the community. Sir Travis did very well even after I convinced him to stop using his powers, mostly because he wasn't a prideful ass. Some of the players there just kept raising the stakes because they couldn't bear to fold."

"I know the type," Gwen said. Some of them grew bored with gambling and went looking for more exotic pursuits, such as the so-called Worshipful Order of Ancient Wisdom, or were eventually cut off by their parents and forced to seek gainful employment overseas. "Do you know how much Sir Travis was paid? Was gambling his main source of income?"

"I never enquired," Sir Charles said, stiffly. "But given what he did for the government, I am sure he received a more than fair salary. And all of our expenses were refunded, no questions asked."

Gwen nodded, thoughtfully. It was unlikely that Lord Mycroft would have refused to give Sir Travis a proper salary. If nothing else, a resentful man made a poor employee. It was a shame that more money wasn't enough to overcome those who resented Gwen's elevation to

Royal Sorceress, but the only thing that would satisfy them would be a male Master Magician – themselves, for preference.

"And Lord Bracknell would have satisfied himself that Travis could keep his daughter in the style she deserved," Gwen mused. "Did he know about the Golden Turk?"

"I don't know," Sir Charles admitted. "It was founded just after the Swing – a number of gambling halls were destroyed and the owner saw a chance to establish himself. Lord Bracknell might not have even known of its existence. *He* doesn't go gambling."

"I'll have to investigate," Gwen said, shaking her head. David had spent time in gambling halls, but young ladies of good breeding *never* gambled. "I have to visit Ambassador Talleyrand tomorrow – and then Augustus Howell."

Sir Charles jerked in surprise. "You actually mean to visit *him*?"

"He's a suspect," Gwen said. Who was Howell that so many different people had bad reactions to him? She seeded her voice with as much Charm as she dared. "Do you know what he wanted with Sir Travis?"

"I wouldn't dare to guess," Sir Charles said. Again, he seemed utterly unaware of the Charm. "But I do not believe that he had anything to do with Sir Travis's murder."

"It has to be investigated," Gwen said.

"No doubt," Sir Charles said. He smiled at her. "Can I take you for lunch after you meet the Ambassador?"

Gwen hesitated. Lunch with a man, even lunch in a public place, would be used against her by her enemies. If they'd known that she'd eaten with Lord Mycroft in private – more than once – they would have enjoyed spreading rumours... and Sir Charles was far less powerful than Lord Mycroft. On the other hand, he was famous and popular and the rumours might backfire...

And she enjoyed his company. More, perhaps, than she wanted to admit.

"I'd be honoured," she said, and meant it. "Where do you want to eat?"

Sir Charles made a show of being thoughtful. "Glisters, I think," he said. "I believe the food there is generally considered excellent. Sir Travis used to love it."

Gwen nodded. "That would be suitable," she said. It wasn't as if she could invite him to Cavendish Hall. She looked up at him as a question returned to her mind. "How did you know where to find me?"

Sir Charles made no pretence of being puzzled by the question. "I asked the Inspector," he said. "He was quite happy to tell me where I could find you."

"Ah," Gwen said.

She climbed out of the carriage and started to walk towards Cavendish Hall. The coachman had stopped a small distance from the building, just so she wouldn't be seen getting out of the carriage right in front of it. Discreet, she considered, although probably not as discreet as he thought. Gwen wasn't *that* unrecognisable.

Shaking her head, she walked into the building and headed up to her office. She could check the clerks, make sure they'd done a good job, and then head to bed. Tomorrow was going to be a *very* busy day.

Chapter Fifteen

wen hadn't slept very well after climbing into bed, even though she'd been exhausted. The nightmares about the undead crawling through London – where her powers seemed to have failed and all she could do was stare helplessly as they approached her – had been particularly bad. The undead seemed to have had the faces of her family... she had woken up at six in the morning, drenched in sweat and hadn't been able to get back to sleep.

"You have some letters," Martha said. Somehow, her maid always seemed to know when she was awake. "Three of them look quite important."

Gwen scowled. She'd briefed the clerks carefully on what they could handle, what could be passed to Doctor Norwell and what had to be put aside for her, but she expected some teething problems. At least Doctor Norwell could supervise them for a couple of days, after which she would have to place her trust in the young men. But anything addressed to her personally would probably be given to her...

She took the letters from Martha and inspected them carefully. Five of them looked to be letters from people who expected the Royal Sorceress to drop everything and help them with their problem; she put them aside for later attention and looked at the important letters. One of them was clearly from Lord Mycroft – she recognised his clerk's handwriting – but the other two were unfamiliar, even though one of them was written in a feminine hand. Puzzled, she opened the envelope and scanned the letter quickly.

"Lady Elizabeth Bracknell requests the honour of Lady Gwendolyn Crichton's company," she read out loud, "and would be happy to host her at Bracknell Hall..."

It was a puzzling letter; Lady Elizabeth had written as if she'd been writing to a man, rather than to another woman. Gwen's position in London was somewhat atypical, but she didn't need to be so formal. And if she were inviting Gwen to a ball, why not say so? It sounded more like she wanted a private discussion. There was certainly no time or date attached, suggesting that Gwen could set her own time.

She reread the letter to see if there was anything she'd missed, but found nothing. At a guess. Lady Elizabeth was unused to sending letters requesting *anyone's* presence, which did make a certain kind of sense. One didn't send formal invitations to one's girlfriends to visit... unless a formal ball was planned, whereupon sending an invitation was officially required. But Gwen was hardly one of Lady Elizabeth's girlfriends...

Gwen sat down at her desk, found a writing pad and a pen, and sketched out a quick reply, promising to visit the following morning. Lord Bracknell had a flat in Pall Mall – like everyone else with the connections and money to secure one – but his wife and daughter lived out on the edge of London, near some prime hunting ground. Gwen made a mental note to check up on the family's finances before visiting, just in case they had an additional motive for murdering Sir Travis. But it seemed unlikely that they would murder him and then ask the person investigating his murder to visit their home.

Once she'd sealed the reply in an envelope and dropped it down the chute to the mail room, she opened the second letter. David had ordered it sent, the cover letter stated; it was a copy of Sir Travis's will. The writer had added a note saying that she would have received a copy anyway, something that puzzled her until she looked at the top sheet of the will. Sir Travis had appointed the Royal Sorcerer as the executor.

He must have meant Master Thomas, she thought, as she checked the date. The will had been written nine months ago, back before Gwen had been an apprentice. Sir Travis, like everyone else, must have assumed that Master Thomas was effectively immortal, if only because no one had wanted to think about what would happen when he died. And if Master Thomas had known about him...

She scowled. There was probably an explanation somewhere within Master Thomas's notes, but she had yet to find it. Just another matter that he hadn't had time to tell her before he died, if he'd decided to share it at all. For all she knew, Sir Travis had been quietly delighted not to have to report to a slip of a girl.

Pushing the thought aside, she skimmed through the will quickly, looking for anything that might have provided a motive for murder. There was almost nothing; the estate was to go to his closest living relative, along with almost all of his possessions. A set of notebooks and a small sum of money were to go to Sir Charles – there was a wry comment in the will that they should help him write his dispatches that made Gwen smile – and another small sum of money was to go to Polly. Not enough to let her avoid working for the rest of her life, Gwen noted, but enough to give her a few options she wouldn't otherwise have. But there was no mention of any jewels.

And no mention of Lady Bracknell, Gwen thought, as she read it a second time. But that wasn't too surprising either. The marriage had been arranged after the will had been written; Sir Travis wouldn't have rewritten it in favour of his wife until after they were actually married. In fact, the only clause that stood out was a request that certain trophies Sir Travis had taken while in India were to be donated to the Diogenes Club. The list included several tiger heads, a set of artefacts from Central Asia and a handful of books written in Arabic.

Shaking her head, she wrote out a short message for Norton to meet her in her office in thirty minutes, dropped it down the chute and opened the third envelope. It was a brief note of introduction to Ambassador Talleyrand, signed by Lord Holdhurst, the Foreign Secretary. Stripped of its flowery language, it requested that the Ambassador grant Lady Gwen an audience; the covering note explained that there was no way they could *force* Ambassador Talleyrand to agree to speak to Gwen. He was a diplomat and had diplomatic immunity; if he was proved to be the murderer, he couldn't be punished beyond being expelled from the country.

Gwen put the note – and Sir Travis's will - in her purse, then walked down to her office and checked the letters the clerks had left for her to inspect. Most of them were unimportant, although one of them concerned the sighting of weird creatures up near Loch Ness in Scotland and probably merited investigation. If people could become werewolves, why not mermaids? She put it aside for later contemplation and threw the remaining letters – mainly ones complaining about her appointment – in the fire. She didn't need to reply to those.

"My Lady," Geoffrey Norton said, as he entered the room. "How may I be of service to you?"

"Master Thomas was appointed to serve as the executor of Sir Travis's will," Gwen said. She didn't bother to explain. By now, everyone in London would probably know about the murder. "I assume that duty has also devolved onto me?"

"Almost certainly, unless there was a specific provision in the will against it," Norton confirmed. "May I see the document?"

Gwen produced it and handed the document to him, then waited as patiently as she could for him to finish reading it. He took much longer than her, but he *had* been a lawyer before Mycroft had recommended him for the Royal Sorcerers Corps. He'd be sure to read every line before committing himself to an opinion.

"There's nothing too unusual in this will, although some of its terms are rather vague," Norton said. "You'd have to compile a list of everything Sir Travis owned, assign it to the person laid down in the will and then certify that you had done so... it could be challenged by his family, but I suspect that they would be unsuccessful. He wasn't trying to prevent them from claiming Mortimer Hall and everything else was his to dispose of as he pleased."

"And when," Gwen demanded, "am I meant to find the

time to do that?"

"Oh, you could appoint a surrogate," Norton said. "Master Thomas often used a lawyer working for the Corps to take care of such matters – this is hardly the first time he was named as the executor for a magician's will. You'd have to read their final report before distributing the various bequests, but you could leave him to do the rest of the work."

Gwen nodded. "Could you handle it?"

"Perhaps, if you didn't mind me spreading the work over the next week," Norton said. "I could focus on it exclusively, but it might not speed the process up; I'd have to send enquires to various banks and suchlike and they don't always respond rapidly..."

"Do it as quickly as possible," Gwen said. She hesitated, then asked the next question. "Could you also inspect his mother's will?"

Norton frowned. "Perhaps," he said. "But I assume that was handled by someone else...?"

"There was a bequest in it to give her jewels to the serving girl," Gwen said, shortly. "I would like to discover if she received those jewels – and, if not, what happened to them."

"It wouldn't be the first time someone just kept quiet about a specific bequest," Norton said. "I shall certainly look into it... however, I should warn you that it may be difficult to force them to surrender the jewels. The court might just rule that the will was overridden by Sir Travis's will and as he made no mention of the jewels..."

"Let me know what you find out," Gwen said. Given how Polly had been treated, both by Sir Travis and the police, it would be a good thing to make sure she actually got the jewels she had been promised. "One other question, then; do you know anything about the Bracknell Family's current circumstances?"

"Lord Bracknell is a judge," Norton said. "He will have had plenty of opportunities to enrich himself, even if he didn't have old money. I wouldn't have thought that they'd be in any trouble. The Swing only bankrupted families who kept all of their property in London."

Gwen nodded. It was looking increasingly unlikely that the Bracknell Family was responsible for Sir Travis's death; hopefully, she would be able to confirm that when she visited Lady Elizabeth. At least that would reduce the number of potential suspects...

"Thank you," she said, as she stood up. "Contact me once you have completed your first survey of the estate."

The dining hall was surprisingly full so early in the morning. Sir James and three of his comrades had taken over one of the tables and were arguing over a large map of London, trying to determine the best way to protect the King when he toured his city. Gwen suspected that the simplest answer would be to wrap the King in a protective bubble the moment he left the Palace, but George IV wouldn't like that idea. He'd spent too long estranged from his subjects before the Swing had shaken his faith in the government.

She took her chair, ordered breakfast and picked up a copy of *The Times*. The headline proclaimed there to have been an OUTRAGEOUS MURDER AT MORTIMER HALL, with a few details of the crime scene that were largely inaccurate. Someone had probably been speaking to the policemen who'd been ringing the building, Gwen decided, rather than the ones who'd seen the dead body. An underlying note stated that the police already had a suspect in custody; the writer had outdone himself describing the savage nature of the Africans, as if Polly hadn't been a child when she'd been rescued. It concluded with a strong suggestion that hiring such people as servants was inherently dangerous.

Maybe that reporter won't have a career for much longer, Gwen thought. It didn't take much to whip up racial hysteria – and slave-owners would not appreciate demands for any laws that threatened their human property. They had enough problems with Royal Navy officers refusing to help slavers, or cracking down on them at the slightest provocation. Strings would be pulled and the reporter would find himself out of work.

She read through the rest of the article quickly. There was a brief outline of Sir Travis's career in India, but no mention of his magic – or of his visits to Istanbul. Or, for that matter, of an engagement to Lady Elizabeth. Anyone who knew about the engagement was unlikely to mention it to the press; if no one knew about it, the engagement might as well have never happened. It was unusual for a man to object to marrying a woman who had been previously engaged, but it had been known to happen. The Bracknell Family would probably prefer not to take that chance.

There was no mention of her involvement, Gwen was pleased to see. Whoever had provided the information to the reporter clearly hadn't known that she was there. Still, the reporter had done quite enough damage. Gwen would have been surprised if the heirs waited until tomorrow before registering their claims. Mortimer Hall might have been allowed to grow a little unruly – Polly couldn't have hoped to keep it clean and tidy indefinitely, at least not without additional servants to help – but it *was* in a good part of London. Someone who moved in and cleaned it up would be well-placed to join the next social season.

Lord Brockton entered the dining hall and started to take his seat on the other end of the high table. Gwen waved to him and pointed to a seat next to hers; reluctantly, he left the seat he'd been holding and came to join her. No doubt he'd been hoping to avoid her as much as possible.

"I am required to investigate the murder of Sir Travis, one of our magicians," Gwen said, when he sat down. "During that time, I expect you and the other Head of Departments to continue running your sections; Doctor Norwell and Sir James will handle any disputes over resources, training facilities and suchlike. Should something happen that requires my attention, you may use a Talker to summon me."

A complex range of emotions flickered over Lord Brockton's puffy face before he nodded. "As you command, Milady," he said. He didn't sound happy; if something went wrong while Gwen was away from Cavendish Hall, it would be hard for him to blame her for it. Not that would stop him trying, of course. "However, Sir James..."

"Has a great deal of experience melding the different talents," Gwen said. She wondered – with a faint glimmer of amusement - just how he planned to object. No one could question Sir James's masculinity – or his experience. Indeed, if Gwen hadn't existed, he would have been the best choice for Royal Sorcerer. "And, for that matter, in not making other departments feel that they have to fight."

Lord Brockton scowled at her, recognising the unsubtle jab for what it was. There were nine members of the Royal Committee – not counting Gwen – and six of them could override her, if they voted together. But Lord Brockton was too good at alienating the other Head of Departments to convince them to block her on the Committee. As long as she was careful, she could keep them from uniting permanently.

"Very good, Milady," he said, finally. He sounded as though he were making a great concession, but as long as he accepted it Gwen was prepared to ignore his tone. "I shall respect his judgement."

Gwen ordered breakfast, ate quickly and then left the room, pausing just long enough to order Sir James to follow her. Once they were outside the hall, she briefly outlined what she wanted him to do – and warned him to be careful of the Royal Committee. It would be far too easy for Lord Brockton to claim all of the training resources for his Blazers, which would annoy the Movers... and the Charmers tended to cause trouble if left unwatched. The Changers and Infusers required less supervision, but they didn't like being talked down to by the Blazers... there were times when Gwen wondered if she'd really been asked to supervise a nursery, one where the slightest misspoken word could cause years of hurt feelings.

"Don't worry," Sir James assured her, when she'd finished. He seemed glad of the distraction from Merlin's routine duties in the capital. "I'll have Pete keep an eye on him."

"Thank you," Gwen said. Lord Brockton would find it harder to cause trouble if he were supervised by another Blazer, particularly one with such close ties to the Movers.

"I shall leave it in your capable hands."

Her carriage was waiting outside, as she had ordered. She took a moment to check her appearance, then climbed inside and sat down, forcing herself to run through the meditation routines Master Thomas had taught her. She didn't know if Talleyrand was a magician – there were rumours about every foreign politician who made himself known to the British public – but the French definitely had their own magicians now. Jack had taught them how to isolate and train the talents in return for being allowed to hide out in France and recuperate, before returning to Britain. It was quite possible that the French diplomat would be accompanied by a Talker or a Sensitive.

Why not? She thought, wryly. It was undiplomatic, but everyone knew that everyone did it – once they had the magicians, at least. These days, Ambassadors were either escorted or never told anything useful. *We send Talkers with our diplomats.*

Chapter Sixteen

he French Embassy was a huge building, protected by wrought-iron spikes and a handful of armed policemen. It was the most important embassy in London, but also the most vulnerable; youths had been gathering to throw stones over the wall every night since the general public had been told that the French had been responsible for the undead plague in London. Gwen had heard that the protests were causing diplomatic headaches for the Foreign Office; sooner or later, someone was going to get seriously hurt and the headaches would become a nightmare.

She climbed out of the carriage and walked towards the gate, nodding brusquely to the policemen on duty. A French officer, wearing a resplendent blue and gold uniform, stopped her as she reached the gates and demanded to know her business. Gwen gave him the letter of introduction Lord Mycroft had sent her and smiled as the guard gave her a sharp look. The Quality might claim that women in trousers was a French invention, designed to subvert the social order, but he hadn't realised that she was female until he'd read her name.

"Lady Sorceress," he said, hastily. His English was oddly accented, but understandable. "I shall have to speak to my superior."

Gwen waited as he stepped back inside the guardhouse for a brief conversation with another officer, then returned and bowed to her. "Ambassador Talleyrand will be pleased to see you," he said. "If you will come with me, I will take you to him."

The interior of the French Embassy was luxurious.

Gwen was tempted to stop and look at each of the portraits separately, remembering names and faces from lessons her tutors had tried to drive into her skull. The various French kings were instantly recognisable, but the others were harder to place. One of them was of Jacques Necker, the Swiss-born statesman who had saved the French financial system and staved off outright revolution. If he'd failed and the uprisings in Paris had spread to the rest of the country...

She gathered herself as she was shown into a large stateroom. Talleyrand - Charles Maurice de Talleyrand-Périgord, Ambassador to the Court of St. James – rose to his feet to greet her, holding out one hand to take hers. Behind him, a young girl sat on a chair, her gaze flickering between Talleyrand and his visitor. She couldn't have been much older than Gwen.

"Charmed, my dear," Talleyrand said, in French. He kissed the air just above her hand. "My humble home is honoured by your presence."

"Thank you, Your Excellency," Gwen said, in the same language. Most educated men spoke French, which didn't always endear them to the lower classes, who blamed France for everything that went wrong in their lives. "I regret that I had to come on business."

She sat down on the chair he indicated and studied him thoughtfully. Talleyrand was, according to Lord Mycroft's file, seventy-seven years old, but he looked remarkably fit for his age. The only sign of vanity was the fashionable wig he wore on his head and a surprising amount of powder on his face, probably concealing the wrinkles. His eyes, however, were bright and clear, studying Gwen with open interest. Lord Mycroft considered him an equal. That, if nothing else, confirmed that he was a very dangerous man.

The file had been unusually detailed. Talleyrand had limped from a very early age and his family had stripped him of the right to inherit their title, claiming that he was too disabled to uphold their proud military tradition. Instead, Talleyrand had entered the Church and trained as a priest – then become a politician during the unrest that had swept over France in the late 1790s. He'd gained wealth and titles through good advice and diplomatic achievements, even if he *had* failed to prevent the War of 1800-2. And he'd abandoned his former family to start a new one of his own. Gwen could understand *that* impulse.

"When a pretty girl is involved, business is always pleasure," Talleyrand assured her. He switched to English. "And we may converse in your language, if you wish. I would not like to discomfit you."

"I need to practice my French," Gwen said, which was true enough. It would also force her to think about what she said before she said it. Talleyrand might be flirting with her – the file had stated that he had a remarkable reputation for womanising – but he would also be measuring her for his report to the King of France. She *was* the Royal Sorceress... and if war came, Gwen would be charged with leading Britain's magicians into war.

"I am happy to allow you to practice on me," Talleyrand said. "I must confess to some curiosity, my dear. Why have you sought out my company?"

Gwen looked at the other girl, then lifted an eyebrow.

"My daughter Simone has my full confidence," Talleyrand added. "She has served as my secretary for the last two years. And she was quite interested when I told her about you."

Someone must have told him that I was coming, Gwen thought, coldly.

"I'm glad to meet you," she said, giving Simone a smile. "Maybe we can chat later about other matters."

The girl looked very shy; indeed, it was hard to see any resemblance between her and Talleyrand at all. Her skin was so pale that it was almost translucent, leaving her dark eyes standing out in her face. The yellow dress she wore attracted the eye *away* from her beauty. It was quite possible, judging by what had been written in the file, that Talleyrand merely *thought* that she was his daughter. But there was no way to know for sure.

She looked back at Talleyrand. "As you may have read in the papers" – and someone at the Foreign Office had probably told him, she added inwardly – "Sir Travis

Mortimer was murdered two days ago. You were one of the people who saw him before he died."

"I heard," Talleyrand said. "The papers were full of speculation. I particularly enjoyed the suggestion that his family had killed him after he refused to sell them Mortimer House."

Gwen scowled. "I need to ask you some questions," she said. "What did you and Sir Travis have to talk about?"

Talleyrand studied her for a long moment, as if he were trying to peer into her soul. "I would prefer not to discuss confidential matters with you, my dear," he said, in a surprisingly light tone. "However, under the circumstances, there may be little choice."

He sighed. "I was aware that Sir Travis had served the British Government as a secret diplomat," he added. "It was my hope that he could help me to negotiate directly with the Prime Minister and the King."

Gwen frowned. There seemed little point in denying it. "How did you know that he was a secret diplomat?"

"There were French agents in India during his time as an emissary," Talleyrand said. "One of them identified Sir Travis and reported it to Paris."

Sir Charles had talked about a mission to Bukhara where they'd discovered that the Russians already had influence over the Emir. Could the French have been involved too? Or, perhaps, the Russians traded the information to the French in exchange for something they wanted? But then, it was no secret that the French had agents in India; they'd never quite given up on the subcontinent, even after they'd been evicted from the mainland in 1800. Talleyrand might well be telling the truth.

"So you thought he could help you," Gwen said, thoughtfully. "Why didn't you make a more open approach?"

Talleyrand gave her a sharp look. "You are aware that your countrymen seem to believe that we unleashed undead monsters on London?"

Gwen flushed, uncomfortably. That made sense; if the Airship Treaty had to be kept secret, if only because the terms might upset someone, any discussions with the

French would have to be even more secret. The Prime Minister could not allow a hint of weakness to slip out or he would be challenged in the Houses of Parliament. And that might weaken his position to the point where the opposition could force a vote of no confidence through the house.

"So you approached Sir Travis," Gwen said. "What happened then?"

"He was reluctant to talk about his time in India," Talleyrand said. "But after I had convinced him that we had honoured the unspoken convention of not revealing such information, he was willing to approach his superiors for us. I had believed that he would keep his word – I never anticipated that he would be murdered that same night."

Gwen suspected that he was probably telling the truth. Logically, the French gained nothing from murdering Sir Travis, particularly if they needed him to do something for them. And besides, if Talleyrand were to be blamed for Sir Travis's death it would almost certainly start a war, particularly after the Battle of London.

"The timing must have been very poor," she mused. "Do you know if you were the last person to visit that night?"

"My appointment was for just before midnight," Talleyrand informed her. "And Sir Travis looked tired. I might well have been the last."

"Which puts you at the top of the list of suspects," Gwen pointed out.

Talleyrand smiled at her. "How – exactly – do I benefit from murdering Sir Travis?

"At the very least, I would be returned to France in disgrace and my career would be over," he said. "My enemies in Paris would see to that, even if they didn't manage to convince the King to hand me over to your country. And I have been working hard to prevent a war between Britain and France. That war might well *start* if a French diplomat murdered a British citizen. Your people fought a war over one man losing an ear. What will you do if an Ambassador murders a diplomat?"

Gwen scowled. He was right.

"I have to ask," she said. Carefully, she infused a little Charm into her voice. "Did you murder Sir Travis?"

Simone coughed.

"There are gentlemen's agreements that Charm is not to be used as part of negotiations," Talleyrand said, reproachfully. "But you are no gentleman."

"No," Gwen agreed, irked. He'd detected the Charm... or had *Simone* detected the Charm? Might there be more than one reason he kept her around? "I'm afraid that no one has ever accused me of being a gentleman."

Talleyrand didn't sound offended. "I didn't murder Sir Travis," he said. It was impossible to tell if the Charm had affected him or not. "Like I have told you, I gain nothing and lose much from the act."

He stood up and bowed. "And I am afraid that I have given you too much of my time," he added. "I would be interested in meeting you again, Lady Gwen, but in less stressful circumstances. It is quite possible that we could come to a proper understanding."

Gwen rose, recognising the dismissal. "Thank you for your time," she said, sincerely. "And I have enjoyed meeting your daughter too."

She held a hand out towards Simone, who hesitated and then took it. Her touch was feather-light, but there was no mistaking the faint tingle that suggested the presence of magic, recognisable to any other magician. She looked up into the girl's eyes and saw the recognition on her face, followed by a faint touch on Gwen's mind. A Talker, then... no wonder she'd sensed the Charm.

"The guards will escort you out," Talleyrand said. How much of the byplay had he sensed? "And I hope you do find the killer, Lady Gwen. Sir Travis did not deserve to die."

Gwen kept her mind tightly shielded until she was out of the embassy and standing on the street. Irene Adler, the most capable Talker in the British Empire, had taught her how to shield her mind, but Gwen lacked the skill of an experienced Talker. How capable was Simone? It was quite possible that *Jack* had taught her how to use her powers...

And if she hadn't coughed, Gwen would never have noticed.

She walked over to the coachman and scribbled out a short note for Lord Mycroft. He would have to be informed, if only to ensure that Simone didn't have another chance to read information from an unwitting mind. Given her exotic looks, it was quite probable that she could pull information from besotted officers while they were trying to court her. Irene did precisely the same thing.

"Take this to Lord Mycroft," she said, once the note was finished. "Then you can take the rest of the day off."

The coachman blinked in surprise. "You won't want me later, Milady?"

"It's a good day," Gwen said. "I'll walk."

She contemplated the situation as she headed into the centre of London, barely distracted by a mob of children watching an airship as it made its way towards the Thames. Airship service over London had been badly disrupted by Jack hijacking one and using it to raid the Tower of London – making the magicians on guard look like fools in the process. Master Thomas had intended to use the debacle as an excuse to get rid of some dead wood before he'd died. Now, the airships were slowly returning to London town.

Glisters was a two-story building on the outskirts of Whitehall, managed – Gwen had heard – by an Italian family that had escaped the French invasion that had secured control of Italy. It was a very exclusive restaurant; anyone who wanted to eat there had to book in advance and the staff turned away anyone who hadn't reserved a table. Gwen suspected that the Royal Sorceress – and certain other very high-ranking people – could demand a table anyway, but it didn't matter. Sir Charles had already booked for them both.

"I took the liberty of ordering iced tea, rather than wine," he said, as she sat down facing him. The booth would provide a limited amount of privacy, as long as they kept their voices low although Gwen was sure that *someone* would recognise both of them. "I understand that magicians don't touch wine."

"We prefer to avoid it," Gwen said, touched. No one else had shown her that sort of consideration, even David. "Alcohol can cause magicians to do something stupid."

"Just like the rest of us," Sir Charles pointed out, as the waiter brought them two glasses of iced tea. "There's a buffet of cold meat, vegetables and bread, if you like that sort of thing, or there's venison stew... that, I am informed, tastes very good."

"It would," Gwen said. Most people in England could afford pork or chicken, but beef and venison tended to be reserved for the wealthy – venison in particular. Lady Mary had once served venison and then complained that she could have served four whole cows and it would have been cheaper. "The stew would be lovely, I think."

Sir Charles ordered, then turned to face her. "How was your meeting with the Frenchman?"

"Interesting," Gwen said, neutrally. "Have you ever met Ambassador Talleyrand?"

"I believe that I saw him once, across a crowded hall," Sir Charles said, mischievously. "He didn't pay any attention to me. And why should he? I was just a gentleman adventurer, hardly worthy of his attention."

He scowled, suddenly. "Do you think he could have killed Sir Travis?"

"I think he would have to be insane to try," Gwen admitted. France would just lose too much if Talleyrand were blamed for the murder – and the only constant in the Ambassador's career was that he worked for France, always. "Did you know that he'd approached Sir Travis?"

"I didn't," Sir Charles admitted. "But I hadn't seen Sir Travis before his death, so... I don't know if he'd spoken to Talleyrand. I can't see why, though."

"The Ambassador claimed that he hoped to enlist Sir Travis in opening up a secret channel to the British Government," Gwen said. "Does that sound plausible?"

"If they knew that Sir Travis had... contacts in the government, it might be reasonably plausible," Sir Charles said. "Otherwise... he was just another nobleman."

He thought about it as the waiter returned with two plates of stew. "If they found out, I'd bet good money that it was from someone in the Viceroy's Palace in India," he added. "Those idiots never know when to keep their mouths shut. Even the Viceroy had been known to drop a hint or two of secret dealings in the wrong ears from time to time. Did you ever hear of McMurdo?"

Gwen shook her head.

"Officially, he was an accountant," Sir Charles said. "Unofficially, he worked for the Viceroy. There was a Rajah who was having... dealings with the French and McMurdo was charged with discovering enough evidence to allow the Viceroy to act. But someone leaked and the Rajah realised what was happening. McMurdo was brutally murdered and his corpse... was desecrated. The Rajah tried to blame it on the Thugs, but everyone knew the truth."

He changed the subject, noticeably. "What are you doing after lunch?"

"I need to visit Mr. Howell," Gwen said. "And..."

Sir Charles stared at her. "I think I'd better come with you," he said, after a moment. "I can -"

Gwen scowled at him. "Just who *is* Howell that everyone is scared of him?"

Sir Charles hesitated. "I think you should make up your own mind," he said. "But you really shouldn't go alone."

"Then you can ride with me," Gwen said. She was *sick* of the mystery. After she got back to Cavendish Hall, she was going to force an explanation out of someone. "But you'll have to remain outside the house."

"Fine," Sir Charles said. "But shout if you need me, understand?"

Gwen allowed magic to flare over her hand, just for a second. "I'm the Royal Sorceress," she reminded him, as his face was illuminated in a brilliant glow. "What do I have to fear?"

Chapter Seventeen

he occupants of Hampstead had been lucky, Gwen decided, as the carriage rattled to a halt in front of Howell's house. They might have been forced to flee as the Swing ravaged Central London, but they'd escaped having their houses looted for the most part, although a handful of servants had taken the opportunity to rob their masters and vanish into the chaos. Howell's house was clearly one of the more expensive houses in the district, complete with its own garden and gatehouse. And, she couldn't help noticing, a handful of private guards.

"Wait here," she ordered, as she clambered out of the carriage. "I'll shout if I need you."

She marched over towards the gatehouse before Sir Charles could protest. It was nice to have someone caring for her, but it was also irritating; she'd taken care of herself in much worse circumstances. The guards looked up at her as she approached and frowned, clearly trying to place her. Gwen smiled at them as she reached into her purse and produced her calling card.

"Lady Gwendolyn Crichton to see Mr. Howell," she said, briskly. If she had been dealing with another magician, she could just walk into the building – with or without Howell's permission – but she had no automatic right to face a non-magician. "Please let him know that I'm here."

"Certainly, Milady," one of the guards said. "I shall enquire of the Master."

Gwen kept her face impassive as the guard left the guardpost and ran towards the house, leaving her waiting outside the gate. That was rude; protocol dictated that she should have been offered a seat in the guardhouse while waiting to see if Howell would agree to speak with her. Leaving her outside implied that she was unwelcome... which she might well be, she conceded. Very few people wanted to *meet* the Royal Sorceress.

The guard took nearly ten minutes to return to the guardpost. "The Master is ill, but will see you," he informed her, as he pulled open the gate. "If you would please accompany me..."

Gwen felt her senses twitch as she followed him up the lane and into the house. The farm had been plastered with psychic residue from the hundreds of women who had been confined there against their will, creating impressions that would last for a thousand years. Howell's house felt... spooky, almost as if she were stepping into another nightmare. And yet, unlike the farm, there was nothing sinister about the building. Indeed, if she hadn't been the Royal Sorceress, she would have thought that she was imagining it.

Whatever Howell did for a living, she decided as the butler took over her escort, it had to be very lucrative. His house was littered with paintings and expensive decorations, including several that would have been banned in polite company. He also seemed to have a small army of servants at his beck and call, some of whom eyed her curiously as the butler led her though the house. Gwen's mother could not have wished for a more aristocratic house.

And yet Howell was no aristocrat. Gwen was sure of that, if only because she couldn't imagine an aristocrat with a title refusing to use it. A businessman, perhaps? It was possible, except that a businessman who had seen such great success would almost certainly be offered a knighthood, if not a peerage. The Establishment believed in trying to co-opt talent where possible, even if society's matrons didn't really like the idea. They'd sooner marry their daughters to Frenchmen or even Russians before letting them marry a former commoner.

"The Master is in bed," the butler informed her, as they

stopped outside a heavy wooden door. "Please don't go near the bed, Milady. You could catch his illness."

Gwen nodded, impatiently, as he opened the door and showed her into a darkened room. The only light came from a gas lantern that had been turned down low, barely giving enough light for her to see the man lying in his bed. There was a faint smell of something unpleasant in the room, reminding her of the hospitals Lucy had been setting up for the poor. She hesitated and then cleared her throat. She couldn't help feeling guilty for disturbing a sick man.

"Lady Gwendolyn," Howell croaked. The sheets rustled as he turned to look at her. "I'm sorry not to be in a better state."

"I'm sorry to have to disturb you," Gwen said. She was slowly becoming used to the darkness. "I can arrange a Healer to attend you, if you would wish."

"It's just a cold," Howell said, after a moment. He sounded rather peevish at the whole suggestion, although Gwen couldn't understand why. "It will be gone in a few days."

Gwen peered at him. Howell didn't *look* very dangerous at all, certainly not dangerous enough to scare a man who had gone tiger-hunting in India. He looked rather like a middle-aged uncle, a man secure enough in his own position to offer friendship to his nephews and nieces without reservation. His face was pleasant enough... until she saw his eyes. There was something snake-like about them that sent chills running down her spine.

"I hope you will get better soon," she said, as she gathered herself. What could he do to disconcert her? "I need to talk to you about Sir Travis."

"I assumed as much," Howell said. "I read about his death in the paper. Terrible business, My Lady, simply terrible."

Gwen nodded in agreement. "I won't waste your time," she said, bluntly. "What was your business with Sir Travis?"

Howell studied her for a long moment, his icy regard making her shiver again. "It was my intention to offer him a loan," he said, finally. "We were discussing the precise terms of the loan, but failed to come to an agreement."

"A loan?" Gwen repeated. "Did he need money?"

"I assume so," Howell said, sardonically. "People do not generally try to borrow money unless they have some desperate need of it."

Gwen resisted the urge to scowl at him. His story was plausible; there were certainly no shortage of aristocrats who were rich in everything, but money. A title didn't automatically confer wealth on its holder. And Sir Travis had not been very wealthy. Most of what he'd owned belonged to the family, rather than to him personally. He could not have sold Mortimer House without his family's permission.

She looked up at Howell and saw his eyes resting on her face. "And you," she said, "were going to loan him the money? Is that what you do for a living?"

Howell smiled, but the smile didn't touch his eyes. "There are some... individuals who would prefer not to have to ask a bank for a loan," he said. "Those individuals place discretion ahead of anything else, even security. They eventually come to me."

Gwen had listened to her father's business dealings, back before Master Thomas had offered her the chance to join him. The banks were rarely completely discrete; the bankers shared information with one another, information that eventually leaked out onto the streets. If one aristocrat was heavily indebted to one bank, the other banks might well know it and refuse to loan him anything else. And yet there had been no clue that Sir Travis was indebted to anyone.

She put that thought to one side for a moment. "And you loan them the money?"

"Indeed I do," Howell said. "My repayment schedules are quite generous. And often they have more to trade than simply money."

"Sir Travis didn't have much income," Gwen mused. She might not have been expected to handle money – if she'd been a normal girl with a normal husband, the husband would have handed all of the money affairs – but she knew enough to know that Sir Travis might have been a bad investment risk. "Why did you want to loan him money?"

"He called me," Howell said. He gave her an odd smile. "It was up to *him* to convince *me* to loan him money."

Gwen gave him a sharp look. Olivia had told her more than she'd ever wanted to know about life in the Rookery – and how loan sharks could bleed a person dry, once they got their claws into someone's life. Their victims would take out a relatively small loan, but the interest would just keep mounting up until they were forced to take out a second loan just to cover the first one... for a person with limited income, it might be impossible ever to get out of debt. And then the loan sharks would move on to their children.

"Right," she said, sharply. "And did he say *why* he wanted the money?"

"Of course not," Howell said. "We merely discussed his ability to repay the loan, should it be made."

"I see," Gwen said. There was nothing *illegal* in offering to loan someone money, but the whole concept still bothered her. "What did he have to offer?"

Howell sighed. "Relatively little, I'm afraid," he said. "He claimed that he was going to marry the daughter of a High Court Judge – and take up a more prestigious position at the Foreign Office. But I am not so inclined to believe vague promises of future wealth, Lady Gwen. I asked him for an agreement that would give his house to me, if he failed to repay on schedule. He refused to provide such an agreement."

"He couldn't have, legally," Gwen said. "Mortimer Hall belongs to the family."

"But they might have been willing to settle," Howell said. "I *would* have had a claim on the estate..."

He shook his head slowly, deliberately. "We failed to come to a meeting of minds," he added. "I have no claim on his estate."

Gwen nodded. "When did you visit him?"

"The appointment was for ten o'clock," Howell told her. "I was early, of course. Punctuality is *so* important."

"Ten o'clock," Gwen repeated. That would suggest that

David had been the first visitor, followed by Howell... with Talleyrand the last person to see Sir Travis alive. "Did you happen to notice if anyone else visited that night?"

"I saw no one," Howell said. "Indeed, Sir Travis was opening the door himself. That is *not* a sign of wealth and power."

Gwen suspected that Lady Mary would have agreed. The unwritten laws of etiquette insisted that servants – a butler or a housemaid – should meet guests and help them to make themselves presentable before they saw the master or mistress of the house. It was rude to wear a coat when entering a house, but if the servants were the only ones to see it could be overlooked. Polite Society had plenty of rules that were ignored as long as no one actually had to take notice that they were being broken.

And he was right. Even the poorest upper-class families would have at least three or four servants. Sir Travis had had just one. And even then, Polly should have greeted everyone at the door. Sir Travis doing it himself wouldn't leave a good impression.

I wonder what sort of conclusions Talleyrand drew, she thought. *David would have known, of course...*

She studied Howell for a long moment. "Did you know anything else about Sir Travis's life?"

"Nothing," Howell said, blandly. "His family weren't speaking to him or his mother... although I dare say that they will already be demanding that Mortimer Hall is handed over to them. The closest branch of the family to Sir Travis is known for being grasping, I'm afraid."

Gwen scowled. There was probably a letter at Cavendish Hall waiting for her from the family, if they'd seen a copy of the will. And they might just be tempted to try to move into the building *before* Gwen had completed her investigation, even though it was still under police guard. If they were wealthy and powerful enough, they could ignore formality and present the world with a *fait accompli*.

She wasn't entirely sure that she believed Howell, but for the moment there were no grounds to ask further questions. "I should warn you that you are a suspect," she said, instead. "Please don't leave London without permission from the police. I may have to talk to you at a later date."

Howell's eyes glittered in the dim light. "I have told you all I know that is relevant to your investigation," he said, flatly. "Should you continue to harass me, I shall be forced to take steps."

Gwen met his eyes, resisting the temptation to take a step backwards. "It is a step in the investigation," she said. "I'm afraid that there are no legal grounds for objecting, unless you can present proof that you did *not* kill Sir Travis."

"I am not required to prove my innocence," Howell reminded her. His voice became mocking. "How can the Royal Sorceress be unaware of *that*?"

That was true, Gwen knew. The police were required to prove someone's guilt beyond reasonable doubt, not force someone to prove their own innocence. If Howell *hadn't* been the last person to see Sir Travis alive, there was good reason to believe that he *wasn't* the killer. She couldn't blame him for being indignant at the merest suggestion that he was a suspect...

And if I have a bad reaction to him, Sir Travis's reaction would be far worse, she added, in the privacy of her own mind. *He wouldn't step down his Sensitivity while talking to him at all.*

"However, you are a suspect," Gwen said, instead. "We can request that you stay in London until the investigation is concluded."

Howell's face seemed to twist, becoming *dangerous*. Gwen had known many dangerous men, including Master Thomas and Jack, both of whom could have taken Howell's house apart without breaking a sweat... and yet, it was impossible to escape the sense that she was looking at a very dangerous man indeed. Not a violent man, not a thug or a genteel magician... something far worse. She felt her skin crawling as she reached for her magic, preparing to shield herself. And yet there was no obvious threat...

"Maybe I will," Howell said. The sense of danger

refused to abate. "How is your mother, these days?"

Gwen blinked at the *non sequitur*. What did her mother have to do with any of this?

"You might wish to ask your mother about me," Howell said. He turned over, showing her the back of his head, then reached for the bell and gave it a ring. "Jarvis will show you out."

"What," Gwen demanded, "does my mother have to do with you?"

"Ask her," Howell said. She couldn't see his face, but she could hear the amusement in his voice. "I am sworn to silence."

Gwen opened her mouth to demand answers, then the door opened to reveal the butler. She shot an angry look at Howell's head, briefly considering trying to force answers out of him, before deciding that it would be futile. Even if she succeeded, it would give her enemies too much ammunition. There were strong laws on the books against mind-reading without a warrant, most of them too strong for their own good. Too many Talkers were in breach of them as soon as they came into their powers.

"Good day, sir," she said, icily.

Howell made no response.

She allowed the butler to lead her back down the corridor and out of the house, unable to escape the sense that she had just escaped with her life. It was illogical; there had been no danger, certainly nothing that she could see. And yet her senses had been warning her that she was in very great danger indeed. But of what?

Sir Travis would probably have *known* what the danger was... but Sir Travis was dead. His Sensitivity had failed him at the last.

The guards opened the gate for her, allowing her to step out onto the street. Gwen couldn't help noticing that the gate was stronger than she'd realised, carefully designed to make it hard for someone to break it down without explosives. An angry mob might not be able to push it down by naked force. If Howell had enemies – and loan sharks would have plenty of enemies – maybe it made sense, but... somehow, she was sure that he hadn't told her the complete story.

Sir Charles jumped out of the carriage and held out a hand to help her into it. Gwen ignored his hand and scrambled up herself, her mind too jumbled to care that she was being rude.

"I need to go to Crichton Hall," she said, once he'd joined her in the carriage. "Can you have the coachman take us there?"

"Of course," Sir Charles said. He opened the slot and issued orders to the coachman, then closed it with an audible *snap*. "Is there something the matter?"

"It's not something I can discuss," Gwen said, shortly. What *was* her mother doing mixed up in the whole affair? As far as Gwen knew, Lady Mary wouldn't have known Lady Mortimer – and the thought of her knowing Sir Travis personally was laughable. "I just need to go there."

Sir Charles settled into his seat as the carriage started to move. "It won't take long to reach your home," he said. "Do you want me to come inside with you?"

"No, thank you," Gwen said. It was going to be hard enough talking to her mother without a single man being with her. And then it struck her that she was being incredibly rude. "I... I can make my own way back to Cavendish Hall."

Sir Charles grinned, relishing her discomfort. "There's a formal ball this weekend for Ambassador Talleyrand," he said. "I would be delighted if you would accompany me."

Gwen hesitated. She had received an invitation, but she hadn't intended to go. And yet... the last ball she'd attended had been fun, at least until Jack had arrived to reintroduce himself to Polite Society.

"I'd be delighted," she said, although she had the vague sense that she'd been outmanoeuvred in some way. "But we'll have to talk about that later."

Chapter Eighteen

wen couldn't help a surge of mixed emotions as she stood in front of Crichton Hall, waiting for the butler to open the door. The Hall had been her home; she'd never been anywhere else, save for a couple of brief visits to the countryside. She had played with David in the garden – until he'd grown all stuffy – and practised with her magic in the trees. They'd even spent one summer building a treehouse, before Lady Mary had decided that it wasn't ladylike to climb trees and ordered Gwen not to do it any longer.

And yet the Hall had also been a prison. She had been confined within its walls, held by invisible chains of social propriety... and the shame her mother felt at giving birth to such a child. What would have been a source of great joy and pride if she'd been born male had damaged her mother's social standing when she'd had a daughter. That, at least, wasn't going to happen on Gwen's watch. She'd already started recruiting upper-class women who happened to have been born with magic.

The door opened, revealing a familiar face. "Mistress Gwen," the butler said, gravely. "Welcome home."

He'd been new when Gwen had left to go to Cavendish Hall, which was probably why he was still working for the family. Most servants had been too scared of Gwen to stay for long, even though the rumours were wildly exaggerated. She had *not* turned a pair of maids into her dolls. Even the most skilled of Changers would have been unable to do *that*.

"Thank you," Gwen said, as he took her hat and coat. "Is my mother home?"

"She is in the Flower Room," the butler said. "Should I bring tea and biscuits?"

"Please do," Gwen said, although she had no idea if her mother would be pleased. She'd spent too long avoiding her mother in the months since Master Thomas's death. "I can find my own way there."

Lady Mary had been redecorating since Gwen had left, she saw; over the years, Gwen had destroyed dozens of pieces of china with bursts of accidental magic. In hindsight, she wondered why Lady Mary hadn't killed her - or given her up for adoption. Her mother had been a stronger person than she'd realised, she saw now. Perhaps, now that they were both mature adults, they could get along better. But Lady Mary might always see her as the little girl who'd thrown tantrums and pushed her tutors away.

The Flower Room had once held David's toys, before he'd grown up and had most of them transferred to his new house. Now, Lady Mary – in line with the ineffable dictates of fashion – had turned it into a hothouse where she was trying to grow exotic plants imported from the Far East. Gwen smiled as she smelled the flowers, wondering why her mother didn't take such good care of the garden outside. But then, that would suggest that the family was too poor to hire a gardener.

"Gwendolyn," Lady Mary said, as she looked up from a potted flower. "How... *nice* to see you again."

"Thank you, mother," Gwen said. Her mother could always make her feel like an ungrateful child – and, in truth, she had a great deal to be grateful for. "It has been too long."

She sat down on a bench and studied her mother as she worked on the flower. Lady Mary's hair was slowly going grey, but apart from that she looked like an older version of Gwen herself. Gwen had wondered, more than once, about her own paternity; if Jack could have been adopted by a well-connected family, why couldn't someone else have adopted her, if she'd come out of the farms. It was sometimes hard to see anything of her father in her. But then, the farms wouldn't have sent an untested girl out for adoption. It was much more likely that Gwen was her parents' child.

But David doesn't have magic, she reminded herself. *If I do, why doesn't he?*

"I heard that you were spending time with Charles Bellingham," Lady Mary said, without looking up from the plant. "You are comporting yourself with all the dignity of your station, I trust?"

Gwen scowled, inwardly. It hadn't been more than a couple of hours since she'd had lunch with him. Word moved faster than horses and carriages in London... someone had probably spotted them in Glisters and sent a note to Lady Mary. The elder women always kept an eye on the younger girls.

"Yes, mother," she lied. Few girls of her station would share a carriage with an unrelated man, unless they had a chaperone. On the other hand, she suspected that she wouldn't have enjoyed herself so much if Lady Mary had been there. Some of Sir Charles's stories would not have amused her mother at all.

"There is some... question over his family," Lady Mary added. "But on the whole, you could do worse for marriage."

Gwen scowled, openly this time. *Trust* her mother to start wittering on about marriage, as if her life would only be validated when both of her children had left the nest and started building households of her own. *David* had a wife and a child on the way... she didn't need to worry about Gwen. And besides, surely being related to the Royal Sorceress was something she could brag about in Polite Society.

Or maybe not, she reminded herself. *Master Thomas had no close relatives when he died.*

"I have no intention of getting married yet, mother," she said, tightly. "I am young..."

"You are growing older," Lady Mary reminded her. "Most girls your age are not only married, but bringing up children. It is rare indeed for a young woman to marry a suitable young man after she passes twenty-five."

"There are no suitable young men," Gwen said, dryly. If

there had been another Master, she was sure that she would have been urged to marry him and see if two Masters could produce more Masters. Master Thomas had had children through the farms, but unless the suggestion that Jack had actually been his son was correct, none of them had been Masters. "And those you keep pushing at me don't want to marry the Royal Sorceress."

Lady Mary scowled at her, then walked over to sit down next to her. "Your father and I only want what is best for you," she said, as she gave Gwen a hug. "In many ways, you are lonely. You were *always* lonely."

Gwen had to admit that she was right. Being a so-called devil-child had left her almost friendless; very few girls of her generation had been willing to play with her, even before the rumours had grown far out of proportion. And, even as Master Thomas's apprentice, her femininity had isolated her. She could never be too friendly with the other magicians.

And now? The great and the good hung on her every word, or privately disdained her when they thought she wasn't looking, but none of them were her *friends*.

"You're perceptive," she said, numbly. "Why were you never this perceptive before?"

Lady Mary surprised her by laughing. "While I was a child, my mother was a thoughtless old biddy who tried to run my life," she said. "When I grew up, I realised that my mother had only wanted the best for me."

Gwen nodded, slowly. Her maternal grandmother had died when Gwen had been very young, before she had discovered her magic. It was difficult to imagine Lady Mary as a naughty young girl, but she must have been ... once upon a time.

She would have liked to have chatted to her mother for hours, just trying to enjoy her company, but duty called.

"This trip isn't for pleasure," she admitted. She felt a pang of guilt as she realised that she might not have visited her mother *unless* she hadn't had a choice. "I need to ask you about someone."

"Not Sir Charles, I presume," Lady Mary said. "But I will definitely look into his family tree."

Gwen gave her a cross look, which washed off her mother like water from a duck's back. Now, she could tell that her mother often concealed her intelligence behind a facade... although she wasn't sure how much of the facade truly was a facade. If all she'd wanted was some flowers to impress visitors, it would have been simpler to buy them – or hire a proper gardener to take care of the plants.

"Not Sir Charles," Gwen said. "Augustus Howell."

Her mother's arm shook. Gwen looked up and saw, to her alarm, that her mother had gone pale.

"*Mother?*"

Lady Mary stared at her. "*Where did you hear that name?*"

Gwen hesitated, then answered. "I have to find out who murdered Sir Travis and he's one of the suspects in the investigation," she said, honestly. She could trust her mother, she suspected, to keep *that* to herself. "He suggested that I should talk to you..."

Her mother clutched Gwen's arm. "What did he tell you?"

"Merely that I should talk to you," Gwen said, alarmed. Who was Howell that so many people had bad reactions to his name? Lestrade, Lord Mycroft, Sir Charles... and now Lady Mary? What did those people have in common? Maybe she should have asked David; stuffy or not, she could usually get answers out of her brother. "Mother..."

"Nothing else?" Her mother demanded, her grip tightening. "Nothing at all?"

"No," Gwen said, quickly. "Mother... who is he?"

"No one," Lady Mary insisted. "Just... just don't go near him, all right?"

Gwen stared at her. Lady Mary had been flustered before, particularly after she'd heard about some magic-related chaos the young Gwen had caused, but she'd never been on the verge of outright panic. Even when Master Thomas had come to invite Gwen to study under him, Lady Mary hadn't *panicked*. She'd just fainted with shock.

Briefly, she considered trying to Charm her mother. In hindsight, it was clear that she had used Charm on the servants, although she hadn't really known what she was doing. She'd resented her ignorance at the time, even though it might have worked in her favour. If she'd really known what she was doing, would it have twisted her as badly as it had twisted Lord Blackburn?

And she *couldn't* Charm her mother. That would be morally wrong.

"I need to know," she said, quietly. "Mother..."

"Don't talk about him," Lady Mary insisted. She let go of Gwen and stood upright, shaking so badly that Gwen was sure that she was going to fall over. "Just... leave him alone." Her voice hardened. "That's an order, Gwendolyn."

Gwen felt a flash of *déjà vu*. Her mother had been fond of that phase when Gwen had been a child, using it to remind her daughter that certain orders were not up for discussion, even though Gwen – and David – had spent considerable time and ingenuity looking for loopholes in her instructions. And yet... how *could* her mother issue orders concerning Gwen's post and expect them to be obeyed? Gwen was no longer hers to command.

"I need to know," she repeated. "Mother, this is *important!*"

"He won't have murdered Sir Travis," Lady Mary insisted. She turned and strode off towards the door. "Dinner is at five o'clock sharp, Gwendolyn. You *will* join us, won't you?"

The door banged closed before Gwen could formulate a response. What was Howell if the mere mention of his name pushed her mother into a state of near-panic? Somehow, Gwen doubted that a loan shark could cause so much shock. Her family might not be as wealthy as some families, but they were comfortably well off; her father's investments in airships were definitely bringing in the money. Given time, David would probably ensure that they were richer than anyone else.

Besides, Lady Mary didn't handle her own money, apart from her dowry. She was the youngest daughter of her family and hadn't inherited much when her father had passed away... Howell would surely have considered her a bad investment risk, far more so than Sir Travis. Unless... he'd expected Lady Mary's husband to pay? But a husband wasn't legally obliged to pay his wife's debts unless he'd backed them...

"Nothing about this makes sense," Gwen said, out loud.

She briefly considered asking her father, then dismissed the thought. If her mother was scared... how would her father react? Instead, she walked over to the door and stepped out into the corridor. Unsurprisingly, there was no sign of Lady Mary.

Gwen hesitated, wondering if she should just go – but her mother would be mortally offended if she didn't stay for dinner. And it had been months since she'd spent any time with her parents... shaking her head, she turned and made her way up the stairs to her room. Lady Mary, as was tradition, had left it strictly alone. Even the maids had refused to go inside and dust. But then, they'd been scared of Gwen...

It struck her, as she stepped inside, just how *small* the room seemed. Her bedroom at Cavendish Hall was much larger – and, she realised slowly, was designed for an adult. She looked around, remembering the dolls she'd played with as a young girl – and how she'd accidentally burned one to ashes when she'd been experimenting with her magic. The stuffed donkey she'd been given one birthday still sat on her bed. She couldn't help reaching for the toy and cuddling him to her chest. And to think that she'd almost forgotten him!

Most of the wardrobe had been cleared out – she'd had her dresses transferred to Cavendish Hall or simply given away when she'd become the Royal Sorceress – but the secret compartment at the bottom of the wardrobe was still untouched. She couldn't help smiling as she sensed the magic she'd used to hide it; a clumsy job, by her current standards, but very unusual for a child. Another magician would probably find it with ease; the maids, on the other hand, would have completely missed it.

Inside, the books were still there. One copy of *Edmund: A Butler's Tale*; a fast-flowing book, crammed with sizzling gypsies. She'd hidden it for David after Lady

Mary had caught him with its sequel, reading the book whenever she'd had a spare moment until she'd completed it. It had been a fun read, even though she'd had to look up some of the words in her dictionary. Lady Mary would have been horrified to know that Gwen had read it.

She put the book to one side and picked up the next one, a copy of a play her father had been asked to finance, years ago. *The Bloody Murder of the Foul Prince Romero and His Enormously Bosomed Wife*, the playwrights had called it, claiming that it was a philosophical work. Their covering letter had explained that the violence of the murder and the vastness of the bosom were justified artistically. Lord Rudolf had thrown the manuscript in the wastepaper bucket without bothering to read it; Gwen had filched it before the maids could throw it out. The dialogue, which seemed to be nothing more than a list of horrible things the actors intended to do to the Prince, had made her giggle.

Maybe I should see if they ever performed it, she thought, as she pulled out the next two books. One of them had been a gift from an uncle who didn't like Lady Mary and had no compunctions about saying so. Gwen had enjoyed reading the copy of *Letters From America; Being The True Story Of The Battle Of New York*, but it hadn't been very helpful in developing her magic. The writer had hedged so much in his work that it was difficult to draw the line between what was real and what had been added to confuse readers. After a moment, she put it on the bed, silently promising herself that she would reread it when she had a moment. The Luke and Saul mentioned in the book had to be Master Thomas's old friends. No one knew what had happened to them.

The other book was a guide to the natural world, a thinly-veiled tome about the human body. She'd badgered David for weeks before he'd agreed to buy it for her, back when her body had started to change. Not that it had been much help – the male writer spoke in riddles or outright concealed certain subjects – but it had been interesting. Gwen had decided that she wanted to become a doctor for a few days before going back to her magic after reading the book, if only because the writer had been stupid. His book was written for women – and it was clearly inaccurate in places.

Maybe I could find a Healer and patronise her so that she can write a book, she thought. But Healers didn't really know much about *what* they did. Their powers were largely governed by instinct. *Or maybe one of the Trouser Brigade would be happy to study medicine. I could certainly hire a private tutor if the universities wouldn't allow them to study there.*

There was a tap at the door. "Lady Gwen," an unfamiliar maid said, "Lady Mary would like to know if you would like to stay overnight."

Gwen looked at her old bed, then shook her head firmly. It just wouldn't have felt right. Besides, she had a feeling that dinner was going to be awkward...

"No, thank you," she said, feeling a pang of guilt – again – at the flash of fear in the maid's eyes. Had she really been such a monster as a little girl? "I will take a carriage back to Cavendish Hall."

Chapter Nineteen

s Gwen had expected, dinner was a fraught affair; her mother seemed oddly nervous, while her father was happy to chat about the latest developments in airship construction – but not about anything else. Certainly, he'd passed most of the family's involvement in political affairs over to David, yet he should still have maintained an interest. Maybe he just didn't want to talk about it in front of his wife.

Afterwards, she took a carriage back to Cavendish Hall and fell asleep, only to be woken early the following morning by Martha. Lord Mycroft had sent a request for an immediate report on her encounter with the French Talker, so urgently that Gwen realised that Simone had passed completely unnoticed until she'd come too close to Gwen. Maybe the Talkers who generated mental hisses to cover diplomats might have shielded them, preventing her from reading their minds... or perhaps not. Gwen called for coffee, wrote out a brief report and then went down to breakfast. There was little else she could do about the French girl.

There was a letter beside her plate on the High Table. Gwen scowled down at it, noted the masculine hand that had scratched out her name, and then opened it. There was a formal invitation to the Ambassador's Ball and two dance cards – one of which had already had all of the dances marked off. Gwen couldn't help a smile as she studied it, then put the cards and invitation into her purse. Traditionally, a man would only ask a woman to dance one dance – unless he was very serious...

What, Gwen asked herself, *if he is serious?*

She liked Sir Charles, but it had only been three days since they'd met. Certainly, she'd spent more time with him than the average girl her age would spend with a potential suitor – and without a chaperone at that – and he'd treated her more like an equal than any other man she'd met, apart from Jack. Even Master Thomas hadn't treated her as an equal... and she *hadn't* been his equal. She had been an ignorant young women when she'd been offered the chance to study under him.

In some ways, it would be a good match, she decided. Sir Charles was a hero in his own right, but not someone high-ranking enough for her marriage to cause political problems – or require the consent of the King. And, as he wasn't a magician, he wasn't under her command; she wouldn't have to worry about jealousy or accusations of favouritism. There was the question Lady Mary had raised about his family, but she could look into that...

And she was wasting time, she told herself angrily, as the servant put her plate in front of her. She should be concentrating on finding Sir Travis's killer and bringing him to justice, *then* she could worry about Sir Charles's intentions... and if he would make a suitable husband. Crossly, she ate her breakfast and then called for her carriage. Her note to Lady Elizabeth hadn't given a precise time, but Gwen had promised to be as early as possible.

She ran into Sir James as she left the dining hall. "Everything went well yesterday," he assured her, without the smirk that she knew Lord Brockton would have given her if he'd had to make that report. "There's a full outline on your desk."

"Thank you," Gwen said. "How did the training go?"

"We should have two new teams ready by the end of the month," Sir James assured her. "If the French try to cross the English Channel, they won't manage to land before being sunk."

"Let us hope so," Gwen said. The Royal Navy was the most powerful navy in the world – but the French Army was vastly stronger than the British Army, at least without considering magic. If the French managed to land on

British soil, the defenders might be in some trouble, even if firearms ownership had skyrocketed since the Swing. "The French have their own magicians now."

"I don't see how they figured it out," Sir James said, once she'd told him about Simone. "They should still be trying to brew potions and turn people into frogs."

"Professor Cavendish figured it out," Gwen said, hoping that it would misdirect him a little. The truth – that Jack had taught the French a great deal during his exile – was known to only a handful of people, just like the truth about the undead plague in London. If both secrets came out, the British public would have problems deciding which one of the guilty men to hate more. "And the French aren't *stupid*."

"They should have listened to the Pope," Sir James growled. Like most scions of older families – his ancestors had served Queen Elizabeth - he was a proud Protestant. "He wanted them to burn witches and crack the skulls of warlocks."

"There's too much advantage to be had from magic," Gwen reminded him. Master Thomas had been quick to abandon the prejudice against female magicians when it had suited his purposes. "And besides, these days the Pope does what King Louis tells him."

She nodded to him, then headed down towards the main entrance, where she ran into Norton. "There are some legal letters for you," he said, as he offered her a leather folder. "All from Sir Travis's family, I'm afraid. They need your personal attention."

Gwen scowled at him. "I thought I appointed you as my representative..."

"You did, but these letters are not entirely connected to my job," Norton explained. "You may have to reply personally."

"I'll read them as I drive to Bracknell Hall," Gwen said, taking the folder. "Let me know if there's anything else I can do."

She walked out of the entrance before he could reply and climbed into the waiting carriage. "Bracknell Hall," she ordered the driver, as she opened the folder. "And don't spare the horses."

The first letter was nothing more than a demand that she confirm – in writing – that Norton was actually her appointed representative. Gwen recognised it as a delaying tactic, although she had no idea why they were actually bothering. It wasn't as if Norton was enquiring into *their* financial affairs. She scribbled a quick reply, then an additional note to Norton asking him to look into why the family was trying to waste time. It hadn't taken her too long to realise that something that seemed pointless to her might not be so pointless to someone else.

"Idiots," she muttered, as she opened the next two letters. Both of them demanded that she move at once to distributing Sir Travis's property, particularly the house. The police were still investigating the building... but they seemed to expect them to leave at Gwen's command. "Don't they have any idea how long this could take?"

She wrote out a brief, but formal reply, informing them that she could not begin distributing the estate until there was a full accounting of both Sir Travis's property and the reason for his death. After a moment's thought, she added a note to the effect that Norton was her designated representative and all other communications were to go through him. Finally, she opened the fourth letter. Its tone was very different.

That I, a respectable married woman, should be expected to answer imprudent questions about the contents of my jewellery box is beyond the pale. To pry into matters long over is pointless, particularly when the jewels in question were promised to me by my Aunt. Should your representative continue his imprudence, you will be hearing from my lawyer.

She must have taken the jewels that were left to Polly, Gwen realised, after reading the letter a second time. Norton, true to his word, had made enquires when it had become clear that the jewels were nowhere to be found in Mortimer Hall. The threat of legal action would have stopped a normal investigator stone dead, particularly as the legitimate owner of the jewels was of no account. But Gwen was far from normal. She wrote out another note to

Norton, sealed the fourth letter inside, and put it back in the folder, just as the carriage rattled to a halt.

"Bracknell Hall, Milady," the coachman said.

"Thank you," Gwen said, as she dropped down to the pavement. "Please wait here for me."

Bracknell Hall was huge, large enough to hold several families comfortably. Gwen strode up the immense marble steps, knocked on the door and waited. It opened a moment later and a butler – an elderly gentlemen who seemed unwilling to do anything, but look dour – ushered her into the building. Gwen gave him her hat and coat, then allowed the butler to show her into the drawing room. Lady Elizabeth Bracknell entered the room two minutes later.

She looked to be a perfect aristocratic daughter, so perfect that Gwen would have hated Lady Elizabeth on sight if it hadn't been clear that she'd been crying. Lady Mary would probably have approved of the way the girl held herself, but Gwen could see tears in her eyes and half-hidden streaks running down her face. She was a beauty – long brown hair framed a heart-shaped face – even though she was wearing a plain dress that matched her hair. But if she was in mourning, shouldn't she have worn black?

No one knows about the marriage contract, Gwen reminded herself. *Too many people would have asked who she was mourning – and why.*

"Thank you for coming," Lady Elizabeth said. Even her voice – soft and warm – was perfect. "You really are the Royal Sorceress?"

Gwen looked at her, then held up her hand and summoned flames to dance over her palm, warming the air. Lady Elizabeth let out a strange sigh, staring at the flames almost as if she were mesmerised. Gwen clenched her fist, long enough to suppress the magic, then forced herself to relax.

"I killed him," Lady Elizabeth said. Her voice might have been perfectly composed, but it was easy to hear the grief – and guilt – behind it. "He died because of me."

Gwen stared at her. *She* had had some training in how to fight physically, rather than using magic, but she was the

Royal Sorceress. Very few girls were taught how to fight – even how to use the shotguns and hunting rifles used on every noble estate – in the confident expectation that their menfolk would protect them. And Lady Elizabeth didn't look strong enough to inflict the blow that had killed Sir Travis. How could she have inflicted such damage?

"You killed him?" She asked, reaching out with her senses. The girl certainly *seemed* sincere, but that didn't mean that she was telling the literal truth. "An experienced man like Sir Travis and you killed him?"

"I didn't kill him myself," Lady Elizabeth said. "I..."

There was a crash as the door burst open. "Elizabeth," a harsh voice demanded. "What are you telling our guest?"

"Mother," Lady Elizabeth stammered. "I..."

Gwen rose to her feet. Lady Bracknell looked formidable, certainly far more stubborn than Gwen's mother, but Gwen had faced worse. Besides, she *had* been invited. "I was called to speak with Lady Elizabeth..."

"You were not invited into our home," Lady Bracknell thundered. "You may dress up as a man, but that doesn't give you liberty to *act* like one."

She swung round and glared at her daughter before Gwen could reply. "And *you* should know better than to send out invitations without asking our permission!"

That was a contradiction, Gwen noted, but there was no point in telling her. Who would have thought – Gwen certainly hadn't – that there was a mother worse than Lady Mary in London? But Lady Mary hadn't really been that bad... she felt a moment of sympathy for Lady Elizabeth, who'd had a harpy dictating her every waking moment. It was a miracle she hadn't turned out any worse.

"That smelly little lesbian is not welcome in our house," Lady Bracknell continued, one hand raised to strike her daughter. "And..."

"Shut your mouth," Gwen ordered, drawing on all of her Charm. Lady Bracknell's mouth snapped shut with an audible crack. The Charm was far from subtle, but it would take a very strong mind to escape its grasp. "Go to your bedroom, sit down on the bed and stay there until your daughter comes to tell you that you can leave. And I suggest that you treat her better in future."

Lady Bracknell stared at Gwen with unconcealed hatred, mixed with shock, but she obeyed.

Gwen watched her go, then turned back to Lady Elizabeth. The young woman looked absolutely terrified and it was hard to blame her. Even if she hadn't been scared of the magic Gwen had demonstrated, her mother would not be happy when the Charm wore off. And it would, Gwen knew. Nothing lasted forever.

"Now," Gwen said, quietly. She kept the Charm out of her voice this time. Even if Lady Elizabeth didn't sense it, the Charm might not work right on someone who was clearly distraught. "Why don't you tell me what happened?"

Lady Elizabeth started to tear up again. Gwen sighed inwardly, removed a handkerchief from her purse and passed it to the girl, allowing her to dab at her eyes. Maybe using so much Charm so blatantly had been a mistake. But Lady Bracknell had deserved to be slapped down hard.

You could have held her upside down until she fainted, a quiet voice in the back of her head pointed out. *Or you could have put her to sleep, or...*

She angrily told the voice to go away as Lady Elizabeth finished wiping her eyes. "Mother and father don't let me go out very often," she said. "Mother was always talking about how I would have to find a good match and how they weren't going to let me join the season until they were good and ready. And then they introduced me to Sir Travis and I discovered that I *liked* him."

Gwen considered her words, thoughtfully. The choice of Sir Travis seemed odd, given the harridan the poor girl had for a mother. He wasn't a very high-ranked nobleman... but then, he worked directly for Lord Mycroft. Maybe Lord Mycroft or the Duke of India had put a good word in Lord Bracknell's ear for Sir Travis. It was certainly possible.

And besides, if Sir Travis were to be raised in the peerage, as was certainly possible if he brought the Airship Treaty to a successful conclusion, all objections would simply melt away.

"He treated me like a queen," Lady Elizabeth said. "I discovered that I *loved* dancing with him... we couldn't dance together too often, my parents said, but he was so much better than the others... and when my father told me that I was going to marry him, I was overjoyed."

Because it would take you away from your parents? Gwen thought. She couldn't think of a better reason for Lady Elizabeth to want to be away. Even if Sir Travis turned out to be a monster, he might not be as bad as her parents – and if they went to live somewhere overseas, she would be away from them for good.

"I wanted to tell the entire world," Lady Elizabeth continued. The bitterness in her voice was almost overpowering. "My parents wouldn't allow it – they said that no good came of announcing a wedding before it was about to take place. I had to wait, but I dreamed of him all the time..."

Gwen rolled her eyes, but said nothing.

"... And I promised myself that I would be the best wife he could hope for. And then the letter arrived."

"The letter," Gwen repeated. Had she found out something about Sir Travis that her parents had considered murder, rather than simply terminating the contract? "What letter?"

"I burned it," Lady Elizabeth admitted. "But it was already too late."

She reached out and clutched at Gwen's hand. "Can I trust you? *Really* trust you?"

"Yes," Gwen said, simply.

"You can't tell anyone, ever," Lady Elizabeth insisted. She sounded almost hysterical. "Ever! Not my mother, not my father... not whoever you report to... no one!"

Gwen almost pointed out that she'd just confessed to murder in front of the person investigating the case, but kept that to herself too.

"I won't," she promised, and hoped that it was a promise she could keep. "What did the letter say?"

Lady Elizabeth looked down at the carpeted floor. "I..."

She shook her head. "I shouldn't talk about it," she said.

"But I must. I fell in love, you see."

Gwen scowled as part of the puzzle clicked into place. It wasn't a very pretty picture.

"I was thirteen when Uncle Moresby came to stay," Lady Elizabeth said. "He was my father's second cousin – and his son Jonathon was fifteen. I fell in love with him and he with me – we exchanged letters for a few months, before they left London and went to the colonies. Those letters... they were passionate. I should never have written them."

Gwen leaned forward. "Did Jonathon come back into your life?"

"The letter I got included a copy of one of the letters I sent to Jonathon," Lady Elizabeth said. "And then that terrible man visited and said that if I didn't pay him the sum of seven hundred pounds – he called it a trifling sum – my marriage to Sir Travis would never take place. I knew that once Sir Travis read the letter, he would break the contract – and my parents would kill me. But I couldn't pay! I had no money!"

Her voice rose to a scream. "And then that man went to Sir Travis and... and he *died*! It was my fault! I killed the best man I'd ever known!"

Chapter Twenty

lackmail, Gwen thought.

Her mother had never mentioned the concept, but there had been a little about blackmail in *Edmund; A Butler's Tale*. It was simple – and evil. People had secrets, secrets they would pay to conceal... and if someone else happened to find those secrets, they could use them to force the victim to pay or see the secret revealed to the world. Blackmail. A very simple word for a very ugly concept.

Understanding clicked in her mind. *Howell*. A man who seemed harmless – and yet everyone seemed *terrified* of him. And he was a wealthy man who clearly had enemies, enemies who might ignore the law and strike directly at his home. If he was a blackmailer, it might explain everything... no *wonder* no one had wanted Gwen to get involved with him. But she'd been given no choice.

"Howell," she said, out loud. "He did this to you?"

Lady Elizabeth nodded. "I *couldn't* pay," she said. "He will have taken the letters to Sir Travis and... he killed himself."

Gwen frowned. She wasn't an expert in the many ways people could commit suicide, but there was nothing about Sir Travis's death that suggested that he'd killed himself. Even a Mover would have had problems hitting the back of his head with enough force to cave in his skull. Hanging or poison would have been much more likely for a suicide – or Sir Travis could simply have shot himself in the head. And he'd looked peaceful, rather than tormented, when he'd died.

"Tell me," she said, slowly. "What makes you think he

killed himself?"

"He *loved* me," Lady Elizabeth insisted. "And he would have seen me as a betrayer!"

That made no sense at all, Gwen knew, although Polite Society might have agreed with that viewpoint. A woman was not supposed to develop attachments to any man, at least before the wedding was arranged and formally announced. It might come back to haunt the happy couple – just as it had come back to haunt Sir Travis and Lady Elizabeth. But she hadn't even *known* Sir Travis when she'd written those letters.

"And Howell had the letters," she mused. "How did he even know they existed?"

"I don't know," Lady Elizabeth protested. "Jonathon wouldn't have given them to him – he just *wouldn't*. But I don't know how else he could have got them!"

Gwen scowled, inwardly. Polite Society often overlooked the small army of servants that everyone who could afford it employed, servants who were sometimes mistreated and started looking for ways to get back at their masters and mistresses. Perhaps one of Jonathon's servants had discovered the letters and stolen them to sell to Howell. Or maybe Jonathon had been desperate for cash and hadn't been as honourable as Lady Elizabeth assumed. A man could survive such a scandal far more than a young woman could.

"I shall enquire," she said. "Why do you think that Sir Travis killed himself?"

"Father said the newspapers never got anything right," Lady Elizabeth said. "And Howell told me that he was going to visit Sir Travis that night..."

"I don't think he killed himself," Gwen said, quietly. She reached out and squeezed Lady Elizabeth's hand. "Someone killed him."

Howell? It was possible; Sir Travis might have looked at the letters, then reached for a weapon and threatened Howell. Someone who'd spent so much time in India might not be so concerned about what Polite Society had to say about his wife – or more inclined to fight rather than surrender to blackmail. But Howell had said that he had visited Sir Travis before Talleyrand, which suggested that he *hadn't* killed Sir Travis – or that he had simply lied to Gwen. Could he have been *beaten*? Was that why he'd been in bed?

In that case, Gwen mused, *the whole story about offering him a loan is nonsense.*

Or was it *entirely* nonsense? Lady Elizabeth couldn't have hoped to pay Howell – but could Howell have loaned Sir Travis the money to pay himself? It sounded too complicated for words... and yet it did make a certain kind of sense. If Howell found something that he could use to influence Sir Travis, particularly after he started to work in a more public role, it might be worth whatever he paid him. And Sir Travis might not even *know* where the money was actually going.

She shook her head. It sounded like too much of a gamble.

"But those letters are still out there," Lady Elizabeth said. "What happens if he sends them to my mother?"

Judging from Lady Bracknell's words, Gwen had a feeling that she would *not* be kind to her daughter if she saw the letters. She might simply disown her daughter – or she might seek to arrange a marriage at once to someone who wouldn't care if her daughter had been *tainted* by scandal. And Lady Elizabeth would find it hard to refuse...

Would Howell release the letters? Gwen considered it, trying to think like a blackmailer. Very few people knew that Lady Elizabeth had been engaged at all, so he might well consider simply keeping the letters and waiting to see who she became engaged to next. But if she couldn't pay – and it was clear that she had little money of her own – it might be pointless to wait. Why *not* send the letters to Lady Bracknell – or her enemies in society?

"It might not be good," she said, with studied understatement. "What did you want to do with your life?"

"I was going to be a helpmeet," Lady Elizabeth said, bitterly. "I know French, Spanish, Russian, Turkish and Hindi – I could have gone with Sir Travis and helped him in his work. Or I could have handled other matters for him, if he'd had to go on business..."

Her voice trailed away. "But instead I killed him," she added. "I caused him to die."

"I don't think so," Gwen assured her. She made a mental note to ask Lestrade to search Mortimer Hall for the compromising letters. They hadn't been discovered in the safe she'd cracked open. "Like I said, someone killed him. And there is no reason to believe that it was something to do with your letters."

Lady Elizabeth looked up at her through tear-filled eyes. "You really think so?"

"Yes," Gwen said, firmly. It would have been nice to have the case solved there and then, but Lady Elizabeth wasn't the murderer – and she was sure that Sir Travis hadn't committed suicide. "You are not to blame.

"But I need to know," she added. "Did you have any other suitors?"

"Mother kept them away from me," Lady Elizabeth said. "She even supervised my dance card. No one could add their name twice..."

Gwen winced in sympathy. She hadn't attended many balls with her mother, but even Lady Mary had refrained from being *that* controlling. But then, Gwen's mother had had an unfair advantage. Very few young men had wanted to dance with the girl they'd been told was a devil-child. If Lady Elizabeth had been under *that* sort of control, it was a surprise that she'd even managed to write *one* letter to Jonathon. Maybe Lady Bracknell just hadn't considered him a serious candidate for her daughter's affections.

It was possible, she supposed, that Lady Elizabeth had an admirer that she didn't know about, someone who had fallen in love with her after just one dance. Such things did happen and they were considered major scandals when they finally came to light, if only because the girl would be blamed for leading the poor man on. But anyone who had been seriously interested in her would have tried to court her more openly... unless Lady Bracknell had refused to let it go any further.

"Charming," Gwen muttered. She would have to ask

Lady Bracknell who else had tried to ask for permission to court Lady Elizabeth. "What do you want to do now?"

"Mother will probably send me to a convent," Lady Elizabeth said. "Or try to find another man."

The latter was more likely, Gwen decided. After all, no one knew about the engagement – or about the compromising letters. And Lady Elizabeth would be a good catch for anyone, as long as her reputation remained unblemished.

"And she's not going to be happy about what you did to her," Lady Elizabeth added. "Can't you make her forget?"

"I don't think so," Gwen said, ruefully. A skilled Charmer could make someone forget something, but it never seemed to go away permanently. It was merely buried at the back of someone's mind, awaiting something that would release the memory. "It wouldn't stay forgotten."

Society's rules said that she should leave Lady Elizabeth to her fate, no matter how little she deserved punishment. And Lady Bracknell *would* punish her daughter for compromising herself so badly – of that, Gwen had no doubt. If she'd had even a hint that the letters existed, she would have married Lady Elizabeth off as quickly as possible.

Gwen shook her head. No one should have to be treated like that.

"I have an idea," she said. "Would you like to come work at Cavendish Hall?"

Lady Elizabeth stared at her in absolute disbelief. "Are you serious?"

"Yes," Gwen said. "You're an educated girl – and I need a secretary who happens to be female. And you have a high position in society, so my detractors can't complain that someone from the lower orders is looking at their letters."

"Oh," Lady Elizabeth said. She smiled, wanly. "Too few men willing to open your letters?"

Gwen nodded. She received hundreds of letters every day – and Doctor Norwell had proved himself reluctant to open them when she wasn't at Cavendish Hall. Lord

Mycroft's clerks didn't have that reluctance, but she couldn't keep them indefinitely. Lady Elizabeth would make a good secretary – and she could say that she was keeping the girl somewhere where she could see her, if anyone asked. On the other hand...

"Howell might see your new position as a chance to force you to spy for him," she added, slowly. "You would have to refuse if he contacted you."

Lady Elizabeth paled. "I'm never going to get away from it, am I?"

"It could be worse," Gwen told her, sharply. "You could have people whispering that your mother lay with a devil before you were born."

"But if the letters did come out," Lady Elizabeth said, "you would have to sack me..."

"Why?" Gwen asked. "I don't care about your reputation in society – and neither should you."

She shook her head. "As long as you don't actually betray *me*, you will always have a place at Cavendish Hall," she said. "And if Howell contacts you, you can tell me and we can work something out."

No one would have dared blackmail one of Master Thomas's people, not when he took a paternal interest in his subordinates. But Gwen's reputation was nowhere near as fearsome...

Yet, she told herself. Something would definitely have to be done about Howell.

"If you want to come with me, pack a bag of clothes and we can go now," she said, firmly. "Or you can come later..."

Lady Elizabeth stood up. "I'll come now," she said. "Just let me get cleaned up before I pack."

Gwen watched her go, then closed her eyes and concentrated on a mental impression of Gareth St. Peter, one of Cavendish Hall's Talkers. *Gareth*!

Lady Gwen, his mental voice echoed back, two seconds later. As always, it felt difficult to push her thoughts so far. And to think that a Talker could send a mental message right around the world! *What can I do for you*?

Gwen concentrated. The problem with mental

communication was that it was hard *not* to send plenty of unwanted impressions along with the message. Talkers tended to be more than a little neurotic, simply because they had few secrets from their brethren. And very few people had secrets from them.

Lady Elizabeth is going to be staying at Cavendish Hall for the foreseeable future, Gwen sent. *Have one of the smaller suites prepared for her, then have one of the sealed offices next to mine opened up and cleaned out.*

Understood, he sent back. *I shall pass on the message. Inspector Lestrade left another message for you, Milady. He needs to see you at Mortimer Hall.*

Gwen blinked. *Did he say why?*

No, Milady, Gareth said. *He just said that it was important.*

I'll go there directly, Gwen said. *Tell Martha to help Lady Elizabeth settle in.*

She broke the mental connection and staggered, feeling sweat forming on her forehead. Laymen claimed that mental communication should be effortless, proving – once again – just how little laymen actually knew. Even experienced Talkers had problems maintaining a link without eventually collapsing – or risking madness. Master Thomas had warned Gwen to use mental communication as little as possible... although she'd had the impression that it was to prevent her from giving away too many secrets while she was using the talent. It was so hard to control one's thoughts.

It wasn't far from Bracknell Hall to Mortimer Hall, she reminded herself. She could put Lady Elizabeth in the carriage and have the coachman take her to Cavendish Hall, while Gwen herself walked or flew to Mortimer Hall. Or she could just have the carriage take her there first and pick up another cab to take her back home afterwards. Shaking her head, she stood up and called for a servant. The maid who answered didn't seem to find it odd when she asked to be pointed to Lady Bracknell's room.

Lady Bracknell was sitting on the bed, a thoroughly murderous expression on her face that became fear when she saw Gwen. Clearly, her mind wasn't formidable enough to break the Charm outright, although that wouldn't last. Charm, particularly blatant Charm, rarely did, unless it was renewed time and time again. Gwen couldn't help being torn between two different emotions; pleasure that Lady Bracknell had finally run into someone stronger than she was and guilt for acting too much like Lord Blackburn. He'd believed that magicians were naturally superior to non-magicians and Charmers were superior to ever other kind of magician.

"Your daughter is going to be taking up employment at Cavendish Hall," Gwen said, without preamble. "It is a very important job that only an educated woman of high birth can do, so I trust that you will raise no objections. Should someone ask, you can tell them that you are honoured that your daughter is serving her country."

Lady Bracknell's face seemed to darken with unspeakable rage. She would probably be horrified at the thought of her daughter being outside her control – and only realise that most of the magicians in Cavendish Hall were either male or from lower class backgrounds later. Gwen made a mental note to ensure that *someone* was serving as a chaperone before Lady Bracknell even realised that was going to be a problem. *Gwen* might not have any suitors, but the same couldn't be said for Lady Elizabeth.

"She will be in a much stronger position for making a good match," Gwen assured Lady Bracknell, "*if* she chooses to marry. There are quite a few magicians who rank higher than your family, socially, and they would have a chance to meet her..."

She had to smile at the woman's expression. They weren't *that* high up the social tree – but that would change, if they found a really good match for their daughter. Which raised the question of just why they'd agreed to allow her to marry Sir Travis... had someone told them that he was going to be further ennobled? Or was there something going on that she wasn't seeing? She made a mental note to enquire of David – or Lord Mycroft – and then concentrated on Lady Bracknell.

"I don't blame you for being upset at how her

engagement ended, but you should understand that it wasn't her fault," she added. "If you give her a hard time, she might simply decide not to come back to your home. I suggest that you give her some time to recover – and that you take the time to meditate on what is actually important."

Hypocrite, a voice in her head pointed out. Had she treated her own mother any better? And Lady Mary hadn't been anything *like* as bad as Lady Bracknell. How could she blame Lady Elizabeth if she lived on her salary from the Royal College and never went back to Bracknell Hall?

"Now" – she allowed Charm to slip into her voice – "you can wait here until after we're gone, then you can leave the room and do whatever you see fit."

She stood up, took one look around the ornate bedroom – with only a small bed, suggesting that Lord and Lady Bracknell never slept together – and then strode out of the room without looking back. Lady Elizabeth had packed with commendable speed and was waiting in the lobby, a servant carrying a massive trunk standing next to her. Gwen made a show of picking it up with one hand – actually, she used her magic to hold it in the air – and carrying it out towards the carriage. It was easy enough to secure it to the roof.

"I've made arrangements for you to be met when you reach Cavendish Hall," she said, as she followed Lady Elizabeth into the carriage. "And I'll be back as soon as I can."

Lady Elizabeth blinked at her, nervously. "Where are you going?"

"I just need to visit Mortimer Hall," Gwen told her. She couldn't blame Lady Elizabeth for being nervous. Gwen had been nervous when she'd gone to study under Master Thomas... and she'd always wanted to use her magic. "Don't worry. I'll find my own way back home."

Chapter Twenty-One

ost of the reporters seemed to have decided that Mortimer Hall wasn't going to give them anything more newsworthy and left, leaving only a handful of junior reporters to watch the gates. Gwen rolled her eyes as she jumped down from the carriage, said goodbye to Lady Elizabeth and walked up towards the policeman on duty outside the gates. He looked surprisingly pleased to see her.

"Too many relatives have come to try to see the house," he explained, as he opened the gates. "Several of them even wanted to argue with the Inspector when I refused to let them in."

Gwen had to smile as she walked up to Mortimer Hall. It might have been falling apart, but it was still in a very wealthy part of London. Whoever owned it could use it to boost their status – if, of course, they had the money to renovate it. They might discover, eventually, that they had inherited a white elephant. Gwen knew enough about household management, thanks to Lady Mary, to know that parts of the house would simply rot away without constant maintenance. A single servant could not have hoped to keep pace with everything that had to be done.

"Lady Gwendolyn," the Sergeant on duty at the door said. "The Inspector is in the reading room, studying the late owner's papers."

"Thank you," Gwen said, keeping her amusement hidden. She knew that Lestrade *hated* paperwork – and if the case wasn't so political, he would have passed it down to someone lower in the department. But then, she felt the same way too. "I'll see him in there."

The reading room was a small library in its own right, Gwen realised as she stepped through the door. Each of the walls were lined with bookshelves, mostly copies of history's finest works of literature. The complete works of Cicero, Cato, Caesar and hundreds of other famous Romans dominated one wall, while another held more recent books from England, France and Russia. One section held a number of books written in Arabic; Sir Travis must have brought them back from Turkey. And there were even a couple of books on magic, one written by Benjamin Franklin in his final years. Franklin's contribution would never be officially recognised, but he'd added greatly to humanity's understanding of some of the talents.

Lestrade was seated at a desk, a cup of tea beside him, reading through a stack of papers. He looked pleased to see Gwen too, if only because he had an excuse to put the papers to one side. Gwen couldn't help wondering if Mycroft had sent some of his clerks to recover anything classified before Lestrade started his investigation, before deciding that it probably didn't matter. Lestrade might have had only a very limited imagination, but he was one of the most trustworthy men in Scotland Yard.

"Thank you for coming," he said, as he turned the chair around to face her. "There was a curious development earlier this morning."

Gwen sat down on a rickety sofa and smiled at him. "What happened?"

Lestrade rang the bell for Polly. "Polly can probably explain it better than I can," he said. "She was the one who took the message."

Gwen looked up as Polly entered the room. "More tea, Inspector?" She asked. "Or for Lady Gwen?"

"Not right away," Lestrade said. "Can you tell Lady Gwen what happened this morning?"

Polly bobbled a short curtsey to Gwen. "I was responsible for settling bills with the tradesmen," she said. "Even... even after the Master died, I was still responsible for it."

That was... *odd*, Gwen knew, but it did make sense. Sir

Travis hadn't had the wealth to set up permanent accounts with the businesses that handled food deliveries into the capital, so he would have had to pay tradesmen every week. Giving the money to Polly and allowing her to handle it might have seemed better to him than doing it himself. After all, what sort of nobleman allowed himself to be seen shaking hands with a businessman?

My father, she thought, ruefully. Lord Rudolf had rebuilt the family fortune through business – which might have reflected badly on him in society, if his daughter hadn't been a devil-child.

"They'd heard about his death and come seeking payment before all of the money was locked away," Polly continued. "I had to pay everyone... until the Turk arrived. He demanded four *thousand* pounds – again."

Gwen stared at her. Four thousand pounds was a minor fortune. A person with even a thousand pounds in the bank would be considered wealthy. He might not be able to afford a home in Central London, or even rent a flat in Pall Mall, but he could live comfortably for a very long time.

"Again?" she asked.

"He'd come a few times, always when the Master was out," Polly said. "He just dismissed the debt when I passed on the message. But now...

"I couldn't pay," she admitted. "The Mistress never gave me more than a hundred pounds every month to buy food. So I had to explain that he would have to ask you – and then he insisted on leaving a letter, explaining what Sir Travis owed."

"Here," Lestrade said. He passed Gwen an opened envelope. "You'll need to read it carefully."

Gwen took the paper out of the envelope and unfolded it. It was printed on cheap paper, topped with a faint series of Arabic letters. The rest of the paper, however, was in English – and devastatingly clear. Sir Travis had gambled at the Golden Turk, lost heavily – and owed the manager four thousand pounds. The note ended with a warning that if the funds were not provided within the week, the manager would begin legal proceedings against Sir

Travis's estate.

"He was a Sensitive," Gwen said, out loud. "How did he manage to *lose*?"

But Sir Charles had said that Sir Travis was a man of honour. If he'd been able to control his talent to the point where he could dampen it down, or even suppress it completely, he would have been playing on an equal level to the other gamblers. And without that talent, he might have managed to lose – and lose badly. Four thousand pounds wasn't bad – it was *disastrous*.

Lady Mary had told David, after her brother's first fling with the tables, that gambling was dangerously addictive. She hadn't known that Gwen was listening as she'd outlined horror stories of young men who got themselves so deep into debt that their families had to pay vast sums of money just to keep them out of debtor's prison – or make the best marital arrangements they could, just to raise funds. One family had even had to sell its ancestral home. The message must have sunk in; David had rarely gambled since then, at least as far as Gwen knew.

"That seems to be a major chunk of Sir Travis's estate," Lestrade said. "At least, the parts of it that actually belonged to him outright. A lawsuit, however, might have to be settled before it went to court, or the hall itself might be at risk."

Gwen nodded. A court wouldn't care about the family's heritage; if the debt was upheld, it would have to be paid in full. Sir Travis's family would be better advised to find the money now, rather than risk losing the hall in court. What had Sir Travis been *thinking*? He'd been about to get married!

"I'll look into it," she said, reluctantly. "He *really* must have been keeping his magic under control."

"More than that," Lestrade said. "How much do you know about gambling halls?"

"Nothing," Gwen admitted. She'd never been in one; young ladies didn't, although she knew that some gambled at home with their friends. "Why..."

Lestrade gave her an odd smirk. "The average gambling hall doesn't often allow such debts to be run up," he explained. "When it does, they're sure that the gambler can back his debts or that he has a backer, someone who will pay if he cannot."

Gwen nodded. Her father had once backed a bill for a friend – and grumbled for weeks after the bank served him with a writ for fifty-seven pounds.

"But four thousand pounds would be beyond most backers," Lestrade added. "Even the most devoted friend of a gambler would have objected to guaranteeing that much. I'd be surprised if anyone backed more than a couple of *hundred* pounds."

"That makes sense," Gwen mused. The next question was obvious. "Who backed the debt?"

"It doesn't say," Lestrade said. "Between you and me, Lady Gwen, the Golden Turk has a comfortable relationship with law enforcement. We cannot just demand answers from them..."

"But I can," Gwen interrupted. "I am the executor of the will, am I not?"

"In that case, there are more letters for you," Lestrade told her. "I was going to forward them to Mr. Norton."

"Please do," Gwen said. Sir Charles had mentioned the Golden Turk too – and she would have to go there. Maybe she could ask him to escort her and question him on the way. "Legally, this debt would have to be settled before the estate was parcelled out?"

"Probably," Lestrade said. "Unless someone else paid the debt, cancelling it."

Gwen nodded. *That* seemed unlikely.

"I'll follow up on it," she assured him. She nodded for Polly to leave the room, then continued. "But there's been another matter."

She explained, briefly, about Lady Elizabeth – and Howell. "Why," she finished, "don't the police arrest him?"

Lestrade sighed. "We've had our eye on him for a long time," he admitted. "But he's a cunning one, with too many friends in high places. Even if someone swore out a complaint, it would be hard to prove anything – and without proof we couldn't search his house. Maybe we could get him a few months in jail, if someone stood up in court and provided evidence, but the witness would be ruined immediately afterwards."

Gwen gritted her teeth. She'd once had to give evidence in front of a jury, a month after she'd been confirmed as Royal Sorceress, and it hadn't been a pleasant experience. The defending attorney had torn into her, questioning everything from her competence to her impartiality. It was his job... but Gwen had found it hard to remember that afterwards.

And she'd just been a witness. If someone had stood up and explained that she'd been blackmailed, the entire secret would have to be discussed in open court. It would have been around London before the session had finished and all over the Empire within a week. And even if Howell spent some time in jail, what would it matter to his victim? Her life would have been ruined beyond repair.

"His reputation is terrifying," Lestrade added. "Oh, he's an honest man in his way; if someone pays, he stays bought. I've known some blackmailers to demand constant payments or else – but Howell just looks for one payment and never asks again."

That was cunning, Gwen had to admit. If Howell had kept demanding money, his victim might have snapped and fought back. A single payment would be far less dangerous – and his victim might even have seen it as a bargain. But what was to stop the victim demanding the return of all of the compromising letters?

"He'll keep something to ensure his own safety," Lestrade said, when she asked. "But he won't go after someone twice..."

Gwen had never fainted, not in her entire life. Women might have a reputation for fainting when shocked, something that she suspected men believed because they thought it proved that they were superior to women, but she had never fainted. Yet she came as close to it as she ever had as the awful realisation finally crystallised in her mind. Why would Lady Mary have even *heard* of Howell, let alone have been so scared of him... unless she'd been one of his victims! Her own *mother* had been blackmailed.

"Lady Gwen?" Lestrade said, alarmed. "Are you all right?"

Gwen opened her eyes, silently relieved that she had been sitting down. If she'd been standing, her legs would have buckled and she would have collapsed. And if she'd fainted in front of Lestrade... he might have seen it as proof that she was nothing more than a weak and feeble woman. Angrily, she took control of her emotions and thrust them to the back of her mind. There would be time to think about what Howell had done to Lady Mary later.

"I'm fine," she growled. "Did you find any trace of Lady Elizabeth's letters in his study?"

"None," Lestrade said. "We've been through everything in his drawers, the safe you opened and a neat little hidden compartment underneath a chair. There were some financial notes, a set of observations on various Indians and Turks he'd had to deal with... but nothing that might have been compromising letters. The only thing we found that was anyway dubious was a set of French playing cards."

Gwen sighed, inwardly. One of the students at Cavendish Hall had ended up in hot water after his tutor had discovered a set of French playing cards in his room. They were considered indecent, not entirely without reason, but that didn't stop them being passed from hand to hand by young men. The pack the young man had owned had been incinerated by a Blazer... and he'd probably found a new one before the ashes had even cooled.

"No letters," she mused. "Do you think he burned them?"

"It's possible," Lestrade said. "But we did check the fire to see what might have been burned and there were no traces of paper ash."

Gwen considered it, carefully. If Howell had taken the letters to Sir Travis, would Sir Travis have allowed him to take them *away*? Perhaps, perhaps not... and Howell hadn't seemed like a physically strong man, even when he wasn't ill. Could he have intimidated someone who had ridden all over India, getting into scrapes and then getting out of them? Somehow, Gwen doubted that Sir Travis would have allowed Howell to scare him. He couldn't be as bad as a mad mullah from the North-West Frontier.

But Howell had definitely walked away alive...

"Nothing about this makes sense," she muttered. Howell hadn't destroyed Lady Elizabeth's reputation the following morning – and he could have done so, *before* he realised that Sir Travis was dead. That suggested that he'd had some reason to stay his hand, but what? Had Sir Travis promised him the money to buy his silence?

She called for Polly, who had been standing on the other side of the door. "Polly," she said, slowly, "how often did Mr. Howell visit Sir Travis?"

"He came the morning before he died," Polly said. "The Master was out, so he left a note promising that he would call in the evening. And then he left."

Gwen shook her head, tiredly. "Was that the first time he came?"

"I think so," Polly said. "Sir Travis might have met him outside the house."

Maybe, Gwen thought. Had Sir Travis been gambling to raise money to pay off Howell? It was possible, but if he desperately *needed* the money – and he did – why hadn't he used his powers? Was there someone at the Golden Turk who would have sensed his magic, if he'd tried to use it? That was unlikely; unlike Talking, Sensitivity was a passive power. It was hard to notice unless one was a Talker.

And the timing seemed odd too. Lady Elizabeth hadn't been allowed to talk privately with her fiancé – and Lady Bracknell had known nothing about the blackmail. Gwen was sure of *that*. She would have paid if she'd known, before sending Lady Elizabeth to a convent or marrying her off to someone who wouldn't ask too many questions. How could Sir Travis have known that she needed money, or started running up such a high debt in the handful of days he would have had before Howell came to see him?

And just who had killed him?

"I'm going to have to go to the Golden Turk," she said,

shortly. She needed to think carefully. Maybe if she slept on it the whole case would make more sense. "Did you locate any of the jewels?"

"It seems that Lady Mortimer's jewels were taken by her cousin," Lestrade said. If the change in subject threw him, he didn't show it. "They ignored what it said in the will."

Gwen nodded, sourly. She would have a few sharp words with whoever had served as Lady Mortimer's executor. The terms of a will could not be set aside at the behest of a relative, certainly not unless they proved that Lady Mortimer had been mentally unsound before she died. And there had been nothing to suggest that was the case.

She stood up. "I'm going back to Cavendish Hall," she said. "Please let me know if anything changes."

"You've got his journal and a few other papers," Lestrade reminded her. "The rest of his documents seem fairly straightforward, so I'll forward them to you along with a report when I've finished. However, I haven't located anything that relate to gambling debts – or Howell."

"They don't get written down very often," Gwen said. Lady Mary had told her that much, back when she'd been trying to hammer housekeeping into Gwen's head. Some financial matters were never written down, or simply left with a coded title so that anyone else wouldn't recognise them for what they were. "I'll go through the journal and then tell you if I come across anything that might be important."

She stood up and allowed Polly to escort her back to the entrance. There were several police carriages out there and she could have used one, but instead she chose to walk back to Cavendish Hall. She needed time to think.

Chapter Twenty-Two

octor Norwell had once told her that if she was perplexed, it was better to think about something else for a while and then return to the original subject with a fresh mind. Gwen tried to think about personal assignments instead of the murder investigation, but her mind refused to cooperate; she couldn't help wondering just what Howell had on her mother that had terrified her so much. What had she *done*?

Lady Mary's greatest shame was no secret, Gwen knew; everyone in Polite Society knew about her daughter, the devil-child. Howell could hardly blackmail her with something that was already public knowledge; she would have laughed in his face. But what else could there be? It was impossible to imagine her staid mother doing anything like Lady Elizabeth...

Or could it have something to do with me? She thought. *What if I did come from the farms*?

Jack had been shocked by the realisation that his family wasn't his real family – and he'd eventually turned against the Establishment, leading a revolution that had almost brought the British Empire to its knees. If Master Thomas had arranged for her to go to an aristocratic family, he would have made sure that Gwen never found out the truth. But how would he have known that she had magic before she used it when she was six years old? It was very rare to sense magic in a child...

But he had too many secrets, she reminded herself. *What if he had one for locating magicians from birth*?

She could ask her mother... but Lady Mary would refuse

to discuss it, just as she refused to discuss anything that was even slightly improper. And Howell... could it be that he'd *already* started to pressure Lady Mary into trying to convince Gwen to leave him alone? No, that couldn't be possible; the timing simply didn't work.

But who could have killed Sir Travis?

She was sure that David hadn't killed him; he had nothing to gain and a great deal to lose. Ambassador Talleyrand had nothing to gain either... and even though *he* might escape punishment, murdering Sir Travis would almost certainly start a war. And Howell... he didn't seem to be the murderous type. He preferred to assassinate someone's character from a safe distance. If he'd fought with Sir Travis...

And yet he'd been alive afterwards, with no signs of a real struggle.

Polly was locked up until morning, Gwen thought. *She couldn't have killed him; it was clear that the body had been dead for hours before it was recovered. And besides, I Charmed her; she couldn't have lied to me. She didn't kill him.*

She shook her head, wearily. Maybe Lord Bracknell *had* hired a killer... but the Bracknell family didn't benefit either. They were wealthy enough not to need anything from Sir Travis ... could it be that they didn't *want* her married off? But if that was the case, why would they agree to the contract at all? They could just have refused to grant permission for Lady Elizabeth to marry him.

The happy couple might have already planned to elope to Scotland and marry there. But why would they bother? They already had a signed agreement that they would marry. The only motive for a quick marriage that made sense was pregnancy – it was known to happen, even in Polite Society - but Lady Elizabeth hadn't been allowed enough latitude to *get* pregnant.

And if she were pregnant, that would be a cause for an immediate marriage, not murder, she told herself. *And they could have married at once with her parents' permission...*

She scowled. The more she thought about it, the less it

seemed to make sense.

Howell goes to Sir Travis, intending to reveal Lady Elizabeth's secret... and Sir Travis is alive afterwards, she thought. *Nothing happens to reveal her secret before the news gets out that Sir Travis is dead. Why doesn't Howell tell the world?*

The blackmailer had told Gwen that he'd gone to Sir Travis and offered him a loan, rather than blackmail. That was probably a lie, Gwen decided... she almost swore out loud as she realised that it hadn't been the *only* lie Howell had told her. Keeping her at a distance ensured that her rudimentary Sensitivity wouldn't be able to pick up on a lie. No doubt he'd faked his illness just to ensure that Gwen stayed back. The semi-darkness had even helped to muffle her senses.

But he'd talked about a loan – and Sir Travis, who was in debt to the tune of four thousand pounds, might have needed one. And he was an up-and-coming government servant. Gwen had seen enough of Master Thomas's patronage network to see the value of having contacts in all walks of life. Howell could have offered Sir Travis a loan and then insisted on being repaid in information, rather than money...

Gwen stopped and stared down at her hands. Could it all be a wild coincidence?

That can't be right, she told herself, after a moment. Coincidences did happen, Mycroft's brother had told her, but the more unlikely they were, the less likely it was that they *were* a coincidence. Howell would have to have visited both Lady Elizabeth and Sir Travis on different matters within a few days... no, it didn't seem likely. The odds were that there was a connection there somewhere. She made a mental note to find out exactly what Howell had said to Lady Elizabeth – he'd clearly known about her impending wedding, even if Polite Society as a whole hadn't known – before going to visit her intended.

And yet none of it answered the real question. Who had killed Sir Travis?

She reached Cavendish Hall and stepped through the gatehouse, walking up into the main hall. Doctor Norwell came out of his office and waved frantically to Gwen, as if he'd expected her to just ignore him. Sighing inwardly, she allowed him to lead her into his cramped office and took one of the few visible chairs. The others were buried under piles of books and paperwork.

"I'm glad I caught you," he said, before she could say anything. "You do realise that hiring Lady Elizabeth is unprecedented?"

Gwen blinked in surprise, then realised that Doctor Norwell was worried about his job. As a non-magician, his position at Cavendish Hall was never truly secure, no matter how long he'd served as a theoretical magician and researcher. He could be fussy and pedantic, but she rather liked the old goat. Besides, he wasn't spending half of his time trying to undermine her position.

"You've had problems opening some of my letters," Gwen reminded him. It was absurd – no one sent romantic notes to her at any time, let alone under her official title – but men were often silly. "Lady Elizabeth will work as my personal assistant rather than anything more... general."

"Her presence has already caused comment," Doctor Norwell warned her. "The Head of Movers was complaining about her at some length."

Gwen lifted an eyebrow. "Is there anything I can do, short of finding a male Master and resigning in his favour, that will *please* His Lordship?"

Doctor Norwell gave her an odd little smile. "Probably not," he admitted. "I suppose you could just vote in his favour at Committee meetings..."

"Which would annoy all of the other Heads," Gwen pointed out. "I think I have reached the point where I will try to have him replaced by another Mover..."

"That might be unwise," Doctor Norwell said. "Lord Brockton has a great many influential friends. Colonel Sebastian did not. If Lord Brockton happened to leave, he could do a great deal more to damage your position than writing nasty letters about you to *The Times*."

Gwen shrugged. He was right, but there were always options. If the Airship Treaty passed, *someone* would have to go to Istanbul to help the Turks set up their own magical school – and who better than Lord Brockton? How could the Turks *not* take him seriously? He was related to some of the foremost peers of the realm. With a little work, Gwen might even be able to create an impression that he was going against her will...

"Never mind that," she said, after a moment. "How is Sir James working out?"

"He seems capable of keeping Lord Brockton reasonably pacified," Doctor Norwell said. "The only other person to have complained is Earl Amherst, apparently on the grounds that Charmers are poorly represented in Merlin and therefore Sir James cannot be trusted to keep the balance between the various talents."

"Oh," Gwen said. "And how did Sir James take that?"

"Offered to create more posts in combat teams if there were more Charmer volunteers," Doctor Norwell said. "The Earl shut up after Sir James invited him to try out for another team."

Gwen hid a smile. She'd only met a couple of Charmers who weren't physical cowards.

"But there's another matter I wished to discuss with you," Doctor Norwell said. He looked oddly embarrassed. "You were seen eating with Sir Charles."

Gwen kept her face under tight control. What made him think that it was his business?

She knew the answer to *that* a moment later. Everyone considered her business *their* business.

"Indeed," she said, flatly.

Doctor Norwell seemed unable to meet her eyes. "How much do you know about his family history?"

"Nothing," Gwen said. She'd meant to look into it, but she'd never had time. Besides, her mother was probably already collecting gossip as well as hard facts – and probably giving more credence to the rumours. "Why is that important?"

Doctor Norwell gave her a look she remembered from some of her old tutors, a look that suggested that she was being stupid on purpose.

"You should know that birth is important," he said,

crossly. "Even after the Swing, it is unthinkable that certain social classes should co-exist in holy matrimony."

Gwen crossed her arms under her breasts and scowled at him. "And?"

"And Sir Charles came out of the farms," Doctor Norwell said. "Didn't you know that?"

"... No," Gwen said.

"He might not actually know," Doctor Norwell admitted. "He was a healthy baby boy, so he was... ah, *farmed* out to the Bellingham family. His adopted mother and father were quite low on the family tree, so there would be no unpleasantness with titles and inheritance and whatnot."

Gwen nodded, impatiently. Few aristocratic families would have refused to take an orphan into their homes, particularly if they believed him to be of noble blood, but they wouldn't be happy with the possibility of the adopted child inheriting instead of their true children. And if the child didn't *know* that he'd been adopted, it would be difficult for his 'parents' to disinherit him while keeping the farms a state secret. Common practice had been to insert the adoptees into the family *after* a legitimate heir or two had been born.

Her lips twitched. It had occurred to her, just after she'd gone through the files, that quite a few aristocratic families had diluted their blood, without anyone else ever realising it. Her mother would have fainted away on the spot if she'd ever found out.

"So he was adopted," Gwen said, when it became clear that he was waiting for a response. "So were quite a few other children."

Doctor Norwell nodded and rushed onwards. "He didn't show any trace of magic," he said. "There wasn't even enough to justify the normal experiments – putting a potential magician in danger to see if panic brought out the magic. Eventually, the Royal College just lost interest in him."

"Oh," Gwen said. Panic – and fear, and rage – did bring out magic, if the potential was there. Her life hadn't been in any danger back when her magic had first blossomed, but it had certainly felt that way. "There was nothing at all?"

"Nothing," Doctor Norwell confirmed. "There wasn't even a hint that he *should* have had magic, the same hint you see when we discover a previously unknown talent. I don't blame the researchers for deciding that they were wasting their time and letting him find his own path through life.

"And then something happened – there was a major row within the family. I don't know the exact details because no report was ever filed, but I'd guess that he discovered part of the truth of his origins. And then they bought him a commission and sent him off to India."

Gwen winced. Not too long ago, according to her mother, a wealthy professor had taken a flower girl from the streets and turned her into lady, training her how to conduct herself in Polite Society. She'd fooled everyone, even society's grand dames... and she had *known* that she wasn't truly one of them. But someone raised to think of themselves as aristocratic right from the start? They might well have *believed* that aristocrats were naturally superior to everyone else before they found out the truth.

Jack's sanity had been damaged. Who knew how Sir Charles would have reacted?

"He showed commendable bravery in India and the Viceroy knighted him," Doctor Norwell said. "But his birth threatens his future."

"Except that no one *should* know about his birth," Gwen pointed out, coldly. "Or did his family start talking about the farms?"

"No," Doctor Norwell said. "But some people have worked out that there was... *something* odd about his birth."

Gwen was privately surprised that it hadn't happened more often. It was traditional for a pregnant woman to withdraw to the countryside when her pregnancy became noticeable, just to ensure that the baby breathed in the sweet smell of the country rather than London's ever-present smog. Few people would attend her until the baby was presented to London society – and girls were not always presented to society – but even so, someone might just realise that a woman had either managed to give birth astonishingly quickly or that the child hadn't been hers at all. But then, as long as the formalities were observed, it was unlikely that anyone in society would be so gauche as to comment on it.

"And they said that I was a devil-child," she said, tartly. There were times when she resented Master Thomas for not coming to take her earlier, even after it had become clear that she was using more than one talent. But the reluctance to employ women at any level had been too strong until it had become clear that Master Thomas wouldn't be around for much longer. "Why should I hold his birth against him?"

"Others will hold it against you," Doctor Norwell said. "You know how talkative some people can be..."

Gwen felt her temper flare. "There isn't a single one of the recruits who hasn't been to one of the brothels I'm not supposed to know about," she snapped. In prior days, they'd gone to the farms; it hadn't taken them long to find an alternative once she'd shut the entire program down. "Am I supposed to *care* about what they think of me?"

"You are expected to serve as their leader," Doctor Norwell said, very carefully. "Every time Queen Elizabeth's reputation was threatened, she lost prestige and her position was undermined. And your position is very much like hers."

Gwen felt magic shimmering just under her skin, demanding release. She clamped down on it as hard as she could.

"Her *father* had six wives and plenty of mistresses," she hissed. "Why exactly was *that* not held against him?"

"The position of a woman is different," Doctor Norwell said. "There has to be no doubt over who is the father of your children. For your reputation to be compromised..."

Gwen surprised herself by laughing out loud. "Doctor, my reputation was monstrous even before Master Thomas rescued me," she reminded him. "I didn't *ask* to be born with magic, or to be left alone to learn as best as I could before the Royal Sorcerers Corps decided that it *needed* me. Right now, I sleep in a building inhabited by hundreds of young men and spend half of my time dealing with male officials without a chaperone. What do you think that Polite Society thinks of me?"

She went on before he could say a word. "If men were so... concerned about their own chastity, I might be more understanding," she added. "But a man who dips his wick" – she wasn't supposed to know the street slang and using it made Doctor Norwell pale – "is considered a hero, while the woman he deflowers is considered a villain? I see no logic or justice in that, *Doctor*. Is it not just as worrying to the young woman he marries later when she realises that he might have fathered another child out of wedlock?"

Her lips twisted into a bitter smile. "Oh, right; I *forgot*. A bastard child is naturally blamed for her own bastardy. Somehow, the cunning little mite must have influenced her father to fall prey to the seduction of her mother and impregnate her, despite not even being *alive* at the time. Tell me – how can you blame an unborn child for the sin that conceived her?

"Besides, if they can ignore Lord Nelson and Lady Hamilton, they can ignore me."

"The world isn't fair," Doctor Norwell said, after a long moment. "It is the way it is..."

"It is the way it is because certain people find that it keeps them in power," Gwen interrupted. "And if that power is nothing more than the ability to determine which particular style of dress is *in* or *out*, it's pathetic. Let those who are without sin throw their stones at me, Doctor. It's caring about society's opinion that will get me into trouble. If they want to talk, they can talk. I won't let myself care.

She gave him a sweet smile. "My reputation is mud," she added. "Who *cares* if it gets worse?"

Chapter Twenty-Three

only heard a few rumours about Mr. Howell," Lucy said. "We were told never to go near him."

She'd aged in the six months since the Swing, Gwen realised, silently berating herself for not spending more time with the Healer. Lucy's once-red hair was shading to grey, while her face was lined and worn. All magic took a toll, but Lucy might be being pushed too far – and yet, Healing was an incredibly important talent. There were hundreds of men and women who would live full lives because of her.

"I guess he had little to do with the Rookery," Gwen said, as she studied the hospital ward. Healers automatically had a great deal of authority – and Lucy had used hers to insist that the hospital be thoroughly cleaned before she started to treat patients. Doctors had known about germs for several years, but a surprising number of them had refused to take any precautions until after the Swing. "No one to blackmail there."

"Probably not, no," Lucy agreed. "And most of the people there would resort to violence if blackmailed. It only works if you have someone who would rather pay up than fight, or accept public exposure."

She gave Gwen a sidelong look. "But that wasn't really what you came to talk to me about, was it?"

Gwen nodded, reluctantly. She'd forgotten just how perceptive Lucy was – but then, she'd grown up in the Rookery, where the slightest mistake could bring death.

"No," she admitted. "I need advice."

She briefly outlined her meeting with Sir Charles – and

how she'd lost her temper at Doctor Norwell, after he'd questioned her. Lucy listened in silence, without leaping to judgement; few people from the Rookery cared much about society's protocols. Gwen had been shocked the day Jack had shown her the Rookery and the horrors that lurked within the poorer parts of London. Even after the Swing, the problems blighting the area had not been banished overnight.

"Sounds like you have it bad," Lucy observed, when she finished. "Or perhaps you just want to rebel against your parents."

Gwen snorted. "My parents?"

"Metaphorically speaking, of course," Lucy said. "Young men seek independence at the earliest possible moment – or become mummy's boys, if the mother keeps them tied too close to her. Girls, on the other hand, don't seek independence until they're much older. You're old enough to feel that you should be carving out your own destiny."

She winked at Gwen. "You're also at the age where you could make some *really* bad decisions," she added. "Do you know how many mistakes you could make? You could wind up pregnant and married to a man who is genuinely unsuited to you, or an unmarried mother, or... or dead, if you took the wrong substance. Why do you *think* that girls are allowed so little freedom at your age."

Gwen scowled. She'd always considered that such social controls existed to allow the parents to draw the maximum advantage from their female offspring – after all, a girl couldn't carry on the family name. But were they also there for the girl's protection? Would she prefer the right to make her own mistakes, and suffer the consequences, or to be wrapped in swaddling cloth and shielded from the ills of the world?

"I think I'd prefer to make my own mistakes," she said, finally.

"That's what my previous employees used to say," Lucy said. There was a tart note to her voice. "And you know what happened to *them*."

"They became prostitutes," Gwen said, tonelessly.

"I was one of the good ones," Lucy said. "I never worked my girls to death. There were others who took girls who had nowhere else to go and forced them to work until they died... or worse. People who make really bad choices can fall a very long way."

She smirked, suddenly. "There's a Lord who has been here three times in the last six months," she added. "He... likes it rough, I think. If it wasn't for me, he'd be crippled by now."

Gwen didn't want to know the details. "Is it wrong of me to want to blaze my own path?"

Lucy turned to look at her. "Correct me if I'm wrong," she said, sardonically, "but aren't you *already* blazing your own path?"

Gwen flushed. "I meant with a man, not with magic," she snapped. "Is it wise of me to let Sir Charles court me?"

"He seems rather pushy," Lucy observed. "But then, just how *does* one approach the Royal Sorceress? You may well be emancipated from parental controls – in that case, he would have to approach you rather than your family."

That was true, Gwen knew. Lord Rudolf had signed her over to Master Thomas – and Master Thomas was dead, without naming a Guardian for Gwen. Given that she was already seventeen, she was effectively in charge of her own estate – rare, but not unusual for a young girl. One of David's attempts at courtship had been aimed at a young girl whose parents had died in India, leaving her alone in the world. She'd had a freedom Gwen had envied at the time.

And if Gwen was emancipated, anyone who wanted to court her would have to court *her*, rather than her family.

"You toffs do make life complicated for yourselves," Lucy added. "I really shouldn't complain. My business wouldn't have been so profitable if you hadn't wrapped sex up in all manner of complex rituals."

She chuckled as Gwen blushed furiously.

"My advice?" She added. "If you want him, run – but don't run too fast. Men tend to hold something they've worked for in higher esteem than something they were given freely. But if you don't want him, tell him as bluntly as you can. Men, the poor dears, are *very* bad at picking up on subtle hints."

She shrugged. "Other than that," she said, "make sure you work out a solid marriage contract. The law gives a man control over his wife's assets unless he's already signed his rights away. I've known girls who have run into trouble because they thought that love would conquer all and didn't take a few precautions."

Gwen rolled her eyes. "I'll see how things go," she said. "What if..."

Lucy smiled. "You're reluctant to discuss the practicalities? That's not a good sign."

There was a knock at the door. "Bring her in," Lucy carolled. "We're decent."

The door was pushed open by a pair of young women wearing white, who stared at Gwen before remembering themselves and wheeling in a bed. Gwen grimaced as she saw the young girl lying on the bed, her left hand badly mangled and her face twisted with pain.

"A factory accident," Lucy said, all humour gone from her voice. "They still like using young children, because they can pay them less... but when they're injured, they're put out to die. Until now."

Gwen silently promised herself that she would have a few words with Lord Mycroft and have the girl's factory inspected by dour-faced government officials. The new laws, passed after the Swing, should have restricted the employment of young children, but it was often difficult to enforce them. Children were smaller and often nimbler than adults; it was common for them to serve as everything from chimney sweeps to apprentice craftsmen. And, if they breathed in too many fumes while they worked, their lives would be blighted forever.

Damned workhouses, she thought, angrily. There were always orphans in London... and many of the orphanages specialised in sending their children to work, claiming that it was part of their education. In reality, the managers were trying to make as much money as they could. She promised herself that she would have a few of them inspected too, particularly the ones she helped fund. There was no *way* she was going to collaborate with *this*.

Lucy nodded to her. "Do you want to try to Heal?"

Gwen hesitated. Healing should be one of her talents, but she'd never managed to master it – unless she had been Healing herself all along. She'd never really been seriously injured until after she'd become Master Thomas's apprentice... yet she couldn't recall any cuts and bruises lasting more than a few hours. And there were other issues...

"I'll try," she said. Healing was an odd talent; very few of the Healers had managed to produce *any* explanation of what they did. They were governed by instinct. "Can you hold her still?"

The body *wanted* to heal, Lucy had told her, when she'd agreed to join the Royal Collage as the nation's first Healer. All the magician really did was smooth the way, providing energy that would allow the body to heal itself; the trick to Healing wasn't so much directing the process as it was pushing the body into healing faster. But Gwen suspected that there was more to it than that. Changers and Infusers both pushed magic into objects – or people – and yet neither talent could be used to heal. At best, a Changer might be able to rebuild a broken arm – and yet the results had never been good.

Gwen closed her eyes as her fingertips touched the girl's arm, trying to feel the life energy flowing through the girl's flesh. Or maybe it was magic. No one had ever come up with a real explanation for how magic actually worked... some talents seemed to make sense, others seemed inexplicable. Doctor Norwell seemed confident that the answers would come one day, but it might be years before they were fully understood. Gwen concentrated and felt out the girl's injury. She heard a moan as her magic shimmered against the girl's body... and stopped.

Careful, she reminded herself. Back before she'd known that there were separate talents, she'd actually managed to get them to work together, an achievement in ignorance that had impressed even Master Thomas. But if she accidentally hurt the girl instead of healing her, simply by drawing on the wrong talent, she would never forgive herself.

"Focus on the wound," Lucy murmured. "You want to encourage it to heal."

Gwen tried, but the magic seemed to refuse to enter the girl. "It isn't working," she said, opening her eyes. Why didn't it *work* for her? She could feel the potential within her magic, so she had the talent... she just couldn't use it. And Master Thomas had never developed it either. "Can you deal with her?"

Lucy nodded and stepped forward, pushing Gwen away from the girl. "Watch," she said, as she pressed her hand against the girl's arm. "I begin..."

Gwen opened her mind and watched the magic ebb and flow. Lucy was pushing magic into the girl effortlessly, as if it was the easiest thing in the world; moments later, the girl's flesh and bone started to knit itself back together. Within seconds, it looked as good as new, apart from the pale skin. It would take days before the girl's skin tone was uniform once again.

And there were people who called it a mark of witchcraft, Gwen reminded herself. *She might have to stay here for a week.*

"I don't understand it," she said, in frustration. "Why doesn't it work?"

"Maybe you just need to practice more," Lucy said. She smiled as Gwen scowled at her. "Or maybe you can't Heal because of all the other talents."

That made sense, Gwen decided. Blazing and Moving worked well together, but Charm seemed to supersede both Talking and Sensitivity. Her Changing and Infusing were both very limited, although *that* wasn't always a disadvantage. An Infuser could do a great deal of damage without any real skill. And Seeing needed her to lie on a bed – or in the bath – and meditate to get any value out of it.

"Maybe I need someone willing to risk his life to have me experiment on him," she said, finally. "I might accidentally Blaze him instead."

"There won't be any shortage of volunteers," Lucy assured her. "Let me know when you want to experiment and I'll find someone."

Lord Brockton, Gwen thought, before deciding that it was unlikely to happen. The Head of Movers loved hunting, but his powers would protect him even if he fell off his horse. Besides, she couldn't justify experimenting on him – or denying him a proper Healer.

"Thank you," she said, as the nurses wheeled the girl back out of the ward. "For everything."

She walked back to Cavendish Hall, slipped in through the side entrance and walked up to her office. Doctor Norwell had put Lady Elizabeth in a guest suite, an unsubtle way of hinting that she wouldn't be staying very long. Irene used the same suite when she visited Cavendish Hall, which was as little as possible. Gwen understood, now, why Irene spent so much time away from England. It was easier to be a free sprit if there were no relatives around.

Gwen tapped on the door and stepped inside. Lady Elizabeth was lying on her bed, reading a heavy tome; Doctor Norwell had to have found it for her from the Hall's library. *A History of Magic* had been written by a government hack and contained so many inaccuracies that anyone trying to use it to understand magic would find it impossible. On the other hand, it *was* a reasonably accurate – if generalist – picture of just what the Royal Sorcerers Corps had done since it was founded.

"My mother is probably screaming for her lawyers right now," Lady Elizabeth said, as Gwen sat down facing her. "Do you think that you'll get in trouble?"

"Maybe," Gwen said. "We need to talk about your duties – but I have something I need to ask you first. How did Howell even find out about your engagement?"

Lady Elizabeth frowned. "I don't know," she said, slowly. "No one knew."

Gwen lifted an eyebrow. "*No one* knew?"

"Well, I knew," Lady Elizabeth said, crossly. "My parents knew; Sir Travis knew... but I don't think that there were many others. There were a couple of witnesses... they wouldn't have told anyone, would they?"

"Not if they were sworn to secrecy," Gwen said. A marriage had to be announced in public – the banns had to be formally read – before it could take place. The contract, on the other hand, could have been kept secret indefinitely. "So how did Howell know that you were engaged?"

She couldn't fault the blackmailer's timing. An engagement made a girl's reputation all the more important – and she would do whatever it took to preserve it, even if it cost her much of her fortune. But Howell had demanded an impossibly high sum... surely he'd *known* that Lady Elizabeth couldn't pay. Or had he intended to bargain?

"I don't know," Lady Elizabeth insisted. "Who could have told him?"

"That might solve part of the mystery if we actually knew," Gwen muttered. David had known, Sir Charles had known... she would have to ask them both if they'd shared the information with anyone else. Perhaps someone *had* intended to court Lady Elizabeth and one of the witnesses had quietly told him that she was already engaged. "Did your servants know? Your maid?"

"I never tell Janet anything," Lady Elizabeth said. Her face reddened, suddenly. "Do you realise that she spied on me for ten *years*? She was never *my* servant."

Gwen felt a moment of sympathy. A servant, particularly a serving maid, was in a good position to know *everything* about her mistress, even the details that would normally remain strictly private. Gwen's maids had been too terrified of her to stay long, but Lady Elizabeth wouldn't have that advantage. Her maid would have reported her to Lady Bracknell if she'd done anything even remotely questionable.

"I wonder if your father told someone," Gwen mused. She would have to ask – or, more practically, arrange for David to ask. "Does he have an assistant?"

She pushed the whole issue aside a moment later. "Let me show you your office," she said, standing up. "And introduce you to the clerks."

"Mother will have another fit," Lady Elizabeth observed, glumly. "I'll be *working* for my pay."

"At least you'll *get* pay," Gwen reminded her. Girls rarely had any money of their own, or even control over their trust funds. "You'll be free to spend it as you wish."

She took Lady Elizabeth to the office Doctor Norwell had opened up for her and started to go through the correspondence the Royal Sorceress received. "Separate them out for me," she explained. "Anything concerning future deployments for trained magicians can go to Mr. Norton – he'll take care of it, as long as the magicians don't leave the country. Hints of new magic should be forwarded to Doctor Norwell; he's charged with organising their investigation."

The memory made her scowl. Only one new kind of magic had been discovered in a decade – and it hadn't been the Royal College that had discovered it. Gwen had a private suspicion that allowing more researchers to share in the knowledge the Royal College hoarded would lead to new kinds of magic, but it was unlikely that the Committee would agree to share. She couldn't really blame them either. Anything shared widely enough would reach the enemies of the realm within a week.

"And hate mail can just be dumped in the fire," she finished. She smiled at Lady Elizabeth's expression. No one had ever sent her hate mail in her life, no doubt. She'd seemed practically perfect in every way. "I don't bother to reply to that sort of junk."

While Lady Elizabeth practised with the latest intake of letters, Gwen picked up a sheet of paper and dashed off a quick note to Sir Charles. Tomorrow, she would go with him to the Golden Turk... and she was looking forward to seeing him. And who cared if the rest of Polite Society disapproved?

Chapter Twenty-Four

t's nice to see you again, Lady Gwen," Sir Charles said, as she climbed into the carriage.

"You too," Gwen said. She took the seat facing him and forced herself to relax. The carriage lurched into life a moment later. "We need to go to the Golden Turk, I am afraid."

"It isn't the sort of place I would bring a normal young lady," Sir Charles said. "But you're a very extraordinary young lady."

"Flattery will get you nowhere," Gwen said, with a smile. To her surprise, he smiled back. "But I have to go there, if only to see what Sir Travis owed – and who backed him."

"It wasn't me," Sir Charles said, quickly. The carriage rocked as the coachman turned a corner. "I don't have the money to back up gambling debts."

Gwen considered asking him about his family, before realising that it was likely to be a sore subject. She didn't like talking about her family either. Besides, Sir Charles had created a reputation that was all his own, unlike many others of nobler birth. There was only so far one's family name could take someone.

"Four thousand pounds, according to the demand note," Gwen said. "And they want it paid at once."

Sir Charles frowned. "Gambling debts have always been tricky things," he said. "Sometimes they get passed down to the heir, sometimes they disappear when the debtor dies... but four thousand pounds couldn't be written off so easily. The Golden Turk will be out of pocket, at the very least."

"And at worst, there will be a chain reaction of debt," Gwen said. Her father had made David study the South Seas Bubble of 1720, where the sudden collapse in share prices had ruined countless investors, many of whom had only had a vague link to the South Seas Company. If the gambling debt was written off, the Golden Turk might be unable to meet its own commitments and go out of business – and that might take out other businesses. "No wonder they're demanding immediate repayment."

She'd forwarded the demand note to Norton for his attention, but as far as she knew the executor had around a year to carry out his duties. However, the Mortimer Family weren't being patient – and as Lady Mortimer had died less than a year ago, the legal web was more tangled than anything Gwen had seen. No doubt they would argue that Sir Travis's will overrode his mother's, leaving Polly's jewels in the hands of Lady Mortimer's niece.

"They might not be able to wait," Sir Charles said. He gave her a sharp look. "Are you armed?"

Gwen had to giggle. "How many girls have you asked *that* question?"

"It's a wise precaution in India," Sir Charles said, not in the least abashed. "You never know what will happen, particularly if you live outside the cities."

"I've got my magic," Gwen reminded him. Master Thomas had believed in carrying concealed weapons – and ordered Irene to teach Gwen how to conceal some on her own person – but he'd also warned her never to discuss them with anyone. "Are *you* armed?"

"I brought my service revolver," Sir Charles said. "The Golden Turk is meant to be safe – even if the young bloods do think that going there gives them a hint of roguish dealings – but you're going to tell them that it might be a while before they see their money."

"If they ever do," Gwen said.

The Golden Turk was situated at the outskirts of London's dockyards, not too far from the Rookery. Gwen couldn't help noticing that there were a surprising number of Turkish immigrants in the area, including a handful who looked quite well off. Lord Mycroft had told her that the last change of power in the Ottoman Empire had sent hundreds of corrupt officials scurrying out of Turkey – not unlike Lord Blackburn going *into* Turkey, she had to acknowledge – and quite a few of them had ended up in Britain. The troubles with France had somehow made Turkish food fashionable, giving some of them a chance to make money and renovate the area. Given time, it might end up looking like Istanbul.

"Most of the Turks who came here were upper class," Sir Charles said, softly. "They didn't take coming here well, but it beats having their heads removed by the new Sultan."

Gwen nodded.

The Golden Turk was a large building, unmarked save for a single crested image out of Turkish mythology. Gwen recognised it as a genie, an entity who would grant three wishes to anyone who gained possession of its lamp, but would often twist the wishes until the unlucky person would throw the lamp away. The discovery of magic had started a search for magical artefacts, even though no one had ever encountered a genie or any other supernatural creature in recorded history. Gwen suspected that the Royal College had quietly encouraged the search in order to trick Britain's enemies into wasting time.

She led the way through the main door and found herself standing on a balcony, overlooking a gambling hall. Dozens of men were sitting at tables, throwing dice, spinning wheels or playing with cards, while women wearing wisps of clothing moved from table to table, whispering encouragement in male ears. Gwen had to force herself to look away from one dark-haired beauty whose clothes concealed absolutely nothing. She couldn't *imagine* wearing such a revealing outfit anywhere, even in the privacy of her own home.

"Those tables are minor," Sir Charles explained, as they made their way around the balcony towards the office. "It's unlikely that anyone will win or lose more than fifty or so pounds."

Gwen gave him a puzzled look. Fifty pounds could keep someone alive for weeks on the streets – if they were allowed to keep it.

"Gambling is addictive," Sir Charles added. "The richer men down there will be urged to join the senior games, the ones that are by invitation only. Once there, they will begin gambling for *real* money." He pointed to golden coins on the tables. "Those are made of wood – most gamblers hand in their money to the cashier and exchange it for gambling chips, which are useless outside the building. Then they take their winnings and exchange them for cash."

"Real money," Gwen repeated. "Don't they know that fifty pounds is *real* money?"

"Of course not," Sir Charles said. There was a hint of bitterness in his voice. "Most of the people with regular tabs here don't actually sully their hands *earning* money."

He leaned over until he was whispering in her ear. "And in many of the games, the odds are slanted in favour of the house," he added. "Smart gamblers know better than to play *those* games – and yet I don't see any empty tables. Do you?"

Gwen shook her head. She'd never learned how to gamble and couldn't follow what the players were doing, but it didn't look as if many of them were winning. If they wanted to just give away their money, there was no shortage of charities – and the hospitals were always looking for donations from wealthy aristocrats. Or maybe she was simply unable to follow what was going on. The ones who looked like losers might be winners.

They reached the booth at the far end, manned by a dark-skinned girl who gave them both a warm smile. "Good morning, Gentlemen," she said, in oddly-accented English. "What would you like to play today?"

"I am here to see the manager," Gwen said, passing the girl her card.

The girl jumped, clearly not having realised that Gwen was female.

"I shall have you shown to his office," the girl said, quickly. She glanced at the card, turned and called out several words in a foreign language to someone out of sight, and then looked back at Gwen. "A guide will be here in a moment."

"She called you a witch," Sir Charles whispered in Gwen's ear. "I don't think she likes you."

"I've been called worse," Gwen reminded him.

A side door opened, revealing a young girl of indeterminate age wearing a thin sari that covered her body, but concealed almost nothing. Gwen shook her head in disbelief as the girl pressed her hands together, gave her a half-bow and then beckoned for them to come through the door and into a darkened staircase. Like Cavendish Hall and most aristocratic residencies, the Golden Turk was honey-combed with corridors and stairwells intended for the staff, keeping them out of sight. The girl led them up two flights of stairs and into an office that overlooked a set of smaller rooms. Gwen looked down and realised that each one had a table and a handful of men sitting around it, gambling.

"The more formal games," Sir Charles said, quietly. "Down there, entire fortunes are moving from hand to hand – and the house always takes its cut. Or other things are being gambled – I knew a man who tried to gamble away his wife."

Gwen stared at him. "That *can't* be legal," she protested. "You can't sell a wife."

"It wasn't," Sir Charles said. "But he still tried. The laws, such as they are, don't always apply here."

"Royal Sorceress," an accented voice said. "I confess that I have no idea of how to address a Royal Sorceress. How does one address you without causing offence?"

Gwen looked up. A light-skinned man was standing there, wearing long white robes decorated with golden strands and a simple white skullcap. His beard was neatly trimmed; Gwen couldn't help noticing that he seemed to have spent more time on personal grooming than any other man she knew. He wore a curved blade at his belt, ready to be drawn and used in a fight, although she had no idea how well he could use it. His robes didn't hide the fact that he was considerably overweight.

"Lady Gwen is sufficient," she said. She wasn't going to let herself be called *Mistress* Gwen, even though it was the feminine version of Master Thomas's title. "I am currently serving as the executor of Sir Travis Mortimer's will."

"Ah," the Turk said. "I am Abdullah Bey Defterdar, owner and manager of this fine establishment. Welcome to the Golden Turk, a little piece of our home for us poor exiles."

His face shifted into a sombre mask. "It is customary among our people to chatter about nothing first," he said, as he led them into his office. "But you English are a hasty folk – and I am minded to be hasty too. Please, be seated."

Gwen sat down on a cushion and watched as he produced a set of account books from a shelf on the wall. "We keep careful track of all debts owed to us," Abdullah informed her. "As many of our players often gamble beyond what they are carrying on their person, we allow them to run up gambling tabs – provided that they can prove that they can repay us or that they have a backer who can repay us. Many of your young English noblemen try to use their father as their backer, which can cause problems when the father refuses to back up the debt."

He passed the first account book to Gwen. "In this case, you will see that Sir Travis ran up a series of debts over the last four months," he explained. "Those debts were not, at first, backed – but his luck held and he won a place at the advanced tables."

Gwen looked up at him. "The *advanced* tables?"

"Those who prove that they can pay can be invited to the advanced tables," Abdullah said. "It causes no shortage of embarrassment when a player is pushed out because he cannot continue to match his competitors, even without actually *losing*. We prefer to avoid such scenes where possible."

"I can imagine," Gwen murmured.

"Sir Travis started to lose – not all the time, but he lost enough to run up a debt," Abdullah said. "We asked him to find a backer or withdraw from the games; he found Hiram Pasha, a wealthy man, to back up his debts." He produced an envelope, withdrew a sheet of paper and passed it to Gwen. "The Pasha promised to pay if Sir Travis proved unable to meet his debts."

Gwen glanced at the paper, then frowned. "It is in Arabic," she pointed out. "I cannot read it."

Sir Charles took the paper and read it quickly. "It's very florid, but it basically commits Hiram Pasha to guaranteeing the debt and paying the Golden Turk if Sir Travis proved unable to pay," he said. "Do you want a precise translation?"

"No, thank you," Gwen said. She looked up at Abdullah, who was watching her expectantly. "I know very little about gambling, but Sir Travis is clearly unable to pay his debts. Why haven't you collected the money from Hiram Pasha?"

"We attempted to contact the Pasha when we heard about Sir Travis's death," Abdullah explained. "However, he did not answer his door and the messenger was reluctant to try to do anything that might attract his attention. He was known to have a dark temper when crossed."

Gwen knew far too many people like that, starting with most of the Royal Committee. "So you resorted to sending a demand note to the estate?"

"We need that money," Abdullah admitted. "Legally, we have a claim on part of Sir Travis's estate."

That was questionable, Gwen knew... but Abdullah was between a rock and a hard place. Sir Travis might not have owned very much, yet if it were auctioned off the proceeds would definitely be more than four thousand pounds. In that case, Abdullah would have to try to get the money from the estate first, *before* trying to claim it from Hiram Pasha. After all, Sir Travis *could* still pay his debts... if the estate were sold instead of passed down to the closest male heir.

"So it would seem," Gwen said. "Who *is* Hiram Pasha, anyway?"

Abdullah gave her a surprised look. "How can you not have heard of him? He runs an import-export company, importing food and materials from home to make our exile a little more comfortable – and exporting British produce to Turkey. The" – he spluttered a number of words Gwen didn't recognise – "who calls himself the Sultan has a mania for British goods. He is obsessed enough to allow us exiles to dabble our hands in business, just as long as he gets his imports. Hiram Pasha is one of those who serve as a link in the chain from here to Istanbul."

"A very wealthy man," Gwen guessed. "Does he have a reputation for paying his debts?"

"Of course he does," Abdullah said. "If he hadn't, we would never have accepted his word of honour."

Gwen nodded. The courts *might* grant Abdullah his debts – either from Sir Travis's estate or Hiram Pasha's pockets – or they might not. Polite Society disapproved of gambling debts, which was ironic as most of them were run up by aristocrats, and they might not allow the debt to be passed on to someone else. And that might destroy the Golden Turk. Even a prolonged legal battle might be disastrous.

"His debts were backed," she said, slowly. "Did Hiram Pasha back any other debts?"

Abdullah gave her an odd look. "No," he said, slowly. "Sir Travis was the only one he backed."

Gwen looked over at Sir Charles. "How did they know each other?"

"They might well have met," Sir Charles said, slowly. "The simplest way to practice another language is to speak to a native – and the native might well know more about what was actually happening in Istanbul than a diplomat. Sir Travis could have learned a great deal from him."

"Could be," Gwen said.

Abdullah cleared his throat. "This is all very interesting, but I must have my money," he said, quickly. "I cannot afford to write off such an expense. If you do not present me with the money, I will be forced to start legal action."

"I need copies of your accounts," Gwen said, firmly. "We are currently in the process of working out what Sir Travis actually owned and what belongs to the family. Once that is completed, we will try to settle his debts."

"I need the money quickly," Abdullah insisted. "Within a week, perhaps two - or I shall be forced to hire lawyers..."

Gwen nodded. "We will deal with it as quickly as we can," she said. She stood up. "For the moment, we need to visit Hiram Pasha. Do you have his address?"

Abdullah found another book, flicked through the pages and showed her a particular page. Hiram Pasha lived close to the Thames, Gwen saw, near the giant warehouses that stored goods shipped in and out of London. And near one of the bases Jack had used to conceal his army for the planned uprising. She wondered, as she copied down the address, if Hiram Pasha had ever known what was hidden nearby.

"Thank you for your time," Gwen said, taking the account books under one arm. "We will contact you as soon as possible."

The manager insisted on escorting them back down to the ground floor personally, rather than summoning his young servant to do the honours. Gwen wondered, absently, what sort of relationship there was between the two; the girl seemed too dark-skinned to be Abdullah's daughter, yet she seemed more than just a servant. She puzzled over it as they were shown outside with a final handshake, then asked Sir Charles as they walked back to the carriage.

"Many of them were Ottoman nobility, fleeing the purge," Sir Charles commented. "*Pasha* isn't a surname; it's a title. And many of them brought their servants with them when they fled. That girl is probably someone who grew up with noble children and played with them, but isn't really noble. You should pity her."

Gwen nodded.

Chapter Twenty-Five

ot a very impressive house," Gwen commented, as they climbed out of the carriage in front of Hiram Pasha's home. It was a dark two-story building, one of many built for London's merchants and traders. "You'd think he could have bought a proper home."

"He might not have wanted to stay in London permanently," Sir Charles pointed out. "If he was not completely barred from Istanbul, he would merely have wanted a place to stay in London, rather than a proper home."

Gwen nodded as she walked up to the solid wooden door, found the knocker and tapped it firmly. There was no response. She waited two minutes, then tapped again. Surely Hiram Pasha would have a manservant or a maid, even when he wasn't at home. His partners might come to visit and need somewhere to leave their letters or cards.

"Maybe he fled the debt," Sir Charles suggested. "Four thousand pounds is a *lot* of money."

"Could be," Gwen said, as she stepped backwards. The curtains were drawn over the ground floor windows, but the upper floor windows were uncovered. She glanced at Sir Charles, then levitated herself up into the air until she could peer into the windows. The first window showed a small bedroom, completely deserted; the second revealed a man lying on the ground, unconscious or dead.

"Someone's wounded," Gwen said, dropping back to the ground. "I saw a body."

She stepped up to the door and reached out with her magic, pressing against the lock. It clicked, allowing her to push the door open. The interior of the house was as dark and silent as the grave; Gwen concentrated, generated a ball of light and sent it drifting forward, illuminating the hallway. A second dead body was lying on the floor.

Sir Charles bent down to study the body. "Her neck's been broken," he said, grimly. "I saw something like it in India; the killer came up behind her, caught her neck and snapped it with one twist. She wouldn't have had time to fight back."

Gwen winced. The girl – the maid, given how she was dressed – didn't look Turkish; she had to be one of the country girls who came into London in hopes of finding a better life. Many of them had tried to tough it out with the young Gwen; it hadn't been until years later that Gwen had realised that her maids had been among the lucky ones. Some others had faced worse than a bad-tempered girl who couldn't or wouldn't control her magic.

She stepped into the next room and scowled. A man was sitting on a chair in front of a desk, half-hidden in the semi-darkness. Gwen created a second light and swore as it revealed blood on the floor. Up close, it was clear that someone had cut the man's throat with a knife, probably before he even knew that he was under attack. The man – she guessed the dead body belonged to Hiram Pasha – seemed almost peaceful.

Leaving the light globe in the room, Gwen walked back into the hallway and headed up the stairs. There were three bedrooms on the upper floor, one containing another dead body. She studied the corpse quickly, but found no obvious cause of death. Poison? Magic? Or maybe it was something physical. There was no way to know.

She glanced into the other two bedrooms, trying to determine who had owned them. One – the larger one – probably belonged to Hiram Pasha. The next one, she suspected, belonged to the maid, unless there was another woman in the house. All the clothing was clearly feminine. And the third one... must have belonged to the second dead man, she decided. But who was he?

There was a loud rapping at the door. "Police," a voice barked. "Who are you?"

Gwen blinked in surprise and headed back towards the stairwell. Someone must have seen them entering the house and sent a runner to the police, who'd responded with surprising speed for the area. The Bow Street Runners were normally more careful around the docklands, if only because drunken sailors thought it a hoot to attack policemen and steal their hats. Hiram Pasha must have definitely brought in the money.

"Lady Gwen, Royal Sorceress," she said, as she came down the stairs. One of the policemen was holding a truncheon, threateningly. Sir Charles looked about ready to go for his throat. "You need to inform Inspector Lestrade that our investigations might well have hit a dead end."

The policemen looked at her in disbelief. "You?" One of them asked. "You're the Royal Sorceress?"

Gwen scowled, reached out with her magic and lifted both policemen into the air. "Yes, I am," she said, as tartly as she could. "Now, one of you can stand guard outside and the other can send for Inspector Lestrade. He is handling the police aspect of this case."

She put the two policemen down and watched with a certain amount of amusement as they scrambled to do her bidding. Sir Charles looked rather more amused as she stepped back into the study and looked down at Hiram Pasha's body. At least he wasn't scared of her...

"You have to be careful not to touch the body," Sir Charles said. "The police won't thank you if you mess up the crime scene."

"I suppose not," Gwen said. Apart from Mycroft's brother, there were relatively few detectives who bothered to study the scene of the crime. Scotland Yard tended to prefer to grab the nearest suspect on the automatic assumption that he was guilty. "Can you tell how long it was since they were murdered?"

"More than a few hours, less than three days," Sir Charles said. He smiled as Gwen blinked at him. "We know that there was no response after Travis died, so he might well have died at the same time. Besides, the bodies haven't really started to decompose."

"True," Gwen agreed, impressed. They would have to ask around to discover when Hiram Pasha had last been seen alive, but that wouldn't be difficult. "Do you think that the two deaths are connected?"

"They must be," Sir Charles said, quietly. "What are the odds on two people who knew each other coincidently being murdered on the same night?"

"Don't forget the others," Gwen said, quietly. The man who'd killed Hiram Pasha had also killed his maid and the other man, whoever he had been. A son? A business associate? A bodyguard? "Did Polly only survive because she was locked up in her room?"

She walked around the desk and started to study the papers Hiram had left out in the open. A freshly-bound Bradshaw, outlining every means of transport within Britain, from the newly-built railways to canal barges; a book examining the merits of different forms of sailing ship for transporting bulk goods across the Atlantic; a copy of the latest stocks and share prices from London... nothing seemed too out of place. The only oddity she found was a copy of a cheap novel about a woman who entered a Sultan's harem; it was officially banned, but copies had been popping up everywhere for years.

"I've seen harems," Sir Charles commented, when she showed him the book. "It's nothing like that."

Gwen smiled. "What were you doing in a harem?"

"It was our escape route out of Bukhara," Sir Charles said. "The guards just screeched to a halt when they realised we'd entered the forbidden room."

"Oh," Gwen said, suspecting that she was being teased. "And what *else* did you do in the harem?"

Inspector Lestrade arrived before Sir Charles could answer, flanked by a small army of policemen. "Dear me," he announced to all and sundry. "This is quite a scene."

Gwen stepped backwards and allowed the policemen to start their work. Lestrade had shown the foresight to send a policemen to Hiram's office to find someone who actually knew him, allowing the body to be identified quickly. The unknown man turned out to be the son of one of Hiram's business associates in Turkey, who'd been staying with Hiram to learn how to act in Britain. Gwen felt a moment of pity for the poor man's father as the policemen slowly carried the body out of the house. As a foreigner, the body would probably be shipped back to Turkey rather than cremated. God alone knew what would happen to Hiram; his legal status, she suspected, was rather indeterminate.

"Hellfire," Lestrade said, thirty minutes later. He had started to probe through the drawers that Gwen hadn't been able to touch before they arrived. "Lady Gwen – look at *these*."

Gwen took the papers, glanced at them... and nearly jumped out of her skin. Sir Travis's handwriting was distinctive – and the numbers on the top of the page matched the papers that were missing from the safe. Lestrade would crow over finding them before the Royal Sorceress, but it hardly mattered. The *real* question was how they'd come to be in Hiram Pasha's house.

"Those are Travis's papers," Sir Charles said, looking over her shoulder. He sounded badly shaken. "What... what are they doing here?"

"Good question," Lestrade said, briskly. "Did your friend and confidant tell you anything about this foreigner?"

"Nothing," Sir Charles said. "But I didn't know *everything* he did."

"It seems that they had a bit of a relationship going," Lestrade grunted. "The person who killed Sir Travis could easily have been the same person who killed the three victims here."

He might well be right, Gwen decided. If someone had managed to sneak up on a Sensitive, they wouldn't have any trouble dealing with Hiram Pasha's household. The maid would have been almost childishly easy to kill; the others might have been a little harder. But an assassin might not have had any real problems with them.

"Find out when he was last seen alive," Gwen ordered. She would bet half of her fortune that Hiram Pasha had last been seen on the same night Sir Travis died. "And then..."

She scowled. Every time she thought she was putting the pieces together, something appeared to force her to reconsider.

"I spoke to the manager of his shipping company," Lestrade said. "He was last seen alive three days ago."

Gwen nodded. Hiram Pasha had died on the same night. That could *not* be a coincidence.

Lestrade raised his voice as more policemen arrived. "I want this entire house searched *thoroughly*," he ordered. "Full procedure; anything out of place should be brought to me at once, after it has been carefully logged. Anyone who makes a muck of it will be patrolling the docksides after dark for the next ten *years*."

"Tough guy," Sir Charles muttered. He didn't seem to like Lestrade. "But how well would he do on active service?"

"It doesn't matter," Gwen said, tightly. "He isn't being *judged* on active service."

The policemen were very efficient – and thorough. Everything in the house, starting with the bedrooms, was carefully inspected and catalogued, then removed while the policemen felt around for secret compartments. The search was so thorough that they would probably have found Gwen's hidden compartment at Crichton Hall, although they would probably not have been able to break in without a magician's help. They even removed the maid's clothes and inspected each of them, separately.

"Come and look at this," Lestrade said, ten minutes after the search began. "I think it's magic."

The compartment had been hidden at the back of the kitchen table, an odd place for a secret of any kind. Inside, the policeman had found a pair of crystals, a handful of papers and a strange clockwork device that seemed to resemble an unsealed watch. Gwen touched one of the crystals and scowled as she recognised the magic infused into the rock. Hiram Pasha had been very paranoid – or he'd had something to hide.

Lestrade scowled at them, as if he took their presence as a personal affront. "What *are* they?"

"Privacy crystals," Gwen said, slowly. "They prevent magicians from spying on you."

Seeing was one of the most unreliable talents, even though it was immensely useful when it worked properly. Magicians couldn't see the future, but they could spy on someone – if they knew enough about the person or location to focus their minds properly. As far as Gwen knew, Hiram Pasha had never been spied on by Cavendish Hall, but there were no shortage of Seers who might decide to work for someone else. And it was quite possible that there were other Seers who might have remained completely unregistered. The talent could be very useful if no one knew that a particular person was a Seer.

"He would have had something to hide," Sir Charles said, when Gwen had finished explaining. *"What* did he have to hide?"

"A very good question," Lestrade said. He gave Gwen an unreadable look, then picked up the other crystal and studied it. "How common are these things?"

"Too common," Gwen said. An Infuser with enough talent to make them could earn enough to retire on within a few months. *Everyone* wanted a blocking crystal. "They don't last indefinitely, but even an unskilled Infuser could recharge it once it was created."

She picked up the clockwork device. "What is this?"

"Code wheel," Lestrade said, after a moment of hesitation. "I've seen them before, once or twice. You spin the wheel, then use it to produce a simple substitution cipher. It can be difficult to break without knowing the key."

Gwen studied the device for a long moment, admiring the workmanship, and then put it down on the table. "What sort of person would own one?"

Lestrade made a face. "Most shipping owners do write their orders in cipher," he admitted. "It isn't uncommon for their rivals to try to steal an advantage where they can. But this... combined with the papers we found, suggests that Hiram Pasha was a spy."

Sir Charles clenched his fists. "Are you suggesting that

he *spied* on my friend?"

"It is also possible that Sir Travis sold him the notes," Lestrade said, his face darkening. "He had gambling debts to pay..."

"I will not listen to such insinuations," Sir Charles thundered. "Sir Travis risked his life for his country while you ran around London threatening to arrest innocent maids. Where were *you* when we were surrounded by a million holy warriors bent on cutting off our manhoods and then burning us to death? I *demand* that you retract your allegation at once!"

Lestrade purpled. "It is my duty to consider all possible reasons for the crime," he snapped back. "Sir Travis gambled! What else might he have done?"

"He would never betray his country," Sir Charles insisted. "Never! Do you know what he went through when we were caught...?"

Gwen stared from one to the other, unsure of what to do. She couldn't let them start throwing punches, or Lestrade would have to arrest Sir Charles... and God alone knew where *that* would end.

"You arrested an innocent girl because you couldn't be bothered to look for the real murderer," Sir Charles snapped. "Lady Gwen does all of the investigation and you use what *she* finds to try to tarnish Sir Travis's reputation!"

Gwen hesitated, then generated a light ball between the two men, bright enough to make them stumble backwards and cover their eyes.

"Enough," she said. Both men stared at her, but relaxed. It dawned on her that neither of them had really *wanted* to start throwing punches, at least not in front of her. "There is nothing to suggest that Sir Travis willingly handed over his private papers to Hiram Pasha – or, for that matter, no conclusive proof that Hiram Pasha was a spy."

She stared at them both until they calmed down. "Now, this has clearly become *political*," she added, with the private thought that the whole case had *always* been political. "I need to speak to Lord Mycroft to discuss where we go from here. I'll take the rest of the papers from Sir Travis with me – the Inspector can see to it that I get a list of everything else in the house, particularly the paperwork."

"Yes, Milady," Lestrade said.

"I need you to arrange for Polly to be brought to Whitehall," Gwen continued. There was no time to go to Mortimer Hall and question her about Hiram Pasha. "Mortimer Hall can remain under guard until we have completed the investigation; Polly... can go back there once I've finished asking her questions. But she isn't a prisoner and you are not to treat her like one."

Lestrade scowled, but nodded.

Gwen turned to Sir Charles. "I overlooked something," she said, briskly. "I want you to go back to the Golden Turk. Don't tell them about Hiram Pasha's death; just ask Abdullah if Howell was backing any debts on the gaming tables. If so, find out who and when. I have a hunch."

And it will keep him busy, away from Lestrade, she added, silently.

"Of course, Milady," Sir Charles said.

Gwen led the way outside, wondering if she'd ruined their budding relationship... if they *had* a budding relationship. Men were so hard to understand at times.

He caught her arm as she started to walk towards Whitehall. "Take the carriage," he said. "Jock will see you there safely – and it isn't that far back to the Golden Turk. And" – he leaned forward to whisper in her ear – "will you come with me to the dance tomorrow night?"

Gwen hesitated, then nodded. If nothing else, she would be making a point. She was not going to allow others to dictate the path of her life.

And Talleyrand will be there too, she thought. *Maybe I can ask him about Hiram Pasha and see how he reacts. Or would he bring Simone? That would be interesting to see.*

Chapter Twenty-Six

iram Pasha being involved in this affair is... worrying," Lord Mycroft admitted. "His death is even more so."

Gwen frowned, sipping the cup of tea Lord Mycroft's assistant had brought her. "You knew him?"

"I was aware of his existence," Lord Mycroft said. "He was serving the Sultan of the Ottoman Empire as a spy."

"A spy," Gwen repeated, shocked. "He was spying on *us*?"

"Everyone spies on everyone else," Lord Mycroft said, dispassionately. "The Turks might want us to be their allies, but they spy on us anyway – as we spy on them. You never know when some domestic policy issue will weaken the alliance without any formal announcement that it is being terminated."

"It doesn't seem cricket," Gwen muttered, crossly.

"The French and the Spanish don't *play* cricket," Lord Mycroft reminded her. "There are certain things we have to do, no matter how distasteful, to protect the British Empire. Spying and counter-spying are merely two of them."

He gave her a droll smile. "We became aware of Hiram Pasha shortly after his arrival in London; his cover story was just a shade too convenient for our tastes, so we kept an eye on him. Eventually, we realised that he was slipping information back to the Sultan, who seems to have a mania for intelligence gathering."

Gwen stared at him. "Why didn't you arrest him?"

"Better to have someone we know than someone we don't know," Lord Mycroft said. "This way, we get to feel out his spy network and prepare to round them all up if the situation changes. So far, he hasn't sent much back to Turkey beyond some reports on the post-Swing political changes."

"That you know about," Gwen said.

"That we know about," Lord Mycroft confirmed. "This game is always risky."

He pressed his fingertips together, contemplatively. "But this raises a worrying question," he added. "How did Hiram Pasha obtain Sir Travis's documents?"

Gwen scowled. Sir Charles had been insistent that Sir Travis was no traitor, but the gambling debts suggested a strong motive for treason; Hiram Pasha's backing of Sir Travis's debts might be nothing more than a subtle way to pay him for his services. And yet, if that were the case, who had killed Hiram Pasha – and why? And why leave the documents there for the police to find?

"There was no report of Sir Travis meeting with Hiram Pasha," Lord Mycroft continued, "but that doesn't prove anything. He was not obliged to report such a meeting – and we could only watch from a distance without arousing Hiram Pasha's suspicions. A Sensitive would be hard to shadow in any case."

"So where does that leave us?" Gwen asked, bleakly. "Sir Travis a traitor?"

"Worse than that," Lord Mycroft said. "There are people who will argue that the Airship Treaty is too favourable to Turkey. Right now, they can argue that the Turks *paid* Sir Travis to write a treaty that will give them considerable advantages – without repaying us in equal coin. The Airship Treaty would be a dead letter."

"But there would be no conclusive proof," Gwen pointed out.

"It wouldn't matter," Lord Mycroft said. "The mere suspicion would be enough to scuttle the treaty – and destroy any hope of an alliance with Turkey."

Gwen shook her head, thoughtfully. "But who murdered Sir Travis and Hiram Pasha?"

"We may never know," Lord Mycroft said. "The Sultan is a sneaky fox – and his intelligence officers are trained to seize every advantage they can get. If one of them killed Sir Travis, then Hiram Pasha, it would break the chain that would lead us to Turkey – and make it impossible for us to *prove* anything. Except that still doesn't explain the documents. What were they doing in Hiram Pasha's house?"

"Maybe Hiram Pasha didn't know that he was about to be sacrificed," Gwen said, looking over at the chessboard. "The assassin might not have known that they were there."

"Perhaps," Lord Mycroft said. "I understand that you brought Sir Travis's maid to Whitehall?"

"Yes," Gwen said, flatly.

"You must find out what, if anything, she knows about Hiram Pasha," Lord Mycroft said. "And then we need to wrap this whole affair up as quickly and quietly as possible."

Gwen shook her head. "How could someone as... loyal as Sir Travis be a traitor?"

"Very few men are villains in their own mind," Lord Mycroft said. "It was only three years ago that we caught someone slipping information to France in the belief that it would help prevent a war, which didn't stop him accepting a hefty sum of money every year. Sir Travis... went through hell in India, which would be arguably worse for a Sensitive. And he had gambling debts. He might well have decided to switch sides at some point.

"Or he might have genuinely believed that an alliance with Turkey was vitally important," he added, "and compromised himself to ensure that one would be formed. Except now there will be no alliance, at least until every last line in the treaty is scrutinised by diplomats..."

David is not going to be happy, Gwen realised. He'd been Sir Travis's superior, his contact in Whitehall... and now his career would be blighted by being too close to a presumed traitor. What would *that* do to their relationship? Would he blame Gwen for the disaster? Or would he simply go back to business, leaving politics alone?

She looked down at the papers they'd found in Hiram Pasha's home. "How do you decrypt them?"

Lord Mycroft smiled. "Each of the number sequences refers to a word in a particular book," he said. "In this case; *Jewels of the Orient: Tales from the Harem.* You look up the word, then write it down... and by the time you finish, you have a complete paragraph in English."

Gwen winced. "There was a copy of that book in Hiram Pasha's house," she said.

"That isn't good," Lord Mycroft admitted. "The code is close to unbreakable without knowing which book served as the key. Sir Travis would have had to have *told* Hiram Pasha which book he was using to encode his messages. And that would make him an outright traitor."

"Yes," Gwen said, slowly. "Can I take the papers and decrypt them?"

Lord Mycroft raised an eyebrow. "Do you have a reason for that?"

Gwen hesitated. "I want to play a hunch," she said, although she couldn't have put the hunch into words. "It just strikes me as important."

"Feminine intuition is always powerful," Lord Mycroft said. "Very well, but take care of them. *Don't* show them to any of your staff."

"Understood," Gwen said. She stood up. "With your permission, I will see to interrogating Polly."

"After that... we will have to wrap the whole affair up as quickly as possible," Lord Mycroft reminded her. "Sir Travis's family will have the house; you can start handing out what remains of his fortune to the people he named in his will. The gambling debts... will have to be left unpaid."

"The Golden Turk might sue," Gwen pointed out.

"Pointless," Lord Mycroft said. "They can claim their funds from Hiram Pasha's accounts – I can give that a quiet push if the banks start to balk."

Gwen nodded and walked out of the door, heading down towards the guest suites on the ground floor. They were, she'd been told, comfortable prison cells, used when someone of high rank had to be held prisoner – or when someone had to be held without *realising* that they were held. There were no iron bars or sarcastic gaolers; instead, there was quiet supervision and good food. Gwen nodded to the guard and stepped through a door that locked silently. Polly looked up as she entered.

"Lady Gwen," she said. "Is the house all right?"

"I think so," Gwen said. If the maid was innocent, she must be on the verge of panic, wondering just what was happening to her. "I'm afraid that I have more questions to ask you."

She took one of the comfortable seats and sat down facing Polly. "I need you to answer truthfully," she said, lacing her voice – once again – with Charm. "Did a man called Hiram Pasha ever visit Sir Travis?"

"No," Polly said, immediately. The Charm seemed to have affected her profoundly. Lord Blackburn would have made snide comments about the weak minds of the lower orders, but Gwen suspected that it had something more to do with her youth and general isolation from society. Someone more cynical might be more resistant to the Charm.

Gwen frowned, thoughtfully. "Did you ever hear Sir Travis mention his name?"

"No," Polly said, again.

But that proved nothing, Gwen knew. She didn't tell *her* maid everything...

A thought struck her and she looked into Polly's eyes. Charm could never be truly trusted, any more than Charmers themselves. She'd asked Polly a question and received a truthful reply, but it might well be incomplete.

She composed the question as carefully as possible. "Did you hear anyone *else* mention Hiram Pasha's name?"

"Yes," Polly said. "You."

Gwen winced. "Anyone else?"

"The visitor from the Golden Turk," Polly said. "He mentioned the name once."

"Ah," Gwen said, feeling a flicker of triumph. "What happened, exactly?"

She listened carefully as Polly explained that a man from the Golden Turk had visited twice before, hoping to collect the debt that Sir Travis owed the gambling hall. Polly had taken a note each time and passed them on to Sir Travis, but he'd said nothing about it. She didn't know who Hiram Pasha was or what, if anything, he had to do with her employer.

Gwen scowled, convinced that she was missing something.

"He just tore up the notes," Polly explained. "I don't think he cared."

Think about something else, Gwen told herself. *Maybe you'll realise what you were missing.*

A thought struck her. "Did *Howell* come to the house before the night Sir Travis died?"

"He came in the morning of the same day, but Sir Travis was absent," Polly said. Her voice had started to slur, indicating that the Charm was taking its toll on her. "I took a note for him..."

Gwen's eyes narrowed. "What did he actually *say* to you?"

"He asked all sorts of questions about Sir Travis," Polly said. There was a hint of pride in her voice. "I told him nothing, of course, even when he tried to slip me a guinea. The Mistress had always warned me to keep my mouth shut."

"He asked you questions," Gwen repeated. "And you told him nothing..."

She cursed mentally as the pieces fell together. Irene Adler, the most capable Talker in England's service, had explained how easy it could be to read a person's mind, without digging so deeply that the victim might notice even if he lacked a spark of magic. The Talker just asked questions and the answers floated to the top of the victim's mind, even if he didn't say them out loud. Someone could be interrogated and walk away convinced that he'd told the interrogator nothing.

Polly had no way of knowing that she'd betrayed Sir Travis. She certainly hadn't *intended* to betray Sir Travis. But what she'd intended to do didn't matter.

Gwen thought her way through it, step by step. Howell had discovered that Lady Elizabeth was secretly engaged, probably through reading her father's mind. He'd attempted to blackmail Lady Elizabeth, only to discover that she was unable to pay, even though she was devoted to her prospective husband. And so he'd gone to Sir Travis's house, intent on destroying the marriage... and discovered, through reading Polly's mind, that Sir Travis had gambling debts. Instead of destroying Sir Travis's engagement he'd offered to pay his debts!

It made sense, she decided, once she had tested every last link in the chain. Destroying Lady Elizabeth would no doubt scare any other potential victims, but it ran the risk of a physical confrontation with Sir Travis, who had a long history of serving the Empire in India. Paying his debts, on the other hand, would create an obligation that would be hard to break – and if he took up a position in the Foreign Office, he would be in a good position to repay his benefactor. And Howell could keep Lady Elizabeth's letters in reserve, just in case Sir Travis sought to break free of his web.

No *wonder* Howell was such an effective blackmailer. He could read minds!

He would have other advantages, she realised. Given a little careful work, he could isolate the people who would bow to his pressure... and never confront those who would resort to violence, even if their social ruin would follow immediately afterwards. And he could ensure the loyalty of his servants; their minds would be open books to him. She shuddered as she thought through all of the implications. Irene had admitted, once, that minds could be terrible things to read, which was why quite a few Talkers ended up in the madhouse. Howell... had chosen to immerse himself in the worst of humanity.

And he might have found out about Lady Elizabeth's letters through reading her mind, Gwen thought, and gritted her teeth. She could never tell Lady Elizabeth *that*. Polite Society would have a collective heart attack if they realised that someone like Howell had been poking through their minds for years...

She shook her head. Howell was a rogue magician, completely unregistered. Dealing with him was her responsibility.

He'll expect mother to call me off, Gwen realised, as she

remembered how Howell had pretended to be ill. It had kept her far away enough to prevent her from sensing his magic. *What does he have on her?*

She hesitated, wondering just what she should do. If she went to deal with Howell, her mother's life might be destroyed... but if she did nothing, Howell would be destroying other lives for years to come, until someone finally killed him. She couldn't leave him free. If his secrets got out, Polite Society would hate her... but then, they hated her anyway. Besides, she could always force him to destroy the evidence before throwing him in jail.

"You're going to stay here for a few days," she told Polly. The maid looked alarmed. "Don't worry about the house; the police will keep their guard on it. You can have a rest here."

She stood up, winked goodbye and walked out of the door. "Make sure she eats properly," she ordered the guard. "And if she wants more books to read, find her some."

"Yes, Milady," the guard said, clearly used to taking care of the prisoners. "When should she be released?"

"I'll deal with that," Gwen said. Of course; there would be no formal jail term for Polly. She wasn't *really* under arrest. "Just make sure you take care of her."

She felt cold rage growing in her breast as she walked up to the ground floor and headed out of the building. Howell had to be stopped – and squashed like a bug, if he refused to come quietly. Master Thomas would just have gone to confront him at once; Gwen could afford to do nothing less, not if she wanted to build up a reputation of her own. She spied Sir Charles as he climbed out of a cab and waved at him. He smiled back at her.

"Apparently Howell paid several debts," he said, as they walked towards his carriage. "But I didn't find anything linking him to Travis..."

"I found it," Gwen said. She explained quickly about Howell's talent. "He offered to pay Sir Travis's debts."

Sir Charles paled. "How long has he been reading minds?"

Gwen shrugged. "He's clearly mastered the talent," she

said. "That probably means that he developed it when he started to mature into an adult – I don't think there's ever been a child with the talent who remained sane. We can ask him after we arrest him."

"You intend to arrest him?" Sir Charles asked. "Don't you need a warrant?"

"I am the Royal Sorceress and he's an unregistered magician," Gwen explained, as she climbed into the carriage. "It is my duty to deal with him – and I don't need a warrant as long as I have a good reason to believe that he *is* an unregistered magician. Testing him would only take a few seconds, after all."

"You might want to consider not taking him alive," Sir Charles warned. "How many friends do you think he has in Polite Society?"

"You mean people who are too scared of him to say anything," Gwen snapped. Master Thomas might well have considered not trying to take Howell alive. She couldn't afford to do that, not when she knew how far her tutor had been prepared to go at the end. "We can have him tried by the Royal Committee, should I be proved right. If not... it might prove embarrassing."

She looked over at him. "If you don't want to come..."

"I'll come," Sir Charles assured her, quickly. "You're going to need someone to watch your back."

Gwen sat back as the carriage rattled onto the streets, composing herself as best as she could. It would be nice if Howell came quietly, but she had a feeling that he wouldn't, not when he had so many enemies who might just take advantage of his indisposition to burgle his house or simply have him assassinated while he was in jail. Maybe they would decide that they were going to be ruined anyway and lash out at Howell while they could.

She looked back at Sir Charles and smiled. Somehow, his presence felt comforting, rather like the times she'd played with David before he'd grown up. It felt *right* that he was there.

"Let me do the talking," she said, flatly. Lestrade would throw a fit if Sir Charles gave the impression that he was working for the Royal College. "You just look tough."

Chapter Twenty-Seven

wen hefted her cane – passed down from Master Thomas – as she jumped down from the carriage and landed neatly on the pavement. It felt reassuringly solid in her hand, although if she had to use it as a weapon she would be in some trouble. Behind her, Sir Charles checked his revolver before jumping down beside her. He gave her a grin that suggested that he was ready for trouble.

"Park over there," Gwen ordered the coachman, "and stay there until we come for you."

She looked up at Sir Charles, wondering how he managed to look so confident. Gwen *always* felt nervous before wading in to arrest a rogue magician; very few of them came quietly, even after the Swing's aftermath had created a general amnesty for unregistered magicians who registered themselves with the Royal College. Howell might be a Talker, but there was no reason why he couldn't have other magicians on his side.

"Follow my lead," she said, quietly.

Sir Charles nodded. "Understood," he said. "I'll be right behind you."

Gwen hid a smile – very few men in London would have been happy letting a girl walk first into danger – as she strode over to the guardhouse, pasting a confident expression on her face. The guard looked confused, then startled, as she held up her card rather than passing it to him. That *always* meant trouble.

"Lady Gwen and Sir Charles, here to see Mr. Howell," she said. Legally, she could have informed the guard that Howell was under arrest, but he might well be more loyal to his master than the law. "You will take us to him at once."

The guard hesitated. "I will have to call the house and..."

Gwen cut him off. "This is a matter of vital importance to the Royal Sorcerers Corps," she said, sharply. "You will take us to your master at once."

She prepared Charm, ready to force the guard to surrender, but he gave way before that was required. He led them up the path towards the house, glancing around nervously as if he expected someone or something to leap out of the bushes at any moment. Gwen puzzled over it – Howell didn't seem the type to keep dangerous animals on the grounds, even if they had been large enough for such creatures – before realising that Howell had to be a dangerous master when crossed. The guard had to know that they had no appointment.

Inside, they were met by the butler. "You will take us to Howell, at once," Gwen said, flatly. The guard who'd escorted them so far made his escape while the butler was preparing his rebuttal. "We need to speak with him."

The butler was clearly made of sterner stuff than the guard. "Do you have a warrant?"

Gwen scowled at his tone. "I have blanket permission to raid houses if I suspect that unregistered magicians are operating within," she said, tartly. "Now, take us to Howell or I will place you under arrest for obstructing me."

The butler bowed – so deeply that it was clearly meant to be insulting – and turned, leading them towards Howell's sickroom. Gwen found herself wondering if Howell would pretend to be sick again, before pushing the thought aside and concentrating on her surroundings. The other servants seemed to be nowhere in evidence.

She frowned as the butler opened a different door. "Lady Gwen and Sir Charles, sir," he said, announcing them. "They have no warrant."

Gwen stepped past him and into the room. Howell was sitting in a comfortable armchair at the far end of the room, a humourless smile playing over his lips. He wore a suit instead of a nightshirt, somehow looking far more dangerous. In the light from the gas lamps, he seemed far more dangerous than Gwen had realised. There was something almost serpentine about his appearance.

"Well," he said. "*This* is a surprise."

"Mr. Howell," Gwen said, flatly. She'd memorised the whole routine at Lestrade's insistence. "You are under arrest on suspicion of practising magic without a licence or registration papers. It is my duty to warn you that you do not have to say anything at this time, but anything you do say may be taken down and used against you in a court of law. I must also test you for magic now..."

Howell lifted a finger. A second later, the side wall exploded inwards, throwing chunks of debris towards Gwen and Sir Charles. Gwen shielded herself automatically as she sensed two sources of magic coming through where the wall had been, both illegal magicians. Magic crackled through the air, picking up more debris and slamming it towards Gwen. Both magicians were Movers, she realised. If there were any others, she couldn't sense them.

She pulled her own magic around her, then reached out towards the lead magician. He was strong, but untrained; it was easy to slam enough magic into his shield to send him staggering backwards. The other seemed to be more determined; Gwen had barely a second's warning before he picked her up with his magic, shield and all, and threw her into the far wall. She winced as her shield slammed into the wall, then drew on her magic, directing a beam of raw energy towards the Mover. There was a brilliant shimmer of light as magic crackled over his shield. She couldn't help noticing that he looked surprised... didn't he know who he was fighting?

Gwen yanked herself forward and slammed her magic into his, sending him staggering backwards. He had more raw power than she'd realised, but he hadn't quite grasped what it meant to fight a Master Magician. Gwen borrowed Sir James's idea, reshaped her magic and poked into his protective bubble. He let out a yelp and jumped backwards, barely avoiding the beam of magic she threw at him.

"Sit down and surrender," she ordered, pushing as much Charm into her voice as she could. "Give up!"

Both magicians seemed to hesitate, before shaking off the effect. Gwen cursed inwardly and scooped up several pieces of debris, infusing them with magic before hurling them at the two magicians. Their bubbles wavered alarmingly as the debris exploded, shaking their confidence as well as their magic. And then they returned to the attack.

A blast of light struck Gwen's bubble; a Blazer had entered the fight. Gwen looked up, saw a man wearing a servant's uniform and drew on her magic, picking him up and hurling him into the wall. A Blazer had no protective bubble to shield him; he struck the wall hard enough to crack his skull. Gwen grinned, knowing that she'd regret it afterwards, and looked up at the two Movers. If they'd had the same skill and experience as Merlin, she would have been dead by now. But as it was, they seemed to want to retreat.

"Give up," she said, again. "I promise you both a fair hearing..."

They hit her together, slamming their power into her bubble. Gwen felt it buckling and stepped to one side, barely noticing that Sir Charles was fighting two other servants, both of whom seemed to be carrying clubs rather than firearms. One of the Movers leapt forward, trying to grab hold of her magic; she reached out with her own, tangled the two magic fields together and slammed him into the wall. There was a fearsome crash as parts of the roof started to cave in. The Mover turned, his magic flickering in and out of existence, and she drove a beam of energy through his skull. His entire body caught fire; Gwen heard, or thought she heard, a scream before he crumbled to the floor.

She turned to face the other Mover, who picked up and threw a grand piano at her with the force of his magic. Gwen winced, realised that she couldn't hope to block it and jumped upwards, using her magic to fly over the piano as it hurtled underneath her. A moment later, she threw her own magic into direct conflict with his, pushing against his protective bubble. His face was twisted with effort as he tightened his defences, keeping her out. Gwen pushed down, smiling inwardly at the expression on his face. From his point of view, the foolish female was actually strengthening his shield.

Gwen met his eyes, then nodded downwards as she sent magic crawling through the floorboards. Her infusing talent was nowhere near as developed as a pure Infuser, but it hardly mattered. The blast was uncontrolled, yet confined within the Mover's protective bubble. It collapsed a second after its creator was blown to bits. Gwen staggered backwards as the backlash struck her, then shrugged it off. There was no time to collapse herself.

Sir Charles had knocked down two servants and was battling three more. He seemed to be enjoying himself, although Gwen was sure that three-to-one were bad odds. She lashed out with her magic and slammed two of them back out the doorway and into the corridor, then turned to find Howell. He had crept away during the fighting... cursing, Gwen ran after him and saw the blackmailer heading out of a side door. No doubt he thought he could be over the wall and away before the fighting came to an end. She reached out, caught him with her magic and pulled him back inside.

"Sit down," she ordered, as she slammed him into the armchair. Changing wasn't her forte either, but it was easy enough to reshape the chair to produce makeshift handcuffs. Howell struggled against them, glaring up at her; thankfully, he wasn't strong enough to break the wood. Gwen would have had to do something less pleasant to keep him still if he had been. "And be quiet."

Sir Charles finished knocking down the servant and looked over at her. "Jesus Christ," he said, as his gaze moved from Gwen to the half-destroyed house. "Is this what it's always like for you?"

Gwen winced inwardly, wondering if he would decide that he no longer wanted anything to do with her. The house had seemed solid until Howell's Movers and Gwen had fought at point-blank range; now, it seemed on the verge of collapse. One of Gwen's tutors had spoken about supporting walls and pillars that helped keep the roof up; the fight might well have knocked one or more of them out of position. And a solid wall was so badly damaged that a large wardrobe had been knocked down, revealing another hidden safe beyond. It looked large enough to allow someone to step inside without feeling cramped.

"Sometimes," she said. Apart from the practice skirmish with Merlin, she hadn't fought a battle of such violence since Master Thomas had died. One Mover would have been easy to kill. "Can you check the bodies?"

"You'll regret this," Howell informed her. "Do you know how many friends I have in high places?"

"I have a vague idea how many people you have blackmailed," Gwen said, tiredly. "Did we kill all of your horde of magicians or are there others out there?"

Howell merely smirked. "Even you must realise that you have overstepped yourself," he said. "And you" – he looked up at Sir Charles – "are not untouchable either."

"I've been threatened by experts," Sir Charles said, as he checked the bodies one by one. "You're nothing to an Emir who has been known to have his cooks hauled off and beheaded for having the nerve to undercook his meals. And you really *don't* want to know what he did to his wife when he discovered that she was having an affair with his chief huntsman."

He looked over at Gwen. "The magicians are dead," he said, shortly. "I killed one of the servants, but the others are still alive."

"Find something to tie them up," Gwen ordered. "Then go check the rest of the house; if there are any other servants, they're under arrest too. But be careful."

There was a faint snicker from Howell as soon as Sir Charles had left the room. "You should be more careful, my dear," he sneered. "Don't you know what I can do?"

Gwen shrugged. "The entire world knows what sort of child I was," she said. If they hadn't known, Colonel Sebastian's *hints* would have pointed them in the right direction. "And you had at least three illegal magicians in this house, working for you. Hiring an illegal magician is, in itself, illegal."

She smiled, tiredly. "Speaking of which..."

Howell cringed away as she reached for him and touched his forehead, keeping her mental shields firmly in place. She felt a mental attack as soon as she made physical contact – and sensed magic, bubbling just under Howell's skin. Even without the attack, she would have had the proof she needed. She was right. Howell *was* an unregistered Talker.

"I saw your feelings for him," Howell said, as she broke contact. "Do you know that he's a bastard son?"

Gwen winced. Howell was a better mind-reader than she'd realised. But then, he had had about as much practice as Irene and fewer scruples.

"I know the truth of his origins," she said, softly. "And you know what? I don't care."

She gathered herself as she stared down at him. "Tell me," she said, forcing Charm into her words. "Why did you go to visit Sir Travis?"

Howell glared at her, his lips firmly pressed closed.

"You *will* answer," Gwen said, strengthening the Charm. "Why did you go to Sir Travis's house?"

His lips opened, then he managed to close them. Gwen was impressed, despite herself; few people could resist such strong Charm. But she needed answers.

"You *will* answer," she repeated, then changed tack. "Did you go there intending to tell him about Lady Elizabeth's previous relationship?"

"Yes," Howell said, then clamped his mouth shut again. The simpler question had worked its way through his defences.

Gwen smiled, coldly. "And you found out from reading the maid's mind that he had debts to pay?"

"Yes," Howell said. He spoke on, although she couldn't tell if the Charm was finally breaking him down or if he was trying to overwhelm her with words. "He refused to take my money and ordered me to leave. So I did."

Blood dripped down from his mouth as he changed the subject. "I know your mother's greatest secret," he said, tauntingly. "If you don't let me go, the secret will come out and she will be *disgraced*."

Gwen glared at him, but he hadn't finished.

"I know many secrets," he leered. He sounded almost dazed. "I know things about your previous Master that would make you blush. Or about some of the men you rely on in Cavendish Hall. Why do you *think* I was able to hire so many magicians for so long?"

"Master Thomas is dead," Gwen said, coldly. What did Howell know? She wasn't sure that *she* wanted to know. "And I know too many of his secrets."

"There are ones that no one dared write down," Howell informed her. "I know them."

"Later," Gwen said, as she pushed more Charm into her voice. "Do you know who murdered Sir Travis?"

"No," Howell admitted.

Gwen winced as the trickle of blood from his mouth dripped onto the carpet. "Do you know who might have a motive to murder Sir Travis?"

Howell actually giggled. "The owner of the Golden Turk?"

His giggling grew nastier. "Always rumours about that place," he added. "Some of them were even confirmed. My, oh my, how easy it is for someone to compromise themselves when they get too close to the east. They take it up the rear end, they do."

Gwen had a nasty feeling that she knew what that meant; she certainly didn't want to enquire further. "Do you know anything about Hiram Pasha?"

"Typical shifty Turk," Howell said. The daze in his voice was growing stronger. "Undercuts his enemies by drawing funds from Turkey, the nasty bugger. He can undersell them all and put them out of business, then start jacking up prices. Should be laws against it. Probably are, but no one cares if you have the leverage and I do..."

Gwen frowned. Lord Mycroft had said that Hiram Pasha was a spy for the Sultan, who was presumably bankrolling his business. With that advantage, he *could* afford to undercut everyone else... but it would make him enemies, who might have a good reason to publicly question the value of a Turkish alliance. And it would put British citizens out of work... it didn't take much to spark the fires of xenophobia in London.

Howell's voice suddenly sounded a great deal more rational. "I can forgive you the mess you have made of my home," he said. "You can release me; I'll destroy the evidence I accumulated on your mother and give you what I found on the men who are supposed to work for you. There will be no need to mention this to anyone..."

Gwen felt her temper snap. "Damn you," she snapped, Charm flowing into her voice. "What do you have on my mother?"

"I... I won't tell you," Howell said. Blood was leaking from his nose. It happened to Talkers who pushed themselves too far, but no one was quite sure why. "You'll have to bargain with me."

"No," Gwen hissed. She turned up the pressure as far as she could, hitting him with enough Charm to make an army surrender without a fight. "You will tell me..."

There was a sudden rush of... *something* and Howell slumped in his chair. Gwen swore like a trooper, realising that he'd been pushing against her mind all along, and peered down at him. Drool was dripping from his opened mouth; the stench reaching her nostrils suggested that he'd soiled himself. Carefully, she touched his forehead and sensed... nothing. His mind seemed to have completely gone.

What the hell had she done?

Chapter Twenty-Eight

think I broke his mind," Gwen confessed, as Sir Charles stepped back into the wrecked room. "Did you find anyone else?"

"A couple of maids and a cook," Sir Charles said. "I tied all three of them up and left them in the kitchen."

"Good," Gwen said. She looked down at Howell's twitching body and tried to tell herself not to feel guilty. "I don't know if he can recover from what I did to him."

"There is no shortage of people who will thank you," Sir Charles said, rather dryly. "I dare say that half of London will be singing your praises by the end of the day."

Gwen shrugged. Maybe he was right... or maybe they would just end up more scared of her than ever. Had Master Thomas ever snapped a person's mind? Some talents caused madness, particularly if they were developed too early, but she'd never heard of anyone being driven into a catatonic state by an outsider.

"Maybe," she said, looking over at the safe. "I need you to go get the police – again."

"You'd think that someone would have called them already," Sir Charles pointed out. "This is a wealthy area..."

"Howell wouldn't have thanked them for calling the police," Gwen said. It was quite possible that he'd had something on all of his neighbours, something to keep them minding their own business at all times. "Take the carriage and see if you can find someone senior – and discreet, if Lestrade isn't around."

Sir Charles gave her an odd look, then nodded and

walked out the room. Gwen turned her attention back to Howell and frowned, wondering if his mind was trapped inside itself, unable to break free. Or maybe it had completely departed his body, leaving nothing more than an empty shell. There was no way to know, but Gwen was sure of one thing. The body would die unless someone fed and watered it every day.

She turned and walked towards the exposed safe, reaching out with her mind to study it. In some ways, it was simpler than Sir Travis's safe, suggesting that Howell hadn't fully trusted any magician. On the other hand, even the most competent Mover would have trouble breaking in; the locking mechanism was astonishingly complex. And she would have bet half her salary that Howell had been the only one with the combination to get inside.

Gritting her teeth, she used her magic to carefully unpick the lock. It was clever, she realised, devilishly clever... and if she hadn't been so good at multitasking, it might well have defeated her. Pull the wrong part of the lock with magic and heavy bolts would fall, sealing the safe beyond hope of access. It made her wonder, as the safe clicked open, why someone hadn't simply sealed the safe before. But Howell had just been too intimidating to challenge openly.

She pulled the door open and looked inside. It was larger than she'd realised, easily the size of a small office, the walls lined with shelves. The shelves were covered in paper folders, each one marked in neat precise handwriting. Gwen picked up one of the folders and glanced at it, absently. It was marked Lord Horatio Nelson. Inside, she found a handful of papers and stared down at them, slowly realising that they dealt with the birth of Lady Hamilton's love child. But everyone knew that the poor child was Nelson's illegitimate daughter. There was no blackmail value in *that*.

Slowly, a scandal began to emerge as she read through the papers. Nelson's wife had died in 1805, taken by an illness that – some suspected – might have been poison. What if Lord Nelson had killed her so that Lady Hamilton could take her place? But she hadn't... Lord Nelson had never married her. Had Howell played a role in ensuring that such a marriage never took place?

Carefully, feeling almost defiled, she put the papers back in the folder and returned the folder to its place, before looking along the list of names. Several jumped out at her, including Lord Mycroft; surprised, she opened it and saw a simple note written in the same handwriting. *Where is his sister?* Gwen frowned; Lord Mycroft had never mentioned a sister to her, but then he was an intensely private man. Apart from his brother, she knew nothing about his family, not even where they came from. She turned the note over and read a second piece of handwriting on the back. *Connections to France through Horace Vernet?*

"Not exactly something you could use for blackmail," Gwen muttered to herself. The Royal Family had strong ties to monarchies on the continent, even the French or Spanish. There weren't *that* many upper-class families that didn't have at least a vague connection with the world outside Britain. "But what if he used it at a crucial moment?"

She put the folder back and started hunting for Sir Travis's folder. It was at the front of the safe, suggesting that Howell had looked at it recently; she took it off the shelf and opened it, half-afraid of what she might find. But there was almost nothing, apart from a note stating that Sir Travis owed four thousand pounds – maybe more – to the Golden Turk. The other papers consisted of biographical notes, including the titbit that Sir Travis was a Sensitive. That explained, Gwen decided, why Howell hadn't risked reading Sir Travis's mind. The Sensitive would probably pick up on it and react harshly.

But there was no motive for murder in the files.

Cursing herself, she tossed the folder out of the safe and started looking for others, wondering how many of them she dared read. The Earl of North Hollow was accused of having had his sport with a young noblewoman against her will, although there was no proof and Gwen suspected that it was only good for nasty gossip. She'd met the Earl once and had ended up feeling thoroughly disgusted. His family, equally disgusted, had largely barred him from London.

An oversized folder belonged to another nobleman Gwen knew, someone who had served in India, America and even France during the brief and aborted attempt to capture Toulon in 1801. His folder branded him a liar, a cheat, a braggart and an adulterer – and finished with a note from his manservant, claiming that he'd cheated in a duel of honour with another man in the same regiment. *That* would ruin a man's career, even if the rest of it might be shrugged off. Gwen put the file back on the shelf, then looked down at one marked LADY ELIZABETH BRACKNELL. Bracing herself, she opened the fire and found the compromising letters.

Lady Elizabeth had been a charming – and explicit - correspondent, she realised. Gwen had spent the last nine months in Cavendish Hall and *she* didn't know half as much as Lady Elizabeth had done, when she was younger... how had she found out so much? It was difficult to imagine Lady Bracknell reading the trashy romantic novels that gave printing presses a bad name... but how else? No *wonder* Howell had been so convinced that the letters would destroy Lady Elizabeth's engagement. Poor Sir Travis would have had no choice; he would have *had* to assume that his fiancée was an *experienced* woman.

Gwen pocketed the letters, intending to return them to Lady Elizabeth, then started looking for other names. Somewhat to her surprise, the next one she saw was her own. What had Howell known about *her*? She pulled the folder off the shelf and read through it quickly, allowing herself a moment of relief when she realised that he hadn't really known much, beyond what was already well known to Polite Society. There was a snide suggestion that her chastity might be in doubt – after all, she *had* slept in Cavendish Hall without a chaperone – but little else.

The next folder was marked LADY MARY CRICHTON.

Gwen argued with herself for a long moment. Part of her wanted – needed – to know what Howell had held over her mother's head; part of her really didn't want to know the truth. The secret could die with Howell, unless he'd taken precautions to ensure that his death resulted in all of the information being distributed... she didn't really *need* to know, did she? And then she remembered how often her mother had forbidden her from reading specific books, stunting her education. She'd been so ignorant that she'd thought that she was dying when her body finally started to mature.

She opened the folder and flicked through the pages. The handwriting was different; an older woman's, she decided, written to confuse rather than to reveal. Gwen had plenty of experience with David's handwriting and it was still difficult to parse out the words. But when she did, she almost fainted for the second time.

"She couldn't have," she said, out loud. But Lady Mary had been *terrified* of Howell. She'd known that he had something on her, something that could never see the light of day. "She..."

Abruptly, she felt rage and magic billowing up within her. How could her mother have lied to her for so long? How could she? The temperature rose rapidly; the folders started to blacken, then burst into flames. Gwen, lost in her fury, barely noticed until her trousers started to catch fire, shocking her back into full awareness. Choking for breath, she stumbled out of the safe towards the holes the fight had smashed in the walls. There was fresh air from where they'd cracked the side of the house.

Coughing, she turned and watched as Howell's collection of dirty little secrets were reduced to dust and ash. Pompey would have approved, she thought, remembering the copy of *Life of Pompey* by Plutarch that she'd borrowed from David. He'd burned thousands of incriminating letters after the end of the fighting in Spain, hoping to put an end to the civil unrest gripping Rome. It had worked, for a time.

But it hadn't entirely been her choice, had it? Her own thoughts mocked her. What would she have done if she hadn't lost her temper? So many famous names, so many belonging to people who had mocked and sneered when she became Royal Sorceress. If she'd taken the files, could she have used them to ensure that no one ever sneered at her ever again? Or maybe she should have revealed everything, exposing the hypocrisy and deceit that ran through Polite Society. What sort of mayhem would *that* have caused?

She looked back at Howell, remembering her first impressions of the man. He'd been a monster, far worse than any of the noblemen or criminals Jack had killed in his campaign to unsettle the establishment. Howell's activities had shattered lives, ruined reputations and created nightmares that had never truly ended. Everyone he blackmailed must have been left wondering if they would hear from him again, no matter what assurances he offered. They would have been looking over their shoulders for the rest of their lives.

It would have ruined her, she realised numbly. If she'd kept all the secrets, if she'd *used* them, it would have destroyed her soul. She might have got away with it, but she wouldn't have been the same person afterwards. Master Thomas had stepped over the line to preserve society, the society he'd fought to upheld throughout his adult life. What would *her* excuse be?

And yet she was still angry at her mother. How *could* she?

She put the folder to one side, beside the one for Sir Travis, and then looked into the safe. The papers had been destroyed and the flames were slowly dying down, having scorched the metal walls, leaving nothing but ashes. Gwen watched the final flames flicker away and die, then drew on her power, scattering the ashes so completely that no one, even Mycroft's brother, could hope to put them back together. Perhaps Sir Charles was right. There *would* be thousands of people who would thank her for what she'd done.

"Lady Gwen," Inspector Hopkins said, as he entered the room. "What... what in God's name happened here?"

Gwen smiled, although she felt no real humour. Hopkins had always considered himself a more intellectual detective than Lestrade, but he had never really accepted

Gwen's authority on the grounds that she'd come into her position through good luck rather than earning it fairly. In some ways, Gwen understood him better than she did Lestrade, yet there was no time for an argument. Or even a frank exchange of views.

"It doesn't matter," she said, tightly. "This is very much a magical affair."

She ignored his cross look and continued. "Mr. Howell needs to be taken to the hospital, where one of the Healers can take a look at him," she said. "If the Healers manages to actually *Heal* him, he is to be treated as a rogue Charmer and gagged as well as cuffed. He is to *remain* cuffed and gagged until I see him personally."

Hopkins nodded. Scotland Yard had good reason to be nervous around Charmers – or any other kind of magician, for that matter. They turned the world upside down.

"His servants are to be taken to the nearest jail and kept there, again, until I have had a chance to take a proper look at them," she added. "I think we killed all of the magicians, but there's no way to be entirely sure. You can hold them under Section Five of the Rogue Magicians Act of 1820, if necessary. I don't think that many of them will object."

Hopkins nodded. Section Five covered non-magicians who helped rogue magicians to hide, or employed them. The servants might not be in hot water – it had been Howell, she assumed, who had employed the other magicians – but they might be glad to be in jail, once Howell's enemies realised that his power was broken. They might go after his servants just to see if any of them knew where he might have stored copies of his incriminating documents.

"Yes, Milady," he said. "When will you deal with them?"

"I have another matter to attend to," Gwen said. It was true; besides, she wanted to make sure that Howell couldn't be Healed before she started talking to his servants. "I will consult with Cavendish Hall afterwards, so we can decide properly what charges should be filed."

She scowled at Howell as two burly policemen picked

him up and carried him out of the room. He didn't respond at all to their manhandling.

"After that, I want this house *sealed*," she added. "*No one* goes in or out without my permission, no one at all. If someone comes, you are to take their names and business, but they are to be denied access. Have officers patrolling the grounds; someone might decide to climb the back wall."

"Yes, Milady," Hopkins said. He sounded more than a little irritated at her constant stream of orders, but Gwen found it hard to care. "I shall see to it at once."

Gwen nodded and stood back, leaving the policemen to get on with it. The two maids were loudly protesting their innocence as they were cuffed and marched out of the house, followed by the cook, who seemed to be in a state of shock. A handful of policemen picked up the stunned servants and dragged them out of the building; they probably wouldn't wake up until they reached jail. One of them clearly had a broken leg, but there was no Healer at the jail. He'd have to hope that the prison doctor knew what he was doing...

Some hope, Gwen thought, sourly. Even with the new laws, prisons were far from healthy places – particularly for prisoners who were already wounded when they were brought in and placed in a cell. Unless, of course, the prisoner happened to have noble blood – or a great deal of money.

Sir Charles looked over at the blackened safe. "Those were all of his papers?"

"I think so," Gwen said. The entire house would have to be searched – the *third* house that had been searched since Sir Travis had been murdered. She hoped that Hopkins could trust his policemen if they *did* find something incriminating; the temptation to use it would be incredibly strong. "How many other stashes do you think he had?"

"None," Sir Charles said. He picked up a piece of ash, studied it thoughtfully and then ground it to dust. "Who could he trust to take care of them?"

Gwen considered it for a long moment, then put the matter aside. "I need you to drive me to my mother's house," she said. Her anger was still there, ready to be unleashed. "Can you do that?"

Sir Charles hesitated. "Are you sure you're up to visiting your mother?"

"Yes," Gwen snapped. No doubt Lady Mary would wonder if he'd asked her to marry him when they arrived. She was in for a rude shock. "I have to see her. Now."

Sir Charles nodded and left the room. Gwen started to follow him and then stopped, staring around at the devastation. If three untrained magicians – and her – could do so much damage, what would happen when – if – magicians went to war against other magicians? How dangerous would it be in London if magic were used in an outright fight... or airships were used to drop explosives on the city... or steam-powered warships sailed up the Thames. For a moment, she almost felt sorry for the people who disliked magic and distrusted *her*. Their world was changing and they no longer felt safe.

She looked down at the file in her hand, then walked after Sir Charles. Perhaps he was right and it wasn't the best time to talk to her mother, but it had to be done. She was *not* going to allow her mother to treat her like a child again.

And Lady Mary had to answer for what she had done.

Chapter Twenty-Nine

ord Rudolf is in the study, talking with Lord Flitch-Fletcher," the butler said, as he showed Gwen into her old home. "Lady Mary is in her study."

"Thank you," Gwen grated, as she walked past him. She'd had the whole drive to build up her temper and it needed release, before she lost control of her magic. Even Sir Charles hadn't been able to calm her down.

She stepped into her mother's study – a room she'd rarely been allowed to enter as a child – and closed the door firmly behind her. Lady Mary looked up, surprised and then concerned, as Gwen dropped Howell's folder on the desk in front of her mother.

"I took it from Howell," Gwen said. "What were you *thinking*?"

Lady Mary opened the folder and read the first sheet of paper. Her face paled; for a long moment, Gwen was convinced that she was going to faint. Then she looked up at her daughter, her eyes wide with horror – and shame. Polite Society was unforgiving when someone broke the rules and Lady Mary hadn't just broken them, she'd shattered them into tiny pieces. Gwen refused to look away as her mother swallowed hard. Whatever she'd imagined, she hadn't imagined *this*.

"I had no choice," she protested. "I couldn't..."

"Every day, ever since I was born, you tried to mould me into a perfect young lady," Gwen hissed. "You told me what to do and corrected me ruthlessly; you wanted someone you could marry off to someone of a higher rank than us. And yet you had *this* in your past. How *dare* you?"

"It was your father's child," Lady Mary said. "We... we just couldn't keep it."

"You're lying," Gwen snapped. Everyone knew that a bride could do in six months what a wife needed nine to do. Polite Society wouldn't have commented if the formalities were observed. "When did you plan to tell me about the brother or sister I never had?"

Her voice hardened. "Who did you sleep with to get pregnant?"

Lady Mary shook her head. "I'm sorry," she muttered. "But I had no choice."

Gwen looked down at the documents. Howell had found out – somehow – that Lady Mary had visited an abortionist, three months before her marriage to Lord Rudolf. If it had been Lord Rudolf's child, it wouldn't have been *that* much of a problem... but someone else's would have been a major scandal. The wedding would have been cancelled, leaving Lady Mary forever tainted with a reputation for premarital sex. And the child would probably have been given up for adoption.

Her mother started to cry. "I had no choice," she repeated. "I didn't realise that I could get pregnant until it was too late. My mother arranged the appointment with the abortionist..."

"And you killed your child," Gwen said, coldly. She knew, through Lucy, that abortionists were common in the poorer parts of London, but she had never realised that upper class women went to them too. "I should have had a half-brother or sister, if you hadn't killed the child."

"You wouldn't have existed at all," Lady Mary said, rallying. "Do you think Rudolf would have kept me if there was proof that I..."

"Go on," Gwen sneered. "If there was proof that you gave yourself to another man before your wedding?"

Her anger grew stronger. "Every day, you told me to be the perfect lady," she snapped. "And you were nothing more than a hypocrite! You lied to me!"

"I did what I thought was best for you, even after you became a... a magician," Lady Mary said. "I didn't want you to grow up like me!"

"Always running, fearful that someone would catch you out," Gwen said, quietly. "What did Howell demand from you in exchange for his silence."

"Six thousand pounds," Lady Mary said. "It was my legacy from my grandfather, enough money to ensure that I would be a catch in society... I had to transfer it from my bank to Howell, knowing that my husband might one day want to use it. But I had no choice."

Gwen felt a twinge of sympathy. It was rare for a woman to control what she brought to the marriage; customarily, it was given to her husband to use as he saw fit. Lady Mary's grandfather had been staunchly traditional in such matters; he'd always believed that women were incapable of doing anything unless they were led by men. Her mother might, depending on how the courts looked at it, have stolen from her own husband.

"And Howell promised you that no one else would ever know," Gwen said, remembering what he'd told Lady Elizabeth. "But he kept the files... and I found them."

She looked down at her mother. "Who was he?"

"It doesn't matter," Lady Mary said, softly. "He never knew that he had a child. Our lives parted before I knew that I was with child; I never told him the truth. By then, I was engaged to Rudolf..."

Gwen remembered everything her mother had done, in the guise of teaching her to be a proper young lady. The endless lessons in etiquette, the ritualised banquets when she'd pretended to be hosting the highest aristocratic families, the dresses and... and so much else, all blurred together into a stifling childhood. And if she hadn't had magic, she would have been married off, unaware that her mother's past might overshadow her future. If Lady Mary's secret had come out, Gwen's husband might have separated from her. It was believed that certain tendencies ran in families.

Her mother had kept Gwen when others might have abandoned her, Gwen knew. But that didn't make up for everything she'd done.

"Howell is... unlikely to recover," Gwen said, hoping

that she was right. Part of her wouldn't care any longer if her mother was disgraced, but she knew just how many others would be threatened by the blackmailer's recovery. "I think your secret is safe."

Lady Mary looked up, her eyes stained with tears. "What did you do to him?"

"Broke his mind," Gwen said, flatly. She would *not* share the details with her mother. "I took your file, then burned the rest of them to ash. Howell's collection of dark secrets died with him."

Her mother relaxed, slightly. "Make sure you get the credit for it," she said, softly. "Your reputation will be made."

Gwen shrugged. "My reputation was ruined the first day I used magic," she snapped. She risked a question she would never normally have dared ask. "Am *I* my father's child?"

Lady Mary glared at her, one hand raised as if she were about to slap her daughter.

"You're Rudolf's girl, all right," she snapped. "And mine too, for my sins. There were enough times when I thought you were my punishment for what I had done."

"You killed an innocent child," Gwen said, flatly. Somehow, she would have been happier knowing that she *had* been adopted. "What sort of punishment do you think you deserve?"

"What sort of life do you think the child would have had?" Lady Mary demanded. "A known bastard" – Gwen had never heard her mother use any such word before – "in a society that blames the child for the sins of the parent! He would have been isolated, unable to grow and develop... if I'd kept him. If not, I would have had to hand him over to someone else to raise and I couldn't bear the thought of giving him up..."

"So you killed him instead," Gwen said. "You could have given him to one of the servants to raise..."

"I would have had to see him as a servant, or else favour him," Lady Mary said. "Do you not remember the Duke of Holdernesse?"

Gwen winced. The Duke had had an affair with one of

his chambermaids, eventually getting her pregnant. She'd died in childbirth, but he'd kept the boy, even though he could never have acknowledged him as a heir. And then he'd married a respectable woman and had a legitimate heir... until the day his bastard son's jealousy had got the better of him. The Duke's happy life had died along with his wife and younger son. Polite Society had gossiped for months afterwards.

And even if Lady Mary had given the unborn child the benefit of the doubt, she would still have had to explain her pregnancy to Lord Rudolf. He would have *known* that the newborn baby wasn't his child.

"I should tell everyone," Gwen snapped. Her mother's pale face went completely white. "Why not? You had a child killed because keeping him around would have exposed you."

"I had no choice," Lady Mary insisted. "I..."

"You gave up that choice when you let someone else into your bed," Gwen snapped back, angrily. Or had her mother been as ignorant as Gwen herself? Lady Mary had never read books her mother had forbidden her to read. She might well not have realised that she *could* get pregnant until it was far too late. "Didn't you even *think* about the possible consequences?"

"I was young and in love," Lady Mary said. She looked up at Gwen, eyes pleading for understanding. "Don't you understand why I sheltered you so much? I didn't want you to have to make the same choice!"

Lady Bracknell might have been the same, Gwen thought. If she hadn't been so controlling, her daughter would never have written such compromising letters... and ended up being blackmailed by Howell. And if Gwen hadn't scared so many possible suitors, would she have given herself to someone and ended up compromised herself.

"You would have driven me into rebellion," Gwen said, harshly. "If Master Thomas hadn't come for me..."

"Your place in society was destroyed," Lady Mary said. "You can never be part of Polite Society..."

Gwen started to laugh. "Why would I *want* to be part of

Polite Society?" She demanded. "How much of it is even *polite?*"

Her mother stared at her. Lady Mary had always defined her place in life by her position in society, rising up when she married Lord Rudolf, falling down when her daughter proved to be a magician. To her, a place in society – the chance to determine fashion and look down on those below her - was what made life worth living. It was a validation of her self-worth.

But Gwen would never have that, not even if she wanted it. Polite Society would prefer not to deal with the Royal Sorceress at all. The only person who might be close to her position was a Ruling Queen, a woman sitting in a man's chair and wielding power as a man. Queen Elizabeth's success had come from her refusal to marry, knowing that it would dilute her power... Queen Mary of England and Mary of Scotland had both weakened their positions when they married, even though they had needed to provide heirs. That, at least, wasn't something Gwen had to worry about.

"There were hundreds of files in Howell's safe, mother," she said. "Hundreds of names, some of them familiar, some of them *famous*. How many others in Polite Society have dark secrets like yours? All you really do is conceal your own sins and ruthlessly work over those unfortunate enough to have their sins revealed, hoping that it will save you from your own mistakes. Why don't you just admit to your sins and forget about them?"

"You had the benefit of my training," Lady Mary said, flatly. "You should know that it doesn't work like that."

"Of course not," Gwen snapped. "Who cares about the truth when all that matters is protecting one's good name?"

It hadn't been *that* long since John Wilkes had been forced to flee to France for what he'd written in his newspaper. With all of the new newspapers looking for ways to ensure that they lasted longer than a year, how long would it be before some of them started digging into the lives and times of the aristocrats who ruled the British Empire. The new laws on freedom of the press had been intended to prevent the politicians from covering up their own mistakes; Gwen suspected that it wouldn't be long before they realised that they'd made a dreadful mistake. And if Howell had gathered so much blackmail material, who knew what a newspaper could gather... and print.

"I don't want to see you again, *mother*," Gwen snapped, making the final word an insult. "You're a..."

A hand fell on her shoulder and she jumped.

"Gwen," Lord Rudolf snapped. "Come with me."

Gwen cursed herself as Lord Rudolf steered her out of her mother's study. She should have heard the door opening behind her... how much had her father heard? Lord Rudolf had been more inclined to focus on his son rather than his daughter, but he'd been worried about Gwen before Master Thomas had made him an offer. And yet... he didn't know what his wife had done before they were married. What would he feel if he did?

She had no time for reflection as her father pushed her into his study, a large room Gwen had been barred from for most of her life. David had only been allowed inside after he'd matured and gone to work for the family business; Gwen recalled daring him to slip inside when they'd both been children and bored. The last time she'd been inside was when Lord Mycroft and Master Thomas had arrived to take her away.

"You don't upset your mother like that," Lord Rudolf said, as soon as the door was closed. "The butler said that you were angry, but..."

Gwen scowled openly. There was no escaping the scrutiny of servants, was there?

"This is unacceptable behaviour," Lord Rudolf said. "And you have been pressuring the Milton Family..."

It took Gwen a moment to put it together. Of course; Lady Mortimer's niece, the same one who had taken Polly's jewels, had married into the Milton Family. She found it hard to believe that she'd actually had the nerve to complain to Gwen's *father* about it, but it did make a certain kind of sense. Most fathers had absolute authority over their offspring until they were married – and even then, they maintained some influence. Gwen was young and unmarried... and wouldn't be expected to do anything without her father's permission.

She couldn't help smiling. Was Lady Mortimer's niece completely insane?

"This isn't funny," Lord Rudolf thundered. "You are my daughter and I cannot afford to have you doing anything that would threaten the family name. I *order* you to abandon whatever you are doing with the Milton Family."

"No," Gwen said, flatly.

Lord Rudolf stared at her, then reached for his belt buckle. "You are my daughter," he repeated. "I will not tolerate disobedience..."

"I am *not* your daughter," Gwen said. The anger she'd felt towards her mother grew stronger; how *dare* anyone, even her father, try to pressure her into doing anything? "You signed me away to Master Thomas, remember? He became my legal father the moment you signed the papers."

"And he died," Lord Rudolf snapped. "You reverted back to me."

Gwen met his eyes, refusing to budge. "I read the legal papers very carefully," she said. "There was no formal provision for anything of the sort – I dare say that Master Thomas suspected that you might try to use me for your own political schemes. His death emancipated me – after all, you already cut me off from my biological family. And I have his fortune. Do you want to start a legal battle that would make you a laughing stock?

"I'm not under your authority any longer," she added, a moment later. "We can talk, as mature adults, if you like, but you can no longer command me."

She felt an odd moment of bitterness. What would her life have been like if her father had taught her, rather than her mother? David had become a stuffed shirt, a businessman and then a politician, but would Gwen have gone the same way? But then, Polite Society frowned on trade and would definitely frown on a *girl* handling trade... even though quite a few small businesses were owned and operated by women. Gwen's value lay in marriage and that had been destroyed the day she'd first used magic.

Her father glared at her, but he took his hand away from his belt. Whipping a son or daughter – or a servant – was common in society, but striking an aristocratic adult would have been assault; the victim could have sued or challenged him to a duel. She watched him thinking, hoping that he drew the right conclusions. The last thing she wanted was a public struggle between her and her father.

But he knew that Gwen was right; he had *no* legal claim on her... and if he did try to sue for her guardianship, he'd make himself a laughing stock. And then there was the problem of Master Thomas's fortune; Gwen could afford a long drawn-out legal battle, if she was determined to maintain her independence.

And I have friends in high places, she thought, quietly.

"So it would seem," Lord Rudolf said, softly. For a moment, she wondered if he'd read her thoughts before realising that it was unlikely. "But I do insist on you apologising to your mother."

"Later, perhaps," Gwen said, as she headed for the door. The anger that had driven her to come to her father's house and demand answers from her mother was still there, but mixed with sadness... and guilt. "Right now, I have to go home."

"*Gwen*," Lord Rudolf said. "Until you apologise, you will not be welcome in this house."

"Duly noted," Gwen said, opening the door. "And tell your friends that I will not fail in my duty, no matter what pressure they bring to bear upon me."

With that, she walked out of her father's study, leaving him alone.

Chapter Thirty

hat happened to you?"

Gwen climbed into the carriage, silently thanking God that she'd asked the coachman – and Sir Charles – to wait for her. Having to walk back to Cavendish Hall would not have been the best thing to do, even if she'd only walked as far as the nearest cab station.

"I had a... disagreement with my parents," Gwen said, as she sat down. Now that she was away from them, she was shaking, although she couldn't tell if it was rage of fear. The anger that had driven her onwards had become muted, overridden by bitterness and despair. How could she have been so horrible to her own mother? But how could her mother have been so horrible to her?

Sir Charles tapped the wall separating them from the coachman. "Take us to Cavendish Hall," he ordered, then looked at Gwen. "Do you want to talk about it?"

Gwen hesitated, unsure. She *wanted* to talk, but did she have a right to share her mother's secret any further? But she trusted Sir Charles; he'd gone with her into Howell's lair and helped her arrest his people. And he'd had his own problems with his family. Maybe he would be able to offer good advice.

"Howell had something on my mother," she admitted, and then went through the entire story. "I don't know what to do any longer."

Sir Charles put his hand on her shoulder. "Don't think about it while you're angry and hurting," he said, softly. "When you calm down, you can think about it rationally."

Gwen scowled at him, angrily. "Every time I think

about it I get angry," she said, crossly. "Does it ever get better?"

"You're young," Sir Charles said. "Trust me on this; everything hurts badly at first, from the pain of discovering the truth about your mother to learning that you've been sent into an ambush by some paper-pusher in London who can't read a map. The further you are from the event, the less anger you will feel. Then you calm down and deal with it."

"Wise advice," Gwen said, sarcastically. "How did it work out for you?"

"I went to India and had no contact with my family for years," Sir Charles said. "They gave me the name and nothing else; I built my own legend. Everything I mentioned in dispatches was all my own work. My family might want to embrace me again, but it is far too late."

Gwen had to smile, despite the bitterness and anger and rage. "They might think better of you now," she said. "You're a hero."

"That won't count in the long run," Sir Charles admitted. "Why do you think Lord Nelson is one of the loudest voices demanding war with France?"

"Because... he needs a war to boost his reputation," Gwen said. Lord Nelson had been famous for thrashing the French – and burning Tripoli to teach the Barbary pirates a lesson – but it had been nearly twenty years since he had last gone to war. The public would eventually forget why they loved him and then his enemies would pounce on him – and Lady Hamilton. "Are *you* going to start a war?"

"We were trying to prevent one in Central Asia," Sir Charles reminded her. "I think we succeeded, for the moment."

Gwen sighed. "I don't know what to do about my parents," she said, softly. "I didn't even know that my mother could *do* that."

Sir Charles snorted. "What makes you think that she was the only one who had an abortion before she married?"

"... Nothing," Gwen admitted. She was still astonished

that her mother and grandmother had known where to go to get an abortion. "How many others are there?"

"Maybe you shouldn't have destroyed those papers," Sir Charles said. "You could have found out."

Gwen shrugged. Part of her would have been tempted to use them if they had survived.

"I tell you this," Sir Charles said, softly. "There isn't an aristocratic family alive that doesn't have a dark secret buried in its past. Someone born on the wrong side of the blankets, someone killed because they were in the way, someone pressured into voting against their interests... sex, drugs, French dancing... it's all there, hidden in their memories and little else."

"I know," Gwen said, miserably. "I just... I just never thought that it could happen to *my* family."

She'd heard the stories, the whispers that moved faster than horses or even mental communication between Talkers. The families that had locked a mad aunt or child in the attic, refusing to even admit to her existence; the families that had concealed magicians far less uncommon than Gwen herself; the families that had muscled their way into Polite Society through a mixture of intimidation and bribery... but she'd never really grasped that her own family could have secrets. Or more secrets; Lady Mary would have kept Gwen herself a secret, if she could have done so.

Lord Rudolf had gone into trade, she recalled, when few aristocrats would sully their hands with actually earning money. What questionable deals had he made when he invested heavily in airships? How many of them would come back to haunt him now that he was respectable, with children at the forefront of their professions? And how many problems would David inherit when he took control of the family? There was no way to know, short of asking her father – and he was unlikely to give her a truthful answer. Her mind shied away from using Charm on him. It would have been worse than anything Howell had ever done.

"Me too," Sir Charles said. He looked down at the wooden floor, seemingly unwilling to meet her eyes. "I used to think that I was my father's son – I still think of him as my father, after everything that happened. But I wasn't... and I only found out when I discovered that my younger brother was named as the Heir in the will. If I'd been magical, maybe it would have been different for me..."

Gwen felt a pang of guilt. The men who'd operated the farms had insisted that magical children be treated exactly the same as children who had been born to their adopted families, but they'd had problems convincing the adoptive parents that they should treat the farm children as their firstborn heirs. No one had anticipated Sir Charles's older brother – his adopted brother – dying shortly after Sir Charles was adopted, leaving him as the nominal Heir. It must have been a terrible shock to discover that he had been effectively disowned – and then that he was no true blood relation of the Bellingham Family.

"Maybe," she said, softly. "Polite Society is cruel, isn't it?"

"It has always been cruel," Sir Charles said, with surprising fury. "I loved India, Gwen, because my birth or status didn't matter there, not among the natives. All that mattered was being able to represent the Empire; to fight and show the natives that we were the ones who *deserved* to rule. You'd be surprised how many India hands come from families that would prefer to be rid of them, or how little they want to go home."

Gwen wondered just how true that was. She'd never really thought about the world that existed outside Polite Society until Jack had rubbed her nose in just how many horrors there were in London, scant miles from Whitehall and the heart of the British Empire. The toffs either never realised that the poor were there, any more than Gwen had, or exploited them ruthlessly. Quite a few of the aristocrats who were forced to visit the Healers had contracted something unpleasant from visiting cheap brothels near the Rookery.

But India might be the same; a handful of aristocrats, British and Indian, ruling over a vast country, teeming with natives. Who knew just how happy the Indians were with their new overlords? Sir Charles had told her that one rebellion had been nipped in the bud, but how many others would there be in the future? Jack had brought the British Empire to its knees. What might an Indian do if he developed magic?

"Others go off to America," Sir Charles added. "Even after the rebellion, the Americans have been less concerned with status and society than ourselves."

Gwen nodded, tiredly. "It's worse for women," she whispered. "Apart from a few independent women, most of us are completely dependent upon our husbands."

"That might be why your mother chose to abort her child," Sir Charles pointed out, gently. "What sort of future might he have had if she'd kept him?"

"At least he would have *had* a future," Gwen said. She felt tears prickling at her eyes again as the day's events finally caught up with her. "All that time she was teaching me how to behave, my mother was hiding a secret. All that time!"

She found it hard to imagine the scope of Lady Mary's betrayal. If the truth had come out, Lord Rudolf would have had to divorce her, just to protect his own reputation. And if he'd done that, both Gwen and David would have been threatened with being disowned too; David, at least, *looked* like their father. But if Lord Rudolf had reason to doubt his wife's fidelity, he might well have taken the safer step of erasing his children from his family. No doubt he would have justified it to himself by claiming that there was no magic in his family, even if there was magic in Gwen.

And it would grow worse as time went by. David was married, with a child on the way... what would Laura's parents say, if they found out that David might be a bastard son? They might insist that their daughter separate herself from her husband, which would leave David's son without a mother ... or set the stage for a nasty legal battle over custody rights. And Gwen herself...

Her lips twitched. Master Thomas had effectively adopted her, before his death. *Her* position would be relatively secure.

Sir Charles reached for her as she started to cry and pulled her into a hug. For a moment, Gwen resisted... and then allowed his arms to enfold her. Her entire body was shaking as her emotions spun through rage and despair; her stomach suddenly growled, reminding her that she hadn't eaten anything since her fight with Howell's rogue magicians. How much energy had she burned up in the tussle?

And his lips were suddenly very close to hers.

Lady Mary would have said that it was improper for a gentleman to hug a lady, particularly when the gentleman wasn't *married* to the lady, but Gwen no longer cared what Lady Mary thought. Or anyone else... she leaned up and kissed him, feeling his warm lips pressing against hers. He pulled her forward, gently, and stroked her back as the kisses deepened, one by one. Gwen felt a heartbeat starting to race as she became aware of his comforting presence, calling to her.

She sighed as his hand reached down to stroke her bottom, then inch around to the front of her jacket. Part of her mind insisted that it wasn't right, that they were going too far too fast, but she found it hard to care. She *wanted* to have him, although she was no longer sure if it was because she liked him or because she wanted to lash out at her mother. Bracing herself, she touched his trousers... and felt his maleness underneath. The touch excited her...

His hand slipped into her jacket and caressed her breast. No one had ever touched her there and the sensation both excited and shocked her, reminding her of reality. They were in a coach heading to Cavendish Hall, with a coachman outside who might just be able to hear what they were doing. And if she was seen by anyone... she pulled back, wondering if he could stop now. Some of the young students at Cavendish Hall had talked about not being able to stop, when they hadn't realised that she could hear them.

And then he let her go.

Part of Gwen's mind regretted it, instantly. She could pull him to her and allow him to explore her as she explored him; she already knew that he would be willing.

But the rest of her knew better... and also knew that his unwillingness to push her spoke well of him. She looked up into his face and saw his eyes shining and felt... *something* deep within her, as if she were no longer alone against the world.

"I..."

"Don't worry," Sir Charles assured her, placing one finger on her lips. "We have all the time in the world."

Gwen nodded as she fixed her suit, making sure that there was no sign that she had been kissing anyone. Her suit had been rumpled during the fight, but thankfully it was intact; she pulled it closed, unable to repress a shiver as her hand touched where *he* had touched. She touched her lips gently, feeling a ghostly sensation where he'd kissed her...

"They're slightly puffy," Sir Charles said, softly. "But it fades very quickly."

Gwen reached into her handbag and produced a mirror. Peering into it, she muttered an oath; her lips were puffy, her face was flushed and she had clearly been crying. She took out a tissue and wiped her face, wishing that she'd spent more time listening to her mother's lectures on how a young girl should apply cosmetics. But she'd known that she wouldn't be going to many balls and hadn't really bothered to learn.

"Stop the coach near the hall," she said, as she finished wiping her eyes. "I'll fly up and drop into my room through the skylight."

Sir Charles frowned. "Won't they notice...?"

"After what happened today, I dare say they won't worry about it," Gwen said. Maybe she had been wrong to blame her mother. *She* had Lady Mary and Lady Elizabeth as examples of just how badly a premarital affair could go wrong and she *still* wanted to do it. "I normally sleep before writing up the report the following morning."

Sir Charles barked orders to the coachman as Gwen collected herself. Her stomach was still rumbling, demanding food. She'd have to order something as soon as she got into her room; God knew that she didn't dare eat in the hall, not after everything she'd done. Master

Thomas had devised a way of storing magical strength in water, giving himself an unfair advantage against almost everyone, but Gwen had never figured out how he'd done it. All she really knew was that it required a Master to make it work.

She gave Sir Charles a shy smile as the carriage finally came to a halt. "I... thank you," she said. She'd been worried that he wouldn't want to see her again, after he saw what her magic could do, but it seemed that she didn't have to worry about that. "I'll see you again soon."

"Tomorrow," Sir Charles said. "It's the ball, remember?"

Gwen cursed herself. She'd forgotten.

"I won't forget," she promised. Should she wear a dress or her suit? Queen Elizabeth had never had to worry about such problems, had she? "And I'll see you at seven in the evening."

She dropped out of the coach, gathered her remaining magical strength and levitated herself into the air. Flying had been the first major skill she'd mastered and she still loved the sense of freedom it gave, even though flying over London carried its own risks. She watched as the carriage drove away, then turned and headed towards Cavendish Hall. Master Thomas had installed the skylight to allow him to come and go without being noticed. Gwen had rarely used it. She dropped into the room and rang the bell.

"Lady Gwen," Martha said, as she entered. "I..."

She broke off, staring at Gwen's face. "I..."

"Don't worry about it," Gwen said, feeling her emotions spinning again. What if Martha decided to betray her? Howell had exploited servants who'd been abused ruthlessly. "I need you to get me some food, then run me a bath. I'll deal with anything else in the morning."

"Yes, Milady," Martha said, with a bow.

Gwen smiled as she left the room, then looked over at the mirror. It – and the dressing table – had been a present from her mother, just after Gwen had become the Royal Sorceress. There was a small fortune's worth of cosmetics in the drawers, which Gwen had barely looked at, let alone used. She sat down in front of the mirror and looked at herself. She didn't recognise the person staring back.

Normally, she wouldn't have hesitated to take off her clothes in front of Martha. The maid should have been completely trustworthy, but now... Gwen waited until Martha returned with a plate of cold meats and bread, then started to eat as Martha filled the bath and withdrew again. Once the maid was gone, she undressed and looked down at herself. There was a faint red mark on her breast, but nothing else. She couldn't help wondering what it would be like if they had gone further...

Shaking her head, she finished the meal and headed for the bathroom. Once she'd washed, she could go to bed. She would have to write a report, but it could wait. By now, Hopkins would probably have reported to his superiors, who would have reported to Lord Mycroft. The destruction of Howell's papers would be a weight off their minds.

She smiled as she warmed the water and climbed into the bath. It hadn't been her first kiss, but close enough – and no one had ever touched her body. Who knew how far they could go?

Your mother, a voice at the back of her head reminded her. *She knows all too well.*

Chapter Thirty-One

artha brought her breakfast in bed the following morning, which was lucky as Gwen didn't feel like facing the stares of everyone in the dining hall. Howell had cast a long shadow over the aristocratic world, one that might even have reached into Cavendish Hall. Who knew how many of her subordinates had been in his power?

"You have hundreds of letters," Martha said, as she set the tray down beside the bed. She would never have been allowed to bring Gwen breakfast in bed at Crichton Hall, but magicians who overexerted themselves sometimes needed to eat before they got up. "Lady Elizabeth says that most of them are notes of thanks, often unsigned."

Gwen smiled. Polite Society, the same Polite Society that had forced her mother to keep her devil-child out of public view, were actually *thanking* her. She doubted it would last long – she was much more disquieting than Lord Nelson – but for the moment it should buy her some friends and allies. Maybe they'd even start wondering if Gwen had *seen* any of the papers she'd destroyed.

"Good," she said, finally. "Did Lucy send a report from the hospital?"

"I shall ask Lady Elizabeth," Martha assured her. "Your face, you'll be glad to know, is back to normal."

Gwen allowed herself a moment of relief. She'd seriously considered summoning Lucy and asking her to hide the evidence, before realising that would cause even more rumours. Her enemies would wonder if she had been seriously hurt in the fight.

She tucked into breakfast as Martha withdrew, returning

a few moments later with a sealed envelope. Gwen opened it and skimmed through it quickly; Lucy had checked Howell, but had been unable to do anything for the blackmailer, who remained in a catatonic state. He had to be fed, watered and washed at the hospital if anyone wanted to keep him alive, she'd concluded. Wherever his mind was, it wasn't anywhere humans could go and return safely.

Gwen scribbled a short note on the rear of the letter, ordering Lucy to have Howell killed and then burned to ashes, then gave it to Martha to pass along. It was impossible to regret Howell's death after she'd seen his stash of secrets – and watched her mother break down in despair as she'd realised that her secret was known to her daughter. Gwen wondered briefly if her father had sent a note, before deciding that she wasn't going to ask. Instead, she finished her breakfast, washed herself and pulled on a suit. She would have to write a report for Lord Mycroft.

Martha hadn't exaggerated about the letters she'd been receiving. Dozens of them had been placed on her desk, others had been stored in boxes on the floor. Gwen picked up a couple of the opened envelopes and read them, shaking her head in disbelief at the florid tones the unnamed writer used to congratulate her. Polite Society was *definitely* more than a little relieved that Howell was safely dead.

She sorted through the letters until she found a brief update from Hopkins, who had searched Howell's house *thoroughly*. They'd found very little of note, apart from a cellar filled with imported wines from France and Spain. Hopkins had added a note suggesting that Howell might have brought them into the country illegally, without paying the excise tax, but there was no way to be sure. He might just have anticipated war and stocked up on French produce, intending to sell them when the prices skyrocketed after the war began.

"I think I love you," Lady Elizabeth's voice said. Gwen looked up to see her standing in the doorway, holding another pile of letters in her hand. "You freed everyone."

"I think so," Gwen said. She was reasonably sure that Howell hadn't kept any copies outside his house, but there was no way to be *sure*. "Do you still want to stay here?"

"Yes," Lady Elizabeth said, quickly. "My mother doesn't come here."

Gwen had to smile. "Work through the letters, then put the signed ones aside so I can write a response," she ordered. "The others can be counted; Doctor Norwell will probably want them for the archives, even if we don't know who sent them. It's probably best that we don't enquire, either."

"Probably," Lady Elizabeth said. She rummaged through her pile of letters, finally producing one that stood out from the others. "Lord Mycroft wishes to see you at your earliest convenience."

"Unsurprising," Gwen said, looking down at the half-written report. "Tell the coachman that I want to go in fifteen minutes. That should be long enough to finish the first draft of the report."

She finished writing, dropped the report in her handbag and walked downstairs, pretending to ignore the half-admiring, half-scared glances most of the students seemed to be throwing at her. The reminder that she *was* a Master Magician – and had just bested three other magicians on her own – might have taught them some respect. She smiled inwardly as she climbed into the coach, remembering the previous night, and ordered the coachman to take her to Whitehall. As always, Lord Mycroft was in his office.

"Lady Gwen," he said, looking up from the chessboard. "You seem to have won some more friends and admirers."

"Thank you," Gwen said. As far as she could tell, Lord Mycroft was playing against himself. "Why...?"

"Ambassador Talleyrand plays Chess," Lord Mycroft said, tapping the board. "He would have become a grandmaster if Chess had been his consuming passion. Instead, he plays with live pieces."

"Such as his daughter," Gwen said.

"Quite," Lord Mycroft said. He didn't take his eyes off the board. "I've studied the few games he has played publicly, ever since we started playing Chess as a competitive sport. Talleyrand is deeply conservative, reluctant to advance to the offensive, but equally unwilling to allow himself to surrender the initiative. As such, games against him tend to be slow and unwieldy; there are few moments of consuming drama where one player launches a daring attack on the other. Talleyrand prefers to build up his position and advance slowly, but surely, towards the end."

Gwen frowned. "But if he refuses to take the initiative," she said, slowly, "wouldn't that mean that he was permanently on the defensive?"

"Until he turns an opponent's daring stroke against him," Lord Mycroft said. "The key to understanding Chess is to realise that it is how the pieces interact that is important, rather than their relative power; even a king can take a queen, if the other player makes a dangerous mistake. Talleyrand plays to weaken, then go for the kill. He has rarely been beaten publicly."

He looked up and met her eyes. "Just like in real life," he added. "Talleyrand is a survivor, never making a mistake that would see him lose everything."

Gwen frowned. "And what about yourself?"

"We have a great deal in common," Lord Mycroft admitted. "A game between us would be... interesting."

"But you already play," Gwen realised. "Don't you?"

Lord Mycroft nodded, then changed the subject. "Unfortunately, the investigation into Sir Travis's death seems to have run into a brick wall," he said. "Those of us involved with the secret negotiations have been forced to conclude that Sir Travis might well have been paid by the Turks to ensure that they got a very favourable treaty. The Privy Council will be meeting in four days to discuss the matter, but I do not believe that they will recommend that the Airship Treaty be ratified."

Gwen winced. "But that doesn't explain Hiram Pasha's death," she said. "Why would he be murdered along with Sir Travis?"

"We may never know," Lord Mycroft admitted. "The Airship Treaty was passed to Sir Travis's superiors before his death. His paymasters may have believed that killing both of them would cut the links between the Treaty and Sir Travis. If the gambling debts remained hidden, there might have been no evidence to suggest that Sir Travis ever had any reason to be grateful to Istanbul."

"Sir Charles insists that Sir Travis could not have been a traitor," Gwen said. "And really – if he wanted to commit treason, he had ample time to do it before we entrusted him with negotiating with the Turks."

"Treason is an odd little habit," Lord Mycroft said. "The American – Arnold – was perhaps the most capable commander the American rebels had at their disposal. And yet they treated him badly, to the point where he saw his chance to return to us and took it. Had *he* been in command at New York, we might have lost the battle."

"Or if Washington had escaped, Arnold might have thought better of treachery," Gwen said, remembering the lessons successive tutors had tried to hammer into her head. "As it was, he only came over to our side when the war was effectively won."

"Howe was always too forgiving," Lord Mycroft agreed. It was an assessment, Gwen knew, that was shared by many others from that time. "Although, to be fair, the chance to bag the last organised rebel army before it could disperse was worth holding his nose and dealing with a traitor."

He shook his head. "Arnold wasn't the only traitor to jump off a sinking ship – and that is far from the only motive for treason," he added. "Quite a few German princes made deals with the French that allowed them to keep their crowns and castles, even as they sold their population out to foreign overlords. Other traitors had good reasons to hate the society that had birthed them – or were just greedy and wanted money."

"Or could be blackmailed," Gwen said, quietly. "What would you do if someone in your employ came to you and said that he was being blackmailed?"

"His career would be at an end," Lord Mycroft said. He held up a hand before Gwen could protest. "I wouldn't have a choice. Someone who could be blackmailed could be subverted by someone else..."

"But he wouldn't want to lose everything," Gwen objected. It didn't seem fair that someone's life could be destroyed by what they'd done in the past. "He'd lose both his career and his reputation."

"Life is far from fair," Lord Mycroft reminded her.

"Howell's notes asked what happened to your sister," Gwen said, wondering how he would respond. She hadn't even *known* that Lord Mycroft had had a sister. "What happened to her?"

Mycroft didn't look surprised at the question. "She... chose to make her own way in the world," he said, flatly. There was something in his tone that warned her not to press any further. "I rarely see her; few people do, even when she is right in front of them."

Gwen nodded, slowly. "What are we going to do about Sir Travis?"

Lord Mycroft looked down at his hands. "I'm going to have everything transferred to Cavendish Hall," he said, after a long moment of thought. "You are going to start working your way through everything, from the text of the treaty to the papers that were recovered from Hiram Pasha. Read his journal, study the letters he sent back home... find something, *anything*, that we can use to salvage the treaty."

Gwen frowned. "You believe that the treaty is that important?"

"France has gobbled up Spain, to all intents and purposes, and is in a loose alliance with Russia," Lord Mycroft reminded her. "We have a window of opportunity to forge an alliance with the Turks that we can use to counterbalance the two European powers. That window must not be wasted, but it is closing. If we have to renegotiate the treaty, the Turks may assume that we weren't serious and make whatever deal they can with the French and Russians. The Ottoman Empire could easily serve as a land bridge to India, if they allowed the French free passage."

He looked over at the map on the wall. "The Turks have an agreement not to allow hostile warships to pass through the Dardanelles," he added. "If the Russians manage to force them to break that agreement, we might discover that between them and France our position in the Mediterranean would be seriously compromised. The Turkish navy is badly outmatched without our help, but the Royal Navy would have too many other demands on its fleet if war did break out. More to the point, the Russians could build up a fleet in the Black Sea and then surge forward through the Dardanelles just before the outbreak of war."

"Giving them a significant advantage," Gwen said.

"More than you might think," Lord Mycroft said. "The Sultan recently recovered Egypt from the Mamelukes. Most of the unhappy survivors and anyone else who dared object to his new laws have found themselves digging a canal. Once dug, the canal will allow ships in the Mediterranean to transit through into the Red Sea, which will give them access to the Indian Ocean. In short, the French and Russians will be able to shift their forces around quicker than the Royal Navy, giving them an advantage at the main point of contact."

Gwen considered it. "Do you trust the Sultan?"

"I expect him to do what he considers to be in Turkey's best interests," Lord Mycroft said. "We can hardly expect him to stand up to the French or Russians for us if we don't make it worth his while. Or give him a decent chance, for that matter."

"So we need a reason to avoid renegotiating the treaty," Gwen said, slowly. "And if we prove that Sir Travis was innocent..."

"That would help," Lord Mycroft said, dryly. "I suggest that you take his maid with you, back to Cavendish Hall. She might be able to help."

"Of course," Gwen said, dryly. "What about Howell?"

Lord Mycroft gave her a surprised look that didn't fool her for a moment. "What *about* him?"

Gwen waited, saying nothing.

"We knew he was a blackmailer and yet he was untouchable," Lord Mycroft said. "And now we know that he was a rogue magician – and had other rogue magicians working for him – very few people will complain about how you dealt with him. The fact you destroyed his papers will make you very popular. I don't think that you have to worry about someone demanding that you stand trial for his death."

"Good," Gwen said. Was it really wrong of her to be relieved that he was dead? "What will happen to his servants?"

"I believe that is your decision," Lord Mycroft said. He gave her a crooked smile. "If you wish, you may deport them to Australia or America – there is no shortage of demand for indentured labourers to open up the new territories to the West. They may even buy themselves out of indenture and set up a homestead of their own. It would be better for them than staying in London."

"Because someone might kill them because their master employed them," Gwen said.

"Indeed," Lord Mycroft confirmed. "You should interrogate them first, just to make sure how much they actually know. Some of them may have been willing allies."

Gwen nodded and stood up.

"One more thing," Lord Mycroft added. "I understand that you are going to the ball this evening with Sir Charles."

Gwen nodded, unable to conceal her shock. How had he known?

"Sir Charles bought you both tickets," Lord Mycroft said. "Lady Fairweather – you will recall her, of course – sold tickets to raise money for orphaned children; Ambassador Talleyrand served as the major draw, of course. Hopefully, it will be less exciting than the last time you attended one of their balls."

Gwen snorted. The last time she had visited Fairweather Hall, Jack had announced his presence by tossing a dead man's head at the dancers. His brief skirmish with Master Thomas had marked the start of the war to shape Britain's future. Since then, Gwen had largely tried to avoid balls, particularly ones hosted by her mother. If Sir Charles hadn't invited her, she wouldn't have gone to the ball, even if the hostess had sent her a personal invitation.

"Sir Charles seems to have taken the accusations against his friend personally," Lord Mycroft warned her. "I would appreciate it if you could convince him not to do anything rash. Matters are in a very delicate state right now and we don't need a rogue element confusing everyone further."

"Rash," Gwen repeated. The word sound ominous. "Like...?"

"I believe he was talking about challenging Inspector Lestrade to a duel," Lord Mycroft said, diffidently. "Such a duel would not be remotely legal, of course, but the Inspector would be hard-pressed to refuse the challenge without losing too much face. Being a policeman requires physical courage far more than intelligence, as Lestrade has proven on numerous occasions."

Gwen scowled. When had she become Sir Charles's keeper?

Because you like him – and because he listens to you, her thoughts answered.

"It would be very bad if one of them did kill the other," Lord Mycroft said. His voice darkened. "Please try to keep them apart."

It was an understatement, Gwen knew. Lestrade was a police inspector, technically exempt from the *code duello*; Sir Charles could be charged with murder, no matter how willingly Lestrade had entered the duelling ground. And Sir Charles was a public hero. Lestrade's career would be destroyed if he killed Sir Charles, even if he'd been the challenged rather than the challenger.

"I'll do my best," Gwen said, wondering if she could separate the two without losing Sir Charles's respect for her. And Lestrade probably wouldn't be happy either. *Men!* Pride got them killed far more often than anything else. There were times when she was glad that she had been born female. "And thank you for your time."

"Bring us an answer, Lady Gwen," Mycroft said, looking back at the chessboard. "And keep an eye on Talleyrand. You can never trust a Frenchman too far."

Chapter Thirty-Two

ir James met her as soon as she returned to Cavendish Hall.

"I have four Talkers attached to Merlin for this evening," he said, once Gwen had ordered Sir Travis's papers moved to her study. "If that French girl tries anything, we'll stop her."

Gwen nodded. The Royal Sorcerers Corps had been trying to work out how many important people Simone might have met before Gwen had realised that she was a Talker, but it seemed unlikely that they had identified them all. God alone knew how much information the girl had pulled out of their minds and passed on to her father. If Howell could intimidate Polite Society, what could someone like Ambassador Talleyrand do with a mind-reader at his command?

"Make sure they stay close to her," she ordered. "What about the rest of the security?"

"Merlin will remain on guard, along with a number of private guards," Sir James said. "I don't think that anyone will try anything."

"That's what they thought last time," Gwen said. Sir James had been in India when Jack had crashed the Fairweather Ball. "We will take every possible precaution."

Sir James nodded. "You'll be there too," he added. He hesitated, then grinned at her. "Is it so wrong of me to prefer fighting to going to balls?"

"It's a different kind of warfare," Gwen said, remembering some of her mother's stories. The aristocratic balls often served as cover for secret negotiations between different families, or even political factions. People who would never speak to each other outside a ball could do so naturally while dancing, if they saw fit. Or simply borrow a room in the host's house and have a private conference. "But I prefer fighting too."

She ensured that Polly would have a room and a chance to rest in Cavendish Hall, then walked upstairs to where Martha and Lady Elizabeth were waiting for her. Martha had been excited to discover that Gwen was going to a ball, her first in sixth months, and had gone looking for a dress for Gwen while Gwen had been in Whitehall. Gwen didn't see why her maid was so excited – normally, she would have been happy to let Martha go in her place – but decided to tolerate it. Besides, she wanted to look her best for Sir Charles.

"It's a shame your hair is cut so short," Lady Elizabeth said, as they helped Gwen to undress and started washing her body. "Can you make it grow outwards?"

"No quicker than anyone else," Gwen said. Maybe a Changer could have extended her hair, but it would have been unacceptably dangerous. "Long hair just kept getting in the way,"

"Black would have been unsuitable," Martha said, as she produced the dress. "I chose green instead; it'll go well with your hair, as well as making a fashion statement of sorts."

Gwen smiled as she saw the dress. It was simple, thankfully; she strongly disliked the complex dresses that forced the wearer to ask for help to dress or undress. Besides, the Royal Sorceress wasn't expected to wear something too ornate. There was no way of knowing when she'd have to fight. If worst came to worst, she could tear off the dress itself and fight in her underclothes, which were almost as modest

"You won't be showing off too much," Martha added, as Gwen pulled the dress over her head. "Maybe you won't look like a man, but you won't look too much like a young woman either."

Gwen looked in the mirror, then nodded. The Trouser Brigade might shock public opinion by wearing tight trousers – and some girls scandalised Polite Society by wearing dresses that revealed their cleavage – but she looked conservative, yet not too feminine. It wouldn't be good to have people she had to work with thinking of her as feminine, even after she'd proved herself more than once. Men never seemed to like the idea of a woman with more power than themselves.

She smiled, suddenly. Once, years ago, she had considered trying to dress up as a man and sneaking into Oxford of Cambridge. Most of the lectures were barred to women, particularly the ones that interested her – but quite a few women had sneaked in over the years. There had even been a major scandal when Gwen had been a child. Maybe she should have suggested posing as a man to Master Thomas. It might have made it easier to work as the Royal Sorceress.

But I would have had to duck marriage proposals, she thought, ruefully. She hadn't realised how many proposals Master Thomas had received until she'd seen his private cabinet. There had been no shortage of ambitious society dames willing to propose that he marry their daughters or granddaughters, even though he'd been an old man. But that might have been the point. Whoever married him might not be out of their twenties by the time he died.

"You look good," Lady Elizabeth said. She started to work on Gwen's face, dabbing cosmetics against her cheeks. "Do you really need to carry the weapons?"

Gwen nodded. "If I don't carry them, I'll need them," she said. Besides, after six months, she felt naked without them. "Besides, I might want to kill someone without using magic."

Lady Elizabeth suddenly frowned. "Will my parents be attending?"

"I don't know," Gwen admitted. Guest lists were often published prior to the ball, but she hadn't had a chance to look at one. "But I would be surprised if they missed it."

"Tell them that I'm fine and actually doing something useful," Lady Elizabeth said, softly. "I don't want to see them again, ever."

"Forever is a very long time," Gwen said.

She shook her head, ruefully. They had something in common now, didn't they? Gwen didn't want to see her parents again either... no, that was a lie. Part of her mind wanted to mend her relationship with her parents, no matter what they'd done in the past. Lady Mary might have killed Gwen's half-sibling, but she'd also kept Gwen even after it would have been easier to give her away. And they hadn't objected when Master Thomas had come to claim Gwen.

Martha steered her back towards the mirror, allowing Gwen to study her reflection. Her face was fashionably pale, showing off her eyes and blonde hair, while the dress fitted her perfectly. The weapons she had on her person were completely invisible. Gwen picked up Master Thomas's cane and leaned on it, before reluctantly putting it down beside the bed. It couldn't go with her tonight.

"Perfect," Martha said, firmly. "I understand that Sir Charles is picking you up from Cavendish Hall?"

Gwen nodded. It might have been wiser to meet up somewhere closer to Fairweather Hall, away from so many prying eyes, but she was making a statement. She would not be bound by convention, no matter how many of society's grand dames disapproved. Besides, she had good reason to believe that many of society's queens had their own dark secrets. Who would have thought that Lady Mary could kill her own child?

"The side entrance," Gwen said. "Once he arrives, I'll walk downstairs and meet him."

She was feeling a curious mixture of excitement and nervousness when the guardhouse finally called through to say that Sir Charles had arrived. Gwen shared a look with Lady Elizabeth, then picked up her skirts and walked down the stairs, ignoring the handful of students and tutors she met on the way. A couple of them actually gaped at her, as if they were having problems connecting the dark-clothed Royal Sorceress with the blonde girl in front of them. Her modified suit had the distinct advantage of making her look older.

Lord Nelson was a boy when he took command of a boat, she reminded herself. Of course, whoever had heard of a *woman* commanding a ship? There were stories of female pirates, but they'd always been disguised as men. It seemed odd that their crewmen would fall for it, yet Gwen knew how easily the male eye could be fooled. Sometimes, just wearing a male outfit was enough to prevent them from looking any closer.

Sir Charles had hired a larger carriage for the evening, she realised, as he stepped down to help her climb into the vehicle. Gwen smiled at him, feeling a sudden urge to take him in her arms and press her lips against his, even though they were in public. But it would have ruined her face as well as her reputation.

"You look wonderful," he said, as he pulled the door closed. "I trust that I look acceptable?"

Gwen looked at him. He was wearing a white Indian suit, complete with turban, flashing jewels and a sword at his belt. Lady Fairweather had released men from the normally strict rules of fashion, either through a desire to shock or simple boredom; Gwen wondered how many of her guests would have their own Indian outfits. But then, Sir Charles had actually *been* in India. How many of the other guests could make that claim?

"I took it off a nabob who was too dead to complain that I was stealing it," Sir Charles told her. He tapped one of the gemstones on his lapel. "The natives *love* dressing up and wearing flashy jewels. One particular kingdom had an army that was better dressed than any other, but lacked proper weapons or tactics. We had to force the men not to loot after we smashed the enemy formation and crushed them."

Gwen shrugged. She, of all people, understood the difference between looking good and actually *being* good.

The ride was surprisingly smooth, allowing her to relax and enjoy his presence. Normally, even on London's roads, the carriage would have rattled so badly that she would be unable to read or write; she dreaded most of her trips out of the city because she always ended up with a headache when she reached her destination. This time... Sir Charles drew back the curtain, allowing her to see out of the carriage. An odd sense of *déjà vu* ran down her spine as Fairweather Hall came into view.

Jack and Master Thomas had fought, briefly, in Fairweather Hall. The battle hadn't lasted longer than a few minutes, but between them they had done serious damage to the building's structural integrity. Gwen had heard that the Fairweather Family had spent thousands of pounds repairing their ancestral home, yet it had taken months before the building was ready for human occupancy. The ball was about announcing their return to society as much as it was about Ambassador Talleyrand.

"It looks intact," Sir Charles commented. He sounded almost disappointed. "The reports made it sound as though it was a pile of rubble."

"It wasn't quite that bad," Gwen assured him. Still, a few minutes more and the entire building might have collapsed. "And most of the guests survived."

"He probably didn't want to kill them," Sir Charles grunted, as the carriage passed through the gates. "Terror only works if you leave enough people alive to spread the word."

Gwen allowed him to help her out of the carriage as the driver paused in front of the main entrance. There were others coming all the time; the drivers would wait behind the hall until they were called to come and pick up their passengers. She couldn't help noticing a handful of people staring at her, but for once they seemed admiring rather than fearful or condemning.

"You seem to be popular," Sir Charles commented, so quietly that she was the only person who could hear him. "Howell's death did your reputation no end of good."

Gwen smiled as they stepped through the entrance and down the steps into the ballroom. It was very different from how she remembered; they'd expanded the room so it could hold hundreds of people, while hanging new chandeliers from the ceiling to cast a brilliant light over the festivities. One long table held food and drink, while a band was playing a merry tune in one corner. Dozens of portraits hung on the walls, reminding the guests that their hosts belonged to a family with a long history. There had been a Fairweather at many a battle, the portraits said, although they missed out a few details. Gwen's lips twitched; there had been a Fairweather on *both* sides of the Civil War.

"Lady Gwen," a voice said. Gwen turned to see an older woman, wearing a purple dress that drew the eye, stumbling towards her. "I must congratulate you."

Gwen winced as the woman gave her a brief hug and kissed the air in front of her cheek, before staggering off into the crowd. Who *was* she? One of her mother's friends? No, *that* was unlikely. If any of them had known what Lady Mary had done, they would have cut Gwen dead, even if it *hadn't* been her fault. The sins of the mother were borne by the child, according to Polite Society. It just proved that there was nothing really *polite* about it.

"Well done," a man said. He saluted her, then reached for her dance card and marked himself in for a dance. "We all owe you."

Sir Charles elbowed her. "They were Howell's victims," he said. "You freed them from a lifetime of fear."

More and more people stopped to congratulate her as they made their way through the room. Gwen recognised a handful of them, but others were strangers – and yet they all seemed to know her. Sir Charles seemed more amused than the situation deserved, occasionally pointing out one of the wealthier or nobler people who had good reason to thank Gwen. By the time they reached the food table, Gwen was mentally shaking her head in disbelief. How many people had Howell kept in thrall?

"Ladies and gentlemen," the announcer said. His voice effortlessly echoed through the room. "Ambassador Talleyrand of France and his daughter Simone."

Gwen turned to watch as Talleyrand descended the stairs to the ballroom. His gait seemed slower, more deliberate, than she had expected, but then he was around the same age as Master Thomas. And, to the best of their knowledge, Talleyrand had no magic to keep him healthy and alive, although some of Lord Mycroft's intelligence officers had wondered if he had Charm. *Something* had to have kept him in a position of power and influence throughout all of the changes in France. The French suit he wore, cut in the style of Louis XVI, was a droll reminder of his longevity. Gwen couldn't help wondering how many of the guests understood its significance.

Simone seemed even more waif-like next to her father, if he truly *was* her father. Her face was pale even without cosmetics, while her dark eyes were wide, as if it was the first time she'd seen such a gathering. Gwen winced inwardly, wondering how many young men were going to look into those dark pools and lose themselves, telling the French girl whatever she wanted to hear just to keep her attention. And, as a Talker, she could ask questions and pull the answers from their minds...

Gwen smiled as she saw the two escorts from the Royal Sorcerers Corps. Talleyrand would not have been able to refuse their presence; after all, it was quite possible that Londoners would seek revenge for the undead rampage by attacking the French Ambassador. But it would frustrate the girl's intelligence-gathering efforts. Every time she opened her mind, she would feel their presence overriding everyone else's mental signature.

"She's far too young to be his daughter," Sir Charles muttered. "And they don't even *look* alike."

"That doesn't prove anything," Gwen reminded him. "I don't look much like *my* father either."

The Master of Ceremonies started to call the first dance, inviting the couples onto the dance floor. Gwen allowed Sir Charles to lead her onto the floor, keeping one eye on Simone as she gravitated to a middle-aged aristocrat who'd come without an escort. Talleyrand, in the meantime, was chatting to Lady Fairweather and a couple of her cronies, although there was no way to know what they were talking about. It was unlikely that they would be sharing state secrets in public, she decided. But the file had claimed that Talleyrand was a womaniser, with the appetite of a much younger man. Could he really be trying to seduce the hostess in public, in front of her husband?

Stranger things have happened, she reminded herself, as the dance began.

Sir Charles proved to be a very good dancer, leading her around the floor without ever stepping on her toes. Gwen enjoyed the first two dances more than she expected, before reluctantly letting go of him to allow another man to take her onto the floor. He managed to thank her several more times, leaving Gwen wondering just what Howell had held over his head. She couldn't help noticing that he seemed *very* relieved to be free of him.

But Simone had managed to lure Sir Charles into a dance...

Gwen felt her temper flare, forcing her to grit her teeth and keep it in check. How *could* he dance with her? She told herself that she was being stupid, that Simone had probably wanted to see if she could read his mind, but she couldn't help feeling a sense of outrage. The moment the dance finished, she let go of her partner and walked back to Sir Charles, who seemed rather bemused. Simone had let him go and moved on to the next partner.

"She kept asking me about you," he commented, as Gwen scowled at him. "I told her nothing, of course."

"She's a mind-reader," Gwen muttered back. "She could have pulled the answers out of your mind."

It should have been impossible, she knew. Simone *was* being escorted. But it was impossible to be sure, either.

She started to pull Sir Charles back onto the dance floor, then stopped.

"Wait for me," she said, quickly. "There's someone over there I need to see."

Chapter Thirty-Three

ady Alexandra Milton didn't look much older than Gwen herself.

Gwen studied her and her cronies before walking up and introducing herself. Lady Alexandra was shorter than Gwen, with long red hair that seemed to blur into her dress, her lips twisted in a permanent sneer. Maybe not a social queen, not yet, but wealthy enough that her eventual rise to power was unquestioned. Her cronies were probably hanging on in the hopes that she wouldn't forget them after she took her mother's place.

There was no wedding ring on her finger, but she wasn't on the dance floor and she wasn't surrounded by admiring males. Gwen wondered, absently, what *that* meant; even if Lady Alexandra had been ugly as sin, her family and her bank balance would have ensured that she had a stream of admirers. After all, male adultery was winked at, practically condoned... and they would ask who could blame a husband with an ugly wife for looking elsewhere?

"Lady Gwen," Lady Alexandra said. The calm contempt in her voice made Gwen's blood boil. "I trust that you will tell your lawyer to back off?"

"No," Gwen said, tartly.

She had the pleasure of seeing the girl's eyes open wide, just for a long second. "You... I had my father speak to your father..."

"You tried to have me pressured into not doing my duty," Gwen said, keeping her voice as cold as ice. "I take my work a little more seriously than *that*."

She scowled down at Lady Alexandra, daring her to say

anything. "I am going to be blunt," she added. "When your aunt died, you moved quickly and took her collection of jewels – which weren't entailed, by the way – out of Mortimer Hall, claiming them for yourself. I don't know why you believed that you were entitled to act in such a manner, but you did; you stole from your Aunt before her body was even in the grave. And then, I think, you brought pressure to bear on the executor of her will. You ensured that her last wishes were not respected."

"She told me that I could have them," Lady Alexandra said. "They're *mine*."

"Her will says otherwise," Gwen said. "Did you realise where they were meant to go? Did you calculate that a respectable girl from an aristocratic family would win if the matter ended up in front of a court? After all, the person Lady Mortimer had named was a young black girl – we all know what the court thinks of *niggers*. I'm sure you could make a convincing case that Lady Mortimer was insane when she wrote the will. Or do I do you an injustice?"

"I am merely taking what is mine," Lady Alexandra insisted. "Look, you know what it's like to be a young girl. You *need* jewels to boost your status..."

"No, you don't," Gwen said, although she knew that Lady Alexandra was partly right. "I'm sure you think that you can drag this out until a year passes – or have the executor removed from his position because Sir Travis died shortly after his mother. Maybe you're right; maybe you can get a court to rule in favour of the *status quo*. But it isn't going to go in front of a court."

She leaned forward until she could feel the girl's breath on her cheek. "You're going to surrender the jewels to my lawyer," she said. "Or I will see to it that your reputation is utterly destroyed."

Lady Alexandra sneered at her. "You think anyone would listen to you?"

"Think about what I did yesterday," Gwen said, dryly. "How many of them would *not* listen to me?"

She allowed the idea to filter through the girl's mind. Right now, Gwen was *popular*. It wouldn't last, but it would give her the influence to destroy Lady Alexandra, if she decided to push hard. And she suspected that some in Polite Society wondered if she'd stolen Howell's papers, rather than burning them to ash. It was quite possible that Howell had had something on Lady Alexandra or her family.

"I don't have time to force it through the courts, so I'm not going to bother," Gwen added. "Just think how long your position would last if I decided to attack it."

Lady Alexandra's face twisted bitterly, then she nodded. "Very well," she said, sharply. "I will have the jewels delivered to you."

"There was a list as part of the will," Gwen reminded her. Absently, she wondered if Lady Mortimer had anticipated that someone would try to steal her jewels. Most aristocratic women were paranoid about losing their jewels; in many cases, it was the only real wealth they had that was indisputably theirs. "I will check it against the list before I do anything else."

"Of course you will," Lady Alexandra said. "You have no loyalty, have you?"

It took Gwen several seconds to work out what she meant. "I am loyal to those who deserve my loyalty," Gwen said, "and they don't include social queens who sneer at someone who happens to be different from them."

She nodded politely to the girl's cronies and walked off, wondering if Lady Alexandra would keep her word or if she would think better of it, once she got back home. A social queen wouldn't hesitate to ruin someone – or their family – if they thought it benefited them in some way, but the Royal Sorceress had to be more careful. Destroying the Milton Family could have unintended consequences. It wouldn't be the first time a quarrel in Polite Society had affected the nation as a whole.

Simone stepped out of the crowd and offered her a half-curtsey. "Lady Gwen," she said, in her whispery voice. "I was hoping to have a chance to speak with you."

Gwen scowled. Up close, she could smell Simone's perfume, something fashionable and expensive from France. Polite Society had a love-hate relationship with

France, both aping French fashions and condemning French morals, although Gwen suspected that it would be better if it were the other way round. Howell could never have prospered so effectively in Paris, where adultery and fornication were considered part of life.

"Of course," she said, remembering her duty. "What can I do for you?"

"I must formally protest the presence of your escorts," Simone said. Her tone seemed unchanged. "They are fogging my mind."

"You're trying to read other minds," Gwen pointed out, although she knew that she could be doing Simone an injustice. No Talker had perfect mental shields. "And we cannot allow you to do that."

"I suppose not," Simone said. She didn't seem inclined to press any further. "You're quite respected in France."

Gwen lifted an eyebrow. "I am?"

"A woman rising to a position of power among the English," Simone said. "That is vanishingly rare in this country."

"And in France," Gwen pointed out. The French might give their women more latitude than the British, but political power still rested largely in the hands of men. "We had several queens who ruled in their own right."

"True," Simone agreed. "I have been asked to pass on an invitation. My father would like to speak with you in private, later this week. Would it be convenient for you to visit the Embassy?"

"I would have to look at my schedule," Gwen hedged, wondering just what Talleyrand wanted. He couldn't want to talk about the murder, could he? "I'll certainly let you know once I have a free moment."

She hesitated, then asked the question that had been bothering her ever since she'd first met the French Talker. "Are you *really* his daughter?"

The girl's blush told her the answer. Gwen signed inwardly; some things were definitely universal. A Talker who happened to be a beautiful woman would be a *very* convenient partner for a male diplomat. But why claim that she was his daughter in the first place?

She pushed the question aside, nodded politely to Simone and headed back towards where Sir Charles was waiting. Like her, he'd chosen to go without alcohol; instead, he was drinking juice and chatting to a man Gwen didn't recognise. He smiled at her as she approached, then introduced Gwen to Lord Percy, Heir to the Duchy of Northumberland. Gwen concealed her private amusement as she waited for them to finish talking. Once, years ago, Lady Mary had considered Lord Percy a possible candidate for Gwen's hand.

He seems to be smarter than they said, she thought. Rumour had claimed that Lord Percy couldn't count to eleven without taking off his socks. On the other hand, nasty rumours flew through Polite Society without regard to the truth.

"Time to dance again," Sir Charles said, bidding farewell to Lord Percy. "Did you get what you wanted out of her?"

"I think so," Gwen said, as he led her back onto the dance floor. "What about Lord Percy?"

"His brother-in-law has a... relative who wishes to spend time in India," Sir Charles said, dryly. "I was telling Lord Percy how India would make a man of his relative, if it didn't kill him first. Maybe I shouldn't have told him the story of the naked polo team."

Gwen rolled her eyes. A relative of unspecified relation was almost certainly an illegitimate child, she knew. Sir Charles would certainly feel more for the bastard than for the legitimate part of the family. Absently, she wondered how Lord Percy's prim family had ended up with a bastard, before dismissing the thought as silly. It was quite easy to guess the truth.

The evening wore on and couples started to make their departure. Gwen watched Talleyrand from time to time, noticing that he only danced once, while spending most of his time having conversations with wealthy or powerful aristocrats. None of the conversations would be very significant, not if they were being held in a public ballroom, but they would serve the purpose of building up unofficial contacts. Talleyrand had to be looking for someone to replace Sir Travis, now that France needed an unofficial connection more than ever. It might, she realised, be why Talleyrand wanted to see her again.

But he shouldn't need the Royal Sorceress, she thought. As much as she hated to admit it, she was a public figure, something Sir Travis had *not* been. People would notice if she went to the French Embassy and then to Whitehall, particularly if she did it more than once. *Maybe I should speak to Lord Mycroft and get an official unofficial contact set up.*

She smiled at the thought, then looked up at Sir Charles. "Did Talleyrand want to talk to you too?"

"He never approached me," Sir Charles said. He seemed a little surprised by the question. "I don't think I'm important enough for him."

And too famous to replace Sir Travis, Gwen thought, silently grateful that Inspector Lestrade was not in attendance. Keeping him and Sir Charles from killing each other would be difficult.

Sir Charles frowned as he looked around the rapidly emptying room. "Should we go?"

Gwen hesitated, then nodded. Knowing when to leave a ball was a question of timing, rather than anything else; leaving too early could be considered an insult to one's host, while leaving too late could have other implications. She glanced around for Lady Fairweather, saw her standing with several other women and chatting to them about nothing, and then pulled Sir Charles towards the exit. They could write a note thanking Lady Fairweather for her hospitality later.

Outside, the cold night air brushed against them as they waited for the carriage to come around and pick them up. Gwen found herself inching closer to Sir Charles and cursed herself; being too close to him would cause a scandal, no matter what happened. Of course, going in his carriage would *also* cause talk... for a moment, she thought she understood the attractions of France. Quite a few aristocrats who had lost their reputations ended up in France, where they could do more or less whatever they liked. There were times when Gwen could almost understand Lady Bracknell's treatment of her daughter. Even the merest glance or sigh could cause a scandal, if seen by the wrong person.

Sir Charles helped her into the carriage, then muttered instructions to the coachman. Gwen shook her head in amused disbelief; Sir Charles had ordered him to take the long route back to Cavendish Hall. She was tempted to lean back and refuse to play, but part of her *wanted* to kiss him – and do much more. It was easy to fall into his arms as the carriage rolled away from Fairweather Hall. His hands suddenly seemed to be everywhere, stroking her back and caressing her breasts through her dress.

"Don't worry," he whispered, as his hand started to reach under her skirt. "We won't go too far."

Gwen hesitated, then pushed his hand away. Part of her body was *demanding* that she let him touch her there, but she couldn't allow it – not yet. Instead, she moved forward and sat on his knee, allowing him to kiss her again and again. She lost track of time so completely that it was a shock when she realised that they were approaching Cavendish Hall. Sir Charles barely caught her in time to prevent her from falling off his knee and landing on the wooden floor.

"Your makeup is a little smudged, but otherwise you look decent," he said. *He* didn't look too decent; his suit was rumpled, while his face was covered in sweat. "And you tore my suit."

Gwen flushed, then reached into her handbag and found the mirror. Her makeup was *smeared* all over her face... she found a tissue and wiped it all off, before checking again to be sure that she hadn't missed anything. The dress was definitely rumpled; Gwen seriously considered just throwing it out, before deciding that would be a waste of money. It could be washed and repaired.

"I'm sorry," she said, although she wasn't sure what she was apologising *for*. The torn suit... or her reluctance to go any further? "Thank you very much for taking me. I had a lovely time."

"You're welcome," he said. He gave her a smile that made her want to kiss him again, even though there was no time left. "I enjoyed myself as well."

He winked at her. "And they're all glad you killed Howell," he added. "You deserve their praise."

Gwen smiled, then sobered.

"I counted at least thirty people who congratulated me," she said, softly. "How many more were there?"

The thought chilled her. If only a handful of Howell's victims had had the courage to face her, knowing that it would tell her that they had something to hide, there might be many more who would remain unknown. *How* many more? There had been hundreds of files... if each of them related to a different person, nearly two-thirds of Polite Society could have been blackmailed. Howell had cast a long shadow over London... and, even though he was gone, it would take years for the shadow to fade.

"You will probably never know," Sir Charles said.

Gwen couldn't disagree. She might be overestimating it, she told herself; there had been very little in Sir Travis's file, hardly enough to serve as a blackmail tool. And her own file hadn't been very detailed either. Maybe there were only a handful of other victims. If Howell had demanded a few thousand pounds from each of them, he would have had enough to buy his house, hire the rogue magicians and enjoy the rest. But she would probably never know.

"Thank you," she said, again.

He kissed her once more as she climbed out of the carriage. The coachman had stopped near Cavendish Hall, but not close enough for anyone to see her as she disembarked. She waved one hand in farewell, then levitated herself up into the air and flew towards the building. It was easy to drop into her bedroom again, pull off the dress and run into the bathroom. The more complex dresses could be absolute nightmares if the wearer had to go urgently.

She smiled at the thought, then turned on the tap to run a bath. While the tub was filling, she looked in her letterbox and saw a couple of letters. One was a brief follow-up from Inspector Hopkins, another confirmed that Howell was definitely dead and burned to ash... and the third requested a meeting tomorrow morning. No, she realised; it was past midnight. The meeting would be today.

Sam Davis, she thought, remembering the Mover with a fondness for drink. The last she'd heard, he'd been Healed... and she hadn't heard anything from him since then. What did *he* want with her? She put the note to one side, intending to write a reply after she'd washed, and walked back into the bathroom. Her magic seemed oddly imprecise; she had to add more cold water after she heated what was already in the tub. It would have scalded her otherwise.

Maybe its frustration, she thought, remembering an uncomfortable interview with a magician who had been arrested by the police when they'd raided a brothel. He'd had the nerve to claim that he was sexually frustrated and that it was interfering with his magic. Gwen had fined him a month's salary, more for the pathetic excuse than for being caught in a brothel, but now she wondered. Part of her body yearned for Sir Charles's touch.

Be careful, a voice said, at the back of her head. *He isn't your husband yet – and pregnancy would make your life difficult, even if it didn't harm your reputation.*

And it would, Gwen knew. Could she use her magic when a child was growing inside her womb?

She shook her head, washed herself thoroughly and walked back into the bedroom. There was a reply to write, but the bed was so inviting that she collapsed on top and closed her eyes.

And then she fell asleep.

Chapter Thirty-Four

ou made the society papers," Martha said, as she brought Gwen her breakfast the following morning. "All four of the big ones covered the Fairweather Ball."

Gwen rolled her eyes, but looked at the papers anyway. Most of them discussed Talleyrand and his 'daughter', including endless speculation on which of the young blades would win her, *none* of them suggesting that she might be a Talker. Her own mention came lower down, with a note that Lady Gwen, Royal Sorceress, had been accompanied to the ball by Sir Charles Bellingham. There were few other details, for which she was grateful. No doubt the reporters had considered Talleyrand to be the star attraction.

But they would, she thought, wryly. *Lady Fairweather probably vetted the reporters before allowing them access.*

One of the papers included a sketch of Simone that somehow managed to make her look even more waif-like, a child thrown into the political arena by her father and told to sink or swim. Gwen snorted inwardly; the paper's editor, a known Francophobe, wasn't above using Simone to take a few cheap shots at the French, as if no true English father would ever take his daughter to a ball. There was even a call for some young British nobleman to rescue her from her father and keep her in Britain. No doubt that was precisely what Talleyrand was hoping would happen.

"Not a bad mention," she decided, after skimming through the rest of the paper. As always with the society rags, there was little in the way of actual *news*. "Did you find a place for Polly to sleep?"

Martha nodded. "She's in another of the guest suites," she said. "Doctor Norwell was wondering just what you intend to do with her."

"Go through her Master's papers," Gwen said, as she took a sip of coffee. "Once that's done, I'll talk to her about her future."

Which might be bleak, she added, in the privacy of her own mind. Polly would have the jewels – and converting them to cash wouldn't be difficult – but she would also have some powerful enemies. Lady Alexandra and her family wouldn't go after Gwen, yet they'd consider Polly to be fair game. And between her skin colour and sex, it would be very hard for her to fight back. Something would have to be done about that too.

She finished her breakfast, had a quick wash and then dressed in her suit. It had felt odd to be wearing a dress after so long; the suit felt almost like coming home. Once she was ready, she picked up the note Sam Davis had sent her and scribbled a reply, inviting him to meet her at his earliest convenience. She had no doubt that she would be spending most of her day in Cavendish Hall.

Sir James must have been waiting for her to arise, because he met her just outside her office.

"I have a report for you from last night," he said, as he followed her into the room. "The young Talker tried to probe several minds."

Gwen wasn't surprised. "Did you make a list of who she tried to read?"

"Yes," Sir James assured her. "Few of them were actually important, apart from Lord Percy – and his importance comes more in his title than in his current position. I don't think he knew anything useful... by the way, there was no indication of Charm, but Talleyrand seemed remarkably successful in charming many of the older women at the ball."

"He's had plenty of experience," Gwen reminded him. One didn't *need* Charm to charm, or the human race would have died out long before magic first emerged into the open. Love could be dangerous, but it also drew people together and held them close, no matter what else happened in their lives. "And he wanted to be seen, of course."

She glanced down at the list Sir James had produced. Simone had been busy, but she would have found it a very frustrating evening. Physical contact between two people allowed more intimate mental contact and was much harder for outsiders to disrupt. But then, few of her dance partners had known anything important... or so Gwen hoped. It would be easy to underestimate someone just because he looked a fop.

"We will just have to keep an eye on her," she said, tiredly. "Maybe we should also start checking the French staff when they arrive in Britain. Now they know we know about Simone, they might well send someone else."

"That might violate their diplomatic passports," Sir James reminded her. "We'd have to arrange for physical contact by accident."

"Maybe a routine scan by a Healer," Gwen mused. Lucy had been able to tell what was wrong with a patient, just by touching him. "We don't want to risk a disease-ridden person setting foot on British soil."

"They'd laugh at us," Sir James said. "How many problems have we had with diseases from Africa or India that have spread here?"

Gwen nodded, ruefully. He was right.

"Merlin reports that it was a very successful evening," Sir James said, straightening to attention. "And we would really like to go back on the front lines."

"I don't blame you," Gwen admitted. "Tell me; do you think Lord Brockton is capable of fulfilling his responsibilities?"

Sir James hesitated. "I think that he is *too* good at them," he said, finally. He looked more than a little uneasy. Asking him to report on his superior was a gross breach of etiquette. "He is more than willing to fight for more resources for his magicians – and, to be fair, Movers are quite important to us. On the other hand, he is very poor at integrating Movers with other magicians, to the point where I would strongly recommend not having him involved with any cross-talent teams. And he argues over every little detail."

"Even with you," Gwen said. She'd hoped that Lord Brockton would do better with a male superior, but Sir James was in an odd position. Lord Brockton was still the Head of Movers and Sir James's superior, even if Sir James was standing in for the Royal Sorceress. "I think I shall have to remove him."

"His second has been in his shadow for too long," Sir James warned her. "He would be completely ineffective as a Head of Movers."

Gwen nodded. "Would you consider accepting the post?"

Sir James gave her a long searching look. "I couldn't be party to his firing," he said, finally. "Stubborn ass he may be, but..."

Gwen understood. Men didn't like being seen to betray their fellow men, even the ones they should know better than to tolerate.

"I'm going to find him a place to go," she said. Turkey, if the Airship Treaty hadn't been completely destroyed. "If I did, would you take his place?"

"I'd prefer not to deal with the paperwork," Sir James said. "Would I be correct in assuming that Merlin will be based in Britain for the foreseeable future?"

"Probably," Gwen admitted. "Your presence is quite reassuring."

"Let me think about it," Sir James said, finally. "Maybe I can hold the post long enough to groom a better successor."

Gwen nodded and watched him go, then looked down at the small pile of letters on her desk. One of them was from Lady Fairweather, thanking Gwen for attending the ball and wishing her a very happy future. It took Gwen a moment to realise that Lady Fairweather believed that Gwen and Sir Charles were going to marry. She felt colour rising to her cheeks – it had only been a few hours ago when they'd been kissing like mad – and quickly thought about something else. The last thing she needed was to get distracted while she was trying to work.

There was a knock at the door. She opened it with her magic and smiled inwardly as she saw Sam Davis. The Mover looked much better than he had the last time they'd met, but there was something about him that bothered her. He looked... thoroughly uncomfortable even *looking* at her. Gwen put the letter she was reading down and stood up, motioning for him to take a seat. He sat as if the seat had been covered in pins.

"I went to the Healer, like you said," he said, shortly. His voice didn't *sound* drunk. "I then heard that you'd killed Howell. The man deserved to die."

Gwen's eyes narrowed. Had he come to compliment her, like so many others, or was this leading up to something?

"I helped train his Movers," Davis admitted. "There was a recruiter offering money for drink; all I had to do was train a few young sprigs how to use their powers. All of them were unregistered, but they needed training."

"I... see," Gwen said, slowly. "When did you start doing this?"

"A year ago," Davis said. "They were desperate for training."

Gwen scowled. The magical underground hadn't managed to put together a serious challenge to the Establishment until Jack had arrived, but they'd tried. They'd known that *something* happened to lower-class magicians, even if they hadn't known the exact details. Jack, apparently, had never told them about the farms. He'd probably been too ashamed of his own origins to admit to them.

"And some of those magicians probably ended up fighting during the Swing," she said. She'd wondered how Jack had managed to pull together so many so quickly. He'd reaped the benefits of prior training. "What happened to the others?"

"There was an underground recruiting network," Davis admitted. "I never knew names; they took me to a basement, showed me a couple of people I had to train and then took me back again. And I crawled further into the bottle and eventually people stopped asking me to do anything. Until you..."

"I wanted you to get better," Gwen said. Part of her felt sorry for him; part of her remembered fighting the two Movers in Howell's house. "Why are you telling me this now?"

"After I was Healed, I went to a bar," Davis said. "I... wanted to see what my new liver thought of alcohol. And I was met by one of my contacts, who asked me if I'd heard anything about an unregistered Mover who had vanished the previous night. Apparently, money exchanged hands along with names. He wanted to know if we'd arrested him."

Gwen shook her head. No Movers had been arrested, if only because taking them alive was incredibly difficult. Master Thomas's files included a description of a Mover he'd had to poison rather than risk confronting him openly.

"His body was found near the Docklands later that day," Davis added. "Someone had cut his throat."

"The Docklands," Gwen repeated. That *couldn't* be a coincidence. Hiram Pasha had died there... but London had quite a few people die every day. They couldn't *all* be connected. "When did all this happen?"

"The night before you went to Mortimer Hall," Davis said. "I knew that Howell was involved with the underground, so I thought..."

"I think you should understand that you just confessed to a very serious crime," Gwen said, sharply. "Training unregistered magicians breaks just about every law on the books."

She thought, fast. Someone had broken into Sir Travis's home and murdered him; a Mover could have done that, easily. Someone had broken into Hiram Pasha's home and murdered everyone inside; it would have been *easier* than breaking into Mortimer Hall, if only because the owner hadn't been a Sensitive. And then a Mover had been murdered... it seemed unlikely that it *was* a coincidence...

Except Sir Travis had been killed by a blow to the back of the head. Few Movers were that subtle... and Sir Travis should have been able to sense them coming. Hell, the

Mover would definitely have to be in the same room. Killing someone at a distance was beyond anyone, even a Master Magician. Sure, it was *theoretically* possible, but not even Master Thomas had had that level of control.

But if the murderer had hired a Mover to open the doors.

"I know," Davis admitted. "I..."

Gwen rubbed the side of her forehead. "We need to shut this underground down," she said, finally. "Go see Sir James; give him a *full* report of what happened since you were recruited to serve as a trainer. We'll have to arrange a meeting with them; perhaps we can offer them an amnesty, if their hands are not crusted with blood. And then we can decide your fate."

"Yes, Milady," Davis said. "Whatever you decide, I will accept."

He left the room, closing the door behind her. Gwen rubbed her eyes tiredly – why did she feel so tired, when she'd only just woken up? Maybe she should have just stayed in bed.

She stood up and walked over to the wall, where Master Thomas had hung a map of London she hadn't had the heart to take down, even though it was slightly outdated after the Swing had reshaped parts of the city. Someone had used Davis's contact – a Mover – to break into Mortimer Hall, sneak up on Sir Travis and kill him. It should have been impossible; Master Thomas, for all of his power and experience, could not have sneaked up on a Sensitive. She'd gone over that time and time again and yet an answer failed to materialise. If someone had the power to kill at a distance, surely they would have used it for something more dramatic than murdering Sir Travis.

Lord Mycroft would have given his eye teeth for a perfect assassin, she thought, grimly. There were plenty of people on the continent, starting with Talleyrand, that Lord Mycroft might have good reason to want removed. Assassination was rare among the major powers, but that was only because it was hard to get away with it – and detection could mean war. If Lord Mycroft had someone who could kill without leaving evidence, he would have used him.

After Talleyrand visited, Gwen thought slowly, *Sir Travis was killed. Coincidence?*

She shook her head. There was no way to be sure.

Putting the matter to one side, she started to delve into the matters that only the Royal Sorceress could handle. A girl in Newcastle was claiming that her husband had used Charm to convince her to marry him and was requesting that Gwen grant her a divorce. Gwen had no idea why she thought that *Gwen* had such power – only a court could grant her a separation, depending on the exact circumstances – but she would have to send someone to investigate anyway. If the girl had been Charmed, she would probably receive a separation from her husband without further ado. And the husband would go to jail.

The next report, from Haiti, warned that Voodoo practitioners might have managed to find another necromancer. Gwen shuddered at the thought; it had been less than twenty years since the last necromantic outbreak on the tormented island and that had been horrifying, worse than London. Haiti was a worthless piece of rock; whatever value it had once held had long since been destroyed by endless fighting between different groups of settlers. Some wag in London had once seriously suggested giving it back to the French. Gwen was rather inclined to agree.

We might have to send magical reinforcements over there, she thought, as she marked the report for Sir James's attention. The Governor-General of Jamaica didn't have many magicians to call upon and it was unlikely that the Governor-General of British North America would be willing to let go of any of his magicians. *But that would weaken us over here.*

The odd part of the report was a note that Russian traders had been sniffing around Haiti, for no apparent reason. Maybe they were just looking to break into the sugar and slave trade – the Russians had never expressed any moral qualms over slavery – but it was still odd, odd enough to merit a mention in a report concentrated on necromancy. Gwen frowned as she studied it, then added a postscript that perhaps a Talker should ask the Russians a few questions. A trading agreement might help to wean them away from the French... but if they wanted something else, it would be wise to find out exactly what.

Shaking her head, she finished the last letter and headed down to the dining hall for lunch. A number of magicians were still in their morning classes, but there were enough there to cast glances at Gwen as she entered the room and sat down at the High Table. She ignored them, concentrating instead on a copy of *The Times* someone had left for the senior magicians to read. The only article of great interest was a note that Talleyrand had been publicly challenged by an MP to explain France's involvement in the Battle of London.

She was still reading when Norton cleared his throat. "A box of jewels arrived for you from Lady Alexandra Milton," he said. "I have taken the liberty of checking them against the list of jewels in the will and while they are all there, there are also additional jewels that are not included in the list."

Gwen snorted. "Send the ones that aren't included back to Lady Alexandra," she said. There was no point in worrying about why the girl had sent the extra jewels. "And then we can decide how best to present them to Polly."

"I am no expert," Norton said, "but I believe that their sale would bring three to four thousand pounds. Polly would be set up for life, if she were careful."

"I'll see to it," Gwen said.

She finished her lunch and walked up to her study. Master Thomas had designed it, but she'd changed almost nothing. The vast bookshelves suited her too. Picking up Sir Travis's journal, she started to read through it, even though he was nowhere near as skilled a writer as Sir Charles. Perhaps he'd planned to polish it up before trying to publish it.

An hour later, she knew that something was badly wrong.

Chapter Thirty-Five

ir Travis had been methodical above all else, Gwen realised, as she read through his journal. He might not have been quite as good a writer as his friend – in some places, he sounded more like a whiny child than a grown man – yet he was careful to make an entry for every day, even when he had been in Britain. Once Gwen had puzzled out the code he used to refer to his trips to Istanbul, she wrote down a list of dates he had been outside the country and checked them against the records from the Golden Turk.

They didn't match.

For a long moment, Gwen stared at them, puzzled. How could Sir Travis have been in two places at once? No magic she knew could duplicate someone; the most capable Blazer could not have keep the illusion in place for more than a few minutes. The answer was obvious; Sir Travis had not been to the Golden Turk, no matter what the records said. Or had he lied about going to Istanbul?

But he worked for Lord Mycroft, Gwen thought, as she studied the records. Sir Travis had been to the Golden Turk at least once a week for the past six months, if the records were taken on face value, but several of the dates coincided with his trips to Istanbul. *He wouldn't get away with not going to Turkey – and why would he bother claiming to go when he didn't need to fake anything?*

She puzzled over it as she rang the bell for the maid. When Martha arrived, Gwen asked her to find Polly and send her to the study, then looked back at the account books. If one of the records was fake, her father had said while he'd been lecturing David, it was quite possible that they were *all* fake. And if Sir Travis had had no reason to hide what he was doing...

Polly entered, her face grim. "Milady?"

"I need you to recall when your Master was out of the country," Gwen said. "When were you left alone in the house?"

She listened to Polly's answers and compared them to the list of dates. Sir Travis had had no reason to take a second house in London and hide while gambling, not if the pattern hadn't been consistent. He'd been out of the country while the debts were being run up, which meant...

They're not real, she thought. *They can't be real.*

It fitted, she realised slowly. Sir Travis had ignored the demand for money from the Golden Turk – passed on via Polly – because he'd *known* that he owed them no money. But Howell had read *Polly's* mind and believed the debt to be real, giving him the chance to make an up-and-coming government official indebted to him. And Hiram Pasha, who had been supposed to have backed the debt, had been murdered... ensuring that no one would be able to question him. Not even a necromancer could make a dead body sit up and speak.

Means, motive and opportunity, she reminded herself. Why would someone go to all the trouble of faking gambling debts?

Lord Bracknell might have had a motive, if he'd wanted to break off the engagement between his daughter and Sir Travis, but it seemed rather pointless. Howell wouldn't have bothered either, particularly not when the debts could be so easily disproved; his power lay in truth, not lies. And Hiram Pasha... if he had worked for Turkey, why would he want to disgrace the man who had written the Airship Treaty?

"If this had worked," Gwen said out loud, "the Airship Treaty would have been destroyed. But how does Turkey benefit from that?"

Polly gave her a sharp glance. "Milady?"

"Never mind," Gwen said, tiredly.

The answer was obvious; Turkey *didn't* benefit. At best, the treaty would have to be renegotiated and every clause would be harshly scrutinised before the treaty was presented to Parliament. But at worst, the treaty would be utterly destroyed. The Establishment had a long memory and remembered the days when the expanding Ottoman Empire had seemed an all-consuming threat. And it might still *be* a threat. Turkey wasn't too far from India...

She looked at the map Sir Travis had sketched into his journal and considered it for a long moment. The new Sultan had built a powerful army, tapping both the Ottoman Empire's vast reserves in manpower and the very latest in military technology. He'd been using it to restore control over the Empire's semi-independent regions – Egypt, in particular – but it wouldn't stop there. The old nightmare of Turkey invading southern Europe was one possibility; it was equally possible that he might head east, emulating Alexander the Great. Could Persia block the path to India...

... Or would they make common cause against the infidel?

The East had a reputation – fair, unfair; it hardly mattered – for being devious, sneaky and untrustworthy. How long would the treaty last if that reputation seemed to have been proven?

I could take this to Lord Mycroft, she thought, slowly. *But it wouldn't be enough. We'd need to know who faked the gambling debts... and who murdered Sir Travis. Because if he was nothing more than an innocent man trying to do his duty, someone else had to have killed him. And then Hiram Pasha. And the Mover.*

She reached for a piece of paper and wrote out a short note to Inspector Lestrade, asking him to arrange for the Manager of the Golden Turk to be taken into custody... and then stopped. How could they hold him for long? Was faking gambling debts actually a crime? Gwen thought it should be, but she honestly didn't know. If nothing else, he had been trying to claim from Sir Travis's estate – which made it her problem. She crumbled up the piece of paper and scribbled out another one. The manager could be charged with fraud, which would allow the police to hold him long enough for a Talker to ask some pointed questions. It was of dubious legality, but few people would complain. The manager wasn't British.

"Take this to the dispatch room," she ordered Polly.

The maid nodded and left the room. Gwen turned back to the journal and started to read her way through it, right from the start. Sir Travis had gone to India to seek his fortune, as had so many other young men – and his talent had made him quite successful, working for the East India Company and the Viceroy. Maybe he'd intended to hire Sir Charles to rewrite the journal into something more exciting, particularly for the average reader. The journal managed to sound boring, even when talking about death-defying adventures across northern India.

There was a gap midway through the journal, she realised, that corresponded with the time he'd been in Bukhara, locked up in jail. Most of the entries on either side of the gap were even more elliptical than usual, intended to confuse readers. At times, she couldn't help wondering if Sir Travis had been drunk while he'd been writing in his journal. A reference to 'Indian crud' left her completely confused. Other references were even worse.

Sir Charles made his first appearance shortly after Sir Travis had gone to India. Oddly, Sir Travis – who never spent much time writing about his friends – had quite a bit to say about how much he'd enjoyed Sir Charles's company. Gwen wondered just what he meant as she read through some of the more colourful phases, before deciding that Sir Travis had been attempting to link his written work with Sir Charles. She couldn't help a smile as she realised that he'd hoped to attract readers through the link.

But it might not have worked, she thought. *Sir Charles is a good writer as well as an adventurer.*

There was no reference to gambling, she realised, as she read onwards. Instead, Sir Travis noted that he and Sir Charles had moved from kingdom to kingdom, often disguised as traders or preachers. One entry referred to a religious debate with a local priest, which had been a pleasant diversion, and included a whole series of elliptical notations that Gwen couldn't puzzle out at all. What was a 'shortened man?' The only time she'd heard anything like it had been a reference to a man being hanged for murdering his mother.

Sir Charles had made it sound exciting, when he'd been telling her stories. Gwen couldn't help thinking that Sir Travis sucked the life out of everything he touched, at least judging by his journal. Lady Elizabeth might not have found him such a good husband after all... although he would have had to work hard to be worse than her parents. And besides, a Sensitive would be *sensitive*. He would know when something was wrong with his wife.

Part of the journal discussed returning home and securing Mortimer Hall – one entry, relating to Polly, noted that the girl's wages would be raised – and then a series of missions to Istanbul. Gwen had read that section before, but she went through it again, hoping to spot something new. But again, all of the detailed comments were written in a manner that seemed designed to confuse the reader. No doubt Sir Travis had intended to decrypt it before actually *publishing* it. Only medical textbooks could get away with being so elliptical.

Sir Travis had a very lonely life, she realised, as she finished the journal. The last entry seemed to refer to the Airship Treaty, but thanks to the cryptic comments it was impossible to know for sure. *There was hardly anyone he could be near for long.*

It was true of all Sensitives, she knew. Even the most controlled of them were unnaturally aware of their surroundings. Sir Travis had probably refused to hire any other servants because too many of them would make it harder for him to concentrate. And Polly's youth would work in her favour. She would simply have less of an impact on his mind, just by existing.

And yet he'd somehow managed to serve as a diplomat as well as an intelligence officer.

She looked back at the gap in the journal and shuddered. If she'd reacted so badly to the farms, what would Sir Travis have felt when he'd been locked inside a jail? Gwen had seen the inside of a madhouse, back when Master Thomas had been training her, and she'd picked up some of the impressions permanently burned into the stones. An oriental jail would be so much worse. Sir Travis would have had to be on the verge of madness.

And yet... how had he managed to stay so close to Sir Charles for so long?

Flicking through the journal, she found the first entry concerning Sir Charles and read it for the second time.

Met the most extraordinary young officer; a soldier who reeks of nothing, but calm control. The Viceroy says that Charles Bellingham is one of the most accomplished agents in India and I believe him. He radiates almost nothing at all. This will not last, but we can work together until it ends.

Gwen stared down at the lines, reading them again and again. The less emotional a person was, the less impact they would have on a Sensitive; Sir Charles keeping himself under such tight control would have been very welcome to Sir Travis. But there was more to it than that; he couldn't be faking it, he had to be actually calm. Or...

She read through the next section and winced.

The Viceroy knighted Charles today, after we made it back from the Fort. No one deserves it more than him; his calm in the face of adversity saved us both. It was my pleasure to agree to share another mission with him, heading northwards towards Afghanistan. No two sources agree on what we will find there, but Charles is confident. Nothing is quite as dangerous as London, he says.

There were several other references to Sir Charles further on, including one that came just after the escape from Bukhara, written in a very shaky hand.

I am broken. The jail nearly broke me. Were it not for Charles, I would surely have died or gone mad like those poor souls in Bedlam. The Emir is mad and his sons are worse, steeped in such cruelty and hatred that even the worst slave drivers would have shuddered. I touch a bed and see a woman battered beyond belief, a man sliced apart for nothing more than not bowing low enough when the Emir made his appearance. Madness would have taken me if Charles hadn't somehow shared his calm with me.

The Viceroy congratulates us and tells us that there is more work to be done. We can go to Tibet or China or even Japan, if we see fit. But I have refused and so has Charles. I can no longer face the world. I will go back to London.

Gwen shivered. For all of his self-control, Sir Travis must have been pushed right to the brink of madness. If he'd snapped while he'd been held prisoner, he would have died in Bukhara. And if Sir Charles hadn't been there, he would have snapped.

Lord Mycroft wishes me to talk with the Turks. I accept; Turkey is more civilised than Bukhara. I go to Istanbul and talk with them, then come home and talk with Lord Mycroft and his allies. They want a treaty so desperately that I don't need to use my talent to sense it. I give them what they want.

And the final entry.

The Treaty is written. Let us hope that it passes.

Gwen shook her head slowly. The writer didn't sound like the Sir Travis everyone had been talking about, although – as a Sensitive – he would have had to have learned very good self-control. Perhaps he'd fooled everyone, even Mycroft or Sir Charles...

The thought struck her like a spray of cold water. Sir Travis had mentioned, several times, that Sir Charles was impressively calm, all the time. No, worse than that; he'd done something to help Sir Travis survive imprisonment in Bukhara. Gwen shivered as it slowly unfolded in her mind. Sir Charles had come out of the farms, yet had shown no signs of magic at all. Or, as sometimes happened with a new talent, they simply hadn't been recognised.

"No," she said, out loud.

But the conclusion was inescapable. If Sir Charles had been good at avoiding Sir Travis's senses, he could easily have sneaked up on his friend and attacked him from behind. The Mover who had opened the door could have been murdered afterwards, along with Hiram Pasha... after leaving the notes taken from Sir Travis in his drawer, just to make it obvious that there had been a link between the two men. And the death of the Mover might have gone unnoticed. No one had *known* that he was a Mover.

Gwen gritted her teeth as she put it all together. Sir Charles had forced his way into the investigation, offering to help... and pointing her towards the Golden Turk, where she'd picked up the account books that suggested that Sir Travis had been taking money from the Turks. He'd betrayed his friend; no doubt he hadn't known all of the dates when Sir Travis had been in Istanbul. And he'd betrayed Gwen too.

I've been made a fool, she thought, as her temper flared. She'd allowed him to worm his way into her heart, to reach out and kiss her... and do more than kiss her. Lady Mary had aborted her child, but how could Gwen blame her for that mistake when she'd come so close to making it herself? It was worse; she'd *known* what had happened to her mother and yet she'd come so close to repeating her mistake. She'd allowed her desire to blind her.

No one knew, she told herself, but she knew it wouldn't last. Sir Charles might believe his secret to be safe... yet it would come out, once Gwen shared what she'd discovered with Lord Mycroft. Sir Charles would be hanged for high treason, but Gwen herself would be publicly humiliated. She understood just what Howell's victims would have felt now, after coming so close to absolute disaster. All the people who'd claimed that a girl couldn't be Royal Sorceress would come forward to argue that Gwen had proved them right.

She rang the bell. Martha appeared a moment later. "Have my carriage brought round to the front gate," she ordered. "Then have a messenger come here."

Martha nodded and withdrew. Gwen scribbled down a short explanation for Lord Mycroft, then attached it to Sir Travis's journal and the incriminating account books. When the messenger arrived, Gwen passed the whole collection to him with instructions to take it to Whitehall as soon as possible. Lord Mycroft *had* to be informed. No doubt he would be disappointed in Gwen.

She stood up and looked around the study, wondering if she would be allowed to return to Cavendish Hall. They might sack her after the truth came out – and it would, she had no doubt of that. She had sufficient enemies that it would never be allowed to remain a secret... but somehow it no longer mattered. All that mattered was ending the whole affair as quickly as possible.

Shaking her head, she picked up her hat and cane, then walked down the stairs towards the front entrance. Those hoping to waylay her saw the expression on her face and stepped backwards, allowing her to pass unmolested. She paused in the entrance hall, remembering just how proud she'd been the day Master Thomas had brought her to Cavendish Hall... would she be allowed to return?

Maybe not, she told herself, as she walked outside. *But that isn't the important problem right now.*

Chapter Thirty-Six

eople would probably notice if she took a carriage directly to Sir Charles's house, Gwen realised as the carriage clattered through the streets of London, but it hardly mattered any longer. Her reputation was going to be in tatters, both personally and professionally – and while she didn't really care about the personal aspect, she *did* care about losing her professional reputation. But there seemed to be no way to avoid it. She mulled over possibilities for a while, before dismissing them all as impractical.

Maybe I'll have to flee to France, she thought, in a moment of dark humour. *Or maybe even go to India myself.*

Sir Charles had rented a large house on the outskirts of London, an odd decision for someone who wanted to carve out a place for himself in Polite Society. Addresses grew more prestigious the closer they were to Whitehall, even though the flats in Pall Mall were little more than a couple of living rooms and a bathroom. They were a far cry from the great houses of the aristocracy, where a building with twenty bedrooms would be considered *small*. But then, she couldn't fault his choice; it was very hard to do anything in Whitehall without being seen.

"Wait here," she ordered the coachman. She changed her mind a moment later. "No, take the rest of the day off."

She watched him driving off, then turned to look at the house. Oddly, it reminded her of Howell's house, apart from the smaller garden and the complete absence of trees providing cover from prying eyes. Gwen walked up to the gate, hesitated and then pushed the doorbell. There was a long pause before the main door opened and an elderly man walked down towards the gate. Sir Charles's manservant, Gwen decided, after a moment. Very few men in London would be without a manservant, even if they lacked the funds to hire other servants.

"Lady Gwen," he said, as he opened the gate. "The Master said you might call."

Gwen felt her temper flare, forcing her to bite her cheek to keep it under control. Sir Charles had said she might be calling, had he? No doubt he'd believed that Gwen would come so they could make love in private. How arrogant was he to believe she would do that? But she remembered the way her body had felt after they'd kissed for the first time and she knew that he might have been right, had she not realised the truth.

"Thank you," she said, keeping her voice as steady as she could. "Please take me to him."

The interior of Sir Charles's house was almost barren, with only a handful of artefacts looted from India on display. Sir Charles, she suspected, didn't entertain guests very often; a conspicuous display of wealth was part and parcel of living in high society. If the wealthy aristocrats had seen his house, even though it was rented, they would have considered him poor – and wealth lasted far longer than fame. Gwen glanced at one of the artefacts, a golden facemask shaped like a demon, and shivered. It was a truly appalling sight.

"I believe that the Master took that from a Thuggi priest," the manservant informed her, in a tone that suggested that she should be impressed. "The Thugs preyed on their fellow Indians until they were wiped out. Even today, their name is spoken of with fear and hatred."

Gwen shrugged and allowed him to lead her into a study. Sir Charles sat at a desk, writing in a large journal of his own. Merely seeing him caused her heart to race, setting off a conflicting series of emotions that threatened to undo her. He'd killed his best friend and at least four other people, but she still wanted him.

He turned and smiled at her. This time, she realised that

he smiled too much. It was a mask to hide his true feelings, far more suitable than the Indian facemask she'd seen in the hallway... and far harder to see through. Her own admiration for his exploits had blinded her, Gwen reminded herself, again. She could not afford to make the same mistake twice.

"Thank you, Fred," Sir Charles said. "That will be all."

The manservant bowed and retreated, closing the door behind her. Gwen looked at him, feeling oddly vulnerable, even though she knew that she should have nothing to fear. But then, merely being alone with an unrelated man was enough to ruin a lady's reputation... she couldn't help smiling bitterly as Sir Charles stood upright. After everything she'd been fool enough to do, Polite Society would have problems choosing just what they were going to use to ruin her reputation.

"I'm glad you came," he said, huskily. "I missed you after the dance."

He reached for her, but Gwen stepped backwards. "Why did you kill your friend?"

Something flickered through his eyes. "What do you mean?"

Gwen stared at him, trying to feel him out with her senses. She tried not to use that talent – it was weak and imprecise – but there was no choice. He seemed to be nothing, but a void where a person should be. Even the faint disturbance in the air he should have caused as he moved wasn't there.

"You have magic," Gwen accused. "Your talent is the *absence* of magic. A Sensitive would not have recognised that you were there, not unless he *looked* at you. And all you had to do was sneak up behind him and club him on the head. You're a practised fighter; it would have been easy for you to stun or kill him with one blow."

"Travis was my friend," Sir Charles said, coldly. "Gwen, I care deeply for you..."

"Do you?" Gwen asked, sharply. "I think you muscled your way into the investigation to monitor our progress."

"You're a remarkable girl," Sir Charles said. "I allowed myself to fall for you."

"I don't believe you," Gwen said, remembering some of the whispers the junior magicians had shared. They'd all talked about reaching a point after which they couldn't stop – and yet Sir Charles had stopped when she'd told him to stop, without even *trying* to argue. "You didn't have to mention the Golden Turk – and if you were so concerned with Sir Travis's reputation, you would never have *mentioned* the Golden Turk."

She held his eyes, forcing him to look away. "And you talked about gambling incessantly with him in India," she added. "I believed you, yet there isn't a mention of gambling in his journal, not even with you. You were claiming to defend your friend, but instead you were creating an impression that he was addicted to gambling, even to the point of using his powers to cheat. It was quite believable. Men like you and he gamble with your own lives regularly. Why not gambling for money too?

"I went through the account books. There are plenty of debts listed, but a number were entered for days when Sir Travis was out of the country. I have *proof* that he *couldn't* have run up those debts. And Hiram Pasha, who backed the debts, was killed, apparently on the same night Sir Travis died. How very convenient! All the Charm in the world wouldn't suffice to interrogate a dead man."

"You're wrong," Sir Charles said. "Gwen..."

"Prove it," Gwen insisted. "Where were you the night Sir Travis died?"

He had no answer.

Gwen felt magic shimmering within her, demanding release. She wanted to hurt him, to kill him, both for what he'd done to his friend and for making her look a fool. Or worse.

"You killed him," she said, coldly. "You committed high treason. *Why?*"

Sir Charles seemed to relax, suddenly. "Why not?"

Gwen blinked in surprise. "*Why not?*"

He smiled. For the first time since entering the room, it seemed real.

"You know about my family, I believe," Sir Charles said, as calmly as if he were ordering dinner. "I didn't, you see. There was no clue that I wasn't their middle child until I discovered that I'd been adopted. And I only found out through accident."

Gwen couldn't help feeling a flicker of sympathy. She'd been marginalised because of her sex and magic; what must it have been like to know yourself one moment and see it all torn away the next? Jack had had similar motives for turning against the Establishment.

"They treated me as their son, right up until my elder brother died," Sir Charles added. "And then they turned on me. I had an engagement; it was suddenly broken. I had a ticket to the innermost levels of society; it was destroyed. My friends... suddenly wanted nothing more to do with me. And Rachel was so disgusted that she *spat* at me."

"Rachel Wolsey," Gwen said, remembering her mother's views on the girl. She hadn't just fallen from grace, she'd done something Polite Society found even more shocking; she'd *gloried* in her fall. If rumour were to be believed, Rachel Wolsey had slept with every dissolute young man in London. "And *she* spat at you?"

"I was a commoner," Sir Charles reminded her. "She didn't like the thought of opening herself for a commoner."

Gwen shuddered. "And so...?"

"My family – my *adopted* family – paid for me to go to India and bought me a commission," Sir Charles reminded her. "I served there for years, earning plaudits... and yet my family tried to deny me a knighthood. Lucky for me that they didn't manage to convince the Viceroy, after what I'd done. Snobbish prick he might be, but he knew the value of rewarding courage and determination. I was a knight and a famous adventurer. But it wasn't enough."

"And so you decided to betray your country," Gwen said, flatly. "Why did you kill your friend?"

Sir Charles laughed at her. "What made you think he was my friend?"

Gwen stared back at him. "His journal..."

"Sir Travis, the poor aristocrat whose very name opened doors all my wealth could not force, clung to me," Sir

Charles said. "I was never truly aware of my talent until after I met him – and after that, I could never escape him. He was a constant reminder of the mockery my life had become. I did much of the work on our missions; he reaped more of the rewards. Just because he was born on the right side of the blankets!"

He slapped his hands together. "Tell me, *Lady* Gwen, what would have happened to you if you hadn't been born to the aristocracy? You would have been killed – or worse."

Gwen shivered. Lord Blackburn's uncle had seriously urged, back before the Swing had raged over London, that Gwen should be sent to the farms. There, she would have spent the rest of her days drugged out of her mind, giving birth to child after child. If she'd been born to a lower-class household, there would never have been a chance to apprentice under Master Thomas. She would just have vanished into the farms.

"I was lucky," she said, quietly.

"Our entire system is badly flawed," Sir Charles said. "If competence and birth went together, maybe it would work – but they don't go together. For every Duke of India or Lord Amherst, there are ten idiots who think that the world will bow before them, simply because of their high birth. None of them can control themselves and yet they rule our world."

Gwen found it hard to argue. The Committee, at least, was reasonably competent; the same couldn't be said for the lesser nobility, who preferred to enjoy themselves rather than actually work hard to maintain their fortunes. And she had never really understood just how little some aristocratic women knew until she'd discovered why she'd been offered instruction on basic accounting. The women rarely knew the value of money, let alone how to bargain...

She shook her head. "Do you believe that your treachery will change things?"

"It might," Sir Charles said. "The public already has a greater stake in government after the Swing. What will happen if the myth of aristocratic power is called into question?"

366

Gwen couldn't help herself. She snorted.

"Do you really believe," she asked, "that what you're doing is in Britain's best interests?"

Sir Charles shrugged. "Of course not," he said. "But really, when has Britain cared about *my* best interests?"

He pulled up his jacket to reveal a scar. "I was slashed by a knife-wielding assassin while protecting the Viceroy," he said. "My back was lashed hundreds of times while I was in Bukhara, where the Emir believed us to be plotting his overthrow. I even came within bare seconds of being trampled to death by a wild elephant. Time and time again, I risked life and limb to serve the interests of my country. But my country's leaders were so petty that they tried to block me receiving my rightful reward. How many others were knighted for much less?"

"I wouldn't know," Gwen admitted.

"Of course you wouldn't," Sir Charles pointed out, coldly. "All you would know is that someone was knighted. You wouldn't know how many others had been barred from a knighthood because of an accident of birth, or because they weren't considered gentlemen, or... do you know how many aristocrats were promoted into positions where they could get people killed, just because of their birth? I shudder to think what Colonel Robertson would have received if he'd survived the Sikh War. He would probably have been rewarded for walking right into an ambush and seeing two-thirds of his men shot away before someone had the common sense to order a retreat."

He looked up at her. "And tell me," he added, "what would happen to you if they discovered another *male* Master Magician?"

Gwen grimaced. It wasn't hard to imagine at all.

"You would be sacked," Sir Charles said. "What do you *really* owe to the Establishment?"

His eyes bored into hers. "You were treated as a witch when you were a child," he reminded her. "And now, even though you have proved yourself more than enough, they still sneer at you. There are even whispers that you offered yourself to Lord Mycroft to be confirmed in your position. The moment they find a replacement, they will kick you out of Cavendish Hall and exile you to India, where all the *embarrassments* go. What do you really owe them?"

Gwen hesitated. He had a point.

"Come with me," Sir Charles added. "You could blaze your own path..."

"My mother kept me," Gwen said, quietly. It was hard to be angry at her mother now, even after what they'd said to one another. Gwen had come far too close to making the same mistake. "I could have been given up for adoption, but she kept me, no matter the damage to her reputation."

"You were isolated," Sir Charles reminded her. "How many friends did you have growing up?"

"I thought that you were a friend," Gwen said, unable to keep the bitterness from her voice. "But my mother didn't abandon me, even though it would have been easy. Why should I abandon her?"

"The Establishment will drop you the moment it feels it can," Sir Charles said, insistently. "I *care* about you, Gwen; they do not. They cannot. Join me."

Gwen looked up at him. She knew that he was right; her experience told her that aristocracy was sometimes a poor way of choosing leaders. Jack had brought London to its knees and, as far as anyone knew, there was no aristocratic blood in him. Lord Brockton was unable to see beyond his own self-interest; Lord Blackburn had been even worse, before he'd fled to Turkey. And yet...

She'd sworn an oath to the King.

"I can't," she said, quietly. "I gave them my word..."

"They will not reward you as you deserve," Sir Charles reminded her. "How much have you done for them already? No matter what you do, they will always hate and fear you; eventually, they will seek to replace you. One day, your life as the Royal Sorceress will be over."

"You might be right," Gwen said, making up her mind. "But you still killed Sir Travis."

She stared at him, daring him to deny her. "I read his journal. He didn't know how you felt about him – and he clung to you because you didn't upset his talent. I think he cared deeply for you, in his own fashion. And you betrayed him by cracking his skull.

"You're right," she added, before he could say a word. "There are plenty of aristocrats who do not deserve to live. But Sir Travis wasn't one of them. And even if he was, it wouldn't make your actions *right*. You're just seeking to punish everyone for the crimes of a few."

She gritted her teeth at a memory. Six months ago, Lord Blackburn had encouraged Lord Liverpool, the Prime Minister at the time, to send troops into London's poorer districts, stirring up a hornet's nest. The day before, only a handful of them had supported Jack; the day afterwards, they were all rebels and the Swing had begun. Lord Blackburn had played right into Jack's hands.

"I can't let you get away with it," she said, lifting a hand. "Please, come peacefully..."

Sir Charles moved forward, catching her hand in a vice-like grip. "So they can hang me from the nearest tree?" He asked. "Why should I do that?"

Gwen winced at the pain. "Let go of me," she ordered. For the first time in far too long, she felt real fear. Few people had managed to hurt her outside training sessions with combat magicians. "Now."

"Make me," Sir Charles said.

Gwen reached for her magic...

... And it refused to respond.

Chapter Thirty-Seven

Her panic must have shown in her eyes, because Sir Charles began to laugh.

"It was *very* difficult to fine-tune the talent," he said, as he pushed her back against the wall. "Staying invisible to Travis was one thing, but other magicians... ah, *that* was a bit harder. I knew that all magicians are under standing orders to report any strange magical experiences to their superiors and a single mistake would have been far too revealing."

Gwen couldn't help a gasp of pain as his grip tightened. Her magic seemed to be curled up inside her, unable to respond to her commands or reach outside her body. Whatever he was doing was powerful enough to hold her helpless.

"You could have gone to Master Thomas," she said. "*He* would have helped you."

"Or would he have killed me out of hand?" Sir Charles asked. "A talent like mine... think how useful it would be to the enemies of the country. Or even just the enemies of *Master Thomas*. The old man had hundreds of enemies who pissed on his grave after he died. He wouldn't want a talent like mine to become public."

Gwen felt the wall against her back and knew that she was running out of time. "You had to have had help," she said, as another piece of the puzzle clicked together in her mind. "I think you went to work for the French. *They* helped you to control your powers."

Talleyrand had visited Sir Travis... and he'd been the last one to see him alive. It was clear, now, what had happened. Talleyrand had given the signal to Sir Charles and his hired Mover and the murders had begun. Sir Travis had been murdered and his papers had been stolen, then Hiram Pasha had been murdered and the papers planted in his house. And then the Mover had been killed, just to seal off the loose ends.

She brought her knee up, trying to strike between his legs as Irene had taught her. But he twisted to one side, then shoved her to the floor, still keeping his grip on her arm. Gwen gasped in pain as her back slammed against the hard wooden flooring, feeling her head spinning from the force of the impact. Whatever undiscovered talent had allowed her to heal herself, without ever realising that she was doing so, must also have been blocked by his power. And he was far stronger than her, physically.

"Do you know everything I did while I was in India?" Sir Charles hissed. "There were hundreds of details I left out of my dispatches."

He pressed down on her, making it hard for her to breathe. One hand frisked her for weapons, removing two knives and a custom-made revolver Gwen carried in her jacket. He tossed them away as he leered down at her, leaving Gwen in no doubt of what he intended. Without her magic, he could break her... and then take her to France. Jack might have helped them to start up farms of their own. Even if he hadn't, they had to consider the value of breeding Gwen with other magicians.

She struggled against him as his hand started to caress her throat, then reached up to cover her mouth. Gwen saw her opportunity and bit him as hard as she could. Sir Charles gasped in pain and tried to pull free, but Gwen refused to let go. He couldn't pull free without letting go of her wrist.

He grunted and pushed her down, slamming her head into the floor. Gwen saw stars, but somehow managed to hold on to her awareness – and his hand. He let go of her wrist and lifted his hand, striking her across the face. Gwen tasted blood – hers or his; she didn't know – as she felt her magic flare into life. And yet it refused to touch him directly.

Down, she thought, and infused magic into the floor. It

started to collapse a moment later, sending them both slipping down towards the basement. Sir Charles caught hold of her, but her magic refused to be snuffed out this time; she realised, dimly, that his magic might require some degree of physical contact to work. But Charm hadn't worked either... gritting her teeth against the pain, she reached out with her mind, caught hold of his shoes and pushed them away as hard as she could. Sir Charles spun backwards and crashed through the looming hole into the basement. A moment later, Gwen followed.

"Damn you," Sir Charles grunted. "You utter..."

Whatever he had to say was buried behind a dull roar as the rest of the floor started to collapse inwards. Gwen caught hold of her magic, despite the growing pain in her head, and levitated herself upwards, well out of reach. A moment later, she heard a shot and a bullet narrowly missed her; Sir Charles had somehow caught hold of her revolver. She stared down at him, wrapping a bubble of protective magic around her and smiled coldly. A second bullet bounced off her shields.

"You can't touch me," Sir Charles said. He was bleeding from his hand – and a nasty-looking scratch along his face. "And you can't stay up there forever."

"I don't have to," Gwen said. She hadn't felt so drained since the day she'd followed Master Thomas back to London, flying over fifty miles in a single night. If he hadn't sensed her following him, she might have died that night and the undead would have destroyed London.

She wanted to shout, but she didn't have the energy. "I'm the Royal Sorceress, you filthy traitor."

"And what," Sir Charles demanded, "do you think that means?"

Gwen shaped a thought and threw a bolt of energy at him. He stood there... and the bolt dissipated before it even touched him. Gwen scowled inwardly; she hadn't expected that to work, but she had had to try. Instead, she picked up a piece of debris with her magic and threw it at him as hard as she could. He tried to jump out of the way, but it was too late and it slammed into his arm. Gwen heard it break as he staggered, almost falling to the floor.

Somehow, he managed to keep hold of the pistol long enough to fire a third shot at her.

She picked up a second piece of debris and aimed it at his head. Sir Charles opened his mouth, either to curse her or beg for mercy, but the debris struck him before he could say a word. Gwen saw his skull shatter into a mass of bloody chunks, well beyond the ability of any Healer to put back together. The rest of his body dropped to the ground and lay there, twitching unpleasantly. Gwen felt her head swimming and dropped down to the ground, throwing up the moment she landed. It was far too possible that she had a concussion.

"What?" A voice demanded. "What happened?"

Gwen fought her way through the haze that had enveloped her to see the manservant – Fred, Sir Charles had called him – picking his way through the debris towards her. She hoped that he didn't want to start a fight; she doubted that she had the energy to light a spark, let alone stop someone from hurting her. Somehow, she managed to turn to face him, knowing that she had to look terrible. There was blood and vomit all over her suit.

"Call the police," she ordered, as she sank to her knees. The world just kept spinning around her. "Tell them to hurry."

She silently cursed her own mistake as the manservant stumbled off. If she'd had the common sense to bring Merlin with her, or even Inspector Lestrade, she wouldn't have come so close to absolute disaster. She'd been too confident in her abilities, even though she'd had a good idea what Sir Charles could do. All of the other farm children would have to be re-examined, just to see if they had similar talents. Who knew? Maybe there were hundreds of nulls – or whatever they ended up being called – out there.

Slowly, the world stopped spinning around her. Her head still felt fragile, but most of the pain was gone. There was no sign of the manservant... he might have been working for the French and had taken the opportunity to make his escape, rather than doing as he was told. Gwen stood upright gingerly and walked over to Sir Charles.

The body had stopped twitching and was clearly dead.

Damn you, she thought, bitterly.

It had been nice to have dreams of a husband, a man who wouldn't resent her powers or fear what she might do to him if they had a fight. And part of her had fallen in love... or thought it had. But the Sir Charles portrayed in his own dispatches had had little in common with the *real* Sir Charles. She supposed that shouldn't have been such a surprise. The versions of Gwen herself, particularly the caricatures from Grub Street, were almost completely unrecognisable.

Her lips twitched in a moment of black humour. She'd kept and framed the cartoon that had her turning the Royal Committee into frogs. There were times when she wished she could do just that.

She bid the dream a silent farewell and then turned and walked away from him, looking for the way up to the ground floor. The manservant had come down the stairs... she scowled, looking at the mess she'd made of the house, then picked her way up them carefully. She simply didn't feel like levitating herself out of the rubble. Her head still felt fragile.

There was no sign of the manservant, she realised, as she looked around, but the entire building seemed to be on the verge of collapse. She forced herself to move faster as she walked towards what remained of the front door, recovering her hat and coat as she fled. Moments after she made it outside, there was a crash as part of the roof fell in, burying Sir Charles below the rubble. Gwen couldn't help giggling as she realised that she would probably have to pay to rebuild the house from scratch. Her magic had done far more damage than she'd intended to do.

Sitting down in the garden, she removed her stained jacket and pulled the coat on, covering her undershirt. Lady Mary would have said that it was indecent, but Lady Mary wasn't there... Gwen scowled as she realised that she owed her mother an apology. It would have been so easy to allow Sir Charles to take her virginity, no matter the risks. And part of her had wanted just that.

You were lucky, she told herself, sternly. But she didn't

feel lucky.

She looked around, wondering if the police were ever going to come. *Someone* must have heard the building falling inwards... she cursed her own mistake in sending the coachman away, even though she hadn't really wanted witnesses. If she'd left him outside, she could have sent him for the police...

Lord Brockton would sneer in his oh-so-polite manner, wondering out loud just how the Royal Sorceress could have been so stupid. And he would have been right, Gwen admitted to herself; she *had* been stupid. For once, his sarcastic comments and biting remarks would have found a deserving target. Lord Mycroft, on the other hand, would merely be disappointed in her. That, she suspected, would feel worse than Lord Brockton's sneers.

Maybe I should resign, she thought. It was funny how she'd never really considered resigning before, but that had been before her emotions had almost cost her everything. *I could let someone else take the job.*

But there was no one else who *could* handle the job.

She looked up sharply as she felt a touch on her mind, looking around for the Talker who had to be somewhere nearby. Simone was standing just inside the gates, looking at the debris in dismay. Gwen had to smile at the expression on the French girl's face. Talker she might have been, but she had probably never seen the results when two magicians went to war.

A moment later, the French girl began to retreat.

"No, you don't," Gwen said, and reached out with her magic. Simone was pulled forwards, half-dragged by an invisible force. Gwen felt a moment of amusement at the panic in her eyes, before realising just how much she was acting like Sir Charles by *enjoying* someone's terror. But she didn't allow the guilt to convince her to let Simone go. "Why are you here?"

"I have diplomatic immunity," Simone said. Her hands fluttered around her body, as if she was trying to brush the magic holding her away. "You can't do anything to me."

Gwen wondered if that was actually true. *Talleyrand* had diplomatic immunity, but she wasn't sure if that extended to his so-called daughter. Maybe it would have been better if Simone had been classed as an embassy staffer, yet that would have raised eyebrows. She would have been taken for a whore.

"Maybe," she said, allowing some Charm to shimmer into her voice. "Why are you here?"

"I have diplomatic immunity," Simone repeated, after a moment of inner struggle. "You cannot use Charm on me."

"So it seems," Gwen said. The girl was stronger than she'd realised... but then, being a successful Talker required mastery of one's mind. Still, if subtle Charm wouldn't work, blatant Charm would at least keep the girl quiet. "Sit down, put your hands on your head and wait patiently until the police arrive. And then we can go have a few words with your father."

Simone glared at her as her body complied with Gwen's instructions, clearly against her will. Gwen felt another moment of guilt, which she pushed aside savagely. Simone's appearance at Sir Charles's house confirmed her theory that he'd been working for the French... no doubt his powers had helped Simone come to terms with her own powers. Or maybe Jack had taught her personally. There was no way to know.

Maybe your detractors are right, she thought, as she looked at the silent girl. The guilt was making it harder to think clearly, even though her head felt better. *You've become worse than Lord Blackburn. At least he restricted his depravities to the lower classes.*

Gwen felt Simone's glare burning into her back as she stood up and started to pace around the garden. Judging by the constant shuffling, the girl was trying hard to break the Charm or discover it's limits. Gwen briefly considered reinforcing it, just before two police carriages came into view. She shot Simone a triumphant glance as the carriages stopped in front of the house and a number of policemen jumped down onto the streets.

"Inspector Hopkins," she said, in relief.

"Lady Gwen," the Inspector said. He looked past her towards the house, taking in the piles of rubble and barely-standing walls. "What the... ah, what happened here?"

"Magic," Gwen said, tightly. She didn't want to say anything else in front of Simone, not when it would definitely be passed onwards to Talleyrand – and the French magical researchers. Knowing that something was possible was half the battle. "I need you to secure the house, search it..."

"We know the drill," Hopkins assured her. He looked down at Simone. "And who is this?"

"I am a French diplomat being held prisoner against my will," Simone said. She took her hands off her head a moment later, as if she'd only just remembered that they were there. "Your country is in violation of several accords and international treaties that could lead to war."

Gwen blinked in surprise, then remembered that she'd told Simone to stay quiet until the police arrived. "Lady Simone is going to be escorted back to the embassy by me," she said, firmly. There was no point in dragging Hopkins into the affair, not when a diplomatic incident would destroy his career. If there was blame, better it all fell on Gwen. "Can we borrow one of your carriages?"

Hopkins looked as if he wanted to ask questions, before thinking better of it. "There will be other officers on the way," he assured her. "You are welcome to borrow one of the carriages."

"Thank you," Gwen said. She looked back at Simone, still sitting on the ground. "It's time to go and meet your father."

"A formal complaint will be filed," Simone informed her, as she stood up. The Charm seemed to have completely worn off. "You will certainly be called to answer for your crimes."

"You and me both," Gwen said, as she led the way towards the carriage. The Privy Council would be pleased to know that the treaty hadn't been deliberately slanted towards Turkey, but the doubters would still be looking for ways to refuse to ratify the agreement. "You and me both."

Her stomach rumbled, reminding her that she needed food. Probing inside her coat, she found the chocolate bars she'd developed a habit of carrying and took them out, silently relieved that they hadn't melted in the heat. Simone would probably want one too... she hesitated, then passed one of the bars to the French girl. She stared at it numbly for a long second and then put it in her pocket.

Gwen motioned for Simone to climb inside the carriage, then looked over at Hopkins. "I need you to send a message to Whitehall," she added. "Please ask Lord Mycroft to convene the Privy Council tomorrow, as early as possible. I'll make a full report then."

"Understood," Hopkins said. He looked up into the darkened carriage, then back at Gwen. Surprisingly, he seemed concerned for Gwen herself. "Are you sure you know what you are doing?"

Gwen smiled. "For the first time in a week," she said, "I am *absolutely* sure that I know what I am doing."

Chapter Thirty-Eight

I must say," Talleyrand said, "that your treatment of my daughter was abominable."

Gwen tried to conceal her amusement, although she was fairly sure that an experienced diplomat like Talleyrand would have seen it on her face.

"Your *daughter* was involved in a murder, as were you," Gwen said. "I do not believe that she will be welcome in this country any longer."

Talleyrand lifted a single eyebrow. "I do beg your pardon?"

"You went to see Sir Travis on the night of his murder," Gwen accused. "I think you went to see if you could convince him to abandon the Airship Treaty. When he refused, you gave the signal to Sir Charles and his ally and they murdered him, then went to murder Hiram Pasha and leave the evidence in his desk drawer for us to find. You effectively murdered him with your own hands."

"Murder is never diplomatic," Talleyrand said.

"Of course not," Gwen agreed. "But you went and did it anyway."

Talleyrand smiled. "You are aware, of course, that such a course of action might lead to war?"

"But the murder had been committed by an Englishman," Gwen countered. "You might avoid the war altogether. If you were lucky."

She leaned forward. "I used Charm on Simone, I confess," she added. "I didn't ask her any questions, despite the temptation. Tell me – how did you manage to convince him to join you without *knowing* that he was already disloyal."

Talleyrand surprised her by laughing, although there was no humour in the sound.

"You magicians," he said, shaking his head. "There have been betrayers and betrayals ever since the human race was thrown out of the Garden of Eden. We didn't *need* magic to find someone discontented and work on him until he cracked."

He smiled. "But do have fun trying to prove it."

Gwen scowled at him. She could prove Sir Charles's involvement, but it would be much harder to prove that the French had been behind it. The general public already wanted war; the Privy Council would demand considerably more proof before starting one. And now Simone was back in the French Embassy, it would be difficult to *get* that proof.

"We shall see," she said, although she knew that he was probably right. "Until then..."

She stood up. "I dare say that you will be sent back to France," she said, as she walked towards the door. "And, no matter how many admirers she has, so will Simone."

Talleyrand watched her until she stepped out of his office, but said nothing.

The sun was shining brightly as Gwen stepped out of the gatehouse and started to walk towards Whitehall. A moment later, she looked up in surprise as a carriage pulled up beside her and Sir James stuck his head out of the window.

"Lord Mycroft sent me," he said. "Come ride back to Cavendish Hall?"

Gwen hesitated, then climbed into the carriage and sat facing him.

"He said that you might appreciate some company," Sir James said, as the carriage rattled back to life. "Are you all right?"

Gwen honestly didn't know how to answer. Lord Mycroft might have meant well by sending Sir James to her, but she couldn't help feeling that she was being tortured. Seeing him was a reminder that she had compromised herself – and that she might be pushed into resigning as Royal Sorceress. At least Sir James was reasonably competent, she told herself, as she looked up at his handsome face. He wouldn't bungle the job, even if he didn't have the full set of powers.

"I will get better," she said, finally. "Do you feel ready to become the Royal Sorcerer?"

Sir James stared at her. "I can't be," he said, astonished. "I'm just a Mover..."

"Someone may have to take my place," Gwen said. "I made mistakes in the investigation, bad ones. The Privy Council may decide to sack me."

Sir James leaned forward. "Do you really think that Master Thomas never made a mistake?"

"Master Thomas had considerably more latitude than I do," Gwen said, tartly. He'd been Royal Sorcerer for so long that he'd known where all the bodies were buried. "My mistakes could have been disastrous."

"So could his," Sir James reminded her. "And mine, for that matter. There has never been any endeavour where no mistakes were made, no matter how much effort you put into pre-planning the entire operation. You are far from the only person to have made a mistake and then recovered from it."

"Maybe," Gwen said. But a man could make no end of mistakes and survive. A woman needed only a hint of a mistake to ruin her reputation beyond repair. "But they won't see it that way."

Sir James shook his head. "If they offer me the job, I will refuse it," he said. "Quite apart from the paperwork" – he smiled at her expression – "you have done a better job than I think they realise. No one, even a fully-trained man, could have filled Master Thomas's shoes without some problems. And you almost beat all six of us while we were skirmishing. I think you would have beaten us if you hadn't had to hold back."

Gwen nodded, remembering how easy it had been to use her weaker talents against Howell's magicians.

"And then Polite Society owes you a huge debt," Sir James added. "You killed the man who haunted their nightmares for years *and you* destroyed all the evidence he used to blackmail them. I think you have more friends than you realise."

"You probably shouldn't be here," Gwen said, stiffly. She waved her hand around to indicate the carriage's interior. "Your reputation might be damaged."

"I was in India," Sir James said. "My reputation was already damaged."

Gwen remembered Sir Charles and shivered. The general public would probably still see him as a hero, unless the truth came out. And when it did... would they lose faith in all heroes? He *had* been knighted, even though he'd deserved more; the public might start questioning the aristocracy's position, just as Sir Charles had hoped. Who knew where *that* would end?

"It can always get worse," she said, bitterly. How could she have *guessed* the secret her mother had concealed all those years? "You shouldn't..."

"I'm too stubborn to care what other people think," Sir James said. "If they ask me to take your place, I will tell them exactly what I think of it. And there's no better candidate than myself."

Gwen looked up at him, then shook her head. He *was* handsome and he cared about her and... and so had Sir Charles, or so she'd thought. She didn't dare allow herself to be attracted to anyone else, let alone act on it. The rest of her life was going to be very lonely.

Her lips twitched. "Maybe I should go to India myself," she said. "I could get away from Polite Society."

"An understandable impulse," Sir James assured her. "But I don't think that will be necessary."

He shrugged. "Besides, India is hot and teeming with insects," he added. "Plenty of people find it uncomfortable."

Gwen shrugged. "We shall see," she said, darkly. The carriage rattled to a halt. "Do you want to come inside with me or slip in later?"

Sir James gave her an odd look. "I came to pick you up," he said, dryly. "I think everyone knows that."

He winked at her. "Besides, if anyone gives you trouble, I will thrash them to within an inch of their lives," he added. "It will be my pleasure."

Gwen had to laugh. "I have a list of names," she said, deadpan. "Come on."

She gathered herself as best as she could, then climbed out of the carriage with her head held high. Sir James dismissed the coachman and then walked beside her as they passed through the gatehouse and headed into Cavendish Hall. Gwen had half-expected everyone in the building to be waiting in the entrance hall to meet them, but there was no one there apart from a couple of student magicians who were awaiting punishment from the Sergeant. Gwen winced at their expressions, then walked up the stairs towards her office. Sir James stayed with her all the way.

"Lady Gwen," Martha said. *She* would have no trouble realising that Gwen was upset. "Would you like some tea?"

"Yes, please," Gwen said, relieved. Her maid wouldn't pry, thankfully. "Can you bring tea for Sir James and Doctor Norwell too? He'll be along in a moment."

Doctor Norwell bustled around the corner. "I thought that there was no such thing as precognition," Sir James muttered in her ear. "How did you...?"

"Lord Mycroft will have told him to talk to me," Gwen said, ruefully. "And you might as well hear it too."

She raised her voice. "Come into my office," she added, as she opened the door. "We can talk inside."

Martha returned moments later with cups of hot sweet tea. Gwen sipped hers gratefully, silently relieved that the two men were allowing her a chance to gather herself and get her thoughts in order after her ordeal. She didn't want to have to tell them anything, but there was no choice. Doctor Norwell, at least, had to know about the existence of magic-draining magicians. There had to be others out there, perhaps among the farm children who had been believed to be without magic. The normal tests, she suspected, wouldn't work on a null.

Perhaps we should call them leeches, she said, remembering the medical leeches a doctor had offered David, when an illness had left him bedridden for a week. The other magicians would probably call them worse.

Necromancers were executed upon discovery –Gwen had adopted Olivia to save her from certain death – and she suspected that there would be demands that leeches be killed too.

"Sir Charles Bellingham killed Sir Travis," she said. Neither of them showed any surprise, confirming her suspicion that Lord Mycroft had shared the contents of her note with them. "And he had a very unusual talent."

She ran through the whole story, sparing nothing, not even herself. Sir James looked impassive as she confessed to being attracted to Sir Charles, even though she'd missed something that – in hindsight – should have alerted her to the truth. But who would have suspected a known hero of being a murderer? She scowled as she realised that she owed Lestrade an apology as well. The Inspector had seemed concerned about Sir Charles from the start.

Or maybe he was just jealous, she thought, grimly. *Sir Charles's jabs must have rankled.*

"A null," Doctor Norwell mused, when she had finished. "I don't think that our tests would have found someone with a power to absorb magic. They might well escape detection."

Gwen nodded, impatiently. She'd already concluded as much.

"The talent might not be an easy one to fine-tune," she said, tiredly. There were a handful of people who registered as magicians, but had no discernible talent. Sometimes, it took years for their talent to emerge, if it ever did. Master Thomas's notes had included details of several magicians who had never identified their talents. He'd wondered if their talents were completely unknown – or simply useless. "He didn't seem aware of it until he encountered Sir Travis."

"At least we're not looking at another Isabella Thompson," Sir James said. "Hell, we could *use* a null in dealing with such a person."

Gwen winced. Isabella Thompson had been the wife of a British officer in America; utterly unremarkable until she'd fallen and hit her head. She hadn't known that she was an undiscovered Talker; the fall had jarred something loose in her brain and she'd started broadcasting her feelings at everyone within range. The mental broadcasts had caused absolute panic in New York, forcing the magicians on the spot to shoot her from a distance. There had been no other choice, they'd said at the time. They might well have been right.

"True," Gwen agreed. "But we should still take every precaution."

"We will," Doctor Norwell said. Pedantic he might be, and given to repeating himself, but he knew the dangers. "Besides, such a talent will come in handy."

"Let us hope so," Gwen said. She looked down at the papers on her desk, then back up at them. "I have to face the Privy Council tomorrow. They'll want to know everything that happened since the investigation began."

"Ouch," Sir James said. "Do you want me to come with you?"

"There'll be enough blame to go around if you do," Gwen said, sardonically. She shook her head, although she was grateful for the offer. "You don't want any of it on you."

She waited until they'd both gone, then stood up and walked out of the office, heading up towards Olivia's rooms. The girl was somewhat isolated from the rest of the students, but there was no choice. If they'd learned what kind of magic she had, they would have been revolted – or tried to kill her. Olivia had played her own role in saving London, but it wouldn't have mattered if Gwen hadn't adopted her. Necromancers were considered too dangerous to keep around.

Olivia looked up gratefully as Gwen entered, dismissing the girl's tutor. There was nothing wrong with the girl's mind, but she'd had no formal education on the streets and found studying with the tutor to be wearisome, even though Gwen and Lucy had tried to impress the value of formal education on the girl. At least she was no longer squirreling away food from the kitchen, hiding it in her rooms. *That* had resulted in an awkward discussion between Gwen and the Head Housekeeper, who had naturally objected.

"These lessons are boring," Olivia protested, as Gwen sat down in the seat the tutor had vacated. "Do they actually *do* anything?"

Gwen glanced at the papers. "Maths can be very helpful," she said. There were hundreds of girls in Polite Society who never had the chance to learn, simply because their parents didn't believe in educating women. "Once you master it and reading, you can jump ahead of your tutor if you want."

She shrugged. "Do you like living here?"

Olivia gave her a sharp glance – and Gwen winced. Her adopted daughter had learned to trust her, but she didn't trust anyone else, with the possible exception of Lucy. But then, she'd grown up on the streets, disguising herself as a boy to avoid unwanted attention; Gwen had been sickened the day Olivia had told her, quite calmly, what happened to girl-children on the streets. It could even happen to boys. Olivia had made a joke of the time a man had tried to lure her into his apartment, convinced that she was a boy, but Gwen hadn't found it funny at all.

And she'd never quite believed that she would be allowed to remain in Cavendish Hall indefinitely.

"I might have to leave," Gwen said. "Will you come with me?"

It had been hard to convince the Privy Council to pardon Olivia for living – and only the backing of the King had made it happen. And they'd insisted that Olivia stayed supervised for the rest of her life... if Gwen had to leave Cavendish Hall, they might insist that Olivia *stayed*. *That* would raise too many questions.

"Of course," Olivia said. "What happened?"

Gwen hadn't wanted to tell her, but the whole story came tumbling out anyway.

"It sounds like you didn't do too badly," Olivia said, when she'd finished. "You didn't do anything disastrous."

"Thank you," Gwen said, dryly. But then, those who lived on the streets had a more pragmatic attitude to life. A woman's reputation was less important to them, even though it was far from *nothing*. "But I feel a fool."

"Everyone does that," Olivia said. "Or so Mistress Lucy

told me, back when I..."

She shook her head, an old shadow appearing in her eyes for a long second. "I don't think you should waste your time worrying about it," she insisted. *"Really."*

Gwen had to smile. No one was quite sure how old her adopted daughter actually *was* – it wasn't as if her birth had been witnessed and then registered – but she couldn't be far short of puberty. She'd filled out very well once she'd had some proper food and medical care; Gwen's best guess was that Olivia was ten years old. If so, in six more years, she'd be expected to start her season. She wondered, briefly, what Polite Society would say if they knew where she'd come from.

But that's what destroyed Sir Charles, she thought, numbly. *Maybe it's better they never find out the truth.*

"I'll do my best," Gwen said. She stood up and yawned. "I'll let you know what will happen after tomorrow, if they tell me. They might just want to keep me waiting."

She nodded goodbye to her daughter and stepped outside, allowing the tutor to go back into the room. Shaking her head, she walked back to her rooms and stepped inside, locking the door behind her before starting to remove her stained clothes. Talleyrand hadn't said anything, but it was quite possible that he would add a complaint about the smell to his diplomatic protest. Charming his daughter, insisting on an immediate interview... and smelling of vomit. At least it would give the Foreign Office a smile before they tried to think of a diplomatic response.

Once she was naked, she walked into the bathroom and stood in front of the mirror. Her body was badly bruised, but they were already fading away as her skin returned to its naturally pale colour. The bump on her head where she'd cracked it against the floor had already vanished, unnaturally quickly. Maybe the only person she *could* heal was herself.

"Wash and sleep," she told herself. "Tomorrow is not going to be fun."

Chapter Thirty-Nine

he Privy Council had been declining in importance – its role largely taken by the Prime Minister's Cabinet – until after the Swing, when King George had insisted on taking on a greater role in governing his council. Now, it was the highest council in the land, with a roster of members who were exceptionally powerful in political terms. Even the Leader of the Opposition, who commanded a number of votes in Parliament, was a member. If the Privy Council agreed on something, it would happen.

Normally, the Privy Council met wherever the monarch happened to be living at the time, but King George had insisted on basing *his* Privy Council in Buckingham Palace, despite the objections of some of the more traditional councillors. Gwen had visited the Palace several times in the past, starting when she had been confirmed as Royal Sorceress, yet she couldn't help feeling nervous now. The Privy Council had the power to dismiss her, if they felt it was necessary. They'd be tempted to wash their hands of her after the whole affair.

She kept her face as impassive as possible as Lord Mycroft escorted her into the council chamber. The room itself was surprisingly simple; there was a large table, a number of reasonably comfortable chairs and a throne for the monarch, should he choose to attend. Gwen had been warned in advance that King George wouldn't be attending – the matter was considered too politically sensitive for the monarch to be involved – but she couldn't help finding that ominous. The King was one of her strongest supporters.

"Lady Gwen," the Duke of India said, once she was standing in front of them. There was no chair for her, of course. "You may begin."

Gwen bowed her head. The Duke of India had publicly reprimanded a meddling upper-class woman who had sought to close down the brothels near army garrisons, pointing out that British soldiers risked their lives to defend Britain from foreign invasions. He might be a stubborn son of a bitch who thought everyone should do as he said, as she'd heard him called more than once, but he cared deeply for his men. Maybe he would extend some of that tolerance towards her.

"Sir Travis Mortimer was murdered by Sir Charles Bellingham," she said, bluntly. "The murder was planned and authorised by Ambassador Talleyrand."

She waited as the stir ran around the room, wondering just how much they already knew. Lord Mycroft knew, of course, but had he told them? Or had he decided that *Gwen* should have the credit for solving the mystery? It might counterbalance their desire to punish her for embarrassing herself.

"The motive for the murder was simple; the execution was not," she continued, once quiet had returned to the room. "Sir Travis had been intimately involved in drafting a treaty with the Ottoman Empire, a treaty that would have prevented the French from pressing against the Ottomans and allied their formidable land army with British naval might. Added together, we could have swept the French out of the Mediterranean and even invaded Eastern Europe, bringing France to her knees. It was worth any risk to prevent the treaty from ever being signed.

"In order to do that, the treaty had to be discredited. The Airship Treaty made considerable concessions to the Turks in exchange for a long-term alliance. If the motives of the principle writer could be cast into doubt – and he was no longer able to defend himself – the treaty would be delayed, if not destroyed. Sir Travis had to be accused of being a Turkish operative, accepting bribes to write a treaty that favoured the Ottoman Empire. With such an accusation hanging over his head, impossible to disprove, the treaty would not be ratified by Parliament."

She paused, composing her next words carefully. "Public opinion, right now, is strongly in favour of war with France," she said. "The French knew that they were being blamed for the undead rampage in London during the Swing. There was – is – a very real possibility that we would go to war, with or without the Turks. Talleyrand, I suspect, knew the danger from his mind-reading assistant; France could hardly become *more* compromised if they were implicated in Sir Travis's death. If there was to be war, they would have a better chance if it was fought before the treaty was signed.

"I do not know when or how Sir Charles made contact with the French. I *do* know that he possessed an unusual talent, one that nullified magic in contact with his body. Among other things, a Sensitive simply couldn't read him; Sir Travis found him a good companion simply because he could stand to be near Sir Charles without being driven away by a barrage of uncontrollable emotions. Sir Charles did not, unfortunately, share his feelings. *His* motivation for joining the French was to extract revenge on Polite Society for turning on him when his origins became public. Talleyrand was able to exploit his feelings to France's advantage.

"That night, Talleyrand went to visit Sir Travis, perhaps intending to try to bribe him into abandoning the Treaty. Murder is risky, after all, and France might have ended up at war with the British Empire. Whatever was said between them, Sir Travis clearly refused to budge. Talleyrand left Mortimer Hall and gave Sir Charles the signal to move in. With the help of an underground magician, he broke into Mortimer Hall and killed Sir Travis, taking a number of his papers afterwards. Thus committed, he went to Hiram Pasha's house, killed the Turkish spy and left the papers there for us to find.

"Prior to the murder, the French worked hard to create a link between Sir Travis and Hiram Pasha. The Golden Turk, a gambling hall, claimed that Sir Travis owed them money. In reality, the manager took a hefty bribe to forge the debts, ensuring that our attention would be drawn to

Hiram Pasha, who was supposed to have *backed* the debts. They thus created the impression that Sir Travis had been taking money from the Turks all along. The Airship Treaty might therefore have been dictated in Istanbul."

She paused, wishing that she could take a sip of water.

"At that point, chance intervened," she admitted. "The Golden Turk's manager had visited Mortimer Hall several times before the murder, telling Sir Travis's maidservant that he owed the gambling hall money. Sir Travis, of course, dismissed those debts. The maid did not know any better, however, and so when Augustus Howell visited Mortimer Hall and read the maid's mind, he believed that Sir Travis was in debt."

The table rustled again. Gwen smiled and waited for them to calm down before continuing.

"I will have to go back in time here," she warned. "Sir Travis was engaged – secretly – to Lady Elizabeth Bracknell. Unfortunately, Lady Elizabeth had compromised herself earlier in life, allowing Howell to blackmail her. She couldn't pay the price he demanded and so Howell went to Sir Travis, intending to tell him what his intended had been doing before she was engaged to him. Instead, he discovered that Sir Travis owed money and offered to pay his debt. Ruining Lady Elizabeth would have been less profitable than getting his hooks into a government official.

There was a long pause. "Howell met with failure," she explained, "but didn't expose Lady Elizabeth. I don't know what he was thinking, but I think he must have expected Lady Elizabeth to have some influence over her husband – or that the debts would eventually grow to the point where Sir Travis would be desperate for a loan. Howell could wait patiently for the right moment to use his information. However, more or less by accident, he distracted me from the truth."

Her lips twitched. "I was warned by almost everyone not to go near Howell," she said, dryly. "If they'd been more honest about him, I might have realised the truth sooner.

The humour faded. She didn't want to talk about the

next part to anyone.

"Sir Charles worked hard to attach himself to the investigation," Gwen admitted. "I was... rather taken with him and allowed himself to get too close to me. In hindsight, he dropped plenty of hints about Sir Travis gambling, even mentioning the Golden Turk before the manager sent a demand notice to Sir Travis's estate. Eventually, we went to the Golden Turk and discovered the debts, which led us to Hiram Pasha's house. There, we found the papers suggesting that Sir Travis had been a spy. The case against him seemed airtight.

"It wasn't until I read through Sir Travis's journal and his notes that I realised that some of the gambling debts were definitely faked," she said. "There was no logical reason for him to fake a trip to Istanbul; he didn't need to hide in London while gambling – and he certainly hadn't done it on a regular basis. Why should he have? And if some of the debts were fake, it was quite possible that they *all* were fake. Indeed, his journal mentioned nothing about the gambling exploits Sir Charles had told me about. Instead, it talked about Sir Charles having a soothing effect on the Sensitive.

"I went to Sir Charles's house and confronted him. He confessed to having killed Sir Travis, then tried to kill me. I was unprepared for his talent; in hindsight, I should have realised the implications and taken someone else along to provide support. He came very close to killing me outright. I barely managed to escape. When I did so, the first person to arrive was Simone, the so-called daughter of Ambassador Talleyrand – and a Talker in her own right. I went with her to the French Embassy, spoke briefly to Talleyrand, then returned home."

She drew a long breath. "Sir Travis was no traitor," she concluded. "I believe that we can consider the Airship Treaty without worrying about the motives of the writer."

There was a long pause.

"You mentioned that he got close to you," one of the councillors said. "What exactly do you mean?"

Gwen felt her cheeks warm under their gaze. "He attempted to seduce me," she said, bluntly. If they insisted on talking about it, she could talk. "I believe that he felt he could influence me. He was wrong."

"One would hope so," the Duke of India said, scowling at the councillor. "She would be far from the first official to get into trouble with the opposite sex."

He looked up at Gwen before anyone else could say a word. "Thank you for your report, Lady Gwen," he said. "Please wait in the antechamber. We will inform you when we have finished our deliberations."

Gwen nodded, curtseyed to the table and walked out of the room. The antechamber was surprisingly shabby, but comfortable; a maid offered her a cup of tea or coffee as she sat down on the sofa. Someone – she suspected Lord Mycroft – had set up a chessboard in the middle of the room. It was hard to be sure without getting up and looking at the board properly, but it looked like the game he'd been playing with Talleyrand.

She wasn't too surprised when, thirty minutes later, Lord Mycroft came into the antechamber and sat down in front of the chessboard. Or when something clicked in her mind.

"You knew," she said.

Lord Mycroft raised a single elegant eyebrow. "I beg your pardon?"

Talleyrand, Gwen thought, as she stood up. He'd said exactly the same thing, word for word.

She sat down on the other side of the chessboard. "You knew who'd murdered Sir Travis," she said. "Your brother already did the legwork."

"I knew *why* Sir Travis had been murdered," Lord Mycroft said. "There was no other logical motive. But I didn't know *who*. My brother... had other affairs to handle."

He picked up the white queen and held it out to her. "Besides, you needed something to boost your reputation," he added. "Solving the case alone would solidify your position, I calculated, but destroying Howell's blackmailing empire made you immensely popular."

"Popular enough for people to forget that Sir Charles took me for a ride?" Gwen asked, bitterly. "I acted the fool. People won't forget."

"The world is full of people who were foolish in love," Lord Mycroft said. He started to put the pieces back in their starting positions. "You are far from the first person to allow love to blind you. Unlike many, you were capable of realising your mistake and acting on that realisation. Quite a few officials who should have known better allowed themselves to be blinded by love – or lust."

"I'm a girl," Gwen reminded him. "It's different for men."

"Sometimes," Lord Mycroft said. "I have a list of men who cannot be trusted with anything sensitive because they compromised themselves... and then refused to learn from the experience. Compared to many of them, you didn't do too badly at all."

Gwen looked down at the chessboard. "Which piece am I?"

Lord Mycroft shrugged as he picked up the white king. "The king isn't a piece so much as it represents a line of succession," he said. "It cannot be taken, merely trapped; a threat to the king forces all else to be dropped while the king is protected. In our case, the king is England itself. We must protect England, even at the cost of the other pieces."

"You didn't answer the question," Gwen said.

Lord Mycroft tapped one of the knights. Gwen had to smile.

"You aren't so hidebound as many others," he explained. "And that gives you an advantage."

He put the king down and looked up at her. "The Privy Council has decided to commend you for doing an excellent job," he said. "There was some suggestion that you might have allowed your heart to mislead you, but it was voted down by a large majority. Some rumours will slip out, of course..."

"Of course," Gwen agreed.

"... But they will receive no support from the Privy Council," Lord Mycroft concluded, flatly. "Indeed, you will be honoured for your conduct."

Gwen flushed. Praise from Lord Mycroft was rare.

"I made mistakes," she confessed. How close had she come to surrendering completely to Sir Charles? "I..."

"Everyone makes mistakes," Lord Mycroft said. "You have to learn from the experience."

Gwen nodded, mutely.

"There will be no open admission of what happened to either Sir Travis or Sir Charles," Lord Mycroft said. "Sir Travis's death will be blamed on Howell; we can tell a few rumourmongers that Sir Travis refused to be intimidated and Howell killed him in hopes that it would save his life. Few people would question that story. Sir Charles's death will be blamed on one of Howell's rogue magicians. You will be credited with rushing to his rescue and killing the rogue before he could escape."

"There are holes in that story," Gwen pointed out.

"But it will be generally believed," Lord Mycroft said. "Both of them will be buried as heroes – and the Airship Treaty will not be brought into question. The Privy Council will debate it later today and Parliament will, I suspect, have the opportunity to vote on it within the week. If we're not at war by then, that is."

Gwen winced. "The French will know the truth, won't they?"

"They can't say anything without admitting their own role in Sir Travis's murder," Lord Mycroft said. "The truth will leak out, sooner or later, but by then it should no longer matter."

"I hope you're right," Gwen said. She hesitated, then asked the question that had bothered her before she went to sleep. "Is the Airship Treaty a mistake?"

Lord Mycroft snorted. "Every solution to every problem faced by the British Empire, or every other nation, causes problems in its own right," he said. "That's the lesson of history, Lady Gwen. It never really ends."

He tapped the white king. "And we spend all our time trying to prevent the king from being trapped," he added. "That's why the French were so desperate."

"They feared that they might be trapped," Gwen said, in understanding. "*Are* they trapped?"

"Not yet," Lord Mycroft said. "And we don't *want* to

trap them."

He smiled at her. "If you don't want to play," he said, "you can go back to Cavendish Hall."

Gwen hesitated, then risked a different question. "Is it likely that I will ever find love?"

Lord Mycroft showed a hint of surprise before it faded away into nothingness. "You are operating outside society's conventions," he said, finally. "I think you would manage to find someone, if you looked in the right place. But so few of your class marry for love."

"I will be more careful in future," Gwen admitted. She'd never really thought of Lord Mycroft as a father figure before, but who else could she ask for fatherly advice? Doctor Norwell? "Is it wrong of me to feel bad about that?"

"When... something bad happens to a woman, something caused by a man, she may well end up blaming *all* men for it," Lord Mycroft said. He didn't say the word outright, but Gwen knew what he meant. "That you still want to find someone speaks well of you, I think. But just remember to be careful. There are worse things than losing one's reputation that can happen to you."

Gwen nodded and stood up.

"You did very well," Lord Mycroft said. His expression hardened, just for a second. "And the Privy Council will ensure that everyone knows that we are satisfied."

"But it won't be enough to convince Polite Society," Gwen objected. Even the Privy Council couldn't control the gossips. "They..."

"They will do as they are told," Lord Mycroft said. "But I'd suggest that you stayed away from balls for a few months. You're supposed to be in mourning."

"Understood," Gwen said.

With that, she walked out of the room and headed back to Cavendish Hall.

Chapter Forty

I didn't know that you were going to marry Sir Charles," Lady Mary said. "He should have asked your father's permission before asking you."

Gwen gritted her teeth. It had taken her nearly three weeks to work up the courage to visit her mother and in that time the rumours had grown massively out of control. According to the gossip running through Polite Society, Gwen and Sir Charles had been secretly engaged before Sir Charles had been brutally murdered by one of Howell's magicians. It was all Dreadfully Romantic, according to society's queens, and Gwen had been bombarded with commiserations from just about anyone who was anybody.

"He wasn't going to marry me, mother," Gwen said. It was hard enough to say those words, even though she knew that her mother would understand. "The story they told you is a lie."

She ran through everything that had happened between her and Sir Charles, ending with the moment she'd killed him. Lady Mary listened quietly, without saying a word; Gwen found that more worrying than outright shouting. But then, her mother should understand. She'd been through something similar herself.

"I was in love," she concluded, bitterly. "If he'd pressed, I don't know how far I would have gone."

"And you shouted at me for my mistake," Lady Mary said. "What were you thinking?"

Gwen winced. She knew that she deserved that, but it didn't make it any easier.

"I didn't understand what you went through," she said.

Her isolation from society hadn't really helped either. She'd had few of the outlets used by other young ladies. "I think I understand how you must have felt after your relationship failed."

She'd known that her relationship with Sir Charles could have easily destroyed her career, even though she was the only Master Magician known to exist. Lady Mary hadn't had that support; if she'd been discovered to be pregnant, her reputation would have been utterly shattered, ruined beyond repair. Gwen still found it hard to forgive her mother for aborting her half-sibling, but she understood what her mother had felt. God would judge her, in due course. Gwen no longer wanted to try.

"I didn't want to see you make the same mistake," Lady Mary said. She looked up at Gwen, her dark eyes fixed on Gwen's face. "Did you... did you let him go inside you?"

Gwen flushed, but shook her head.

"At least you were wiser than I," Lady Mary told her. "I went too far and paid the price."

She reached out and gave Gwen a hug. "I understand what you must have felt when you found out the truth," she added. "And I forgive you for it. Rudolf... may take longer to forgive you, but I'm sure he will. He cares about you, whatever you may have said to him when you were last here."

"I hope so," Gwen said. At least David didn't know the full story. "And I'm sorry..."

"It's part of growing up," Lady Mary admitted. She smiled, suddenly. "Your grandmother was always very upset with me..."

Gwen nodded. She had never understood her grandmother's tales until now. Hard as it was to imagine Lady Mary as a child, she would have been a rebellious girl at one point... and she had managed to get herself into deep trouble. Now, she had been doing her best to prevent Gwen from making the same mistake. She could understand that too.

"I'll write to father," she said, standing up. "And thank you for seeing me."

Lady Mary stood up and gave her another hug. "That,

young lady, is what mothers are for," she said, firmly. "But you should drop in more often."

Gwen nodded. Spending more time with her mother, now that they knew each other without the masks, would be better for them both, she hoped. And if not, she told herself, it could serve as penance, both for screaming at her mother and growing too close to Sir Charles.

"Goodbye, mother," she said. "I'll see you soon."

Her carriage was waiting outside; she climbed inside and told the driver to take her to Pall Mall, where David was waiting for her. Her mind insisted on replaying everything she'd done with Sir Charles in a carriage, reminding her of her own foolishness. At least she'd survived without doing something *really* stupid, she told herself, although Polite Society might have disagreed. But they seemed to believe the official story.

David had booked them both a table at a nearby cafe. Gwen allowed the waiter to show her to his table and smiled as he looked up from his book.

"So," he said, as Gwen sat down. "How was your meeting with mother?"

Gwen blinked in surprise. How had he known?"

"Father was not too happy about whatever you said to him," David admitted. "I had to remind him that you have plenty of friends in high places and it could be disastrous if he pushed around too much."

"I will write to him," Gwen said, remembering what she'd told her mother. "But I don't know what he will say to me."

"It's a start," David said. "Just be grateful you're not facing him after coming home drunk."

Gwen nodded. She'd been twelve at the time, but she still recalled her father's shouts echoing through the house. He'd been *furious* at David's loss of control, lecturing him on how his uncle had drunk too much as a young man and ended up seriously hurt. Her brother hadn't been able to sit properly for several days afterwards.

"I think what I did was worse," she said, ruefully. "How is Laura?"

"Still pregnant," David said, wryly. "One of your

Healers visited her and pronounced the child a healthy baby boy."

"Father will like that," Gwen admitted. "Someone to carry on the family name."

"You adopted a child," David reminded her.

Gwen snorted. Olivia would never be considered her biological daughter; there was no point in trying to deceive anyone into believing it. Gwen would ensure that Olivia inherited most of her wealth, but she wouldn't be considered a proper heir. And if they learned the full truth, they'd want her dead.

"That doesn't count," she said. "And even if I had a natural child..."

David nodded. If Gwen married and had children, they'd have their father's name.

The waiter returned. David ordered for them both.

"Parliament ratified the Airship Treaty this morning," he said, once the waiter was out of earshot. "It will be formally announced tomorrow in all the major newspapers. We have a working alliance with the Turks."

Gwen smiled. War hadn't broken out in the weeks since Ambassador Talleyrand and his daughter had been declared *personae non gratae*, but there had been some nasty reports, including Franco-Spanish troops mustering near Gibraltar and troop convoys *en route* to Mexico. Apparently, the Governor-General of America was pressing for a pre-emptive strike on Mexico and worrying over the loyalty of Hispanics and Mexicans in Louisiana. Gwen wasn't too surprised; the French had made a big deal over incorporating Hispanics and Mexicans into their empire, even offering them full legal rights. Who knew what they would do if war broke out?

"There will also be an immediate requirement to send magicians over to help the Turks," David added. "Do you have a list of volunteers?"

"Yes," Gwen said, allowing her smile to widen. The mission would have to be led by a high-ranking magician and Lord Brockton was top of the list. If he refused to go, the Privy Council would certainly show its displeasure by pressing for his resignation – or forcing Gwen to sack him.

She would be reluctant, naturally, but she would obey. How could she defy the highest council in the land?

"I'm glad to hear it," David said. "The way things have been recently, it is alarmingly likely that war will break out within the month."

The waiter returned with two plates piled high with food. "This might be the last meal I get to share with you for a while," David added, as his plate was put in front of him. "My gut says that we are about to become very busy."

Gwen couldn't disagree. Little was known for certain about the French magicians, but *her* gut said that Simone wouldn't be the only one. It was quite possible that the French had assembled a small army of magicians... hell, a few Talkers would go a long way towards evening the balance between the two empires. And she had persistent nightmares about the French finding a Master of their own – or two. How many women had Jack impregnated while he'd been in France?

But his children might not be Masters, she thought, grimly. *And even if they were, they'd still be children...*

She tucked into her food as David continued to talk. "The Prime Minister warned the Houses of Parliament that he might be calling up the militia within days," he added, softly. *That* was a surprise; the Duke of India had been on the record complaining that the militia were either skiving farmhands or noblemen who preferred sporting fancy uniforms to actually fighting. "If the French attempt to land we'll give them a warm welcome."

Gwen nodded. Maybe the Duke was wrong – or exaggerating to get more money for the army. These days, the militia consisted of almost every able-bodied male in the country. The war scare – and the Swing – had caused no end of panic and patriotic determination to fight the French if they dared to land on English soil. Sir James had expressed his doubt over the militia's combat value, but Gwen hoped that they at least *looked* intimidating. Maybe the French would think better of trying to land in England if they thought that every bush concealed a rifle.

"Merlin is near Dover right now," she said, although she

had no idea where the French might try to land. On the other hand, the magicians could move much faster than marching soldiers. "And I'll be in London with the reserves."

"I'm glad you won't be in the front lines," David said, quietly. "At least Colonel Sebastian was man enough to admit that he was wrong."

Gwen scowled. Colonel Sebastian had begged an interview with her a week after she'd faced the Privy Council and, puzzled, Gwen had agreed to see him. He'd told her that his niece had been one of Howell's victims and that he had been wrong about her all along. Gwen had thanked him, then arranged for him to join the magicians based near Maidstone. She wasn't really sure if she was rewarding him or putting him somewhere where he might well die. But it had won her some points from the other senior magicians.

"Yes," she said, finally. "Do we have enough time to make our alliance with the Turks work?"

"We should pray that we do," David said. "Besides, even a handful of Talkers would make their operations easier. As far as we know, Russia has few magicians and Persia is still burning any magician they catch."

"Let's hope so," Gwen said. "But we know almost nothing about Russia's research."

Russia was an enigma; they had to have a magical program, but almost nothing had leaked out from the vast country. Even the wars Russia had fought with the Ottoman Empire, after the advent of magic, had revealed little of Russia's magic. It would be nice to believe that the Russians had simply followed the Vatican's lead and concentrated on exterminating magicians, but she knew better than to indulge in wishful thinking.

"The Russians may join France if war comes," David reminded her. "We might find out the hard way."

Gwen nodded. Russia could attack British North America through Alaska, or try an advance through Central Asia to attack India... or, more practically, concentrate on invading Turkey and Persia. Once the British-Ottoman alliance was announced, it was quite likely that Persia would throw in with Russia; the Persians suspected that the Turks would happily crush them if they had the opportunity. The new Sultan's army was far more capable than anything the Persians could build for themselves.

"Yes," she said. Between them, the French and the Russians might have more magicians than anyone realised. "We might..."

She winced as a thought crashed into her head. *LADY GWEN*, the Talker said. Gwen could sense the panic flaring through the Talker's mind, enough to almost infect her own thoughts. She bit her lip to maintain her concentration. *You have to return to Cavendish Hall!*

David stared at her. "War?"

"It could be," Gwen said, as she stood up. Her body swayed; she closed her eyes and centred herself, wondering just who had allowed a half-trained Talker to call her. He hadn't been ready to contact minds that weren't pure-Talkers. "I have to get back to Cavendish Hall."

She walked outside, grabbed hold of her magic and hurled herself into the air. Flying in public still bothered her, but there was no choice. The moment she was high enough, she saw a pillar of smoke rising up from the direction of Cavendish Hall, reminding her of the early hours of the Swing. Thankfully, Cavendish Hall seemed to be the only victim this time.

The damage didn't look as bad as she had feared, she realised, as she flew closer. One of the outbuildings seemed to have exploded; it was commonly used for training Infusers, who might accidentally blow up the entire building if they weren't careful. Gwen remembered her own training sessions with some embarrassment – and she'd had nowhere near the power or dedication of pure Infusers. Quite a few Infusers had been sent to join the army in the hopes that they'd blow up the enemy instead of themselves.

"Lady Gwen," a voice called as she dropped to the ground. She was surprised to hear Martha running towards her. "She's gone!"

Gwen felt a sinking sensation in her chest as she turned to look at her maid. Martha looked terrified. Could the explosion have been intended as nothing more than a diversion? Everyone had run to deal with it at once, fearful of the consequences if the flames had been allowed to spread out of control, clearing the way for someone with bad intentions. They should have prepared better for an assault on Cavendish Hall, she thought, and cursed herself. The Swing should have taught her that chaos could strike at any time.

"Who's gone?" She asked, although she feared that she already knew the answer. "What happened?"

"Olivia," Martha said. Tears were streaming down her face; she'd been fond of Olivia, once she'd got used to the girl's poor manners and worse eating habits. "She's been kidnapped!"

Twenty minutes later, Gwen knew the worst. Olivia was gone – and so was one of her tutors, a grim-faced man who had been teaching Olivia how to write properly. The remaining tutors were dead...

... And there was nothing to lead her to where Olivia might have been taken.

The Royal Sorceress Will Return In

Necropolis

Coming Soon!

Afterword*

he past is a foreign country, as the old saying goes. They do things differently there.

There are times when I am perversely glad that I had such poor schooling in history while I was in my teenage years. What little I did have was centred on such absurdly boring subjects as sheep-farming in Lancashire and a deliberately slanted version of World War One that made *Blackadder Goes Forth* look historically accurate (it isn't). Maybe not quite the Norwegian Leather Industry, as Adrian Mole complained so incessantly, but completely useless (as well as boring) to a growing boy. Had my teachers concentrated on interesting subjects, I have no doubt that they would have managed to suck the life out of them too.

Instead, I read history books – and discovered that I rather *liked* history. I read hundreds of books covering World War Two, then branched out to World War One, the Napoleonic Wars, the American Revolution... and all the way back in time to the Persian Invasion of Greece, which should be studied in every school. (It isn't, even though it was the first moment that gave birth to the 'West.') History explains so much about society; indeed, if the teachers had done their jobs properly, they might have managed to teach us why sheep farming was so important.

But, unless things have improved in the thirteen years since I left school, the general level of historical teaching is still appallingly bad.

It is unfortunately natural that we look back to a long-lost golden age. Very few generations seem willing to believe that they live in a better world than their predecessors. Some

---

* I wrote this after reading some of the reviews of *The Royal Sorceress*.

Britons look back to the days of Empire and consider them superior to the present day; Americans look back to the days of the wild west, before America became the second hyperpower in global history. I have no doubt that the belief in a mythical past existed even in states that were hardly inclined to come up with justifications for building their empires. Even as Rome became an Empire, traditionally-minded Romans bemoaned the loss of the values that had made them so indomitable in the first place. But those values were inevitable casualties of Rome's rise to power.

The problem with this urge to look back is that it tends to concentrate on the good rather than the bad.

Let us consider the many miracles of modern life in Britain, or anywhere else in the West. We have hot and cold running water, purified so that it can be drunk straight from the tap; clean toilets that actually flush; medicine and dentistry that actually works; a reasonable level of sexual equality; equality before the law... and so much else. How many of those do you think existed prior to 1945, let alone earlier? If you have children in the present day, you have an excellent chance of seeing them born and growing to adulthood. In the times of Ancient Rome, even the most powerful Roman was helpless to watch as his wife and children died in childbirth.

The world of Lady Gwen's time was very different from ours. There was no such thing as a secret ballot, for example, which meant that if you happened to vote against your landlord, you could expect to be out on the streets within days. Nor was there any form of social security network; if you were a young boy or girl without a family or a home, you would be lucky if you ended up in a workhouse. *Oliver Twist* provides a good, if grim, depiction of what life was like for the poor – and there was rarely a happy ending.

It was worse for women, even among the upper classes. You may laugh at the social pretensions of Lady Mary and Lady Bracknell, but maintaining such a cloak of hypocrisy was a survival necessity for women. A wife was her husband's chattel – a slave, to all intents and purposes. She could not bring a suit against her husband for adultery, no matter how many times he strayed; a husband could destroy his wife's reputation and ensure that she never married again, even if they remained separated. Indeed, he could legally drag her back to his home and keep her a prisoner, if he saw fit. Given the legal right of the husband to actually *sue* his wife's lover, on the grounds that his property had been damaged, it is surprising that there were any cases of adultery at all.

A girl who was alone with an unrelated man, for any reason, might be considered defiled, even if she could prove that she still had her virginity. Courtship in the 1800s was a heavily ritualised procedure, with the parents involved at almost every stage; if the father disapproved, it was unlikely that there would be a marriage. (The happy couple could run off to Scotland and get married there, but they often suffered the wrath of their parents and had to live on their own resources. A woman might be reduced to effective prostitution to make ends meet.)

With all of this in mind... why would anyone want to *live* in the past?

Christopher G. Nuttall, Kuala Lumpur, 2013.

Elsewhen Press

a small independent publisher specialising in Speculative Fiction

THE ROYAL SORCERESS
CHRISTOPHER NUTTALL

It's 1830, in an alternate Britain where the 'scientific' principles of magic were discovered sixty years previously, allowing the British to win the American War of Independence. Although Britain is now supreme among the Great Powers, the gulf between rich and poor in the Empire has widened and unrest is growing every day. Master Thomas, the King's Royal Sorcerer, is ageing and must find a successor to lead the Royal Sorcerers Corps. Most magicians can possess only one of the panoply of known magical powers, but Thomas needs to find a new Master of all the powers. There is only one candidate, one person who has displayed such a talent from an early age, but has been neither trained nor officially acknowledged. A perfect candidate to be Master Thomas' apprentice in all ways but one: the Royal College of Sorcerers has never admitted a girl before.

But even before Lady Gwendolyn Crichton can begin her training, London is plunged into chaos by a campaign of terrorist attacks co-ordinated by Jack, a powerful and rebellious magician.

The Royal Sorceress will certainly appeal to all fans of steampunk, alternate history, and fantasy. As well as the fun of the 'what-ifs' delivered by the rewriting of our past, it delights with an Empire empowered by magic – all the better for being one we can recognise. The scheming and intrigue of Jack and his rebels, the roof-top chases and the thrilling battles of magic are played out against the dark and unforgiving backdrop of life in the sordid slums and dangerous factories of London. Many of the rebels are drawn from a seedy and grimy underworld, while their Establishment targets prey on the weak and defenceless. The price for destroying the social imbalance and sexual inequality that underpin society may be more than anyone can imagine.

As an indie author, Christopher Nuttall has self-published a number of novels. *The Royal Sorceress* is his first novel to be published by Elsewhen Press. Chris is currently living in Borneo with his wife, muse, and critic Aisha.

ISBN: 9781908168184 (epub, kindle)
ISBN: 9781908168085 (400pp, paperback)

For more information visit bit.ly/TheRoyalSorceress

Visit the Elsewhen Press website at elsewhen.co.uk for the latest information on all of our titles, authors and events; to read our blog; find out where to buy our books and ebooks; or to place an order.

Elsewhen Press

a small independent publisher specialising in Speculative Fiction

Bookworm
Christopher Nuttall

Elaine is an orphan girl who has grown up in a world where magical ability brings power. Her limited talent was enough to ensure a magical training but she's very inexperienced and was lucky to get a position working in the Great Library. Now, the Grand Sorcerer – the most powerful magician of them all – is dying, although initially that makes little difference to Elaine; she certainly doesn't have the power to compete for higher status in the Golden City. But all that changes when she triggers a magical trap and ends up with all the knowledge from the Great Library – including forbidden magic that no one is supposed to know – stuffed inside her head. This unwanted gift doesn't give her greater power, but it does give her a better understanding of magic, allowing her to accomplish far more than ever before.

It's also terribly dangerous. If the senior wizards find out what has happened to her, they will almost certainly have her killed. The knowledge locked away in the Great Library was meant to remain permanently sealed and letting it out could mean a repeat of the catastrophic Necromantic Wars of five hundred years earlier. Elaine is forced to struggle with the terrors and temptations represented by her newfound knowledge, all the while trying to stay out of sight of those she fears, embodied by the sinister Inquisitor Dread.

But a darkly powerful figure has been drawing up a plan to take the power of the Grand Sorcerer for himself; and Elaine, unknowingly, is vital to his scheme. Unless she can unlock the mysteries behind her new knowledge, divine the unfolding plan, and discover the truth about her own origins, there is no hope for those she loves, the Golden City or her entire world.

As an indie author, Christopher Nuttall has self-published a number of novels. *Bookworm* is his second novel to be published by Elsewhen Press. Chris is currently living in Borneo with his wife, muse, and critic Aisha.

ISBN: 9781908168320 (epub, kindle)
ISBN: 9781908168221 (368pp, paperback)

For more information visit bit.ly/Bookworm-Nuttall

Visit the Elsewhen Press website at elsewhen.co.uk for the latest information on all of our titles, authors and events; to read our blog; find out where to buy our books and ebooks; or to place an order.

A Life Less Ordinary
Christopher Nuttall

*There is magic in the world, hiding in plain sight. If you search for it,
you will find it, or it will find you. Welcome to the magical world.*

Having lived all her life in Edinburgh, the last thing 25-year old Dizzy expected
was to see a man with a real (if tiny) dragon on his shoulder. Following him,
she discovered that she had stumbled from her mundane world into a parallel
magical world, an alternate reality where dragons flew through the sky and the
Great Powers watched over the world. Convinced that she had nothing to lose,
she became apprenticed to the man with the dragon. He turned out to be one
of the most powerful magicians in all of reality.

But powerful dark forces had their eye on this young and inexperienced
magician, intending to use her for the ultimate act of evil – the apocalyptic
destruction of all reality. If Dizzy does not realise what is happening to her and
the worlds around her, she won't be able to stop their plan. A plan that will
ravage both the magical and mundane worlds, consuming everything and
everyone in fire.

ISBN: 9781908168337 (epub, kindle)
ISBN: 9781908168238 (336pp, paperback)

For more information visit bit.ly/ALLO-Nuttall

SUFFICIENTLY ADVANCED TECHNOLOGY
CHRISTOPHER NUTTALL

THE FIRST BOOK IN THE INVERSE SHADOWS UNIVERSE

For the post-singularity Confederation, manipulating the quantum foam – the
ability to alter the base code of the universe itself and achieve transcendence – is
the holy grail of science. But it seems an impossible dream until their scouts
encounter Darius, a lost colony world whose inhabitants have apparently
discarded the technology that brought them to the planet in order to adopt a
virtually feudal culture. On Darius, the ruling elite exhibits abilities that defy the
accepted laws of physics. They can manipulate the quantum foam!

Desperate to understand what is happening on Darius, the Confederation
dispatches a stealth team to infiltrate the planet's society and discover the truth
behind their strange abilities. But they will soon realise that the people on
Darius are not all the simple folk that they seem – and they are sitting on a
secret that threatens the entire universe ...

ISBN: 9781908168344 (epub, kindle)
ISBN: 9781908168245 (336pp, paperback)

For more information visit bit.ly/SAT-Nuttall

About the author

hristopher Nuttall has been planning sci-fi books
since he learned to read. Born and raised in
Edinburgh, Chris created an alternate history
website and eventually graduated to writing full-
sized novels. Studying history independently
allowed him to develop worlds that hung together and
provided a base for storytelling. After graduating from
university, Chris started writing full-time. As an indie author,
he has self-published a number of novels, but this is his
fourth fantasy to be published by Elsewhen Press. *The Royal
Sorceress* was the first and *The Great Game* continues
Gwen's story. Chris is currently living in Borneo with his
wife, muse, and critic Aisha.